WALKING

for

BREEZES

JAMES NELSON CAULKINS

authorHOUSE®

AuthorHouse™
1663 Liberty Drive
Bloomington, IN 47403
www.authorhouse.com
Phone: 1-800-839-8640

Published by AuthorHouse 10/11/2013

ISBN: 978-1-4918-2257-9 (sc)
ISBN: 978-1-4918-2255-5 (hc)
ISBN: 978-1-4918-2256-2 (e)

Library of Congress Control Number: 2013917621

Cover art and design by Kirsten Bjore. kirsten@bjoreart.com

This book is printed on acid-free paper.

This book is dedicated to my wife and friend Lorna.

And to every person who considers this Country's constitutional freedoms a challenging opportunity for individual growth.

Thanks to: Robert, Gloria Sue, Mook, Linda, Ang, Nic, Kirsten, and my old friends Mike and Lori. With special appreciation to Mr. Roy Ketchum.

Introduction

Over a century from now the world of people has changed, but the earth still revolves around the sun year after year and rotates on its axis day after day, season after season. God has not struck down humanity, nor has the Earth shrugged off humanity. But people have hurt themselves. And many people have learned. They've learned humility. They've learned that air, water, and soil pollution is no more than animals fouling their own nest. Individuals' nests were clean, humanity's was not. They've learned responsibility. They've learned that population unchecked by reason is no more than animals breeding. Families were healthy, the human race was not. They've learned kindness. They've learned that violence, division, hatred, and crime exist on one side of a perspective. They've learned that maturity and compassion are on the other side. That perspective is found through an awareness and application of "Do unto others."

People have learned that there is individuality within an awareness of humanity. They've learned that the heart and mind are not separated. They've learned that the body and soul are not separated here on Earth. They've learned that reason and feeling are two sides of the same coin. That coin is each one of us and all of us. The learning did not come quickly or easily. Humanity's arrogance caused individuals to miss the basic cause of their own problems.

This country, the Country of Freedom, waited too long to pull back its weapons from the world. Waited too long to choose to reach out to the world with its clean air, clean water, medical, industrial, and computer technologies. Waited too long to grow above greed to compassion. The Country of Freedom waited too long to change its chosen dependency on other countries' energy to the freedom of energy independence. In their own ways, other countries did no better. For all nations and governments are built by people, people for whom the schizophrenic-like division between heart and mind, body and soul, reason and feeling is a standard, not an illness. The organized religions did not help these divisions. They only focused people on obedience to their own structure and affiliation with their own beliefs, thus creating religions' own divisions in people. Divisions that persisted until people learned that when God created man in His image it meant that God created humans as self-determinate beings. For when a being is self-determinate, as God by definition is, all other images of ones self are secondary.

Humans have not done well with this gift of ultimate freedom. They have not done well with the freedom to create their own destiny and their own individuality. They choose to worship God rather than love mankind. They choose to believe that what is better will be given to them by a being greater than they. What they actually need to do is create a better world for all humanity by their own individual effort, their own individual intent. They do not realize that the tough questions for people to answer, the questions whose answers contain enough responsibility to create individuality, are put into religions and then become glossed over with obedience and worship. They did not realize this until with individual intent they learned to bring reason into religion and so build their own individuality. An individuality tempered by the awareness of each person's own humanity, an individuality that unites heart and mind, body and soul, reason and emotions. It is an individuality that causes belief and faith to shift to a firmer foundation but not to be replaced by information and reason. A belief and faith in one's self and one's own individual connection to God instead of belief and faith in other people, their constructs, or institutions. The people in this Country of Freedom learned that the freedoms granted to each individual by their own Constitution could best be lived through the development of value systems, codes of ethics, or religions from an independent perspective with an awareness of humanity.

Over a century ago the world was in turmoil. The turmoil grew as more and more people wanted more and more. Countries who took more than their share were hated and envied and blamed. Terrorists lashed out with hatred in the name of God. Poor countries and poor people wanted what they saw through instant communications that others all around them had. Religions and governments were tools for conformity and group identity. Countries and their people did not stop and look at themselves. They only reacted through their feelings as their feelings were led down a path created by governments through politicians, businesses through CEOs, and churches through their emissaries. It was a path made wide and level by mass media that led to where attacks, slights, and injustices were considered without context. The perspective of people affected by human causes fell to emotional reactions of greed, need, and speed with obligations tossed aside and debts never forgiven. Trees were cut down and deserts grew. Ice caps melted and oceans rose. Living soil was depleted as the variability of food plants diminished. People moved, people starved, people killed. All the age-old divisions, racial, religious, national, and economic, erupted in violence against each other. There had been no true change in people since the century before when millions were exterminated for perceived differences. No change in people that could keep rationality, reason, and perspective alive in the face of cold, hunger, violence, and privation.

After half a century the turmoil quieted down. Not because of an increase in tolerance and a drive to share and work together, but because the numbers of people had fallen and the energy to move large numbers of people vast distances to make war was scarce. People were having too hard a time surviving where they were.

They could no longer wield military power in order to take from others who also barely had enough for themselves. It was then that people began to reflect on what they had done to themselves, why, and what could have been. They began to build instead of destroy. They began to learn that no matter which deity was watching, they were the ones acting. They realized that no ethereal being, nor a technologically advanced species from light years away, had descended to earth to deliver humanity to a promised land in their time of turmoil.

In the Country of Freedom there is virtually no national government. There are city-states that command the area nearby that they use for food and energy production. The governing power of some of these city-states can reach along corridors as much as a hundred miles to protect their energy sources and water. But none of this power is used to administer laws and redistribute wealth beyond city borders. People do not survive in these cities because of the quality of the people who live there, but rather because of these energy sources. The turmoil had swallowed people of quality and good character as completely as the people who found truth in being conformists and followers. The surviving sources of energy have accumulated people from the surrounding areas, but do not support them well enough to comfortably allow them to prosper. Some few can fly to other city-states, but no one can drive through the hundreds of miles of unpopulated and unroaded lands between. Higher education and modest living is desired by many, but earned by only some. Compassion and perspective grow on a base of destroyed resources. People gaze at stars, but there is no exploration away from the Earth. News travels electronically from city-state to city-state and to other countries and other continents, but there are large areas of the Country of Freedom and of the earth that are scarcely populated and have only rudimentary wood, horse, and water power. Some countries choose to have no contact with the Country of Freedom and so are unknowns. Some isolated towns in this country are isolated with their own energy sources, and some people choose to live on their own as in centuries before.

It is difficult to travel from these towns to the city-states, but it is possible.

Into this time and the Country of Freedom in one of the isolated towns outside of the city-state of Denver two brothers are born, Mikhail and Mateen. Their parents had been born in the midst of the turmoil, they as the turmoil began to calm. The younger son, Mateen, bravely travels around the Northern continent and even sails to Hawaii, for the wind still blows and ships still sail. The older, Mikhail, marries and has a son, Eli. Unfortunately, a few years later, Mikhail's wife Rosario dies in childbirth. The baby daughter does not survive either. Mikhail raises his young son Eli until the boy is ten. Then Mikhail is injured and nearly dies in an accident on his farm. Upon hearing of this, Eli's uncle, Mateen, stops much of his travels and chooses to live in the hills near the small town where his brother and nephew live and have been taken in by neighbors. Mateen often travels the relatively short distance for him of about ten miles to visit Eli and his brother, usually staying for a week at a time. After two years of being crippled from his injury, Mikhail passes away. Watching the last two very painful years of his father's life gives Eli a strong sense of the value of an awareness of the dangers around him, physical health, and the complementary value of a good diet. When Eli is a teenager he travels some with Mateen. Then, as a young man, Eli moves back and begins farming his father's land. At first, Mateen helps him, for the fields and orchards had fallen into disrepair.

After a few years Eli meets and then marries Tohlee. They make a home on the farm, and, as the farm begins to prosper, Mateen begins to spend more time on his own land in the hills outside of town. Still traveling but getting on in years, Mateen spends most of his time at his cabin in the woods.

Ten years after marrying, Eli and Tohlee have a son they name Anoo. For the first few years after their son is born Mateen is often at the farm, helping Eli and Tohlee. When Anoo grows out of infancy, Mateen once again spends most of his time at his cabin, but visits the farm relatively often. As Anoo grows into his later teens, he becomes comfortable riding on horseback between Mateen's cabin and his parents' farm. The spring and fall are a time of work on the farm. During the summer Anoo has time to enjoy himself and even visit Mateen at his cabin. After the fall harvest on the farm Mateen, Eli, and Anoo hunt in the hills near Mateen's cabin for meat to last the family for a year.

A few years prior to this, when Anoo was in his early teens, he was living year-round at the farm. He worked all growing season helping his parents and during the winter he attended school in the nearby town. But during his fourteenth summer, Eli, Tohlee, and Mateen decide that Anoo and his great-uncle should spend some time exploring the far reaches of the hills that rise around Mateen's cabin.

This is the world and circumstances these individuals find themselves in. Individuals whose intent creates their perspective and whose experiences are appraised through their own individual perspectives and value systems. They are individuals for whom God the Father has given them the ultimate gift of self-determination by creating them in His image. They are individuals for whom the gift of dominion over life on Earth is a debt owed, not an opportunity. They are individuals for whom Jesus of Nazareth is one of a line of wise men that includes Buddha, Confucius, and Mohammad, wise men who deserve respect and whose teachings should be applied to individual lives through intent. They are individuals who freely choose to intend to unite heart and mind, body and soul, reason and feelings. They are individuals who apply the freedoms of their country at an individual level.

Walking For Breezes

▮▮ Have you finished getting your pack ready, Anoo?"

"Yes, Mother. I thought I was done and then Father checked it and he had me add a few things and take out even more. I guess I over prepared a little."

"It's very understandable that you're excited about your trip and want to bring everything you can think of to make the trip go as well as possible."

"Father said to cover all reasonable possibilities as lightly and compact as possible."

"He's taken similar journeys before with and without Mateen, so I'm sure his advice is well thought out and tempered with experience. I want you to take this with you also. It's a packet of spices, teas, and herbs. The spices and teas are a little treat to make camping food and drink more appealing. I've written down the uses and amounts of the herbs. Make sure you read about them before you leave tomorrow so if you need them you won't be stumbling around wasting time."

"Yes, Mother. I'll read it tonight. I'm not sure I'll get much sleep anyway."

"Your father and Mateen will be up late talking, so I don't think you'll be leaving right at dawn."

"What will you guys be doing while I'm gone?"

"The same things we'd do with your help if you were here. We're also planning on going into town for a few things and we'll see your Aunt Cassie while we're there. I think she's going to come out here for a visit with Jed also."

"I'd like to see her, it's been awhile, and especially if she's visiting here."

"We'll make sure the two of you can spend some time together when you get back. This visit will be more about the two couples getting together."

"That will be nice for you guys. To have time together while I'm gone."

"Yes, it will, but as an opportunity not as a relief, we want you to go, we don't need you to go."

"I understand, Mother."

"This is a time of year when much of the early farm work around here is done and there is time to enjoy the beauty and comfort of late spring and early summer," says Tohlee. "Your father and I will enjoy this idyllic time of year while you have an adventure with your Great Uncle."

"I hope when I get back there will still be some idyllic time for me."

"I'm sure there will be. You've earned your adventure and some quiet time afterwards besides. Your father and I very much appreciate the work you've done this spring, preparing and planting the fields."

"It was hard work but fulfilling. I have to admit though that the reaping is more fulfilling than the sowing," says Anoo.

"I think that sentiment has a long human history," says Tohlee. "Did you tell your friend Kirsten you'll be gone for awhile?"

"I went over there a couple days ago to tell her so she wouldn't wonder where I was. I did tell her earlier I'd be going, but I didn't know exactly when."

"It was nice of you to think of her. I think you'll have some good stories to tell her when you get back."

"Oh! The dogs are barking! And that's their bark when someone is here."

"I'm sure that's your Great Uncle Mateen. Let's go out and greet him."

After welcoming Mateen, Tohlee prepares dinner and Anoo does his early evening chores. He waters and feeds the horses and coops the fowl. Eli and Mateen wander around the farm talking about the spring growth of the crops and the weather Eli is so dependent on. Everyone gets together for a nice dinner and some talk. News and memories are shared. After awhile Tohlee goes inside to sew and Anoo to read. Eli and Mateen stay up late talking around the fire of the many things good friends talk about.

Day One

"I'm sure you're ready for this, Mateen. Do you think Anoo is?"

"Well, Eli, I think that Anoo is as ready for this as you were when you went traveling with me."

"This does bring back memories. I was ready to gain from those adventures because you taught me well and you were patient with me. It was not because of my ability, at the time, to make your ideas into my own individual thought and independent perspective. It took me years to feel comfortable with myself and my own individuality after we traveled."

"What we talked about then was newer to you than it is for Anoo. You've been teaching him all along as he's been growing up," says Mateen.

"That's true. But you were around a lot to help me after I got back from those travels. These days you're not around as much, your talk is more abrupt, and your patience is less with those who cannot readily communicate through a perspective akin to yours or at your level of awareness," says Eli.

"You are the boy's father and will be around for him when he gets back. I was around for you after we traveled because your father had died and I am your uncle. It wasn't because I was the only one who could have helped you. I have no doubt that you will help Anoo after we finish walking together, as I helped you. When the boy gets back, the love you share with Tohlee and your shared compassion for Anoo, will soften any harshness in my manner or in the meaning of the words I use, even if there is some temporary discomfort to him. I feel that I soften as I go deeper into the hills which will temper my delivery, but your concern is noted and I will be aware of Anoo's youthful perspective."

"Soften, yes, but your view of the world is deeper and more individual now than when I went with you. Because of that, your view will appear more abrupt to Anoo than it did to me. Also, a lot of boys see more truth in the words of others than in the words of their fathers even when the words are much the same. Therefore, your words will carry a lot of weight with him," says Eli.

"That is all true. As much as I was around when you came back, you will be around even more for him. He does listen to you. You've been a good father to him and Tohlee will help. She has been a good and loving mother. You've learned a lot since I took you walking. That learning will be a benefit to Anoo. Talking to you and Tohlee, after the boy gets back, will show him different perspectives on all the things he and I will talk about. You, Tohlee, and I all hold similar views of the human condition and the world around us. We express those similar views differently in our lives and in our words. Anoo will see broader possibilities for his own individuality because of the differences in our methods of expressing and living the similar views we hold."

"That is also true; Anoo will see several ways to incorporate similar values and views into life. I think that will help him trust his own decisions and perspective as he creates his own individuality. His youthful perspective on what you talk about with him will not seem as far from what you say once Anoo compares the difference his perspective creates with the differences the three of us hold and are comfortable with in each other. There were things that I needed to learn as an adult from loving Tohlee and from Tohlee herself. Anoo will see in Tohlee and me three different views, a man's view, a woman's view, and the view of a man and woman loving each other. I wonder where these different circumstances since my travels with you will take him. I also wonder how much more you have learned in the last thirty years, Mateen. How much more would I learn if I walked with you now?"

"Perhaps some, my friend, but most things I've learned since our walk I have talked to you about during my visits. As you have told me about things you have learned yourself and through knowing and loving Tohlee. How you have used the things we talked about almost thirty years ago has taught me also. Your individual path of life has brought a perspective to you which in return brought learning back to me. The things you have learned through loving Tohlee I have only in memories, not as a part of my daily life. I admit that this does lessen my patience and causes me to be more abrupt. All these things Anoo will be exposed to on this walk as well as in his life. My losses and age, your fullness of life with Tohlee and hers with you, what Anoo adds to your life and Tohlee's. I don't know how these various perspectives will affect Anoo. I am just helping him along and furthering what you and Tohlee have begun. Anoo's life will be his own adventure."

"Well said, Mateen, let's go over and join Tohlee and Anoo."

As they walk toward Tohlee and Anoo, Eli and Tohlee's farm surrounds them. The morning is cool with the promise of late spring warmth by the afternoon. Vibrant green springtime leaves rustle in the breeze, setting off the blue sky and white cumulus clouds. Turkeys and chickens forage nearby in the orchard as Eli's dog guards them. The horses neigh as they see the men walk away without delivering a treat, only a scratch behind the ears and a pat on the neck. Two cats watch from the barn as they walk by with one of Tohlee's dogs keeping pace beside them. The grass in the yard is growing long as the neighbors haven't brought Tohlee and Eli's calves for the summer yet. Tohlee's second dog rolls and plays in the tall grass as Tohlee and Anoo talk.

"I will miss you, Mother."

"And I you, Anoo. Please take advantage of this time with Mateen. He is an experienced man who has seen and done many things. Listen to him. Ask questions if you don't understand the reason behind his actions or words. Voice your opinion if you don't agree, but voice your opinion with respect and courtesy, as a desire for greater learning, not as criticism."

"Yes, Mother. I'll be open to new things and I'll be polite."

"Do that, Anoo. Mateen, your father and I think that learning and experience put into perspective begets wisdom. Learning, experience, and perspective are explainable. Learning is about facts and concepts and how they are applied to life. Perspective comes from the experience gained through the application of those facts and concepts learned in one's life. You must know the reasons behind another individual's perspective in order to turn their learning and experience into your own individual wisdom. Learning without the pattern of reason is hollow - merely information.

"Collect all the information you can, for it is valuable. But you, Anoo, are capable of being more than a container for information and others' experiences. You will assimilate information in your own way and use it your own way and therefore become your own individual."

"I understand, Mother."

"Obey no human and you will serve no human. Serve no human, Anoo, for you will find that servitude will belittle your potential more than it will comfort you. Be accountable for all your actions and you will be free. I want you to be free. If you accept another person as responsible for your actions, it will lessen your freedom and it will still be an individual decision you are held accountable for. Joy of living and learning comes from freedom. A person physically chained to their work can be free in their heart. A person who does not create their own individuality will not be free in their heart. It won't matter what goods they have or what freedoms they have to move their body when and where they want to. Feel joy at the responsibility for yourself and you will have a freedom of spirit which is a stronger base to live your life from than any human can give you. Be strong in your heart, mind, and body. Trust yourself and cast aside your self-imposed limitations. I have no doubt that what you will find in yourself will be good and that you will grow to be a decent and compassionate man. My love is a freely given gift to you. Take care, Anoo, and go with my love."

"Thank you, Mother; my love is with you also."

"Here comes your father and Mateen."

"Be strong, Anoo."

"Yes, Father, I will."

"Pay attention to what goes on around you. If you find yourself in a time of danger, obey Mateen. When you then find yourself in a place where you can reflect on what happened, ask him why he told you to do what he did. He will not ask for your obedience lightly. To be responsible for your actions you must be aware of yourself. Responsibility for yourself is hollow without honesty. To be honest you must not only be aware of your actions but also of the effect your actions have on yourself and others. Without honesty, the accuracy of your memory will fall to vagueness. A vague memory will decrease the awareness of yourself that you will need in order to create individual responsibility. The awareness which results in a clear memory allows for the reassessment of your actions, a reassessment that individual learning and change can be based on. The circle I've just described is one I enjoy living, Anoo. Be strong and aware. Be honest and responsible. Learn and change. Do these things and you will have a base for your life that will not fail. Not in this life or the next. My love and good thoughts go with you, Anoo. Walk well, my son."

"Thank you, Father."

"Now it's time for us to walk, Anoo. First, we will hike a fair distance to get past some of the nearer farms and town. Pay attention as we go. Pay attention to how your body is working and to what is happening around you. Feel good about walking on this late spring day with the cool breeze blowing away the clouds while you feel its freshness on your face. Peace to you, Tohlee and Eli. Peace to you."

"Peace to you, Mateen, and to your charge."

Tohlee and Eli stand arm-in-arm as they watch Mateen and Anoo walk down their lane and turn south, upriver towards town. Eli knows after they are out of sight Mateen will turn off the road and circle up around town before heading farther up into the hills. Watching until Mateen and Anoo go out of sight around a bend and seeing their dogs running back down the road to their home, they turn to each other and embrace.

"Do you think that was too formal of a parting, Eli?"

"I don't. I think it was not a time for tears or an attitude of what will he do without us."

"I wanted to cry and sob and clutch him to me."

"I think it was a time to part as we will welcome him home, as a young man well on his way towards growing above his need for parental nurturing. We will welcome him home as a friend as much as our child," says Eli.

"You're a wise man, a man who can communicate his perspective with clarity to the benefit of all around you."

"And you are a wise woman, a woman whose love and compassion extends out from yourself and grows in the people around you."

"You melt my heart, Eli."

"You fill mine, Tohlee, and fill me with the desire to melt into you."

"Let's go melt together, but it's too chilly to lay a blanket in the orchard," says Tohlee.

"I think the morning sunny spot in the loft would be perfect," says Eli.

"I'll race you," says Tohlee as she starts to run.

"I'll let you win so I can follow you up the ladder and look up your dress."

"To see this?" says Tohlee as she turns and skips backwards while lifting her dress up to her waist.

"Hey! You're taking the fun out of my peeking game."

Tohlee continues lifting her dress over her head and, pulling it off, throws it at Eli.

"When you change the game, Tohlee, it only makes me wish for a longer ladder."

Mateen and Anoo's walk starts in the pastoral valley where Anoo has lived his entire life. Cottonwood and box elder trees top the river with willow, dogwood, alder, and many smaller shrubs crowding underneath in the patchy shade. The rich bottomland soil fills in any other spaces underneath with tall grasses and forbs. Gravel and sand bars in the river are starting to appear as the high-melt water of spring recedes. Just away from the river, hay meadows that seasonally flood rise to become tilled crop fields and orchards edged by hedgerows. Houses and barns are scattered here and there at the ends of two-track lanes. Above the valley floor shrub land of gambles oak, serviceberry, and chokecherry are interspersed with dry sagebrush-dominated meadows. As the elevation increases the tall shrubs become mixed with small patches of aspen. Higher still, the aspen become forests broken by wet meadows. Farther in the distance the deep green of pine, spruce, and fir darken the hilltops.

"Let's rest and eat here, Anoo. We will go on in a little while."

"How far do you think we've walked?"

"I'd say about six miles. We headed upstream past town which as you know is about five miles from your parents' farm and then we climbed about a mile up this hill. Do you see how the two valleys to the side of us come together down below?"

"Yes, they come together as one big valley which starts where the town is."

"The town grew where it did because of the two streams coming together and the power their joined waters create, especially in spring and early summer. This hill we are climbing becomes a ridge that keeps those two streams separate. There are farms in the valleys below us on either side similar to your father's. They run up their respective valleys for a couple of miles. Then the valleys narrow down too much for farming. My place is about five miles east of here. As I've said when you've visited with your father, the stream that flows by my place goes out of the hills and onto the plains, not into the river to our East that runs into town."

"How far will we go today?" asks Anoo.

"We'll keep going up this hill and then along the ridge for several more miles. That will put us a couple miles past the last farms. After that we'll go farther up into the hills. The hills form the headwaters of the two streams we can see down below us."

"Where will we go in the hills?"

"We will just wander. There are a few places I would like to see again. We will go here and there."

"You've been way up in the hills before?"

"Yes, I've gone by myself and with others many times. I went with your father for the first time about thirty years ago. He was about your age then. We wandered, saw many interesting things, and we talked."

"What did you talk about with my father?"

"We talked about each other, the many aspects to the planet we are living on, and the world we are living in. Much the same as you and I will do. I want you to understand that many things we talk about will be subjects or perspectives you can spend a lifetime exploring if you choose."

"Okay, Mateen, are there people living far up in the hills?"

"No, not really living there. People from the valleys do go onto the lower slopes to hunt, and to gather wood, wild foods and herbs. There are also people who wander through at times, people who have chosen a nomadic lifestyle. So we may see a few people but probably not very many. The valley has richer soil and enough people to keep the wilder predators away. Living in the valley makes for an easier life than up in the hills. But it's not so easy a life that many people go up into the hills looking for adventure or challenge as we are going to do."

"Do the nomadic people move through the hills often?"

"Some years they do, but usually later in the summer. Especially during dry summers they'll bring their grazing animals up to the green grass of the high country."

"Are there many wild predators?"

"There are some, but not so many that we will have to be fighting them off. It's always a good idea to keep your eyes open. You need to remember who and what you are. We aren't carrying any real weapons, just knives and our walking staffs. Most animals will shy away from people, but make sure you give them the opportunity to do so by paying attention and seeing them before they see you. Without weapons you wouldn't want a bear or wolf to feel like you've cornered them or that they must defend themselves against you. Let's just sit back and relax for a little bit, Anoo."

Mateen and Anoo choose to stop on a small rocky rise where they can look down the hill they are climbing. Tall shrubs and short aspens with twisted trunks ring the rise. They sit between some large rocks with sagebrush, clump grass, and a few forbs growing out of the rocky soil. With a quick look around for nearby ant hills they stretch out. After a short nap under the noon sun they rouse themselves and share a snack of dried fruit.

"Tell me, Anoo, what caught your eye as we walked?"

"I noticed a lot of things, the blue sky and white clouds, the breeze blowing the green leaves, birds on the wing. Some were up high, going elsewhere while some were lower, moving from nest to feeding areas. There was a lot of activity on the farms as we went past. Spring is a busy time for farmers like my mother and father. There is planting and caring for the young plants that haven't fully established themselves yet. Most of the farmers I saw were doing similar things. There didn't seem to be many larger animals moving around besides the domestics. I saw a couple of deer as we climbed up this ridge."

"What kind of deer?"

"Whitetails."

"That's right, but I meant were they male or female?"

"They were both female."

"And how old were they?" asks Mateen.

"I guess I'm not sure."

"I think the larger one was fully mature but not old like eight years or more and the smaller one was her female yearling. A female yearling often stays with her mother. She helps the mother with this year's fawns."

"She helps out how?" asks Anoo.

"She mainly watches for predators, or anything that could harm the fawns."

"So that means the mother gets a break sometimes, right?"

"Yes, it does. It also means the yearling is learning how to care for fawns from her mother at the same time she is helping her mother. Most of the larger animals don't move around much in the middle of the day. There are hawks circling the ridge we are on. They like the warm air that flows up the sides of the ridge and then lifts off the crest. Hawks, eagles, and vultures can ride those currents and hardly use any energy at all. For those kinds of birds the heat of day and these breezes are similar to you and me stopping here to rest. They are also safer up in the air than on the ground. Did you see the robin that skipped along next to me?"

"I did. I was surprised we could get that close to it even though robins aren't very afraid of people."

"No, they aren't. But as close as I've come to robins they have never let my shadow cross over them."

"Why is that?" asks Anoo.

"I don't know. Maybe to a robin a person's shadow is just as real as the person is. I really don't know. It's just something I've noticed. I've seen robins in the hills flush two hundred feet away from me and I have also had robins in people's yards let me walk up within a few feet of them. Different individual animals of the same species can have different patterns of behavior. You can learn the basic patterns of a particular species of animal, in this case a bird that hunts animals in the summer and eats berries in the winter. After that basic learning you can start to see that different individuals of the same species have different ways of doing similar things. The robin in a yard, while hunting worms, is more concerned with the cat of the house. The robin in a meadow is more concerned with flying predators while it is hunting worms. Thus the different reactions to a person, the yard robin saw just another person and not a cat while the meadow robin saw unexpected and unfamiliar movement. Much the same as the different farmers we saw are doing similar things in their own way. Each is tending their crops and animals. Each has their own methods of the best way to do this."

"But each of the farmers is an individual," states Anoo.

"And each of the animals you see are individuals also, Anoo. You just have to get to know them as individuals. Most people see robins as a type of bird. They don't separate one robin from another. Robins know one from the other. A person's choice not to see robins as individuals helps create that person's perspective of robins. A person's perspective of robins does not change the robins themselves. For example, a male robin won't feed any female that happens to be on a nest and female robins won't let any male take over incubating their eggs. They know themselves as individuals just as you can get to know them as individuals if you choose. You can look at the farmers you saw today as a group or you could get to know them as individuals if you took the time. The same is true for any animal you run across. Take your dogs, for example. Are your dogs different individuals from each other?"

"Yes, they are. They each have their own personality."

"You see that individuality in your own dogs because you are familiar with them, not because they are the only dogs capable of individuality."

"But people are different in that they think and have souls, aren't they?" asks Anoo.

"How do you know animals don't think or have souls? Just because an animal doesn't tell you that it thinks or what it thinks doesn't mean that it doesn't think. Dogs are very intelligent animals. Have you seen your dogs learn things?"

"Yes, I have. My father taught them how to protect the crops, to bark at strangers, and where the boundaries of our property are."

"Your dogs aren't just copying the actions of your father. I believe they are choosing to act, using their memories of your father's actions and lessons to guide them. Your dogs make that choice partly because of their bond between your father and themselves and partly because of their own territoriality. They choose to act sometimes without your father's commands. Your father has seen them patrol the boundaries of the property and garden at night without having been told. Choosing to act with memories of past actions and learning as a guide is one of the things people consider thinking to be. "I think I'll go visit the neighbors" is considered to be a thought. Creative thought is something different. But then, I don't know many people I consider to have creative thoughts or to have creative thoughts often in any given day. So I wouldn't hold that against dogs or other animals."

"So from your perspective dogs and other animals can think?" asks Anoo.

"I think that we can't say they don't and there is plenty of evidence to suggest they do. I can live my life just fine without knowing for sure. What I don't want is the burden of a negative-unsubstantiated conclusion on me. I don't need to know if dogs can think to feel comfortable with myself. Nor do I need to decide dogs can't think in order to feel good about myself. I would rather accept that I do not know a thing than say or act like I do, just to feel comfortable with myself."

"What do you mean feel comfortable with yourself?" asks Anoo.

"Some people want an order to life. Such as animals are less than people and plants are less than animals. People think, but animals don't. Some people like to have an answer and an order for everything. It causes them to feel comfortable. I feel comfortable knowing what I know and accepting what I don't know. I also don't worry about things I can't know or don't know yet. Many people's answers on a lot of subjects are not well thought out. Those people don't like the feeling of not knowing something or appearing as though they don't know. So they act as though their perspective or information is all that there is on any given subject instead of accepting what they don't know and realizing that they need to learn more about a subject. Truth or correctness for those people is based on how they feel, not the level of accuracy in their answer. There are many things I don't have an answer for and I feel just fine about myself without knowing. I feel comfort from standing on my own thought and experiences. I gain no comfort from other people's thoughts and feelings that I can't verify with my own experiences or perspective. People's thoughts and feelings that you can't verify with your own experience is information with no right or wrong or accuracy built into it. It doesn't matter who is talking or what the source of the thought is."

"Even you and my mother and father?" asks Anoo.

"Whoever the person, whatever the book, or whatever the belief, wherever you find the source, it is only information. The value of that information is found in how you can relate your experiences to that information and so combine that information and your experience into your own perspective. Having your own thoughts means when you hear something said like, "animals don't have souls," you see for yourself if it is true. Whether animals have souls or not is not determined by the perspective of the people commenting on the animals just as people's perspective of robins does not create the individual capabilities of robins. Whether animals have souls is an unanswerable question. Because of that you can be sure that anyone who makes a statement that indicates they do know is more concerned with their feelings than with the accuracy of their statement. Ask yourself what a statement is based on. Why do people think they know what they know? Unfortunately, all too often the reason people think they know something is true is because they want the comfort of an answer. Not because of the correctness of their position. All too often you will find people's truths are based on nothing more than repetition over time. Someone somewhere stated a thing was true and then it was repeated many times over until it was taken for granted. The idea that truth in a thought is determined by the degree of comfort associated with that thought has no more rationality to it than if I said, "It is so because I feel like it is." How can anyone know if animals have souls or not? People don't know definitively what their own souls are. So how can they know an animal doesn't have one? Animals may have souls and they may not. I believe there is more to life than what is in between birth and death on the physical part of this planet. My beliefs do not create life's truths; they create my perspective. I don't need to know the truth of souls to enjoy the breeze on my face. And that enjoyment isn't meaningless to me. Nor are the people I know and the things I see meaningless to me. I am my own meaning. I don't need to think I am above animals or different from them to feel special about myself. I believe that every individual entity is special. That means you, me, your parents, animals, plants, rock crystals, stars, all entities. If, in truth, these things have souls or if they don't is not important to me. All are special and all justify themselves without any help from me or any other person. Are you ready to walk, Anoo?"

"I am. I have a lot to think about. But why is it wrong to believe something is true even when the only reason for that truth is to feel certainty? At least the goal is good."

"When you look beyond a goal and see that the goal requires your conformity to an inaccurate perspective or incomplete information, that transitory goal of immediate feeling is most often not good. Certainty based on shared opinion is not the same as certainty based on available learning and experience. Truths must have accuracy, not just repetition. I'm a person who feels better about myself through accepting what I don't know rather than pretending that I do know something. I find that my mind is more open to new learning when I don't have to dismantle what I've pretended first. Having to dismantle what one has earlier pretended is a common way for people to get in the way of their own ability to learn. An open mind is quicker to learn and change than one closed by an inaccurate conclusion. Pretending to know something is all too often merely a strategy in order to fit in with other people. Accepting another person's perspective as truth instead of thinking for yourself is taking the easy way. If you aren't thinking for yourself, you are not having independent thoughts. I believe that independent thoughts and emotions create soul."

"What, Mateen?"

"You heard me. Let's walk, Anoo. The breeze feels good. Pay attention to where you put your feet. You can put what I've said into perspective just as well by walking and paying attention to what you're doing as you can by sitting and thinking about it. We'll have plenty of time for both over the next few weeks."

The hill they are climbing becomes a gently rising ridge as Mateen and Anoo continue walking. The breeze is cooling but not chilly as the sun has warmed the hills this bright mostly clear day in early June. Shadows from puffy white fair weather clouds move over the hills on the far sides of the valleys they are walking between. The edges of the shadows from the clouds move uphill as fast as they descended into the valleys. The shadows pass over them as shade that causes their eyes to squint when the sunlight abruptly returns. The walkers continue farther into the hills as the afternoon turns towards evening.

"Let's drop down off the top of this ridge into the drainage below us," says Mateen. "It looks like a fine place to camp. It's level down in that area and there's water nearby, a nice view, and we'll be able to see the sunset behind the far ridge. Let's get set up and eat."

"Then what will we do?"

"We'll take a look around and see what else is up and about this coming evening."

"Do we need to set up the tent?" asks Anoo.

"What do you think we should do? Do you think it will be too cold for you? Or that it will rain?" responds Mateen.

"I don't think it will be too cold, but it might rain a little bit by early morning before I'll want to be up."

"You're right that there's often a little early morning rain or heavy dew in late spring when the heat of day has left. But we'll sleep outside tonight. It may rain, but probably not. We should put up the tent anyhow. It doesn't take long to set the tent up or take it down. We'll put our gear inside and then, if it does rain, we just have to get up and go in the tent. After we set up the tent, I'll get our food ready while you gather some firewood."

"Okay, Mateen."

The sun is lowering in the sky as Anoo wanders around finding dried twigs and branches. His small folding camp saw makes short work of even the larger branches he cuts. As a young man he can't resist flexing his biceps and feeling the increasing strength of his arms. After trimming the branches down to carrying size he takes his work back to camp, noticing as he does that the scattered clouds promise a colorful sunset in the long evening of early June. It will be a couple hours after the sun goes down before a spring chill returns to the air. Anoo knows it's better to gather wood in the light than in the dark. That it's better to get camp chores done before a colorful sunset than to have to interrupt one.

"Why don't you get a fire going and tell me how you start and keep a fire going as you do it, Anoo."

"Sure, I'll explain how Father taught me, which is probably how you taught him. First you put down some tinder. Well, first I guess you clear out a spot for the fire. I did that already. Then you put down some tinder like this dried grass and pine needles."

"Where did you get the dried grass and pine needles?"

"They're from under that big ponderosa pine over there where it was drier than out in the open. Then, over the tinder I put a few very small twigs that were still attached to the tree but dead and dry. Dry because they were up in the air not down on the ground. Dry leaves can work as tinder also."

"And your next step?"

"I have a stack of sticks here that are a little bit thicker and ranging up to quite a bit thicker than the small twigs that are already over the tinder. They will be ready to go on the fire after the tinder and twigs are going. Then, there's big wood that will burn awhile to put on after the sticks get going."

"All prepared before you ever light the tinder. That's well done. How will you light the tinder?"

"Well, I have a few ways. Father always says to carry more than one way to start a fire. I have a little candle, some wax or oil soaked paper, matches covered with wax, and flint and steel with me."

"Very good, I also carry a magnifying glass with me just in case. The idea, as your father says is to have more than one way to start a fire and to keep them in more than one place. Never go far from your pack when you're out in the woods, but still keep a fire-making method in your pocket at all times. Then you'll always be able to get a fire going. Fires can be used to signal for help, keep you warm, boil water, cook food, and keep wild animals away. Not just the ones that might hurt you, but the smaller critters that might raid your camp and eat your food. Perhaps most importantly, Anoo, fires are a real comfort if you're in a bad spot. For people in a bad spot, they help create the comfort that supports the ability to think their way out of the spot they're in. For us, on nights like tonight, they are just nice to sit around and look at while talking and enjoying the evening. Where does the flame and heat come from when wood is burned?"

"Father explained that to me. It's the sun coming back out of the wood. Trees and shrubs take energy from the sun through photosynthesis and store that energy as wood. Then, with an ignition source, the wood combines with oxygen in the air, causing the sun to come back out of the wood as light and heat."

"Well said. There's a light breeze blowing tonight that will help feed oxygen to the fire and will move the smoke away from us as we enjoy the fire. After the fire is going good and hot, we'll let it die down to some nice coals to cook over. Then, after we eat, we'll take a look around."

Mateen has set a pot of water near the fire. He puts some dried vegetables and meat prepared the previous fall into the pot. They will soak up moisture as the pot slowly starts to warm from being near the fire. After the food softens, some of Tohlee's fresh spring herbs will be added to the mix. They won't last long and then Anoo's packet of dried herbs will come in handy. The pot will go on the coals to heat up to eating temperature after soaking awhile. The campsite is on a small rise overlooking another of the small streams they've walked above as they traveled along the ridge top. The stream points to the hills on the west side of the valley and has a nice pond in it. While waiting for their food to cook Mateen and Anoo stretch their tired muscles and then relax near the fire. As they look mid-slope across the valley, they see a hillside with isolated groves of pines and aspen with meadows scattered throughout. Up towards the top of the ridge only some rocky cliffs and talus slopes break up the nearly continuous stands of dark timber. The ridge they are on is much the same as the mid-slope of the far ridge with a line of willows and alders marking the stream.

"That was a good meal, Mateen."

"Thank you. A nice long hike is great for the appetite. Let's take a walk down to the pond and take a look around. There is always activity at a pond."

They quietly walk down to the pond, but aren't trying to stay undercover like they would if they were stalking an animal.

"Here's a good place to sit, Anoo. I could watch dragonflies hunt for hours just like I can watch hummingbirds for hours. Both animals move similarly. Very quick, very exact. Both are incredibly well adapted to their own styles of life."

"Father has shown me moths that fly like hummingbirds."

"They are a type of sphinx moth. I like to hear their wings buzz when they are right next to my ear. They come out in the late evening and at night usually later in the summer in cold climes," says Mateen.

"What about dragonflies and hummingbirds? Do you like the way they sound right next to your ear?" asks Anoo.

"Dragonflies clatter too much. Hummingbirds sound good in the ear. But I'm partial to the moths. They are to my ears what a fresh breeze is to my face. They help clear my mind because I give my entire attention to the sound and that aids me in creating my perspective of myself and the world around me because when they move on I look at the world around me without things in my mind tugging at me."

"What things tug at your mind?" asks Anoo.

"Oh, things about my life and the world around me, things I regret about my life or things I don't like about the world around me. We'll talk about things to avoid in your life, things to avoid so you won't have regrets later on that waste your time and energy. I'm not saying that all regrets are bad. A person who has no regrets in life has probably taken baby steps all through their life. Sometimes you have to jump into life with both feet. If you do that, you're bound to make some pretty big mistakes. We'll talk about things you'll be exposed to from the world around you that may have a limiting effect on you. Your parents and I want you to think for yourself. If you accept the thoughts of others as truth or being accurate without question, you will end up with their limits. The limits of others, whoever they may be, were designed around themselves. They never considered you as an individual when they decided what their limits were. Think for yourself. Take responsibility for your thoughts, actions, and emotions. Don't do violence. Know that awareness of self cannot be accomplished without honesty. Know that you cannot learn something new and important without changing yourself. Know that you are strong enough to choose to change parts of yourself and adapt to that change through your own intent. Walk lightly on this earth. Take what you need. Kill only for food and use what you kill," says Mateen.

"Don't I do all those things already? I think, I'm responsible around the farm, I don't hurt things, I'm honest, and I change as I learn new things. I also don't kill for sport or challenge."

"You are a good person, Anoo, and a product of your parents' teachings. I'm not criticizing you. I'm introducing what we'll be talking about in greater detail during our time together. What you are doing now is a base for when you're older and the choices you make are broader and deeper, the applications of principles more subtle. These good things you do now are strongest when they are your choice, when you justify your own actions with your own thought. They will become the base you will live your life from when you make the transition from the existing framework of your parents' lives to your own. There is more power in thoughts coming from a clear mind than I could ever express to you. That power of thought comes from acting well and being straight with yourself. It does not come from accepting the perspective of others. The perspective of others contains no power of your own. The power you obtain in accepting the perspective of others is only what comes from having no doubts. No doubts because you have given up responsibility for yourself. That is a very large price to pay for having no doubts and it is an illusion. The choice you make to follow someone else's perspective or system of beliefs is still your individual choice, still your responsibility. You can achieve the same lack of doubt by being a good and strong person and applying to your own life the principles I'm telling you about. Then you build your own individuality, through your own thoughts and perspective, on your own goodness and strength.

"Sometimes doubt leads you to new thoughts. Not doubt in yourself, but doubt in a line of reasoning or a course of action. You will become strong enough to tear down your own thoughts and beliefs and then build them up again, Anoo. The power of clear thoughts can wipe away limits. Limits that are self-imposed or limits from the world around you. I have found when I take away limits the only base strong enough to stand on is my own thoughts and actions, my own experience and energy. Limits that are imposed by others or by an outside system of beliefs are inherently restraining. Self-imposed limits are limits you have created and are also restraining. They are not limits imposed on you by your condition as a human being living on this planet. Regrets take power from your thoughts and actions like limits do. Learn to turn your regrets into experience so you can move on from those regrets. To intentionally go beyond your limits and so change yourself you must be comfortable with yourself. Your intent applied with your experience will give power to your life and choices. Learn to change your self-imposed limits with the power of your thoughts and your life will be an unending adventure."

With that, Mateen and Anoo take a look around the pond and around themselves, noting where they can only see a few feet and where they can look between clumps of vegetation to areas away from the pond. Mateen situates them where several of the sight lanes come together with some shrubs nearby to hide behind if something comes in close and they want to observe unseen.

"Sit here and listen to what is going on around you, Anoo. Close your eyes and see with your ears what is happening around you. The clarity of mind you need to see with your ears, when focused inside you, will allow you to know your thoughts and emotions. Knowing your thoughts and emotions through the clarity of your mind will allow you to judge their value. Those values felt in your heart and judged by a clear mind will allow you to know the parts of yourself you want to change and the parts you want to reinforce."

"I'll close my eyes and listen, but what is it that I am trying to hear? How do I see with my ears?"

"You are listening for the details of the sounds around you. First, know that I will be doing this with you. After all my years I still need to see details of my hearing for clarity of mind. In the same way that sometimes I still need a fresh breeze in my face to redirect my attention outside myself. Close your eyes. Listen and tell me the details of what you hear. See what you hear as an image in your mind."

After a few minutes and just as many fidgets, Mateen and Anoo settle against the ground. Their breathing and pulse slow and they start to realize the world around them through their ears. First comes the gentle rustling of the breeze in the leaves and grass. Then as they become familiar with those sounds, their ears reach past the rustle out over the pond and around behind themselves.

"I heard a splash in the water very near us," says Anoo.

"It was near us. But what made the splash? Was it a frog jumping in the water from the bank of the pond? Was it a fish jumping after an insect or a kingfisher catching a minnow? Did I throw a rock in the pond? Did a beaver hit its tail on the water? Think about the sound you heard. Think about what you know of sounds and water. What do you think it was?"

"A beaver makes a loud smack when it hits its tail on the water. It wasn't that loud a sound. A frog plops into water from the bank when it's scared. It wasn't that singular a sound. I didn't hear your clothes move. So I don't think you threw a rock. I guess it was a fish or a kingfisher."

"Well done, Anoo. Well done. Have you heard any kingfishers call this evening?"

"No, I haven't."

"Kingfishers are often active with the strong light of day. Not exclusively, but they like the sun higher in the sky to see better into the water. This evening light is not best for them. Also, they are usually around larger streams or lakes. Isolated ponds like this usually can't support a kingfisher. Insects are often more active in the evening than in the middle of the day, but not always or only. It depends on the type of insect. The splash was made by a fish probably after an insect. Fish make almost no sound when they leave the water. Then their bodies make a different sound when they return to the water compared to the sound a kingfisher makes diving into and then flying out of water. I've seen fish jump right out of the water and try and catch an insect as it flies by. Fish bodies sound solid when hitting the water. A kingfisher hits the water hard too, but then there are more sounds as feathers and wings lift the bird back out of the water and water drips down from the bird. But well done! Concentrate on the details of hearing, and clarity of mind will follow. The information you gain of the world around you will end up turning what you hear into a picture in your mind. You will see in your mind the actions you hear around you. In much the same way you can see the actions of animals through their tracks. Clarity of mind and knowledge of the world around you are good things to strive for, my friend. Try it and see for yourself. Close your eyes. What do you hear?"

"I hear leaves rustling. It doesn't sound like the wind, it sounds like something alive is moving them," says Anoo.

"Concentrate. Are they green leaves on the trees? Think what could be moving the leaves."

"There is a pattern to the sound. I'm sure it isn't the wind blowing the leaves. An animal must be moving them. I hear hopping and then rustling in the leaves. Chattering! It is a squirrel, Mateen!"

"Very good, robins sound a lot like squirrels when they move through leaves. Robins usually stop and listen longer, though. They need to feel the vibrations of worms and bugs under the leaves. Squirrels are more likely to be going from one place to another. But they do stop and dig sometimes. Turkeys rustle in the leaves too. But their movements are heavier than what we heard. Play this game often, both with me on our trip and around your parents' farm. Listen and watch the actions of people with the clarity of mind you learn from this game. If you listen and watch people with enough detail and clarity of mind, you will not only see actions the actors aren't aware of; you will also get a perception of their emotions as well. Look into yourself with clarity and you will know the source of your thoughts and emotions. With that understanding, learn to make yourself the source of your thoughts. You need stand on no other person's reasoning for your thoughts to reach the breadth of your own individuality. As you learn to reach with your thoughts, you will find other people's reasoning is not a stable base to reach from. Make sure the source of your emotions can be said aloud to all the people around you. All too often the sources of emotions when people interact with others are petty. That is, until you learn to choose the source of your emotions. If you don't choose the source of your emotions, by choosing who you are and what values you hold, society will force its values on you."

"How do I make myself the source of my thoughts and how do I know the source of my emotions, Mateen?"

"You make yourself the source of your own thoughts by not accepting people's opinions as your own truth. Opinions are not right or wrong or the truth for all involved. They reflect individual values. One particular person be they pope, president, or parent, nor the numbers of people holding an opinion can ever be enough to make an opinion right or the truth for a free individual. Opinions are only information, something to remember and see if your own life or thoughts validate that information. If so, then you stand on your life and experience, not on the individual who gave you the information to begin with. You can know the source of your own emotions by looking into yourself with the clarity of mind and the focus on detail that comes from encompassing the breadth of the Earth while being aware of the individual life around you. A clear mind, inquiring toward the source of an emotion, will receive an answer before petty self-justifications can get in the way. Your clear mind will enable you to focus on detail and encompass the breadth of the Earth around you, ultimately causing you to have thoughts and emotions strong enough to add energy to your soul. I think it is a very tidy little circle of growth and self support. Let's head back to camp now."

When Mateen and Anoo get back to camp Anoo stirs the coals of the fire and adds more wood. Mateen puts their bowls and spoons into the stew pot with some water and places it next to the fire to heat up for washing. The sun has dropped behind the western ridge as they relax around the fire. Reds, oranges, and yellows reflect off the bottoms of the clouds that hang over the ridge. They hold their color even as the campsite is in full shade. Between the colors and warm food in their bellies, neither Mateen nor Anoo feels like talking or moving. After the colors fade and as darkness descends, Mateen washes out the pot and their bowls and Anoo stokes the fire. Mateen fills the pot back up with the water they brought back from the stream. The water they began their day with is almost gone. The pot of water set to boil on the stoked fire will cool off overnight and be ready for drinking the next day. Tired legs and full bellies lead to a short evening of quiet fire gazing. The tired and content adventurers crawl into their sleeping bags as the fire dies down. They both nod off amid their own silence and the rustling of nocturnal creatures.

After Mateen and Anoo left early in the morning, and after their little dalliance, Tohlee and Eli go about their normal routine around the farm. Just around lunch time Tohlee goes looking to see what Eli has been working on.

"What are you up to, Eli?"

"I'm making soil soup to plant these shrubs in."

"Tell me again how you make your soup. I could make it myself but I like to hear your explanation."

"I use part native soil, part aged manure, and part peat moss or rotted crumbly logs. If the soil has a lot of clay in it, I might add some sand or fine gravel also. The idea is to break up the native soil and mix in the manure for nutrients and the peat moss or organic matter so the soil won't re-compact again the way it was before I broke it up."

"How much of each part do you use?"

"It depends on what the native soil is like to begin with. But as a rough guess I'll say I start with 2/3rds native soil and 1/6th aged manure and 1/6th organic matter. That's to start with because I expect to top dress growing beds yearly. I want the shrubs to have a good start in their new and permanent home by rooting well. The better the root system of the shrubs the sooner we can use their fruits."

"How do you know when the soil soup is ready?"

"It's ready when I can stir it up as though a tined garden fork is a giant soup ladle. If I can move the fork through the soil in a figure-eight motion with the tines all the way in, then the soil is mixed and loose enough. Then the roots of the shrubs will have a loose and rich soil that holds water well to grow out into."

"What is it in this soil mix that holds water so well?"

"That is another part the organic matter plays. The organic matter helps keep the soil from compacting and it soaks up water. Dissolved in with the water are nutrients from the aged manure. The nutrients as well as the water are held in the organic matter, but are available to the root systems of the shrubs. This soil will help the shrubs develop a strong and deep root system. Once a strong and deep root system is established, the shrubs will grow up faster and stronger."

"The shrubs sound like a bigger version of the perennials I've been planting."

"How so?" asks Eli.

"I like to think that my perennial flowers sleep the first year, creep the second year, and leap the third year. But of course they aren't really sleeping that first year. It just looks like it on the surface. They are actually concentrating their growth on their roots. Then the plants can use their deep roots as a buffer against extremes of dryness and heat in the summer aided by your soil soup concoction. The second year the surface growth creeps because the perennials need more energy from the sun than the year before to further their root growth and the past year's root growth can support more surface growth. So, the plants put out more leaves than the year before. By the third year their roots are established well enough that the plants can leap up into the air with the energy stored in their root systems. The deep roots can reach water that the large amount of leaves that are grown need in order to stay healthy in the summer sun."

"What kind of perennials are you planting today?" asks Eli.

"A few different kinds, some are herbs for cooking, some are for medicine, and some are just for looks. What kind of shrubs are you planting?"

"Some more Nanking cherries, chokecherries, plums, raspberries, blackberries, and blueberries for more of the delicious jams you make. And some rose for the vitamin C in the hips that nourishes us when we make tea out of them."

"Don't forget how much the birds like to come into our yard for the fruits also," says Tohlee.

"You're right about that. They really add color and song to our day as well as eat bugs that we don't want around, so I don't mind planting extra so we can all get our share."

"Why are you planting the chokecherry and rose when there is so much growing wild all around us?"

"They produce a lot more when they're tended which makes harvest much easier and it leaves the wild berries for the birds," answers Eli.

"And you need all the chokecherries you can get for that good chokecherry stout you make," adds Tohlee.

"That is actually one of my main motivators for planting more," admits Eli.

"Aha! The truth is out now!"

"You've found me out all right. A nice glass of stout to sip in the fall while the trees are changing color and a nice breeze to rustle the dried leaves that have fallen to the ground, all making for a nice afternoon break. It is a wonderful way to relax and think about all that was grown and harvested through the warm season."

"Those are wonderful afternoons with you," agrees Tohlee. "Now I'm going to grab some of the soil you've made and do some more springtime planting."

"Hey, leave some for me, you wench!"

"Never, I say naught but a pittance for you and a large dollop for me."

"Argh, if thou weren't such a comely wench I'd take you over my knee!"

"Perhaps later, good sir, perhaps later!"

After the day spent caring for their plants, and after a quick and simple dinner, Tohlee and Eli are relaxing behind their house, looking out over their gardens and orchards. The sun will be setting soon and the dogs are relaxing with them. The cats are hanging around the barn doors, waiting for night so they can go out and do their hunting. They're hungry after not eating all day, but the cats have been taught that the night, not day, is for hunting. It took Tohlee quite awhile to teach them, but now their predation on her beloved songbirds is at a minimum and the mouse population is being kept in check.

"It is a beautiful evening, Eli."

"Yes, it is. I don't know if late spring is my favorite time of year or if early fall is."

"Luckily you don't have to make a choice about that," says Tohlee.

"You're right. I don't, and I would say that my favorite is whichever one I am enjoying at the moment."

"Did you plant all your shrubs?" asks Tohlee.

"I did. I had about a dozen of each kind come up from seed last year. After a year in pots I was ready to move them out into their permanent spots."

"Your method worked then? For saving the seeds over the winter and getting them to germinate, I mean?"

"It did. I cleaned all the organic matter off of the seeds and then let them dry out before I put them in the shed. There, the seeds were protected from animals and were also in a dark environment. I wrapped them up in an old blanket for protection from extremes of cold and the rare warm day in winter. They were still exposed to below-freezing temperatures for awhile which these shrubs seeds need. Then, around late March I put the seeds in pots with potting soil, but I kept the pots in the shed so the soil wouldn't warm up too fast. In early April I put the pots out where they got some sun, but not the warmest sun. They sprouted in May a year ago. This year, as one-year-old seedlings, they were ready to go in the ground."

"Will you protect them from deer now that they're in the

ground? I know you had the pots up by the house where the dogs keep the deer away."

"I will early on. They are still small enough that I don't want them browsed yet."

"Meaning you'll want them browsed later on?" asks Tohlee.

"I'm not sure. It's something I've thought about but I haven't made up my mind yet. I know that the types of shrubs that grow wild around here get trimmed off by deer. Too many times and the shrubs will be stunted and sprout many twigs at the ends of their branches. But if it's just once or no more than a few times, it does seem that browsing helps to thicken the trunks of the seedlings and make them stronger overall. If they aren't browsed here in the yard should I prune them myself to mimic the positive effect of light browsing?"

"Interesting, you could protect most of them from deer and prune those protected at a couple different rates. Then see what happens in the next few years. Between your different pruning rates and also the unprotected shrubs being impacted by deer, you'll have all the information you need to reach a conclusion."

"That's an excellent idea, my scientific wife."

"Why, thank you, Sir. Perhaps you will write a dissertation on your findings and credit me as your life, your soul, the very breath you take."

"Maybe or maybe I'll just follow up on your idea and see what happens." "Hardly as satisfactory, but I'll take what crumbs I can."

"Oh, you poor unappreciated woman."

"I'm glad you recognize my plight in life," states Tohlee with a straight face.

"Well, I think I've found the pile of manure I'll need for planting tomorrow!" quips Eli.

"Ho-ho, you crack me up sometimes! And what are you planning on planting tomorrow?" asks Tohlee.

"Actually, everything is in the ground now. I'm at a point where my plants can grow on their own for a time."

"Me too, what should we do?"

"Your choice," says Eli.

"Well, I have things I could do in the house in the morning. In the afternoon let's go down to the river for a swim," suggests Tohlee.

"Okay, but in early June it will still be cold."

"Yes, the water will be, but the sun will be warm."

"It's a date for tomorrow then, my love. And what shall we do tonight?" asks Eli.

"The electricity is on for another few hours. Once the sun is all the way down, let's go in and snuggle on the couch with our books. I've had a long day, so I don't think I'll last long before sleep," replies Tohlee.

"Sounds like an excellent way to end the day," agrees Eli.

Day Two

❯❯ Good morning to you, Mateen. How long have you been up?"

"Not long, Anoo. I like to see the colors of the sunrise. My eyes like to take in the colors."

"Take in the colors?" asks Anoo.

"I can feel the colors in my eyes. Sort of like seeing an image in your mind when you hear sounds. But this is a detail of feeling. Something you don't notice unless you're really paying attention. People take into their body through their eyes a lot of blue color from the sky, yellowish-white light from the sun, and green from plants. But there isn't that much opportunity to take in large quantities of red or orange or pink. Some parts of the earth are covered with red rocks. Those areas hold special meaning to some people. The rocks usually aren't as bright a hue as the reds of the sunrise and sunset."

"Are there red rock areas up here in the hills?"

"Not up in the hills but down on the plains on the southwest side of the hills there are. I think we'll end up over there later on in our trip. Another thing about red hues is the way pink light goes through bodies."

"Pink light goes through bodies like ours?"

"Yes, you can see that if you look at your hand with a strong light behind it, especially when the room behind you is dark. You'll see pink where the hand is not too thick with bone and muscle."

"Oh, I know what you mean now. But I thought that was seeing your own blood in your body?"

"Blood in your body not exposed to oxygen is blue. The aerated blood coming from your lungs is red and is carried by arteries to the important organs of the body. Blood with diminished oxygen content is blue like the blood being carried back to the lungs in veins."

"Are you saying arteries carry oxygenated blood away from the lungs to organs that need the oxygen and veins carry blood from the organs back to the lungs for more oxygen?"

"That's exactly what I'm saying. The blood in skin is, oh I'll say, half oxygenated, so it would not be red or pink. What you're seeing is pink light passing right through your skin and smaller amounts of muscle. Another interesting thing about light concerns green plants. What color of light do plants use for photosynthesis?"

"Green because plants are green. But I'm thinking that wouldn't be interesting enough to tell me about."

"Good thinking. The green you see on plants is the light reflected back off the plants, not the light that goes into the plants where photosynthesis occurs, plants mostly synthesize red and some blue light."

"That is really interesting. Are there lots of things like that? Things you have to learn about to really understand?"

"Many times, many, I think we should leave camp set up and just wander around for the day. What do you think?"

"That's fine with me. Is there anyplace near here you want to see again?" asks Anoo.

"No, we're still pretty close to town and my cabin is across the east fork and then only five miles or so, as I said yesterday. So I come through here at times. Let's just see what has been living around here. We'll eat as some of the chill leaves the morning air. Then we'll wander for the day."

It's still early morning, but the sun has warmed some of the morning chill away by the time Mateen and Anoo are ready to leave camp.

They take their day packs and start wandering up the hillside above camp. Some scattered clouds dot the sky, but they don't look threatening at this point. An afternoon thunderstorm is always a possibility to be prepared for, however. They've brought rain gear and some dried fruit and nuts to eat later on after exploring.

"What have you found, Anoo?"

"A dead deer. It's been dead for awhile. The bones are scattered and some have been gnawed by mice."

"Critters like mice and porcupines like to gnaw on bones and deer antlers for the minerals in them. How long do you think it has been dead?" asks Mateen.

"I guess sometime over the winter. I don't know for sure."

"Winter is a good guess. Some of the bones are broken like wolves ate them. It could have been winter killed and then scavenged or the wolves killed it themselves. It's hard to tell after a few months."

"Do wolves really only eat the sick and injured?" asks Anoo.

"I think they select the slow and weak whenever they can. The slow and weak are often the sick and injured. The wolves don't have to work as hard to kill the slow and weak and there is less risk while making the kill. That is why they prefer the sick and injured. I really don't think they would starve to death if they couldn't find any sick or injured. They would select the youngest or oldest if there weren't any sick or injured in the herd. Or they would shift to a different prey source. Sometimes when they are running the prey to see if there are any weak individuals in the herd a mistake can be made. A relatively healthy individual might make a tactical error. Maybe turn the wrong way and separate itself from the herd or run into some thick cover or maybe a snow drift and so slow itself down."

"It sure would be a violent way to die," says Anoo.

"Well, the deer do know the wolves are around. They have seen others of the herd brought down. The deer know what could be in store for them on any given day. Maybe they accept their part in the predator prey cycle? The wolves do have to eat. Do you feel violent or as though you have done violence when you kill for food?"

"No, I don't feel violent. I feel sad at the loss to the woods because I like deer and for the loss of the animal itself. I enjoy their grace and strength," answers Anoo.

"That feeling of loss can be used as motivation to make good use of the animals you kill. Be thankful for all the emotions you have received from deer. From enjoyment over a deer's strength and beauty, sorrow when you kill, all the way to how you feel when you have eaten from an individual animal. An individual animal that you killed and then you consumed the energy that individual had stored in its life for itself. Energy that you took from that individual animal's future and then used to add to your own strength and life. Your hunting and killing of the animal is as much a cycle of emotions as a cycle of predator and prey."

"Do you think the wolves feel those same emotions towards the deer as I do?" asks Anoo.

"I think the wolves know, just as you do, that the deer are prey worthy of respect. They know they have to be at their best and try hard to make a kill. I don't know what emotions are involved with wolves. But I know the same motivations for emotions are there for the wolves as they are for you. They are pushed to be at their best and maybe they appreciate their prey's ability to push them in this way. Wolves are intelligent animals just as your dogs are. Doesn't it seem as though your dogs feel love for you? Sadness when you are leaving? Joy when you return? I think wolves are intelligent, feeling animals. And you certainly don't have enough knowledge to deny them their intelligence or emotions, do you?"

"Of course not, Mateen, that would put the burden of a negative-unsubstantiated conclusion on me like when you talked about dogs thinking."

"Good one, Anoo. Do you think you understand the concept of the burden I was talking about or perhaps only the situation where it occurs?"

"I think there is probably more to the idea than I realize."

"The burden of the conclusion that I am talking about is a burden on your open mind, a burden on your development as an individual. It is a conclusion that if you want to go beyond it, you will have to make the effort to undo it first. Negative-unsubstantiated conclusions are the easy way out. They are a way to avoid thinking about difficult subjects. Difficult subjects contain the most potential for individual development. Whenever you feel that it is better to jump to a conclusion, rather than think about a subject, you are hurting your ability to use your intent to create depth in your own independent perspective."

"Okay, Mateen, I think I see what you mean."

"You need to choose to make yourself see new sides of an issue whenever you would rather just agree with the current tide of common perspective. All too often common perspective has a history of being the easy way out. Taking the easy way out is a method used to avoid a perspective that contains change in it. A method used to avoid choosing the growth that comes from intent."

"Okay! Okay! But I still wouldn't want to be eaten by a wolf pack."

"Nor would I, let's walk around some more. I've seen some very nice flowers blooming," says Mateen.

Mateen and Anoo continue to walk. The sun rises in the sky and continues to warm the earth around them as a gentle breeze moves the air. Patches of aspen, ponderosa pine, junipers, and large shrubs intersperse with meadows. The meadows are sometimes rocky with scattered sagebrush and sometimes lush with forbs and grasses. Mateen and Anoo aren't going anywhere in particular and therefore walk slowly while stopping often. Everything interests Mateen and he knows something about all types of life. At one time or another he has chosen to learn about insects, plants, birds, mammals both small and large, soils, geology, the cycle of water and the weather. He has delved into various specialties closely while his broader views have led him from one area of interest to another.

"Do you know these flowers, Anoo?"

"Mother has shown them to me but I don't remember their name."

"They're fawn lilies, or glacier lilies, or snow lilies, or dogtooth violets."

"Well, which is it?" asks Anoo.

"They are all common names for the same plant."

"Are they lilies or violets?"

"They are lilies. The common names came about in different places and times. One is no more correct than another. The one name that is correct is their Latin name."

"Why is the Latin name the most correct when we speak English?"

"Because that is how types of plants and animals have been organized by people. They each have one and only one Latin genus and species, while they may have many common names. This plant is Erythronium grandiflorum."

"Do you know all the plants' and animals' Latin names?"

"I know quite a few, but not all of them. Glacier lilies bloom early in the spring," says Mateen.

"Why are you calling them glacier lilies if their correct name is Erythum grand flower?"

"Because glacier lily is easier to say than Erythronium grandiflorum is. This particular patch is actually blooming later than most of its kind. Do you know why this particular patch of fawn lilies is blooming later than others of its kind and why some flowers can bloom earlier in the spring than others?"

"These are blooming later than others like it because they didn't warm up as fast."

"That's exactly right. But why didn't they warm up as fast?"

"It's because the sun didn't warm them up as quickly as the other patches."

"Yes, but that's not much of an answer because there's more involved here than just the sun."

"I guess because the trees shaded them."

"The trees shaded them a little but not that much because their leaves hadn't come out yet."

"Then it's because the sun doesn't shine on them as much as others near here."

"Yes, but the sun doesn't pick and choose what spots it shines brightest on."

"Then it's because the ground isn't pointed at the sun right here."

"That's right; this little slope is angled to the north. Most of this hill points west but this little portion points north. North-facing slopes don't receive as much direct sunshine as south or west-facing slopes, so they don't warm up as quickly."

"So the soil here didn't warm up as quickly as the west-facing slope around us and that's why this batch of fawn lilies started later than others," says Anoo.

"That's right, and that means this small portion of north-facing slope is a microclimate on the larger west-facing slope."

"It's a microclimate because this little area has a different climate than the area around it and that causes the same type of plant to act differently right here than others of the same type nearby," says Anoo.

"That's right, and this microhabitat is caused by the sun's aspect," says Mateen.

"What else can cause microhabitats?" asks Anoo.

"A microhabitat can be caused by different types of soils or maybe by being right next to a splashing stream."

"Those types of microhabitats can cause differences in the same types of plants also?" asks Anoo.

"Yes, any microhabitat can. The same types of plants can grow larger or produce more seeds if they are in a more favorable microhabitat than others of their kind nearby, and microhabitats can be detrimental to plants also. A place with compacted soil will cause water to run off it faster than a spot with looser soil which gives less opportunity for plants to absorb the water. Compacted soil also makes it more difficult for roots to grow down into compared to a looser soil."

"Won't one type of plant be replaced by another in that situation not just grow smaller or produce less seeds?" asks Anoo.

"That's a good point and you're right if the microclimate is different enough from the area around it. I was thinking of microclimates that are different from their surrounding area, but not very different. Do you know why glacier lilies are capable of blooming early in the spring?"

"I guess they like the cooler weather of spring and not the heat of summer."

"Yes, but how do they have the energy to bloom so early in the year?"

"It's just what they do."

"Of course it is what they do. They are right here in front of you blooming. But how is it they are capable of blooming so early compared to many other types of flowers?"

"I don't know, Mateen."

"It's because they store energy in a type of root called a bulb."

"Oh, like some of the flowers my mother grows in her gardens."

"That's right. A bulb is made of energy the plant stored from the year before. That energy is used by the plant the following year so it can get a head start on the plants around it."

"What do you mean by head start?"

"Later in the year all the trees above our heads will be completely leafed out and shade this patch of ground more completely. At that time this plant wouldn't be able to get the sunshine it needs to blossom. So it stores food through the winter to give it a fast start in the spring. A fast start so the trees won't shade it too much to blossom and so nearby grasses and forbs won't have had time to overshadow it either."

"Kind of like the fable of the ant and the grasshopper, Mateen?"

"Very good, Anoo! That is exactly what I mean! Some plants live one year and produce lots of seeds. They are called annuals and would be similar to the grasshopper of the fable. It is the eggs of the grasshopper that carry on grasshoppers from one year to the next, not the adult grasshopper overwintering. Just as it is the seeds that annuals produce that carry on that type of plant from one year to the next. Plants like this glacier lily live more than one year. They are called perennials. They also produce seeds but usually a smaller number each year than annuals produce. That's because the perennials have more than one year to produce the offspring that wIll be reproducing after the parent plant has died. That longer life span is how perennials successfully maintain their species while producing fewer numbers of seeds per year than annuals do."

"So you're saying the actual plants overwinter like the ants in the fable. They overwinter and prepare in the fall for the spring. That means there are two different methods to accomplish the same goal just like the different farmers in the valley," says Anoo.

"That's exactly right. You will find in nature that there are many different methods to accomplish the same goal. In the long run that goal is to reproduce a species own kind whether that kind is animal or plant. In the short term the goal is to find food or water, to avoid predators, to find shelter, or to store energy for a time when energy sources can't be found," says Mateen.

"That's what we're doing out here from one day to the next, isn't it?" asks Anoo.

"You're a smart boy, Anoo. Let's head back to camp and relax for awhile."

"Are we still going to stay around here today?"

"I think so. We'll relax and enjoy the afternoon. I want to sit quietly, to stretch, to listen, and to think. This evening we'll catch some fish for dinner out of the pond."

Tohlee and Eli enjoy an easy day of work and light chores before they go down to the river for a mid-afternoon swim. After a brisk swim they warm up on the blanket that they've spread out on the little gravel beach next to the river. Their naked bodies take in the sun and fresh air while the sound of the river and the birds in the trees are the only things they hear. After looking up at the blue and white sky and enjoying the feel of his body in the sun, Eli's attention is taken by the woman lying next to him and the afternoon's beauty is shared by them together.

"Oh, Eli, it's so good when we join together. I love it when you open me up. That you last until I orgasm and then wait for me to come around again."

"I think it only fair that you orgasm twice to my once."

"That doesn't seem fair for you."

"I get enjoyment watching and feeling you, Tohlee. And the longer I wait, the better it feels when I finish. There's no need to hurry, there's nothing that must happen sooner than later. I just like to lie inside you and not move sometimes. When I focus on the feelings you are enjoying I find my orgasm is my own conscious choice to make. I've found that when I pleasure you, I end up pleasured in a way greater than the pleasure of my own release. I like the feeling of sending energy into you when I'm holding you, energy from my being, not from my being physical, energy that comes from receiving a feeling."

"What do you mean by that?" asks Tohlee.

"It's like what I feel from you I want to give back twice as much to you. Not only from the feelings on my body. But also from the way your whole being feels against me and merges with me. When I move inside you I feel energy going from me to you as much as I feel your warm and softly-wet body wrapped around me. By the end I feel as much heat or energy transfer with you as I feel my orgasm into you. I think of our bodies as shaped energy transferors."

"Shaped energy transferors! You've never said that to me before. I send energy into you when we make love. I try to do that. Energy goes up into me from our being joined. Up into my heart and that energy is what I try and send back into you. Then I feel that energy coming back to me from you. Back to my heart that is open from my giving. I think, just as with anything else, this energy is enhanced by having a clear mind. I know I want to be here making love with you.

It is my freely made choice. There is no other place I would rather be and no one I would rather be with."

"And I with you, Tohlee."

"When you are inside me I feel the need to touch your arms and chest, to run my hands over you and kiss you. It feels like I am doing more than touching you when I do this, like I am giving more to you than a touch or a kiss," says Tohlee.

"That Is the energy I am talking about, energy that is in my emotions, emotions that are both physical and spiritual. The emotions that come from both the physical and the spiritual I call energy. I can feel that energy going from me into you and back into me from your heart, from your heart and through your fingers and lips and radiating out from your body. I delight in making love with you, Tohlee. And make no mistake; I enjoy the feel of your body, our differences fitting together. I enjoy the sheer physical pleasure of our lovemaking, especially out here by the river in the middle of the day. But the times I feel closest to you, as though we've shared the most, is when I feel my emotions, not as fulfilling a physical need, but as energy circling from me to you and back again."

"It is the same for me. My emotions start with me. Then grow into something I must give to you as you are giving to me. I give what I truly need to give to you when I'm in a circle of energy with you. You make no mistake either, Eli; I like these romps by the river for what else they are too. Good feelings coming from the body, under a blue sky with puffy white clouds, and with a breeze cooling the sweat running down my body."

A relaxed quiet settles over Tohlee and Eli. They both enjoy the time lying next to each other after their loving. A few clouds are drifting by in the sky moved by a wind as gentle as the breeze that stirs the nearby leaves. They watch the river moving by them and listen to its gurgling in the run, just above the swimming hole.

"I hope it's this way for everyone, Eli. It seems so natural to have these emotions and energies come from our lovemaking. Natural through deciding with a clear mind that you are who I want, natural for being able to see no difference between pleasing you and pleasing me. My choice to give to you causes me to be comfortable with myself. My choices are in line with my heart and mind. I think natural is caused by a clear knowledge of my wants and clear knowledge of my heart. My emotions are let loose by my choices about my life and you, more so than my body alone can do. There is a place on a woman's body you can touch and it will unleash her desires. And that place is her heart. You touch my heart, my love."

"I don't think it's this way for everyone because I don't think all couples are as comfortable with each other as we are. I think that if men and women were honest with themselves about why their lovemaking doesn't satisfy each other to the depths that their sharing is capable of. Honest with themselves as to why men rush or women lay back with minimal participation. The honest answer that would be received is that they actually don't like the person they are making love to at the emotional depths that can be found through making love. Any man can last as long as he would like if he really cares for and is comfortable with the woman he is loving. The man just has to hold a value system where the value of the two bonding is greater than the more transitory need to feel release," says Eli.

"A woman should want to move and touch when she physically shares her emotions with a man. A clear heart and mind leads the body to emotions it could never get by following only the physical. I feel sorry for people who have let life get in between their partners and themselves. Or have let another person get in the way of who a clear heart and mind says they should be with," says Tohlee.

"Letting someone else sway your heart does not produce the clarity of mind that the choice of giving one's heart does. It doesn't produce a base a lifelong decision can stand on. And you know what they say; "Bad marriages have caused more fucking, as compared to making love, than kids romping in a haystack and experimenting with their bodies ever could," says Eli.

"I agree, but who says that?" asks Tohlee.

"I made it up. Hey. Ow! That really hurt," exclaims Eli.

"You're so dramatic! That was more sound than a slap," says Tohlee. "Let's go back and romp in the haystack."

Mateen and Anoo have been relaxing around camp enjoying the sights and sounds of the sky, woods, and hills on this sunny late spring afternoon. They'd hiked the day before with full packs and that morning went up the hill and wandered around. When they came back to camp they were content to stretch and rest in the warmth of the sun.

"Do you have a girlfriend, Anoo?"

"I guess so, but not really."

"And why don't you know for sure?"

"There's a girl I often ski or walk to town with when I'm going in to school and then coming home."

"What's her name?"

"Kirsten. They live about halfway between our place and town."

"Who does she live with?"

"Her parents and she has two younger brothers."

"Do the brothers ski in with you two also?"

"Yes, there are usually a dozen kids going in to town or back to home at the same time."

"But you talk to Kirsten and ski right with her more than the rest?"

"I do. Everyone sticks pretty close together but that means we're all within a hundred yards or so of each other. On the way in we wait at the different lanes for the kids who go in everyday and we all make sure everyone reaches their lane okay on the way home."

"So you two have plenty of opportunity for private conversations and have gotten to know each other as individuals as compared to a part of a family or through classroom interaction?"

"We have, does that mean she's my girlfriend?"

"It's an important first step on a road with many different possibilities. Are you the last to get home of your group?"

"There are two kids that go a little more than a mile farther."

"So no one watches out for them on their last mile after you head down your lane?"

"Not anymore. A few years ago when they were a little too young for that last mile on their own I would go with them and their mother or father usually brought them to our lane on the way in."

"Then you were on your own when you were going back to your place. A few years ago you were almost too young for that."

"I was, but we always checked in with Mother or Father as we were going by our place and Father's dog Tuktu always came with me. Sometimes one or both of Mother's dogs came with me too."

"Dogs are good company for that. How often is there enough snow to ski in to town?"

"School usually doesn't start until November after all the fall harvest is done and the farms are ready for winter. It's usually not until December that snow is staying on the ground. Then in March it starts to get muddy and by April we're usually mud free. School stops by the end of April when the farm work starts up again."

"For several months then you're skiing and a couple more of walking. What's your favorite subject in school?"

"I like everything a little and I guess I like learning about the history of the Earth the most."

"Do you mean the history of the Earth or of the world?"

"I don't know what the difference is."

"I think it's my distinction. I consider the world to be what humans have made and the Earth to be the planet the world of people has been built on."

"Then I guess I like both. I like learning about ice ages and dinosaurs and about knights and castles. But then I really like learning about space exploration and about climates on other planets and what they're made of too."

"It's good to have an interest in different subjects."

"Do you think people will go into space again, Mateen?"

"I think civilizations and societies have risen and fallen throughout human history. In time people will recover from the harm they've caused themselves as they have in the past. The debt will be large and take a long time to pay back, but it will be paid."

With that Mateen and Anoo settle back and think their own thoughts. Anoo about a future time when space travel has put humans on other planets to live, work, and go to school there. And Mateen about what could have been if humanity didn't spend its future on war over and over and over again.

"Are you bored, Anoo?"

"Not really bored - I'm comfortable."

"Good. But it is getting about time to catch some fish for dinner."

"How long do you think the food we brought with us will last?" asks Anoo.

"Oh, comfortably a good ten days I'm sure. We'll find and catch some to supplement what we brought. That will mean we'll have enough for at least a couple of weeks."

"How are we going to catch fish for tonight?"

"Did you bring any fishing line and hooks with you?" asks Mateen.

"I did, Father said to always have some in my pack and a couple little sinkers besides."

"That's good advice. I also carry a few of the more common trout flies with me. Ones that are more generalized as compared to those designed to imitate a specific insect."

"What are some of those?"

"I usually bring a Royal Coachman, Parachute Adams, a Pheasant Tail, and a caddis, as well as a few other nymph patterns. The idea is to carry patterns that will be the most likely to work under different circumstances."

"Will we use flies tonight?"

"I think tonight we'll use bait. Sometimes flies work better for trout than bait, but I don't think we'll have to be concerned with that tonight. We'll cut a couple willow sticks down by the pond and tie our lines and hooks to them."

"What will we use for bait?"

"We can find some worms or grasshoppers or we can look under rocks in shallow water for insect larva. There's always something around to use for bait."

"What kind of fish are in the pond?"

"Brook trout that are around six and up to eight inches long that hopefully will be hungry. The fish are not very big so we'll probably need three or four apiece for a filling supper."

"Is that a lot to take out of this pond?"

"Brook trout often overpopulate a small stream like this one. When they are overpopulated they get stunted in size. If this was a healthy and balanced population they could average over ten inches in a stream and pond system this size. So taking out some will let the others grow larger. That's actually the same way it will work for the willows we'll cut for our fishing poles. The ones that we don't cut will have less competition so more room to grow. Even if we take too many fish out of the pond, others will move in from up and downstream."

"How will the other fish know that we've taken some out of the pond?"

"They won't know. They will just be going from one place to another in the stream. When they get to the pond they'll find a habitat that suits them and doesn't have a lot of other brookies in it to compete against. So they'll decide to stay awhile."

"Why will they be going from one place to another in the stream?"

"They will be looking for spots that are having a bug hatch or where they might find cooler or warmer water. Maybe they're looking for shade or a deep spot of water for protection from predators. They might be leaving a place where there is too much competition from other brookies. There are lots of reasons why fish move around a stream. Let's get our gear rigged up and find some bait."

"Okay, Mateen."

After cutting a couple willow stems and tying on line and hooks, they move off to some large cottonwood trees near the stream.

"Let's look in this leaf litter for worms."

"Leaf litter is a good place to look for worms," says Anoo.

"Yes, it is. I like to look under old pieces of wood that are mostly buried by leaf litter and old grass like this one. Ah see! Grab that one, Anoo. See how this piece of wood has lain here so long there is moist soil under it?"

"You mean compared to a piece that has just fallen and is lying on top of the grass and leaves?"

"That's exactly what I mean, this is prime earthworm habitat. Let's find a few more and we should be all set. The fish aren't that big so we can use a small piece of the worm when we bait up."

"Will the worm die?"

"If we only used the tail half it wouldn't. The worm would grow back the back half. But we'll use both parts. I'm sure there are plenty of worms around here."

"We should thank the worms for their help in our effort to catch food for dinner, shouldn't we?" asks Anoo.

"Yes, we should. And for the willows we cut and the trout when we take their life also."

"That's a lot of killing just for us to eat dinner, isn't it Mateen?"

"Yes it is, Anoo."

With that perspective creating their attitude and a few more worms, they take off their shoes. They move out into the center of the little stream by carefully placing their feet on the slippery rocks. Willows are scattered along the edges of the stream with cottonwoods here and there just back from the willows. The pond is behind an old beaver dam that has been used off and on by so many generations of beavers that it is now mostly dirt with some old logs and branches on top. The stream gurgles through a low spot in the dam.

"Okay, let's stop here, Anoo. We want to sneak up to the pond, so bait your hook here. We'll creep slowly up to that willow that is growing out of the beaver dam. Then we'll crouch down and go around it. Keep your head below the level of the dam. Only show your willow stick over the top. Toss your line out into the water. Don't throw very far past the dam. The deepest water is next to the dam. We didn't put on any sinkers because the water isn't that deep and also so there won't be a big splash when the worm hits the water."

Instead of tossing his line, Anoo holds his stick so his baited hook just clears the dam and then moves out over the water. He slowly dips the stick until the hook dimples the water and disappears under the surface.

"I've got one, Mateen!"
"Pull it in and give it to me. I'll clean it while you catch another."

Anoo baits his hook again and then quietly moves a few feet down the dam before softly dipping the hook below the surface again. This time he feels it sink down until it stops on the bottom. He raises the hook off the bottom a few inches and waits. He feels the sudden tug of a solid take.

"Here's another," says Anoo.
"Very good, now move farther down the dam a little ways, as you just did, and try for more. Keep your head down," coaches Mateen.
"Here's another. Did you say a prayer for them before you killed them, Mateen?"
"I surely did," says Mateen.
"How did you clean them?"
"It's called hog dressing. I cut down behind their head through the spine as far down as the top of their pectoral fins. With small fish like these that first cut kills them very quickly. These fins are the

pectoral fins," explains Mateen. "After that I cut from their vent up to between their gills. Then I cut the pectoral fins away from the body which connects the cut behind the head and the cut up from the vent. That means the head, the pectoral fins, and the guts are all connected and the guts easily peel out of the body cavity when you pull the head away from the body. You finish up by pulling the vent off from the body and then you have to push your thumb along each side of the backbone to get the blood out of there."

"That's the way Father cleans them too. And when he gets a big fish like a three-foot-long pike he cuts a piece of meat off the back and bottom quarter of the gill plate. But these brookies are too small for that. Will you do anything with this pile of guts?" asks Anoo.

"This is the liver. Since this is nice clean water we'll eat that. Everything else we'll toss in the stream for bugs and crayfish to eat. Tomorrow afternoon after we hike around we'll come back to the fish guts and catch crayfish for dinner. Now that we've let the pond quiet down a little, go catch some more and then we'll go back to camp and get a fire going."

After catching and cleaning three more fish they wash in the stream and then sit beside it as their feet dry. Then, with their shoes back on and a half dozen brookies they head back up to camp.

"How are we going to cook these?" asks Anoo.

"When we have a good bed of coals going we'll have a couple of options. We can put them right over the coals stuck on some green twigs if we want a smoky flavor. Or, I can put them in my frying pan with a little oil. What do you think?"

"Let's try the frying pan," decides Anoo.

"Okay. Either way we'll have to pick the meat off the bones. Sometimes when the fish are this size or a little smaller and I have plenty of oil, I deep fry them until the fins are so crispy they are like potato chips. Then I eat the entire fish: bones, skin, and all, minus the head and guts, of course. When you cook fish that small in oil and cook them hot, the bones will be crunchy enough to eat safely. Cooked the way we're going to, with only enough oil to keep them from sticking to the pan, the bones will still be sharp and somewhat flexible. So we'll pick the meat off the bones. Some people like the skin cooked this way and some don't. We'll toss the livers right in the pan with the fish and steam up some taters and veggies in our pot with some herbs."

After the fire has burned down to coals, the food cooked, and served, Mateen looks down at his plate in silence. Anoo also looks down at the food on his plate. He thinks of the fish splashing and tugging at the end of his line. He remembers their bright colors as they first came out of the water and lay in his hands. Then he hungrily eats while savoring the different flavors.

"What do you think?" asks Mateen.

"I think fresh brookies are delicious. I didn't know what I'd think of the fresh liver, but that was good too. When you looked down at your plate before we ate, were you saying thanks again to the fish?"

"It was more of a calm and quiet meditative appreciation. I thank animals as, or shortly after, I take their life and I give thanks when I pull a plant out of the ground or a fruit or vegetable away from its parent stem. Those words and sentiments are directed at the animal or plant whose life I am altering. When those same animals and plants are in front of me prepared for my consumption and sustenance, I quiet myself out of appreciation and in preparation of their energy melding into me. Let's clean up and watch the sun go down. Then we'll start up the fire again and enjoy the evening."

After cleaning themselves and their cookware at the stream they fill the pot and pan with water to boil that night for drinking the next day. Back at camp Anoo puts fresh wood on the fire. Mateen sets the pot and pan full of water on the crackling wood as the lively flames flick up between the cookware. They watch the shadow of the western ridge go past camp as the sun drops out of sight.

Light remains in the sky and the bottoms of the lowest clouds still have a pinkish hue when a gentle-evening breeze begins to move downhill.

"Have you enjoyed our day together Anoo?"

"Very much so, it was a beautiful day and I liked spending it with you."

"And I with you, my young friend. It is a little incongruous, but let's sit around the fire on this quiet evening and talk about violence."

"Violence like what the wolves don't do?"

"Violence as only people can do to each other. Violence like that requires intent. I see no violence in stepping on a bug in the grass that you don't know is there. But going out of your way to step on a bug or not avoiding one when you are able is another matter. The same thing is true with people. You should pay attention to what goes on around you so you don't hurt someone accidentally. You should never intentionally hurt anyone and you should do whatever you can to avoid a violent confrontation. Violence involves intent and there is a feeling that goes along with it. This is not a feeling I have ever found anything good in. That feeling is absent when you defend your home or yourself. In a situation where you are really defending yourself or your home you sometimes must commit actions designed to hurt someone. The feeling of violence does not accompany those actions if they are truly justified. But you must be sure actions designed to hurt someone really are justified before you commit them or you will pay a heavy price in regret. If you disregard that regret you will find yourself turning into someone you don't want to be. You may have feelings of remorse or thoughts of doubt no matter what the circumstances of a violent encounter. Do not confuse survival of health or self with ego. If you can walk away from a fight, walk away, if you are cornered, then act. Don't choose to put yourself in a corner and then think that a violent response to someone has become justified. There are people who put great store in the ability to fight. They run the risk of confusing honor and ego. These people think it is legitimate to fight for honor. Honor and ego can be hard to separate. If someone tries to insult you, your honor is not offended. Your honor is affected by your words and actions, not the words or actions of others. If their words are not true the words themselves will not be enough to create truth. A falsehood does not dishonor you unless you are the deliverer of the falsehood. A falsehood dishonors the giver not the receiver. Do not let a falsehood affect your view of yourself or determine your actions. Be strong in your own truth. Your true friends will know you and not be affected by the falsehood. I cannot think of an insult to your honor that can legitimately result in your committing a violent act. An insult to your honor can certainly elicit a verbal response designed to straighten out the insult, but not a violent response. I am sure you have had confrontations with other boys your age. At some point these childish actions become deadly serious. A mature man can kill with one strike and accidents can always happen. You may not intend to hurt someone badly but it may happen anyway. Do you think if you only intended to knock someone down and they lost an eye hitting an object as they fell that you wouldn't feel bad?"

"I would feel very bad and regret my action," states Anoo.

"As most everyone would, Anoo. Do not open yourself up to those feelings through your own actions. Realize that bodies were meant to be strong and that good feelings come from a properly functioning body. Those good feelings come from a body pitted against itself as easily as they come from one body pitted against another. A fair competition with another can motivate a person beyond their perceived limits. An open mind can motivate itself beyond that same closed mind's self-imposed limits.

"There are limits to what bodies can do. Most people reach mental limits way before they reach physical limits. Violence is not a worthy tool to use to try and reach beyond one's current self. Realize it is good to be able to defend yourself. And realize there is true art in movements of the body. That art can be expressed through dance or the movements found in martial arts. Don't let the intent to harm someone corrupt the good feelings that can come from physical capabilities. There are places in the world and in our society where violence is more acceptable than other places. Avoid those places as you would avoid a direct fight. Push yourself through fair competition certainly, but don't lose your dignity by enjoying a violent confrontation. It has been said that there was a far-off country, long ago, that a virgin with a sack of gold could cross alone and never fear for loss of her dignity or gold. Every part of our society and every individual that exhibits more violence or greed than that country of old decreases our humanity as individuals and as a society.

"Never become callused to violence. Realize that just because people and countries existed in a time previous to ours does not mean they were below average compared to us or this country. They were merely earlier. Standards of societies can fall. Human history is often not a progression towards greater civility and individuality. All too often it is a repetition of past errors. The average of a society, by the definition of average, is less than what individuals can achieve themselves. Create your own individual standards. Do not take your standards from the average of the society you live within. For example, it is said that all is fair in love and war. It is more correct to say that all is fair in love and war only when an individual is too weak to have or hold their own personal code of ethics. As an individual, try to keep the standards toward violence and respect for others of that far-off, long ago, country as your own."

"What country was that?" asks Anoo.

"It doesn't matter as there were more than one and at different times. Just remember to create your own individual standards in all areas of conduct and use that country as a model. I'm going to turn in. Stay up and enjoy the evening if you would like, it's still early."

"Good night, Mateen."

"Good night to you, Anoo."

Day Three

noo has slept in a little after staying up next to the embers of the fire and watching the night sky. He thought about things Mateen said the last two days, but mostly he enjoyed the evening. His calm, quiet mind giving more perspective to the words he has heard than internal debate could. The early morning is cool, but the day promises to be pleasant. Mateen was up before dawn watching the life around him shift from the nocturnal to the diurnal. After breakfast Mateen tells Anoo his plans for the day.

"Let's go for a hike today, Anoo. Then this afternoon we'll catch some crayfish and have a nice supper. Tomorrow we'll move on and see what there is to see. Sound good to you?"

"Sure, we'll just wander around today then?"

"Similar to what we did yesterday, but we'll go farther."

With their day packs on and food for lunch, Mateen and Anoo walk into the woods. They go uphill along the small side drainage they climbed up the day before. At first they move fast, covering ground, giving their bodies exercise and moving away from the smell of their camp and breakfast fire. With their hearts pumping and the feel of their own health running through them, they begin to concentrate on moving quickly and as quietly as their pace allows. After a time they gradually slow and let their senses reach out around them.

They continue walking and their breathing slows with their pace. Their senses begin to reach out past the disturbance of their own movement. They move beyond the woods surrounding them that were disturbed by their initial fast walk. As they continue they go past the area where animals they interrupted and caused to move would have gone thus disturbing other animals. The secondary animals do not know the original cause of the disturbance, but deer for example know that if other deer are disturbed they should be too. The walkers keep going to where the wild things would have no reason to expect them. As they slow even more their movements become silent. They are on a well-worn game trail. It has rained recently enough that the leaves and grasses they brush against and step on are soft. The effect of their presence and movements become a subtlety that is less of a disturbance to the woods than the movement of branches in the breeze or the nearby movements of birds and squirrels.

"Why did you stop, Mateen?"

"Stay still! Something is near to us."

"What is it?"

"I don't know. Wait and be still."

"It is a bear," whispers Mateen. "See it to my left?"

"I do."

"Let's back up slowly. It doesn't know we are here yet. There are cubs with her. Keep quiet. We'll be away from them in just a few seconds. When we drop below this rise we'll be able to move away from them at a faster pace without their sensing us."

"We were lucky, weren't we Mateen?"

"There was no luck involved. I sensed something was near and I did not disregard a warning I received."

"What warning did you get?"

"A feeling that is not quite a voice but still grabs my attention."

"What do you mean?"

"I don't know if I heard, smelled, or saw the bears. But I sensed a presence in a very quick, slight way. I did not realize the importance of the information at first. Then, a feeling came to me that I had missed something going on around me that was important. I stopped and was quiet in my mind. The small piece of information I had not attached the importance to that I should have, came through to me clearly. Not as much through remembering what I had missed, but by directing my senses to the source of the small piece of information I should have taken greater note of than I did. That direction was the direction that the bears were compared to us. Once I focused my senses in that direction I quickly became aware of the bears. Let's head back to camp, Anoo. We'll cross the stream and go up the hill on the other side. We won't have to worry about the bears there."

"Why wouldn't the bears bump into us back at camp or across the stream just like we bumped into them here?"

"Both the bears and us were moving into the wind. We angled in towards each other. If we had not been moving, the bears would have passed in front of us and we would have only seen their tracks. If the bears had stopped, we would have moved upwind of them. The bears would have smelled us and avoided us. It wasn't luck that caused me to see the bears before they realized we were there, although it was coincidence that we almost bumped into each other. Most likely we won't see them again. It's unusual to see a bear when you're out taking a walk. It makes for an exciting hike, doesn't it?"

"I'll say. Would the sow have come after us if she'd seen us?"

"Maybe, it depends on whether she thought there was a safe escape route for her cubs. By herself, she could run away very fast. If there was a safe escape route for the cubs she probably would have taken it. If she assessed the situation and did not think there was a safe escape route, our threat to her and her cubs would have increased dramatically from her perspective even though we had no intention of harming them. Then who knows what would have happened. Probably only a bluff charge, but who knows."

"What's a bluff charge?"

"Black bears are known to charge at a threat and then veer off at the last second. The problem is they look the same as the charge whether it's a bluff or not. It's always best to know the animals are there before they know you are. It's not only best for safety, but also best for learning about animal behavior."

"It seems like animals always know I'm around before I know they're around," says Anoo.

"It takes practice. But if you walk quietly into the wind and move slowly, or when the breeze moves the vegetation around you, your chances of seeing critters before they see you will greatly increase."

"Do other animals bluff charge also?"

"Mice do."

"Who do mice bluff charge?"

"They've charged me a couple different times."

"Were you really, really scared?"

"Ha ha, no, but it was such unexpected behavior it allowed the mouse to get away from me which was the point of the charge."

"Were you trying to catch it?"

"Not really, but the mouse didn't know that. One time I was out at night in the winter. It was a full moon night and the snow was crusty. I had stopped walking and was looking around. A mouse popped out of the snow just to my left and started running in front of me towards a clump of grass that stuck up above the snow. I started running towards the clump of grass, thinking I could get to the grass before the mouse and then it would have been stuck out on the crusty snow next to me. The mouse, realizing I was going to beat it to the grass, suddenly turned towards me and started jumping two feet in the air towards me. I was so surprised I stopped running. The mouse turned and ran to the grass clump and dove under the crusty snow."

"So you were outsmarted by a mouse."

"I have to admit I was. Another time I saw a mouse run into my pantry by going under the door. I knelt down and opened the door. The mouse was up on a shelf at head height and jumped out at me. I reflexively batted it away from my face and it went flying across the room."

"I had no idea mice would do that. I'd much rather have a mouse bluff charge me than a bear."

"Me too, Anoo, me too."

After a short break back at camp for lunch, Mateen and Anoo set out again. This time they go on the other side of the stream from where they saw the bears. After they cross the stream they head straight up a steep hill. Mateen knows that when large animals, both predators and herbivores, come out from cover to look for food they often follow riparian areas. This is because the riparian is richer with plant and animal life than the surrounding drier slopes. From midmorning to late afternoon most large animals have moved back to cover. In this case a stand of trees at the top of a hill. Rather than follow the animals' movements back up from the riparian area into the trees, Mateen has chosen to go straight up the steep hill. This will take Mateen and Anoo into the trees at a right angle compared to the direction the animals probably would have taken. Mateen decided to do this because large animals often choose to bed down where they can watch their own backtrack. Besides often choosing to bed down where they can watch their own backtrack, animals will also choose to bed down with the wind blowing from behind them and therefore down their backtrack. By doing this, they can smell predators coming from the direction that they aren't looking towards. Mateen is hoping that going straight up the steep hill, at a right angle to the animals' probable movements, will keep himself and Anoo out of sight of the animals that are bedded down watching their own backtrack and will also keep their scent from the animals.

"This is a steep hill, Mateen!"

"It will flatten out pretty soon and then we'll get a look at what's in the thick aspen trees we can see up toward the top."

"How do you know the trees at the top will be thick?"

"They look thick from here so it probably isn't a rocky hilltop. As long as it isn't rocky the more level top will allow moisture to soak into the soil better than the sides of the hill where it runs off."

"I see. That will give the trees more time to soak up the moisture through their roots."

"That's right, and it will allow a deeper and richer soil to develop over time."

"Because the little soil particles won't be washed downhill which will create a microhabitat the trees like, right, Mateen?"

"You're a smart boy, Anoo."

"Does that mean the trees are creating their own habitat?"

"The soil particles don't wash down the hill partly because of the shallow slope of the top of the hill, not because of the trees. So that isn't the trees creating their own habitat. But the roots of the trees and fallen trunks will keep soil from eroding downhill. Also in the fall the fallen leaves of the trees will cover the ground, protecting the soil from direct hits by raindrops. Then over time those leaves will decompose, enriching the soil and breaking down to nutrients that the roots can absorb."

"That's kind of self-cannibalistic," says Anoo.

"It is, and it shows that trees do create their own microhabitats."

"How can leaves' decomposing enrich the soil when the leaves came from the soil to begin with?" asks Anoo.

"That's a good question. It's because the sun's energy and the trees' internal processes create chemical compounds using nutrients from the soil that the soil didn't have to begin with. Also, the trees' roots reach down deep enough that they bring up nutrients that would not be a part of the surface life cycle otherwise. That life cycle includes bacteria, worms, and other animals that live off of and break down the leaves. When those animals die and then decompose they supply nutrients to the soil that the tree can use that the soil, tree, and leaves didn't have to begin with."

"And the animals poop too and that's manure like Father uses to raise crops." says Anoo.

"Well done, Anoo, well done."

After reaching the top they stop to catch their breath and then move slowly deeper into the trees. Not only are the trees thick, but the grasses and forbs growing under the trees are already up to their knees. For a little ways all they see are small birds and the occasional mouse. They stop now and then to admire a flower swaying in the breeze with bees or colored hairy flies in it rooting around for pollen. In one spot with some downed aspen trunks and more rocks than they had been seeing, they watch a golden-mantled ground squirrel watching them from a downed trunk with his cheek pouches full. As they're about to start walking again Mateen points out one particular yellow flower of a plant named arrowleaf balsamroot with a similar-colored crab spider in it, waiting to ambush a hungry bee or a fly. After walking a little farther Mateen stops.

"Do you smell that, Anoo?"

"I don't smell anything."

"There's either elk up here or they were here recently."

"You can smell them?"

"Yes, elk are pretty smelly critters."

"I don't smell them."

"Let's move up slow and quiet."

"See, Anoo, they were bedded down here not too long ago. The grass where they bedded down is still flattened out. Those are some of their droppings. They are still shiny and I bet warm if you want to check."

"No way, are you kidding me?" asks Anoo.

"I am a little. You can just push on them with your foot and see if they are still soft and mushy."

"Okay. They're pretty fresh, aren't they?"

"Yes, they're probably not far ahead of us."

"I still don't smell them though," says Anoo.

"Many years ago I was with a friend of mine. We were hunting and he shot a cow elk. When we got up to the animal it had died only a few minutes before. I knelt down next to her and exhaled hard all the air in my lungs out of my nose. Then I bent down until my nose was less than an inch away from her. I took a slow and very deep breath in through my nose. I could actually feel her scent going into my sinuses and then into my brain. It was as though her scent became imprinted on my mind. I've been able to smell elk ever since. Sometimes it's really surprising how far away I can smell them."

"How far away do you mean?" asks Anoo.

"Over a hundred yards I'm sure, maybe a couple hundred if conditions are right. Their scent can linger where they've lain for quite a time, too."

"Did someone tell you how to do that? With your nose I mean."

"Yes, the fellow who took me hunting explained the technique to me. It works for most any kind of smell."

"That's quite a trick. The next time you and Father take me elk hunting, I'm going to learn how to smell them too."

"This year I think you'll get your first elk and that will be the perfect animal to try the technique on. Do you see how some of the beds are oval in shape?"

"Some are, but most are more like rounded triangles," replies Anoo.

"The normal shape of the bed of an animal in the deer family is an oval."

"By the deer family you mean moose, elk, and deer?"

"That's right."

"Then why do most of these elk beds look like rounded triangles?" asks Anoo.

"That's from a calf bedded down right next to its mother. This time of year the calves are still small enough that they bed up close to their mothers."

"What would the bed of the sow and cubs we saw earlier look like?"

"I don't think I've ever seen the bed of a sow with little cubs. The bed of a bear by itself looks quite circular, noticeably different from these ovals. Instead of going up and seeing where the elk are, let's not disturb them. Let's go back to camp and relax."

"Okay by me, and then after relaxing we're going to catch some crayfish for dinner, aren't we?"

"Yes we are, my friend."

Tohlee and Eli have had another quiet day. Tohlee tended her herb, vegetable, and flower gardens. Keeping a careful eye on them for problems from insects and noting their growth and, therefore, knowing if they need any special care like additional fertilizer. Eli has done the same with his orchards, row crops, and the vegetable garden. When they meet in the vegetable garden they enjoy a nice break. They compare notes on the growth of their plants and the presence or absence of harmful and beneficial insects they found along the way. After a light lunch it was more of the same until they decide to take another walk down to the river. It is a summer ritual for them that is so enjoyable they often start it before the river has really warmed up.

"Wow! This water is brisk, Tohlee!"

"It's not that bad, you big baby."

"Well I can certainly see that you're feeling nippy from it! Hey, that didn't deserve a splash!"

"What's the matter? Are you afraid you'll shrink back inside yourself and never come out again?"

"What if I only come back out halfway? What would you think of your teasing then?"

"I think if I applied enough suction you'd come back out bigger and better than ever."

"Now that sounds like an interesting experiment. One that I think requires a long period of intensive studying."

"Well then, we should get out of this water and dry off," says Tohlee.

"I like your thinking," responds Eli.

"Here's your towel. Get yourself dried off. Then come over here, my love. Where you can stand in the sun and look out over the water. This is all for you Eli, all for you."

"Hmmm, Tohlee! Everyday with you is better than the last."

Back at camp Mateen and Anoo drop their packs and have some water. Then, they head to the stream for their crayfish hunt. They take off their shoes when they get to the side of the stream. Their feet aren't as tough as they'll be after a summer of going barefoot. But they're tough enough if they watch where they put their feet. After stepping in up to their ankles and a quick face wash they're ready to hunt.

"Where are we going to find the crayfish, Mateen?"

"They should be right around the fish guts I tossed in the stream yesterday. There could be some eating right now, although, they don't like the bright light of day very much."

"Why don't they like the light of day much?" asks Anoo.

"I think it's partly the way their eyes are and also because some animals that like to eat crayfish like blue herons aren't active at night."

"But raccoons are active at night and they like crayfish too."

"True, but the crayfish have to eat sometime. They'll always face a risk. Night for them is less risky. I have seen crayfish moving around in full light but usually they're in water too deep for herons. So today, in this shallow stream, it's more likely they'll be under rocks near the fish guts, waiting for nightfall before they come out and eat. I tossed the guts from different fish in different places so we could find more crayfish. They've had a whole day now to smell the guts in the water and move to them."

"Crayfish can smell?"

"They sure can, they smell through their antennae. Fish can smell too, but they have noses or sometimes they have barbels which are similar to antennae. Scent is carried in the water similar to the way it is carried in the air. The downstream water flow has direct current and eddies around obstructions like wind currents in the air. The crayfish from downstream will move up, looking for the cause of the scent. The crayfish upstream don't even know this great feast is downstream and available to them. We'll put the ones we catch in my bag with some wet moss and grass."

After moving near to the gut piles they start to turn over the flatter rocks that aren't buried deep in the streambed.

"I see one," Anoo says excitedly.

"Watch out! They aren't all that big, but they sure can pinch. Move up to it slowly and reach behind it and grab it behind the arms."

"Whoops! Hey come back here you!" yells Anoo.

"Next time try keeping one hand in front of the crayfish to distract it. Then reach around behind it with your other hand and grab it. There's another one, try again," encourages Mateen.

"I've got it!"

"Good job, Anoo. We're going for at least a couple dozen so let's find some more. There's one that's too small. Don't bother trying to get him."

"There's another! I got him too!"

"Alright, Anoo! You're an expert already."

After plenty of splashing and some misses their catch has grown.

"Okay, Anoo, that should do it. We've got close to thirty good-size ones and there were plenty of little ones we passed up so they can get bigger. Let's go warm up and settle in to camp."

After drying off and putting on fresh clothes they get a fire going. Mateen sets a pot on the fire with water and spices he's brought. As they wait, they stretch and then sit quietly. They don't move much while being watchful and aware of all that is moving around them. They can see songbirds flitting around the willows down by the stream. A magpie is squawking from a cottonwood. A chipmunk starts showing itself near camp and they watch as it gets bolder. First, they see it running from shrub to shrub. Then it starts to show itself for longer periods of time and moves closer to them. When it sits on a rock three feet from Anoo and scratches itself behind the ears they know they have a camp friend. When Mateen turns and scans the hillside behind them, the chipmunk stops scratching and watches, ready to run. Seeing no movement towards itself it jumps off the rock and starts to forage. Mateen sees and comments on a marmot sitting at the edge of its den hole and a fox moving along the tree line several hundred yards away. Then they return to quiet awareness and the activity of their friend the chipmunk.

"Well, I think they're ready, Anoo. Do you know how to eat them?"

"Like I've read people eat lobsters?"

"Not exactly, crayfish are a lot smaller; the claws are too small to mess with unless you really want to. I usually just eat the tail meat. Pull them apart right here in the middle. Now suck the juices out of the front section."

"No way! You don't really do that, do you?"

"You bet! See! Just like that. Now grab the meat and pinch the base of the tail. The meat will slide out in one piece and that's how you eat crayfish. What do you think?"

"I think we need to have some more crayfish tomorrow night," replies Anoo.

"Well, maybe not tomorrow night, but we'll have them again I'm sure."

"This is an excellent dinner, Mateen. Not only the crayfish but the dried taters and carrots steamed over hot coals are excellent too. I especially like the crayfish cooked up with your spices."

"They were grown by your mother and then I mixed them together into my own crayfish concoction. I'm glad you liked dinner so much, Anoo. Let's get everything cleaned up and then sit around the fire."

"Okay and when I get back I'm going to catch crayfish out of the river and cook them up for Mother and Father. I've seen them in there but never eaten them."

"In bigger water like the river at your place it might be best to trap them or fish for them."

"How do you do that?"

"You fish for them by tying a piece of chicken to the end of your line. You don't need a hook. Just cast near one that you see first and it will grab the chicken with its claws and hold on even as you pull it out of the water."

"So I would do that during the day then?"

"That's right. As long as the water is several feet deep it's too deep for herons to get them so there're more likely to be active in the day. To trap them you make the trap out of woven willows no thicker than your little finger. The shape is a cylinder with one closed end and the other end a funnel. The narrow end of the funnel points in and is in the center up above the bottom. You put a piece of chicken in the trap and the crayfish crawl in through the funnel opening and then they can't find their way back out because the open end of the funnel is above them. Tie the trap to a branch or tree near the water and leave it in all night."

"Then I'll check it in the morning and, yippee, crayfish for breakfast!"

"That's right; crayfish are good fish bait too. If they're big it's usually best to pull the claws off before hooking them through the tail and throwing them in the water. Doesn't your father take you fishing in the river?"

"He does, but he only goes for big pike with his fly rod and flies that are three or four inches long made out of bird feathers or rabbit fur."

"Well then, you'll have to do some exploring of the river on your own both for fish and crayfish."

As Mateen and Anoo are finishing their meal Tohlee and Eli are relaxing by their house, watching the sun setting over their land. The lower clouds are reflecting deeper reds while higher clouds are a soft shade of pink. The night insects are beginning to be active as the warmth of the day lingers. Eli has been actively watching the movements of songbirds nearby and a few ducks flying up and down the river. Several deer are moving through the riparian vegetation along the river. He sees a buck that has antlers that are already quite large for this early in the year. Turning to comment to Tohlee he sees that she has her eyes closed and a faraway look to her face. He waits a few minutes until she stirs.

"You looked like you were far away, Tohlee."

"Hmm, it's been a couple days. I was searching for contact with Anoo. I guess I wondered if he was okay and also hoped that he wanted contact with me."

"And what did you find?"

"No real contact, but I also felt no real need for concern."

"I'm sure they're fine or we would both have known."

"I'm sure you're right. It's interesting how my perceptions of his wellbeing have changed so much over the years."

"Tell me what you mean," says Eli.

"When I was pregnant with him I felt I encompassed all he was. Not just physically, but emotionally and spiritually also. Then, when he was born, I almost immediately began to question if my impressions or feelings of his needs were accurate. I was delighted that Laurel was just down the road and had kids of her own."

"They've been great neighbors for us. You said, at the time, that you really appreciated her visits."

"I did and it took awhile for her explanations and my new experiences at motherhood to coalesce into my own perceptions that I thought accurately reflected Anoo's needs."

"There were a few years when you and Laurel didn't visit as often."

"I still valued her friendship, but we were both busy with our children. I reached a point where I was comfortable caring for Anoo. It seemed I knew what he was going to say or ask for before he did. Some years later when he started to really develop his own identity and perceptions I found I had to communicate with him to keep up with who he was becoming. Now my perception of his physical and emotional wellbeing lets me know when something is bothering him, but I need to talk about it with him. I need him to communicate his concern; I can't just perceive what it is."

"It sounds like your mothering is growing as his individuality is growing. I'm proud of the way you respect who he is. You've stepped back and trusted him to grow without being overbearing. You are an example to him, not someone who tries to manipulate him into who you think he should be. I love you and respect you for that."

"Thank you for saying that Eli, it means a great deal to me. It's as though I've grown as a person and because of that I can allow him to grow also. I found that growth in me has created a broader perspective from which I look out into the world. It's interesting, but it's similar to when I decided I had grown from a young sexual girl to a woman."

"You'll have to explain that to me."

"When I first became sexual I thought the extent of those feelings were physical and also the emotions that are based on the physical. I got a little caught up in manipulating men for my needs. Then I decided I wanted more from myself and for myself. To put it directly, I found how to perceive the world around me through all of that which I am when I learned to hold value systems above my genitalia. I found the breadth of my heart and I found you, Eli."

"But you haven't lost your sexuality, my love."

"No, it was a growth that encompassed all that I had been and I became more. When I grew I didn't have to leave anything behind except my own pettiness."

After Mateen and Anoo clean up camp they relax by the fire. For awhile they don't talk. They are both meditating on the day and earlier conversations. As they sit and the sun sets they hear a family of coyotes about a half mile from camp start to howl from the hills. The male is starting his evening hunt and the excited yips of the young pups can be heard along with the adults as they all sing to the night.

"Let's talk about feelings, opinions, and beliefs, Anoo. Do you think your feelings are unique?"

"They are mine and I'm unique," replies Anoo.

"Yes, they are and you are. Do you think that it is normal for all people on earth to have feelings, opinions, and beliefs?"

"Sure I do," states Anoo.

"Do you think all those people consider their feelings, opinions, and beliefs to be true or false?"

"True I guess. Doesn't everyone think their own feelings, opinions, and beliefs are the truth?"

"I think so. So how many truths do you think there are?" continues Mateen.

"I guess as many as the number of people on earth."

"What about the subjects people talk about? Can they have their own truth?"

"Well I guess so. It's true to say the earth revolves around the sun and it's not true to say the sun revolves around the earth."

"So every person's perspective is their own truth and subjects also have their own truth?" persists Mateen.

"Well I guess so, yes," replies Anoo.

"So there are at least as many truths as there are people on earth multiplied by the subjects that people talk about," concludes Mateen.

"That would be a big number," says Anoo.

"Yes it certainly is. And if all people have feelings, opinions, and beliefs and they are their own truths, can then two different people hold a different opinion on one subject and still both be right?"

"I guess each person could both feel and think that they are right and they would be if the subject they're talking about is not absolute like which revolves around the other, the sun or the earth."

"I agree, Anoo. I think that feelings, opinions, and beliefs are individual truths. They are truths that are not right or wrong as long as we're talking about individual perspective not specific information. Two people can both feel as though their opinions are the truth for themselves even though their opinions differ. The same idea can be said using feelings. Can two different people have different feelings about one subject and both feel their perspective is accurate? Can two different people have different beliefs about a subject and yet both think their own beliefs are the truth?"

"Well sure. It's the same concept, just using different categories of individual perspective as examples of the same idea."

"Well said, Anoo! Do you think that if your feelings, opinions, and beliefs agreed with everyone around you your perspective would be correct?"

"I guess it would depend on the subject."

"That's right. Truth, accuracy, being correct, however you want to categorize it, is not determined by the numbers of people holding an opinion or having a feeling. For example, what if the subject was how you feel when you see the curvature of the earth as you look from a high hill out onto a flat plain? What if one person feels a magnificent awe as they understand the form of the planet Earth they are standing on? While the person next to them feels apprehension as they understand the vast Earth they have been living on has limits? Wouldn't both those different feelings from seeing the same phenomenon be the truth for each person?"

"For each person, yes, but I would rather feel awe towards the Earth than fear."

"Does that make the person who feels apprehension wrong for themselves?"

"No, not for themselves."

"Does it mean that the Earth is not as round for either of the people?"

"No, Mateen, I think it's the individual's feelings that are different from each other. Of course one's perspective doesn't change the shape of the earth."

"So, even though you might agree more with one person or the other, two people can have different feelings about one subject and both people can still be right?"

"Yes, I think so."

"Does the shape of the Earth change based on how many people feel awe or how many people feel apprehension at the realization of the shape of the Earth?"

"No, the shape of the Earth wouldn't change based on who or how many people are thinking about it in different ways."

"In the same way people who conform their feelings, opinions, and beliefs to those of others do not create the truth. They create only agreement. What is true about the Constitution of this country, Anoo?"

"I don't know in relation to what we're talking about."

"The rights of freedom of speech, press, and religion are given to the individuals of this country. They are not rights given to this country so that the society of this country can choose the one perspective it is most comfortable with. They are rights given to individuals so that individuals are free to hold their own independent perspective without fear from oppression by the government of this country. I personally think that this also means individuals who seek out or try to cause conformity in feelings, opinions, and beliefs are belittling the individual potential that the Constitution of this country was written to allow. What I'm telling you is that I think people's feelings, opinions, and beliefs are their own truths and therefore do not contain right or wrong. Information can be right or wrong, but individual perspective is its own truth. Numbers of people who agree with each other do not create truth. Truth and accuracy are caused by the content of what is said, not by who the speaker is. That is why you should always think about what the reasons behind a person's feelings, opinions, and beliefs are. Your parents and I will always try and explain to you why we feel and believe what we do. People who want you to accept what they feel or say as the truth without explaining their perspective are more concerned with your agreement than with the truth. Those people are not ones who will lead you to anything but subservience and obedience. And that, in my opinion, is no way to develop yourself into a mature man."

"In your opinion, Mateen!"

"Yes, Anoo. In my opinion as I explained within the conversation we just had."

"I know Mateen, I get it. You're not expecting me to agree with your opinion; you're expecting me to think about the reasons behind your opinion. I was just being a bit of a troublemaker."

"Well then, young troublemaker, let's let the fire die down some more and look at the night sky."

After some quiet time the fire dies down and their eyes adjust to the darkness around them instead of the flickering flames of an active fire.

"What do you see when you look up at the sky, Anoo?"

"I see stars and planets and shooting stars and blackness and the moon, lots of things."

"Do you see galaxies?"

"We're in the Milky Way galaxy and it's what makes that hazy line of stars."

"Most of the points of light you see in that hazy line are stars in our Milky Way galaxy. Some of the brighter points of light you see in the sky are stars in our galaxy that are closer to us than other stars in our galaxy. Some of the lights in the sky you are looking at are not stars; they are galaxies much farther away from us than any of the stars found in the Milky Way. The stars in our galaxy are our neighbors. There are billions of stars in our galaxy as well as in other galaxies and there are billions of galaxies."

"How many stars does that make, Mateen? As many as the number of people on earth multiplied by the subjects they talk about?"

"That's a good connection to make, Anoo, and I don't know. Billion times billions is too many for me to number. I'm just trying to describe a number so huge it is hard to put into perspective. What

I'm trying to get at is that if life on earth happened by one chance in a million, there are quite a large number of planets in our galaxy with life on them and millions of other planets out in other galaxies with life on them as well."

"Are there really millions of planets out there with life on them?"

"I don't know for sure, I'm just playing the odds. But if there isn't life out there then there's an awful lot of unused opportunity out there."

"Whether it's all just lights in the sky or if it's home to all sorts of other life, it's pretty amazing to me."

"That it is, Anoo, that it is."

"So, no one knows if there really is other life out there?"

"If they do they're not telling."

"Would you tell me if you knew?"

"I would."

"People say they've seen flying saucers and stuff."

"That's what they say. I've never seen a flying saucer. People used to listen with giant radio telescopes for sounds from other civilizations. But they didn't hear anything. I have seen lights in the sky I couldn't explain. But that's different from seeing a flying saucer."

"What did you see, Mateen?"

"One time I saw three lights in a shape like the end points of an equilateral triangle. They were too far apart from each other to be lights on a plane. Plus these lights didn't blink."

"And plane lights do, right?"

"That's right, except for their headlights. These lights were moving in one direction and then they all shifted abruptly and started moving ninety degrees from the direction they were going. Then they sped up until they disappeared from sight."

"What were they?"

"I don't know. I can't explain them. That's why they're called unidentified flying objects. Their appearance wasn't enough to convince me that there is life on other planets, but they were sure enough to make me wonder."

"Maybe we'll see something like that tonight?"

"Maybe."

"There goes a shooting star, Mateen."

"I saw it too."

"Have you seen a lot before?"

"Once during the Perseid meteor shower in August I stayed up all night and I counted over two hundred."

"Wow! That's a lot, Mateen."

"I've also seen several that split into two parts and each part kept burning for a little while. I saw one that exploded with a noise as loud as a sonic boom. I've seen some that were greenish and some yellowish in color. One time I was standing looking in one direction. It was partly cloudy and late in the evening. I realized it was getting brighter and then I had a shadow. I couldn't figure out why I would have a shadow at night. When I turned to see what was causing my shadow, all I saw was a bright light that lit up the clouds around it. I was with some friends of mine. They said they were looking right up toward it and it was the brightest shooting star they'd ever seen."

"I want to see stuff like that, Mateen!"

"If you spend enough time looking up at the night sky you will. There was another time I was awake early in the morning in the winter when it was still completely dark. I went outside to take a look around. As I looked up I saw a few very bright lights coming in my direction high in the sky. After just a few seconds each started breaking up into smaller pieces. A few seconds later there were well over a hundred different lights going across the sky. Some of the lights were colored green, yellow, and blue of different shades although most were white. They kept going across the sky as some lights burned out and others flared up. I had enough time to walk over to the side of my cabin and continue watching them until there were only a few left and those went out of sight over the horizon."

"Were they all meteors?"

"I decided they went across the sky too slowly. I was watching them for a minute or so. I had walked a good forty yards as I moved to keep them in sight."

"What were they then?"

"I think it was a piece of space junk like an old satellite that re-entered the atmosphere.

"That must have been an incredible sight."

"It was absolutely spellbinding and beautiful at the same time."

"Is that a satellite up there?"

"That is a satellite. They don't blink and they move slow and steady across the sky. There are still some in orbit but I don't think anyone is in touch with them anymore"

"Is that a star over there?"

"That's Mars. Jupiter and Mars trade off being the fourth and fifth brightest objects in the sky, but Jupiter usually is."

"What do you mean by trade off?"

"Planets' paths are elliptical and planets travel their ellipses at different rates. Sometimes a planet is closer to the earth than at other times. If Mars is at a point of its ellipse that is closest to the earth and Jupiter is at its farthest, then Mars looks brighter."

"I see, but usually it's the other way around. What are the first three?"

"You tell me, Anoo."

"Well the moon would be first. Then two more planets I guess."

"Up in the sky means during the day also, Anoo."

"Well you can't see anything in the sky but the sun during the day unless you're in a well. Okay! Okay, Mateen! I can see you laughing. What's number three then?"

"The planet Venus. Look! There's another shooting star! That was a pretty bright and long one. You told me about your friend Kirsten. What else do you do with people from town besides your Aunt Cassie?"

"I really like playing the lacrosse games."

"Tell me about them."

"We usually play on one family's land. Do you know how to play?"

"I've never played but I know what the stick looks like and the goal."

"We play on about forty acres of land. There's a goal on either end. Most of the land is hay meadow and pasture and some is orchard and woodlot. There's a small stream running through a corner. From the bottom at the stream to the highest point there's over fifty feet in elevation change. We play with two balls and there are usually at least a dozen people on each team. Plus there's a referee who stays by each goal. The fastest people try to score and the slower are defenders who stay near the goal."

"Which do you usually do?"

"I'm fast, so I'm with the scoring group."

"What happens after a score?"

"Everyone has to go back to their own goal each side with one ball and we start again."

"Forty acres is a lot of ground to cover."

"That makes it more fun. It's hard to tell who has the ball at first. The ball carrier can hide in the woodlot or along the stream while a few others pretend they have the ball and attack the goal from the other side of the field."

"That sounds like a lot of fun. When do you usually play?"

"In the fall, people usually help one nearby farm or another with harvest and then play in the afternoon. Then there's food and drink afterwards."

"I'm sure that makes for a very enjoyable day. I think I'm going to sleep now. Don't stay up too late. We'll pack up and clean up camp first thing in the morning and then hike for quite a ways tomorrow."

"Okay. Good night, Mateen."

"Good night to you, Anoo."

Day Four

Mateen and Anoo wake up early and quickly get to work making a fire and cleaning up camp in the cool morning air.

"Have you had enough for breakfast, Anoo?"

"Yup, I'm good and full."

"Let's clean up the dishes and then take down the tent and finish packing up so we can go to a new place."

"Okay, Mateen."

"Make sure you fill in the hole you dug for poop. Here's the trowel," says Mateen.

"Should I bury our old cans too?"

"No. I prefer carrying them with us to leaving them out here in the woods. You can recycle them back at town. Since we stayed here a few days our packs are going to be a little lighter. So carrying our empty cans with us won't be as hard as walking in here was. Besides, we may end up using them before our trip is through. Make sure you rinse them well so they don't smell and attract critters. There really isn't very much of that kind of garbage as we've mostly brought dried fruits, veggies, jerky, and nuts. The canned goods are just a treat for us. We'll take a look around before we leave and make sure we've left nothing behind that would interfere with another person's stay."

"Should we take our willow fishing poles with us?"

"I don't think so. We'll cut some more at the lake because if we carried these they would get in our way as we walk."

"We're going to a lake?"

"Yup, it's not very big, maybe about ten acres. It was caused by a landslide that dammed up a stream. I'd say it's six miles from here. It'll take about four hours to get there. Then we'll get set up again, probably around noon."

"Ready to go, Anoo?"

"All set, Mateen. Which way do we go from here?"

"We'll start out along this stream. Let's look for a game trail between the riparian and the hillside. Then we'll go up the hill at the end of this drainage and along the ridge before we drop down into the drainage where the lake is."

"Father says game trails never seem to go the same way for very far or in the direction he wants to go."

"That's true when you're covering ground like we'll be. We won't be following one particular trail for the entire hike. Animals tend to move along watercourses so we'll find a better trail at first and then a lighter trail up on top of the ridge. Animals mostly go from bedding to feeding and watering areas. A lot of times those trails only make sense to the animals that make them, until you follow them yourself and learn what kind of animal is doing the making and what it has in mind along the particular trail that you're following. Streams, below the crest of ridges, or passes between hills, are natural pathways for all sorts of critters. So, in those places paths tend to interconnect and, over time, a major travel way can develop. Especially when the larger animals like moose, elk, and bison are involved. Their weight really beats down a path."

"Are there bison around here?"

"Not very many, but we might see some. Once a path gets developed it becomes the easy way to walk through that particular area and gets used over and over by all sorts of critters. The larger the animal the farther the distance that animal tends to cover between bedding and feeding areas. I've seen places where a fallen log was worn halfway through by the little nicks taken off it from repeated hits by the hooves of generations of elk stepping over it. Plus, there are trails that are seasonal migration routes used by animals leaving an area for the winter or heading back into in the spring. Those trails are often braided, not one particular trail, and are caused by the tendency of the migrating animals to stay on one side of a river or a ridge. The animals are moving from one area to another along a broad route, not on a particular path."

The day warms up as they hike along the stream, up the hill, and along the ridge. More clouds appear and it is windier than the past couple of days, especially up on the exposed ridge top. Still it is a day that has warmed up enough so that more summer than spring is in the air. With their full packs on their backs they're getting a good workout. After covering several miles their hands are feeling thick and heavy from their pack straps and they stop to take a quick break. They sit on some large rocks that they can rest their packs on without removing them.

"Look at that grove of aspen trees, Anoo. You can see the breeze move through from one side to the other. Right there the wind really tossed those tree branches around."

"I've seen breezes show themselves like that in Father's hay meadow and in his wheat fields also."

"Sailors watch the water for those kinds of details when they sail. It's amazing how much faster a boat will sail when an experienced captain uses the details of breezes while at the helm. After our break we'll cut over to that little side ridge to the right of us. Then we'll drop down to the stream below, but first let's just enjoy the view from up here."

"How come we didn't go out some of the other side ridges we went by earlier?"

"We weren't ready to drop down to stream level yet. Those other ridges bordered smaller side drainages that run into the west stream. The lake is in the stream in the valley below the side drainage in front of us and that stream is a main fork of the west stream that runs into town."

The walk over to the little side ridge is rocky and uneven but not very far. But a walk like that, after already covering a few miles, means it's time for another break. Mateen and Anoo don't have to turn the hike into a forced march and so they take their packs off and find comfortable places to sit and enjoy the view. The wind is still blowing and the clouds have thickened a little more as the morning has progressed.

"It's a nice view from up here, Mateen. If we had dropped down right to the stream we never would have seen those beaver ponds coming in from the side. I can see the lodge. It's toward the back of the second pond. Do you think we'll see any beaver from up here?"

"They're usually not out as late as mid-morning. Do you see that patch of little aspen going up the bottom of the hill?" asks Mateen.

"I do. Why do the little aspen end and all of a sudden there are really tall ones?"

"That's the line where the beavers stopped going up the hill, or haven't gone past yet. The little trees are where new ones grew up after the beavers cut the larger ones down. Aspen send up sprouts from their root systems if the tree is cut down or dies in a forest fire. Because the new tree is sprouting off an existing root system they can grow really fast."

"How fast is really fast?"

"They can grow four or five feet in a year. Beavers like to eat willows, alders, and cottonwoods, as well as aspen. They eat the ends of the twigs and the bark off larger branches. Then they use the smaller branches for their dams and lodges. After they build a dam, the water backs up behind it and makes a pond where previously there was just a running stream. When the water backs up, the water table rises and that increases the suitable growing area for the types of plants that the beavers like to eat. The beavers are creating habitat favorable to themselves with the dams they make."

"So the dams are kind of like a tool that makes their life better."

"I guess they are. Not like a hand tool, but yes, a kind of tool. The ponds and the lodges are also safer areas for the beaver because they are better swimmers than their predators like cougars, wolves, coyotes, and bears."

"That's a lot of predators."

"That's why the beavers stay near water and are mostly active at night. The farther from water beavers have to go for food the more danger they're in. Also, if the only food around is at the top of a tall thick tree, the more danger they're in."

"Why is that?" asks Anoo.

"Because the thicker the tree, the longer it takes the beaver to cut it down and therefore the longer the beaver has to be away from water. When beavers cut aspen trees, the sprouts that come up are thin and easy for them to cut and eat. If there are a lot of deer and elk around that also eat the fresh aspen sprouts and willows nearest to the pond, the beavers have to go farther from water to find food. That food is at the top of the larger trees where the deer and elk can't reach. At some point, the beavers have to go so far from water for food that the predators will kill them faster than they can reproduce. After that, the beavers are gone from the area and the aspen and willows can grow back unless there are too many deer and elk. If there are enough deer and elk, the wolves and cougars will stay around and kill them too. When there are fewer deer and elk, the wolves and cougars will move off to better hunting areas."

"Then the aspen and willows will grow back for the beavers, right, Mateen?"

"That's right. It's a big circle of animals and habitat and time."

"Wow! But what's the water table?"

"The water table is where water is in the ground. The water in a pond soaks out into and saturates the ground around the pond. That water near the surface can be reached by the willows' roots.

Willows are a type of plant that has shallow roots and likes to have its roots in water."

"The beavers down below sure have plenty to eat, don't they?" asks Anoo.

"That they do. There are the willows in the saturated soil nearest the pond, alders next to the saturated soil, and then the cottonwoods just back from there. Then there's the aspen running up the north and east-facing hillside. I'm sure the beavers living in those ponds raise plenty of young successfully. Those young grow older and head up and downstream, looking for their own places to live. That's where the beavers come from that repopulate an area where they had been killed off. They build or rebuild dams, helping to recreate favorable habitat. Beavers really change the habitat in a valley that's narrow and steep like this one compared to a relatively flat valley floor that has riparian vegetation without the help of beavers. In a narrow valley like this their ponds and the wetlands around them support many more insects, fish, and birds than a tumbling stream could. Many more critters even up to animals as big as that moose there."

"Where, Mateen? Oh I see him, or is it a she? Would it have antlers by now?"

"We'd be able to see the antlers now even though they'll be much bigger by fall. It's a cow and probably has a young calf nearby. Let's drop down to the stream by angling to our right so we don't disturb her."

"We don't want to disturb a cow moose with a calf do we?" asks Anoo.

"That we definitely don't want to do," agrees Mateen.

"Isn't she down lower than moose usually are this time of year?"

"Somewhat, I'm sure she'll head up higher as soon as her calf is big enough."

After swinging wide around the cow moose, Mateen and Anoo walk the remaining couple of miles to the lake. As they do they descend off the ridge that they first walked into the hills on and drop down into the valley of the western stream that runs into town. They follow game trails through stands of aspen and pine and cross meadows already thick with spring growth. As they descend farther into the valley, the west-facing slope they're on becomes drier. The ponderosa pine trees become scattered, the aspen smaller and growing in dense thickets. Farther down, the forest gives way to shrub land as the effect of the rain shadow caused by the high ridge to their west increases.

"That must be the lake, Mateen."

"That's the one."

"Man, the water is clear! Can I go for a swim?"

"Let's get camp set up first. It's starting to look more and more like rain. Later in the afternoon the air will have warmed up some more and I'm sure the water is cold."

Tohlee and Eli wake up early and, after feeding their various animals, have gone inside for their own breakfast. They both like the pattern of waking and being active for an hour or so before a big morning meal. Their midday meal is also pretty large because their afternoons are as physically active as their mornings. Their evening meal is small as the day's activities are behind them.

Eli decides to cook his favorite big breakfast this morning. First he cleans up some potatoes and starts to cook them in a pan. While they're cooking, he cuts up some onions and garlic from the root cellar as well as some dried green and hot peppers. Then he slices up some sausage. The whole bunch goes in another pan with some black pepper. When it's sizzling hot, he pours on a couple tablespoons of soy sauce. This adds some salt and browns everything nicely. Tohlee has grated some cheese and mixed up the eggs she collected from the chickens just a few minutes before with some milk from their neighbors Caleb and Laurel. When everything in the pans has cooked, Eli mixes both pans together. Then he pours the eggs over the whole batch. After the eggs have thickened he sprinkles the grated cheese over the full pan. On top of the melted cheese he adds some of Tohlee's homemade salsa and some sour cream, also from the neighbors. He leaves the pan on the stove for just long enough to take the root cellar chill off the salsa and sour cream. The big breakfast is ready and they sit down with heaping plates.

"Are we going to go into town this morning like you were thinking, Eli?"

"Yes, fair damsel. May I have the honor of your company?"

"Why it would be my pleasure, good sir. I have a list of things I need. It's been over a month since we made the trip, hasn't it?"

"Almost two I think. We haven't made the trip since early April when I needed some things to get ready for planting."

"Well, spring is one of our busy times. Tell me again why you need to go today?"

"I have to buy some boards to fix the steps down into the root cellar and I'm going to add a set of shelves to the left as you go in."

"Oh that's right, and very good! I've wanted more shelf space down there. There's plenty now, but not enough for the fall when we're preserving and stocking up. Are you ready to go?"

"I have all my measurements so I know how much wood I'll need. If we go soon we'll be there before noon and we can be back for the evening electricity so I can make the cuts I need. I should be able to get everything screwed together during the day after tomorrow's electricity."

"Are you going to paint the boards?"

"I'd rather not. I know that the bare wood of the steps rotted out faster than if I had painted them because the root cellar is cool and moist. But I don't want any chemicals hanging in the air in our food storage area."

"I agree and maybe some day we'll have a refrigerator?"

"Maybe, but we'll need more electricity credits than we have now. Not to mention the money up front. I can only grow so much fruit, wheat, sunflowers, corn, and row crops."

"And I can only grow so many spices, cut flowers, and herbs.

Are we going to use dried spices and herbs to get what we need in town? I still have some stocked up from last year."

"Grab whatever you can spare and there are some things in the root cellar we may as well try and barter too, like sausage and honey. Now that the garden is cranking out greens, radishes, and snow pea pods, we can thin out some more stuff from last fall that we never needed through the winter. I bet there is plenty of asparagus and rhubarb we can try and swap too. Not that anyone would want it."

"There's rhubarb but no way for the asparagus, Eli, that's all for me. I'll rustle up a half dozen more eggs instead."

"Okay. Let's get everything together. Then we'll hook up the horses to the wagon. They'll be glad to go. They haven't done much since we plowed the fields together earlier this spring."

"We're going to have lunch at Cassie's, aren't we? I told her last night we thought we'd be coming in today."

"Do you radio your sister every night?"

"Just to check in and it takes less time than you spend listening to the news."

"I do all my own pedaling for our little generator and it's the only news we can get," replies Eli.

"What? Are you kidding me! Cassie the librarian knows everything that's going on in town!"

"I mean real news from outside the valley."

"Oh yeah right, that real stuff."

"Watch out, Tohlee! Your eyes might get stuck up there!"

"I'll risk it. Just buy the town paper to read while Cassie and I chat a little. As long as we're back by electricity time. Or, you could take your saw and the other stuff you need for cutting in the wagon with us. Then you can do it all at Cassie's while she and I chat just a little tiny bit."

"I think this plan was hatched last night on the radio wasn't it?"

"What plan? What radio? What sister? I don't have a clue what you mean, Eli."

Tohlee and Eli get their goods for bartering together, as well as some broken glass and scrap metal, and load it all into their wagon. Then they bring the harnesses out of the barn and hook them to the wagon. The horses are eager to go and walk right over and stand by their traces after they are let out of the corral. They are quickly hooked up and all is ready for the five-mile ride to town. After the short ride down the driveway Tohlee and Eli turn up the valley towards town.

"What are you thinking about, Eli?"

"I was reading a book last night about the way things work. It described the gearing of a small waterwheel that turned a saw blade for cutting lumber."

"I don't think we use enough lumber to make the effort worthwhile, do you?"

"No I don't, but it can also turn a lathe, a smaller saw blade for finer cutting, or grinding stones for turning our wheat and corn into flour. Plus, if we had a copper core we could make a little electricity. Mostly I just thought it was an interesting book."

"I want us to produce our own electricity. But I suppose the copper core would be too expensive just like solar panels are."

"I think everything like that, what little there is, that makes it out of the cities only goes to towns not to individuals. The gradient of the river that runs by our land doesn't have the power to spin a core fast enough for much electricity. Town is better suited with its falls and twenty-foot diameter water wheel. If there were more solar panels or cores for windmills or hydroelectric power available, our town would be able to send out electricity for more than a couple hours every other evening."

"I suppose so. I know that the electricity mostly goes to the medical clinic, the lumber mill, and food storage, as well as the wood, metal, glass, leather and repair shops. They should try going back to water power for some wood and metal working. Then maybe we wouldn't have to wait for the shops to close in the evening for our power. What else was in the book?"

"An assortment of other types of machines most of which wouldn't be of value to us, but the concepts might be able to be adapted to help us."

"Nothing that is more interesting than machines?"

"More interesting? What do you mean?"

"I'd like to read about the way things work like, 'how does the heart work?'"

"What do you mean by that?" asks Eli.

"I mean when you give love, compassion, or emotional generosity, you receive back twice what you gave. How does that work?"

"I'm pretty sure that would be a completely different book about the way things work."

"Perhaps, but by my experience that's the way those emotions work."

"I've found that out too. I'm just a little taken aback by the way you broadened the whole concept of the way things work."

"Well you're very welcome I'm sure, Eli!"

"Now what are you doing, woman?"

"I just want some sun. No one is on the road."

"How am I supposed to keep my eyes on the road?"

"So don't, silly, we're only going a few miles per hour."

"And now oil besides?"

"It feels good."

"Well let me do that!"

"No thanks, you just keep your eyes on the road."

"I thought I didn't have to?"

"Well you just hit a bump! Oh, you troublemaker, you did that on purpose, didn't you?"

"I just wanted to see a little jiggle!"

"You are incorrigible!"

"Me? You don't need that much oil!"

"I told you it feels good."

Tohlee and Eli settle in to their ride to town. The horse's footfalls, the creak of leather and springs, the breeze stirring the trees, and the birds singing are the only sounds. They can see that up in the hills the clouds are thickening, but down in the valley it's a beautiful late spring day with only some fair weather clouds and a bright sun rising high in the sky. There's a lot of humidity in the air for a day as sunny as it is because all the plants are breathing and their moisture is filling the air below treetop level.

"Okay, I'm ready to answer your question," announces Eli.

"What question was that?"

"About the way the heart works."

"Oh okay, what did you come up with?"

"It's spiritual feedback."

"I think you're going to have to explain that statement," says Tohlee.

"It's the spirit world rewarding living humans for correct behavior by giving back twice as much energy as people gave out through their emotional generosity."

"I see, so who is doing the giving?"

"I see several possibilities. Actions that begin on the physical plane but that transcend the physical are difficult to cause so when they do occur their momentum causes twice as much effect in the spirit world where energy is not bound by the physical. The resulting effect that comes back to the initiator of the action is double what was started in the physical. As the spirit world is so closely connected to the physical it is still bound by the laws of physics. The particular law being that for every action there is an equal and opposite reaction."

"Pretty metaphysical even with the law of physics you threw in there. But that would mean from the physical to the spiritual the effect is doubled, but from the spiritual to the physical the effect stays the same, resulting in the noticed doubling of energy. By the law of physics the effect back in the physical should be half the spiritual, resulting in no net gain. Maybe that is where the magic of love, giving, and the spiritual realm comes in. What else do you have?"

"The same sort of idea, but God is actually watching and reward is by the direct choice of a supreme being, as compared to a supreme being having set up the system of physical laws. As you know, I like the idea that we are made in God's image and that image is one of a self-determinate being, a being in charge of its own destiny and entirely responsible for itself. So if God gave us the supreme gift of self-determination, then any actual effect on our lives directly from God would be a confirmation of our own inability to achieve the potential of self-determination that God has given us."

"I would much rather we were self-determinate beings than that our lives, our future, and our evolution are a known plan, even if the plan is hatched by a supreme being. A future open to human potential is thrilling to me. I do not fear the responsibility of freedom. You said you had several possibilities. Is there another one?"

"Yes, there is. I think that the Asian philosophy of the ancestors, the Native American philosophy of spirit guides, and the Christian philosophy of angels are all different societal views of the same phenomenon. In which case spirits connected to the individual would be the conduit for the return flow of the energy you spoke of that comes back double."

"So you're saying the system could still have been set up by a supreme being, giving us total freedom, if the ancestors/spirit guides/angels are humans no longer residing in the physical but still able to influence humans in the physical. And it sounds like that would be most compatible with your belief system. But you're also saying its possible the system could be purely metaphysical and the energy is not being influenced by a value system. To prove that point you have to work out the laws of physics and the doubling of energy problem. The doubling could be a physical energy debt owed to the spiritual. The debt would be a temporary effect with everything balancing back out when the physical entity returns to the spiritual. Your last theory is that God is actively judging us and giving or stopping the return flow of energy based on God's value system or plan for humanity."

"That's an excellent synopsis, Tohlee. I guess I don't have enough experience or understanding or perspective or whatever it would take to prove one perspective over another. But I do prefer the concept that God has given us total freedom and that there are actions humans can do from the physical that can influence energy not bound to the physical. And I prefer to think that some of that influence can come back directly to the individual who created it, while some can also go out to humanity near and far. I also prefer to think that some of that returning energy can be used to hold an individual's perception together when that individual's physical experience is over."

"From other talks we've had, the individual's actions that influence energy not bound by the physical can be mental or emotional. But they are exceptional actions due to intent, concentration, clarity, or out-of-the-ordinary circumstance," says Tohlee.

"That's exactly the perspective my preferred theory is based on. One cannot petition God. Quality has a greater effect than quantity."

"I'm very impressed you could understand my comment well enough just to broach the possibilities you have, Eli. It's just one of the reasons I enjoy our times together as much as I do."

"And I enjoy your inspiration, understanding, and motivation," says Eli.

"You're just buttering me up for some more jiggle!"

"Now that you've reminded me I'm right back to thinking of rubbing that oil on you."

"Get your mind out of the borrow ditch!"

"How can my mind be in the borrow ditch when your breasts are up here next to me?"

"To change the subject where'd the "borrow" of borrow ditch come from anyhow?"

"The ditch became a ditch when rock and soil is borrowed from next to the road and put on the road. That makes the road more level and raises it up above the surrounding soil so the road can drain."

After setting up the tent and unpacking some of their gear so that they're organized for the rest of the day, Mateen takes a break. Anoo takes the trowel and digs a small pit for the morning's needs and then heads out to gather firewood. There's plenty around and it doesn't take long for him to gather a large supply using his little folding saw on the bigger pieces and breaking the smaller ones. As he finishes Mateen shows up to help Anoo haul his work back to camp where they pile it near the fire pit Mateen prepared.

"Is it still too early for a swim, Mateen? I worked up a sweat."

"Let's wait a little bit longer. Tell me more of what you like to do when you're not working on the farm."

"Sometimes a couple friends of mine go around to neighboring farms and see if they need a fox or coyote or bobcat killed that is raiding a henhouse or getting too aggressive."

"How do you hunt them?"

"We usually bring them to us with predator calls. There are trappers around, but they don't like to set traps or snares near homes."

"Do you keep the furs?"

"Whenever the furs are in good condition we take them to the tannery. The meat always ends up at the butcher. The butcher turns the meat into pet or fish food. They cook it up till it's very well done and then grind it into little pieces and mix that with old grain."

"Why do you think the predators come to a call?" asks Mateen.

"It depends on the type of call. Some imitate a kill being made while others cause the predator to think his territory is being encroached on."

"I was at my cabin working in my garden one day," says Mateen. "All of a sudden I heard a loud shrieking. I looked over and saw two birds fluttering and spiraling down to the ground. As soon as they hit the ground the shrieking stopped."

"What kind of birds were they?"

"It was a sharp-shinned hawk taking a flicker."

"Aren't they pretty much the same size?" asks Anoo.

"Yes, that's why the sharp shin couldn't kill the bird in the air or stop it from shrieking. It needed the leverage of the ground to finish off the flicker."

"And if a coyote or fox heard that, it would come and investigate, looking to steal a meal or protect its hunting grounds," says Anoo. "That's why our predator calls work."

"Another time I was sitting by a fire at night when I was out camping. All of a sudden two coyotes started yipping and yapping, running downhill towards me. Every once in a while I could hear a fawn bleat. The coyotes had separated the fawn from its mother and were giving chase."

"Did they catch it?"

"The sound stopped just a hundred yards up the hill from me. I don't know if they caught it and killed it so quickly that there weren't more bleats as it died or if they realized the fire and a human were there and so stopped their chase."

"Maybe the fawn knew you were there and was running to you to use you as protection from the coyotes?"

"I think that is entirely possible," says Mateen. "Have you ever heard a coyote bark like a dog?"

"No, have you?"

"Yes, just once. I was far enough away from any homes that I'm sure it was a coyote."

"They are a type of dog, that's just not a sound I've ever heard them make before," says Anoo. "I did hear coyotes making a different call as an alert once. We were trying to call one in and we decided there were young with parents. They must have known we were people and were alerting their young of danger."

"They are quite vocal animals," says Mateen. "Can you tell the difference between your dogs' barks?"

"Yes, each has their own distinctive sound if you listen close enough. And their barking changes if it's a stranger alert bark or playing bark."

"I think coyotes and wolves know whose call is whose also and different calls are for different circumstances."

"I guess they're doing a lot more communicating than just making noise," says Anoo.

After a quiet, reflective few minutes Mateen starts up the conversation again.

"Let's talk more about why your parents and I want you to think for yourself. Why we want only your own experiences and conclusions to be the base your perspective stands on. Why you should consider other people's opinions, feelings, beliefs, and thoughts as no more than information until your life validates those concepts."

"Isn't thinking for yourself reason enough, Mateen?"

"Yes, and that was an excellent question. It is enough for yourself, but perhaps not enough for other individuals. Your own feelings and opinions are your own truths, but if you want others to value your feelings and opinions you have to be able to communicate to them the reasoning and perspective behind your feelings and opinions. That's how you raise your interaction with others above emotional reaction and above the coarseness of don't think obey."

"Don't think obey isn't how I want to be treated so I shouldn't treat others like that," states Anoo.

"That's exactly right. Over one hundred years ago the world was a very different place than it is now. It was much more technological for many of the people and yet more riddled with superstitions and beliefs."

"Superstitions and beliefs in what?" asks Anoo.

"Many of those people had beliefs about everything that was not at their fingertips and about everything at their fingertips that they didn't understand. There was a lot that people didn't really understand then because technology was changing as fast as it was, changing faster than most people could keep up with. Then the world went through a time of troubles."

"I've heard of the troubles but not with much detail," says Anoo.

"There were famines because the earth's climate only appeared to be stable because of the short view people held about climate and because people took from the earth more than they gave back. There were wars between countries because abundant energy made some people's lives easier and some countries had more energy sources than others. There were wars fought over religions, skin color, and between the haves and have not's. Wars have always been fought for similar reasons but people had put so much effort into perfecting the tools of war that small numbers of people could kill many. Also, diseases had a great effect on humanity because of overpopulation and a lack of education. Natural disasters were compounded by overpopulation and poor housing. As these troubles began to have a greater and greater effect in the world, the same problems caused troubles within single countries."

"Didn't people try and stop all these troubles?" asks Anoo.

"Some tried very hard by trying to talk to people, to get them to stop and look at themselves. They gave examples of many wars fought for religious, social, and political reasons that took a toll on the winning and losing countries involved for generations after the actual fighting was through. They tried to explain that building on the past is better than building from scratch on the rubble of war. They tried to tell people that they should want less for themselves and be more willing to give to others not as fortunate."

"That didn't work? That's just the Golden Rule. Why didn't people just stop hurting themselves and help the less fortunate?"

"Some people did, in some places, and to some degree. But even the people who had enough for themselves became affected by one type of problem or another and so they had less to give. As people's physical comfort was compromised, belief and superstition turned out to be an ineffective way of dealing with the troubles of daily life that arise when technologies stopped supporting the lifestyles of the times. Belief in a supreme being was a pacifier of moods but had no ability to change what was happening in the world. Belief in a supreme being created an attitude of acceptance more than a capability to create something better. The only thing that kept people from degenerating into barbarians even more than they did were the individuals whose conduct and perspective towards the world around them was determined by their own rationality, their own individual value systems. In the face of hunger, cold, sickness, violence, and a loss of leadership, conduct based on belief in a supreme being and hierarchies fell apart. Only individual rationality and perspective weathered the storm of troubles humanity faced."

"So all of civilization was lost and just a few individuals remained?"

"Not all was lost everywhere, but in some places it was. Mostly there was a lessening of knowledge and structure in societies when the comforts and methodologies people were accustomed to were torn away from them. Those who adapted the best were people who functioned from an individual perspective. They were the ones others turned to when societal structures eroded. They were the ones who had the most experience creating their own base to live their life from. The people who had the most trouble were the ones who were the most dependent on existing hierarchies. They were unfamiliar with creating their own base for their own perspective to stand on."

"What is the base you're talking about?" asks Anoo.

"That base is the value systems people use to interact with each other. We live in a free country where it is entirely valid to build your own value systems as long as they aren't violent or illegal. We'll talk more about value systems later. At this point I want you to understand that most people don't build their own value systems in this free country just like most people don't create and live their own religion."

"But why not in a free country whose freedoms specifically allow that level of individuality?" asks Anoo.

"It's because most people don't want that much responsibility for themselves. Most people want a supreme being to be responsible for them or an existing hierarchy like the military. Those are the people who had to learn to build their own base when it was forced on them during a time of violence and privation. They were at a real disadvantage compared to the people who were familiar with building their own base in life because of their own capability and desire. They were the followers who, as soon as they were hungry, joined the mob that had burned down their home while looking for food. Overall, the ability for individuals to rebuild what had been accomplished by society and adapt to changes was really quite extraordinary. Our lives are better for the accomplishments of individuals in those desperate times. The physical troubles people faced were compounded by how lost people became when their beliefs were not real enough to cope with the troubles that came in their daily lives. Prayer and calls to the local authorities did not stop the mob or save their burning house. People became very lost without established structures because they didn't create those structures - they just used them and followed them blindly. Structures like established religion as well as law and order. There was a cascading effect. As daily troubles mounted, doubt in beliefs and the leadership they had chosen to be dependent on grew."

"I don't understand, Mateen."

"There was an overriding belief in those days that God dealt with people on a day-to-day basis. This belief made it difficult for people to understand why sickness, natural catastrophes, wars, and social unrest occurred. God was good and was supposedly active in the day-to-day lives of people. So how could a good and just god allow so many terrible things to occur? There is no real answer to that question if God is active in people's daily lives. So people said "It's God's will" or "God works in mysterious ways." Those justifications are not answers to why epidemics and natural catastrophes occur or why societies make war on each other. Nor do those justifications create in individuals the ability to solve problems. Those justifications create complacency. They are a refusal to admit that humanity itself is responsible for its own daily life. It is a method of avoiding the idea that we are responsible for ourselves as individuals and together we are responsible for all of humanity. From my perspective there is no more a devil that makes me act poorly than there is a god who directs me to my appointed destiny. Whatever plan we are a part of is more dependent on our own forethought and actions than on our following a plan thought through or created by a supreme being.

War is an excellent example of this. If human destiny were the following of the plan of a supreme being, do you really think God couldn't come up with a better way to teach than the experience of war? I don't think that war is somehow a good goal that only a mysterious god can comprehend. War destroys more than it creates except for more tools of war. War is the worst and final choice in any given situation. War is a statement that people made mistakes and lacked forethought. For every war that has ever taken place no supreme being came to people to teach them how to avoid that war, how to avoid the progression of their own actions. War is not good because of what is built afterward. That is an illusion caused by a lack of ability to imagine what could have been without the cost of war. People are talked into going to war by other people, not an anti-God. They are not driven to war by God's mysterious purpose. War won't stop unless people stop war. The best way to stop war and violence of any kind is to realize who is responsible. We are. Not God and not the Devil."

"If neither a god nor a devil were responsible for people's troubles then why did people cause themselves so many problems, Mateen?"

"They caused themselves those problems because of their inability to accept and live their own personal freedom. Personal freedom is to be responsible for one's own individuality and collectively for humanity's destiny. Our freedom means our fate is what we make it."

"Don't you believe in God?" asks Anoo.

"I do. I believe in God as the creator and the sustainer, a sustainer by being the source of the energy that is us and runs through us. Realize this is my belief, not something I can prove to you. It is something for you to think about in connection with your own experiences and perspective. I believe that when God said he created man in his image it means that God created humans as self-determinate beings. Because I think that when a being is self-determinate, as by definition God must be, the only image of oneself that has any real meaning is found through the process of self-determination. I don't believe that God sustains us by helping us in our daily lives. I believe that God sustains us because I believe God is the energy that binds our souls to our physical bodies."

"What does that mean, Mateen?"

"That is getting ahead of things. I believe a being we term God created the universe. I don't know if creation occurred at the moment the being we call God became self-aware and the entire universe grew out from that one moment or just how creation happened. I just think it is probable that when the universe started, it started by intent. Not by the bringing together through coincidence of building blocks or factors that did not even exist."

"And what does that mean?"

"Life on earth may have started through the chance combination of energy and chemicals. No one knows. The universe could not have formed from the chance arrangements of matter. There was no matter. No gravity to form stars into spheres. No stars to have gravity. No gravity to hold atmosphere to a planet. No planet to have enough matter to have gravity."

"There was nothing to have intent then either, Mateen."

"True enough. Yet here we are and far away stars also. That's the part I can't explain, but it seems to me intent must have been involved. It is easier for me to conceive of intent arising from nothing than it is that matter arose from nothing. The holder and creator of this original intent I call God. Energy is present in all things, all things and everything, even things that have never been alive. The root of that energy and the holder of original intent I call God."

"You believe there is energy in all matter, Mateen?"

"The energy in non-living matter is shown at a molecular level by nuclear explosions, gravity, and by chemical and magnetic attractions. The energy in living things is shown by movement, intent, and the ability to transform matter into matter beneficial for itself."

"What do you mean transform matter?" asks Anoo.

"I mean processes like photosynthesis, digestion, beaver dams, people's houses, and varieties of plants we've developed for food, for example."

"Do all living things possess intent?"

"Perhaps the smallest of living things don't possess their own intent. I don't know for sure. But some beings certainly do. All living things can transform matter for their own purposes. Even viruses, which are at the border of living and not living, alter matter when they reproduce. All living things strive to continue themselves as individuals and therefore as members of a group or species. Transforming matter for the purposes of something living separates life from processes that transform matter."

"What processes transform matter?"

"The wind and sand transform rocks to gravel, fire transforms wood to gasses in the air and ash, cold transforms liquid water to a solid which can crack rocks, there are many examples, Anoo."

"Do you think God plays no more a part in our daily lives than what you've described, Mateen?"

"I think that the idea of a god that created a universe with trillions of stars millions of light years away from us and that also directs our individual decisions, is no more accurate and has the same source as the idea that the sun revolves around the earth. That idea is that we're here and we know it, so we think everything must be about us. I am not willing to belittle God by thinking a being as vast as God must be has done nothing else with its creation and can do no better than humanity as it is. And yet, do you think that the source of all that humanity is, this glorious earth and the capability to create our own destiny, is a small thing? No, it is an enormous gift to us, Anoo. It is a gift we could not give ourselves. All that we are is derived from God. Where does the responsibility for us start and God's responsibilities for us end? I think the more responsibility we take upon ourselves and the less we expect God to provide, the more we are living God's plan for us. I believe it is a plan that began with the gift of self-determination. This earth with all its beauty and humanity, with all its potential is an incredible gift from God. Our lives are already an opportunity with boundless possibility. I don't need God to have given humanity the entire universe. God did not need to give me anything more than my life here on earth for me to be eternally grateful. God owes me nothing and I expect nothing more. The gift of being alive and the freedom to exercise my individual intent is gift enough."

After their talk Mateen and Anoo stand on the edge of the cut bank next to their campsite. The sky is blue and white and the gray of water-laden clouds. The greens of the young leaves on the trees and shrubs, of the grasses and forbs all around them are vibrant and varied. Little spots of yellow dot the landscape where wyethia and balsamroot are flowering among larger patches of color from flowering shrubs. The afternoon sun glints on the little ripples of the lake below them like dancing diamonds. The breeze that is causing the ripples brushes their faces. Birds are moving through the air and a squirrel chatters from the tree beside them.

"Are you ready, Anoo?"
    "I'm ready."
    "We can dive in off the rock down below us. Then we can bathe up there at the sandy bar where the stream comes in," says Mateen.
    "It sure is a nice view from up here," says Anoo.
    "This is a great place to watch animals and the stars at night. The side of this hill was very steep to begin with. Then the stream cut underneath it far enough that the whole side of the hill slid down and dammed up the stream. That's how this lake was formed."
    "Did you see it happen?" asks Anoo.
    "I didn't see it happen. But I was up here about forty years ago before it happened. There was just the stream with some beaver ponds then. The next year I was up here and the lake was here and

so was this cut bank. Willows were underwater and water was ten feet up the trunks of the cottonwoods. The trees still had green leaves. It was pretty strange looking. Now you can see that they're just the broken off trunks."

"How deep is the water?"

"The deepest spot is about fifteen feet where we'll dive in off of the rock. Let's go, Anoo."

Mateen and Anoo walk around the steep cut bank down to the lake. The afternoon has warmed up nicely and the hike and work at camp has made them sticky and ready for a refreshing swim. The slight breeze riffling the water and the cottonwood leaves is warm enough as they strip down for their swim. The sun peeks through the clouds now and then.

"Wow! It is cold, Mateen!"

"I knew it would be. Let's swim up to the sandbar and bathe. Sand is great for scrubbing the skin. It cleans off all the old skin and leaves you feeling all freshened up. Just don't put it in your hair. It won't clean the hair oil out of your hair and it gets stuck under there. It's really hard to rinse out."

"Okay. I have the shampoo my mother makes for my hair. She says it won't hurt the water."

"After that we'll swim back and dive off the rock for a final rinse before we give our clothes a washing. Then we'll stand in the sun and warm up."

After cleaning themselves and their clothes in the lake and warming in the sun, Mateen and Anoo walk back to camp. There they spread their clothes out to dry on the lower limbs of the large ponderosa pine tree that stands next to their tent. They both decide to stand in the sun a little longer before putting on their change of clothes. The sun's warmth is temporary and the breeze light. Their skin is refreshed by the sand scrub and the cold water. The sun's rays seem to reach deeper into their skin than usual. Their muscles start to relax in the warm sunshine after the work of their hike and the cold swim. They are getting dressed just as another bank of clouds starts to cover the sun.

"Are we going to go hike around, Mateen?"

"I think we'll just hang out around camp for the rest of the day. We have a great view and we can talk some more."

"What are we going to talk about?"

"Do you know the definition of a wise person?"

"It's someone who has learned a lot and has a lot of experience and perspective."

"Can you explain that to me?"

"Not really, I guess it's just an opinion to me."

"Well said, Anoo. Another way to say the same idea is to say a wise person is someone who knows what they don't know."

"I don't know what that means."

"That's okay. What I mean is that a person needs to be aware of how much could be known about a particular subject so they can put in perspective how much they actually do know. The less a person knows about a subject the more hesitant they should be about voicing their opinion. The more open to other possibilities they should be."

"I'm still not sure I know what you mean."

"When I was your age I used to run around out in the woods all the time. I'd see all sorts of critters and flowers and rocks and stuff. I thought because I was familiar with those various things that I knew about them. I thought if I knew where to go see deer I knew about them. That if I saw squirrels everyday I knew about them. When I was older I sailed to Hawaii and lived there for a few months."

"I didn't know you lived in Hawaii!"

"I did and I enjoyed it a great deal. One day while I was there a Hawaiian hawk landed on a branch just ten feet from me. It sat on the branch and looked at me. I moved a little closer and looked at it. After we looked at each other for a couple minutes it flew away. As it flew away I started thinking. Where was it going? Did it nest in a tree? What did it eat? How many eggs does it lay and at what time of year? How long will it live? I realized how much I didn't know about that bird. Then I realized how much I didn't know about all the animals and plants where I had grown up. The same animals and plants I saw all the time and thought I was so familiar with generated all sorts of unanswered questions for me. I just hadn't been asking those questions. I'd see deer in one particular place all the time. But I had not wondered why - I just went there to see them. Was it the type of plants that were there? Did the wind blow in such a way that they could bed down there and smell danger approaching better than in other nearby areas? Why did I see some flowers growing in one place and not another? Was it the soil or the amount of sun? Did the deer eat them?

"Then I realized I could spend a lifetime walking around a forty-acre patch of ground and never learn all there is to learn about that ground. I'd just have to ask different questions. If I learned all the names of the flowers I could start on all the mushrooms. But maybe I'd wonder what kind of bug was eating one of the flowers. Then I could learn the name of that bug and if it ate other plants and how long it lived. How does that bug live through the winter or where does it lay its eggs for the best winter survival? Do birds eat those bugs? What kind of birds eat those bugs and do they nest on those forty acres and if they don't, why not? If they do, what do they feed their young? Can the young develop on the same diet the adults live on? Do they nest on the ground or in a tree? What is the name of that tree? Why is it growing there? Is the soil different? What type of soil is that? What was the original type of rock that broke down and formed that soil? Is that type of rock common here? What's the name of that rock? Did it start to break apart to form the soil because a lichen was growing on it or did the process of freeze thaw break it apart or both? How long in the spring and fall does the freeze thaw period last? Spring and fall? Why are there seasons? What other planets are in our solar system besides the Earth? What's the name of that constellation up there?

"You get the idea, Anoo. If you ask the right questions about who, what, why, and where on a forty-acre piece of land, you'll end up learning about all sorts of things. You'll become learned in entomology, ornithology, dendrology, astronomy, geology, mammalogy, botany, all manner of ologies. The same is true if you're trying to learn all there is to learn about this lake in front of us or the art of vegetable gardening. What bugs eat what plants in the garden? What plants like what soils? How do you collect and store the seeds of those plants so they'll germinate in your garden next year? What birds do you want to have around to eat what bugs?

"In this lake, how do the plants that grow underwater differ from the plants that grow in the air? What kinds of fish eat what? What bugs grow in the soil on the bottom of the pond and what do they live on? What birds eat the bugs once the bugs leave the water and fly off? Even if you never leave your own backyard, you'll never learn all there is to learn about that yard if you just ask yourself the right questions."

"What happened to the knowing-what-you-don't-know part, Mateen?"

"Oh yeah, I got a little carried away there. Once you learn a lot about one particular subject and then realize how much there is to learn about all the other subjects, you begin to know what you don't know. You learn how much you could learn but don't know yet. How much someone else may know about a subject that you haven't chosen to learn about. When you learn to perceive the world and the people around you from the perspective that life doesn't revolve around you, that the sun doesn't revolve around the Earth, that you're not a conclusion, but a process, you'll begin to gain wisdom."

"I think that's something I'll have to ponder for awhile," says Anoo. "In the meantime, what's a lichen?"

"A lichen results when an algae and a fungus take a liking to each other."

"Ha ha, good one, Mateen."

"That means that a lichen is a symbiotic relationship between an algae and a fungus."

"What is a symbiotic relationship?"

"It means the relationship benefits both parties in the relationship."

"How do lichens break down a rock?"

"They produce a mild acid from their roots that eats into rocks over time."

"How does the relationship benefit the algae and the fungus?"

"When those types of algae and fungus grow together they become more than either can be when they grow separately. I don't know exactly what benefits which and how. That's an area you can choose to learn more about."

"I guess there are a lot of things I could learn more about."

"That's a true statement, no matter who is talking, Anoo. A person could spend a lifetime learning about a patch of woods, or a lake, or their own vegetable garden and never learn all there is to learn about any of them. They just have to ask the right questions and be willing to change their perspective."

Eli and Tohlee trade in their food stuffs left over from the fall harvest and also some fresh herbs, spices, eggs, and salad greens for lumber that Eli is going to use to fix the stairs and make new shelves for the root cellar. Their greenhouses mostly supply them with early greens for themselves, but there is always some to take to town now that the outdoor growing season is in full swing. Besides the lumber, they get some odds and ends that are needed after the long winter. They stop by the community center to trade in books and check the bulletin board for news and to pick up a copy of the local paper. Then they're off to Tohlee's sister's house.

"Hi, Cassie, it's good to see you!"

"Mmm, Tohlee, I'm so glad you guys are here. Thanks for the hug! Get down from there, Eli, and give me a hug too!"

"Hi, Cassie."

"I love your hugs, Eli, and your kisses too!"

"Mmm, it's always nice to see you, Cassie."

"We're going to get lunch ready, Eli. You can take the horses around back and get organized back there for electricity time. We'll see you on the front porch."

"Okay, Cassie. Is Jed around?"

"Not yet, he'll be here sometime after lunch. He's been looking forward to talking with you."

"Was he thinking about anything in particular?"

"He read a book he thinks you'll be interested in and wants to talk about it."

"Okay, I'll be back after I'm set up."

After settling the horses and getting organized for woodcutting Eli joins Cassie and Tohlee for lunch on the front porch. They enjoy a nice lunch of fresh greens, herbs, and jerked elk. After lunch Tohlee and Cassie go inside to clean up and to see what Cassie has been up to in her home the last couple of months. Eli sits on the front porch, sipping chokecherry stout that he and Tohlee have brought. After an hour or so Jed, Cassie's boyfriend for the last few years, comes walking up the drive. Eli pours Jed a glass of stout and they settle into the rocking chairs on the front porch.

"Cassie told me you read a good book you wanted to talk about, Jed."

"I did, Eli. I brought it with me so you can read it next. It's about what happened to our country over a hundred years ago but from a little more philosophical standpoint than some of the other books we've talked about."

"What subject does it start with?"

"It talks about how the choice to be dependent on foreign energy sources sent huge amounts of money out of the country and left us vulnerable to the governments of other countries."

"We've talked about that before. How, after we chose to get more than about fifteen percent of our energy from countries other than our own we turned this country's energy policy from a business decision to a dependency," says Eli.

"That's right, the fifteen percent was a sharing of this country's wealth with less developed countries and so that was a good thing to do. But government and industry didn't stop there. They increased the percentage of foreign energy used by this country to well over fifty percent of total energy use - which left us dependent and vulnerable."

"Did the book say why our country chose that route?"

"The author's idea is that our country needed lots of cheap energy to defeat the Soviet Union in World War III. That cheap energy was used for the weapons of war and to manipulate public opinion. The people of this country were led to think their system was better than the Soviets through the availability of material goods."

"So he's saying that World War III ended, but the effect of the war, even after our country's victory, lingered on for decades and eventually was a major contributor to the great troubles of our country and almost all the rest of the world too?" asks Eli.

"That's right, and a big part of that lingering effect was the use of our military to protect our way of life from the results of our own choice to be dependent on other countries' energy," says Jed.

"So there's the cost of the energy, the cost of the military, and the effect on our society at a personal level due to the dead and wounded soldiers and the time away from their families for all the soldiers," says Eli.

"That's the political and historical base this book starts from. Then the author goes on to say that when the country lost its energy independence it was a sign that the people had lost their independent spirit and individual identity. In the same way that an individual loses their independence and identity when that person lets another person or an institution determine the course of their life."

"Or allows them to define their individual value system," adds Eli

"That's exactly right. This country was born to be structured around the individual. The Constitution of the United States gives the right to its citizens to be free from governmental oppression.

That right is given to individual citizens, not to society as a whole. We have the right to determine our own individuality, not just to determine the collective identity of the society we are in. The governmental oppression our constitution protects us from is from our own government," continues Jed.

"So our government's choice to be dependent on other countries' energy left us, as a country, vulnerable to those other governments' oppression and manipulation, thereby, undercutting our own constitutional rights as individuals," says Eli.

"That's right, and the choice to have that dependency that undercuts our own individual rights was made by our own government and the businesses that were directing our government at the time. I like to think of it as the businesses were in charge of our country, and the politicians in their pockets were more interested in the melting pot of society being a thin, undifferentiated gruel of conformity rather than a thick, lumpy porridge of varying individual tastes and textures," says Jed.

"I like that analogy. So the choice to be dependent on other countries' energy caused our lack of individual rights and thus our lack of individuality?" asks Eli.

"Not exactly, the book is saying that the loss of individuality was going on for quite some time. The individuals in our country had been losing the value that the authors of the Constitution placed on individuality for some time and that is what allowed our government to get away with the choice to be energy dependent and to alter the country the way they did," says Jed.

"So the choice toward energy dependency led to a loss of individual rights. The lessening of the value of individuality, that allowed the dependency to begin with, was a symptom of a larger malaise," says Eli.

"That's exactly what this book is saying and that the choice of energy dependency would have been an obvious statement of societal malaise to the people of the time had they not already lost some of their individual independence," says Jed.

"What are some of the causes of this malaise according to

the book? A malaise that was so severe it took away the value of individuality in this country," asks Eli.

"There are quite a few reasons discussed in the book. It talks about overpopulation, mass education, organized religion, mass marketing, and increased internationality," says Jed.

"Well start with overpopulation. That sounds like the more people there are the more they are treated as a group, not as individuals," says Eli.

"You certainly chose to learn about this topic Eli, and you're right. As there were more and more people everything became mass produced to supply the masses. Food was grown on gigantic farms a thousand times as big as yours and then shipped across the country by trainloads to cities of many millions of people."

"But there were still people who grew food in backyard gardens or small farms," states Eli.

"There were, but they represented a smaller and smaller percentage of actual food production. At the same time raw materials were produced on larger and larger scales, and larger and larger quantities were discarded into landfills. The products that raw materials were used for were produced in ever-larger numbers while variety was lacking and craftsmanship suffered. People used mass entertainment to compensate for their own lack of individual creativity. Backyard music turned into indoor television watching. The entertainment on television was designed to appeal to the masses so that the advertising of products during the shows would reach the most people. Insurance companies to protect the people became gigantic and more interested in their own profits and expansion than in helping their own customers who gave them the money that became their profits. The more people needed help through hard times, the less profit was earned. Helping people was a loss of profits. The more people were conformed, the more accurate the averages the insurance companies used to define the line between profit and loss. Companies became larger and larger and their influence on the government increased. Smaller companies with a product in common banded together so they'd have more influence. The government's entire perspective changed from individual values to the values of these gigantic companies and their affiliates. These gigantic companies supplied everything people used day-to-day from food to insurance, cars, gasoline, medicine, entertainment, and raw materials. A majority of an individual's day-to-day work was made up of doing a small task within a huge process," says Jed.

"So you're saying the whole focus of government became big business and people's perspective on individuality became which product they bought, or clothes they wore, or entertainment that occupied their free time," says Eli.

"That's right; individuality became what people bought instead of value systems individually held. This wasn't hidden from the people. They let it happen. If the people had reacted, the government and big business couldn't have done what they did," states Jed.

"Why didn't they act?" asks Eli.

"Some did in some ways, but not enough to stem the tide of the mass perspective. Some people withdrew from society to protect their own individual lifestyle and values. But this left the government and big business free to do as they pleased. The majority of people went under the sway of this mass business and governmental perspective. The mass education of the time helped promote this shift of values from individuals to the masses. The names of individual inventors were taught in schools at the time, but the focus was not on what caused their inspiration or genius but on the value their invention provided to society as a whole. The process of individual creation was downplayed and the benefits to society of mass production emphasized," says Jed.

"That sounds like socialism taking precedence over individuality at all levels of society and government. Or, perhaps it's fascism as the government was influenced by a relative minority of special interests," says Eli.

"I would say fascism, but that's the idea. Organized religion was one of the motivators. Organized religion taught people to flock like sheep. It taught that all people had to follow one religion for individual salvation. Following and adapting to an existing dogma became more valid than an individual connection to God," says Jed.

"In the way that Christianity focused on the birth and death of Jesus of Nazareth not his teachings in between. Yet Jesus himself stressed, and tried to pass on, his teachings to the individuals around him. It amazes me to think of how much of Christianity is based on what people have decided Christianity should be and how little is based on the teachings of Jesus of Nazareth," says Eli.

"That's right again. A person could be saved by Jesus in one fell swoop without applying his teachings to one's values and actions throughout life. One could have their sins absolved by the authority of a church, thus diminishing the drive to increase individual character. Religion became a club with dues, not a methodology for individual development," says Jed.

"And this focus on Jesus' birth and death was a way to appeal to the masses," says Eli.

"That's the idea. The people chose the easy way out of not relying on their own works in life, but instead having a leader determine their fate. The focus was on praising, exalting, or worshipping the leader, not on individual development or responsibility. A person could ask for forgiveness from the organization instead of living a value system that caused the person not to act in a way that required forgiveness," says Jed.

"Well, as I've said before, I can't be a Christian because I'm not asking for anything from Jesus. I'm not asking for him to save me or for a church to forgive me. I delight in and appreciate some of his teachings but my salvation will be my own responsibility. As Jesus of Nazareth said "there are many rooms in my Father's house. I go to prepare a place for you." I'm not sure what the absolution of original sin was. I've thanked Jesus for that role he seems to have played. But I think he was a man of action and wouldn't have wanted people to praise him or worship him for that. I think he would have wanted people to learn and grow from this new perspective of having original sin lifted from them. I think he would have wanted people to focus on their potential, not to praise him and look to him for their salvation," says Eli.

"I agree completely. One of the effects on the country of this mass religious perspective was to want to corrupt the Constitution from having freedom of religion to the freedom to be any sect of Christianity an individual chose," says Jed.

"That is hardly religious freedom as you well know, Jed. Organized religion is divisive while freedom of religion is inclusive. I consider freedom of religion and the tolerance it necessitates to be more in line with the teachings of Jesus of Nazareth than the divisiveness of telling someone their religion is wrong and they must change their beliefs," says Eli.

"That's a good point. Telling someone their religious belief system is wrong necessitates judging the effects of that belief system on the person as well as their immortal soul," says Jed.

"Judge not lest you be judged yourself, said Jesus of Nazareth. But Christians ignore that teaching and focus on the divisive perspective of a religious hierarchy instead," says Eli.

"The perspective of religious hierarchies that you're one of us or wrong is divisive and arrogant. Freedom of religion is inclusive, just as loving one another is inclusive," says Jed.

"How did the people who wanted to corrupt the Constitution get past the use of the word God in the Constitution? Since all anyone has to do is look up the word in the dictionary to see it is used to represent any supreme being in a monotheistic religion. Hinduism and Islam were religions for not only larger populations than Christianity, but were also well-known religions at the time of the writing of the Constitution. Did the people who wanted to corrupt the Constitution think the Founding Fathers were too stupid to know the meaning of the word?" asks Eli.

"The book doesn't go into that. My guess would be the people were backwards thinkers who let their conclusion that Christianity is the one-and-only religious truth overwhelm their rationality and perspective. Anyway, the idea in the book is that all these factors coalesced into an irresistible drive towards conformity and away from individuality. The final contributor that is mentioned in the book is increased internationality. That means the increased role this country played on the world stage, the increased view of this country as one society, not a country of individuals. That view of this country was both by our own government looking inward at its people and other countries observing us from the outside," concludes Jed.

"How could all of this have happened? Did the people in this country during that time turn the ignition of their cars and just drive away? Did they not realize those cars were developed, over time, by the inspiration and hard work of individuals? Cars they couldn't possibly develop on their own. Did they turn on a light bulb and not consider the individual creativity it took to apply electricity in this way? Did they not think of the work it took to develop electricity itself? Did they not realize that individuals develop society? What have masses of people ever done to further society? Masses of people made the numbers of cars but not the specific engineering of the cars. The great pyramids were only built because of workers who were slaves to kings and the engineers who told them what to do. Was fire harnessed by a society or by an individual? Was germ theory developed by a society or a few individuals? Societies apply individual thought - they don't produce it. Individuals produce individual thought and then give those thoughts to society and the benefits therein. All too often the reward for that individual effort is disdain and a lack of appreciation," Eli rants.

"You're preaching to the choir here, Eli."

"I know Jed, I just get worked up."

"Hey, you guys, we've been listening from inside and have greatly enjoyed your conversation. But now we're having a thirst for some stout."

"Come on out, sweethearts. All this talk has worked up more of a thirst for us too."

"So you guys are saying there was an overall decrease in the value of individuality with a reciprocal increase in conformity throughout society," says Cassie.

"That's right. Take organized Christianity, for example. Conformity was promoted by organized Christianity by valuing salvation over individual learning and the application of the teachings of Jesus of Nazareth. An example the book gave is when hundreds of people lined up in front of a hospital to look at an image of the Virgin Mary on a dirty window. Instead of waiting in line for hours to look at an image because of how it would cause them to feel, they could have volunteered to help the sick people in the hospital. The value system of that time was to go see the image of an icon of their Christian Church in a dirty window rather than help the sick as Jesus of Nazareth taught," says Jed.

"You're saying that the focus of religion at that time was on the symbols of the Church not on the benefit to the souls and health of individuals through applying the teachings of Jesus," says Cassie.

"And that's just one area. Public education was focused on obedience and conformity, not on individual development. Public school didn't focus on promoting the abilities of the gifted; it focused on teaching information to the masses. Scholastic success was measured by generalized tests. The effect was to cause people to think that learning was work or effort instead of a natural function of the mind. The enjoyment of having a thought became the tedium of acquiring information," says Jed.

"So, the government went along with that method of education because masses of conformed people are easier to direct for the aims of government and business," adds Cassie.

"That's right, there are a lot more positions in the center of a large company than there are executives. There are a lot more positions as low-level soldiers in the military than there are generals. The organization became more important than the people in it. People came and went while positions within the organization stayed. Republicans and Democrats were two sides of the same coin. Both political parties promised freedoms and the betterment of society with enough variation to give the appearance of choice. But both parties were controlled by big business. The Supreme Court even decided that corporations had the same constitutional rights as an individual," says Jed.

"But that was just the majority of people and organizations. There were always small businesses developed by individuals and people who learned on an individual level and promoted individuality," says Cassie.

"That's true, and those were the individuals that people in general relied on when large organizations, big government, organized religion, and society as a whole failed. They were people whose established patterns of thought were strong enough to be maintained when societal structures collapsed around them. They were people who created and held their own values and capabilities, they did not just mimic what was happening around them," says Jed.

"You're saying that they were people who did not define individuality by their own appearance or adornment, which brand of product they bought, what form of mass entertainment appealed to them, or what organization they belonged to. They were people whose individuality was determined by the value systems that they themselves held and lived."

"Well said, Cassie, that's exactly what this book is saying," says Jed.

"What I'm curious about is the World War III idea," says Tohlee. "I've always heard that some decades ago World War III decimated the world. I haven't heard what is usually called the Cold War, a century earlier, referred to as World War III. The more recent troubles were World War III because so many countries took sides and warred against each other. Then when the effect of that war was so detrimental to so many societies, civil war erupted within the countries which had participated in that war. People lost so much that they were familiar with and that had given them comfort and security that they warred within their own country, their own state, their own towns and neighborhoods. They warred with each other for what they used to drive down the street and trade little green pieces of paper for."

"You're absolutely right, Tohlee. This author wouldn't argue with you for a second. He's just saying that was World War IV. He's saying World War III was what is usually called The Cold War and that the major battles of World War III were Korea, Vietnam, and Grenada. With a thousand smaller skirmishes besides, and our country never really recovered from the cost of that conflict. It never recovered because a major tool to win the war involved a dependency on Middle Eastern oil. That cheap energy was used to outproduce the Soviets in the arena of military weaponry and to assuage the effects of the war on the populace of this country with material goods. To protect the choice of dependency our country used its political, economic, and military power to influence Middle Eastern governments, culture, and society. In the long run that dependency and the influence to sustain that dependency resulted in a Christian versus Muslim conflict which grew into World War IV. In the end that war became a civil war fought within our own borders."

"I understand Jed, war begat war. So throughout that entire progression what this country needed to do to change the horrors of our history was to choose individual independence over societal dependence. What this country needed to do was reach out to the world, not with its military to protect its chosen dependency, but with freely-given computer, medical, energy, clean air and water technologies. What this country needed to do was value a compassionate helping hand reaching out to the less fortunate more than greed and power. In return we'd have received respect instead of war, growth instead of degradation, life instead of death."

"That is so true, Tohlee, and a perspective that was so little understood and promoted at the time."

After quiet reflection and some sips of stout the mood lightens. They enjoy each other's company and the comfort of friendship. When the electricity comes on Eli and Jed do the cutting and drilling that Eli had set up ahead of time. After buying the boards he had drawn all the lines that needed to be cut, and marked all the holes that needed to be drilled for dowels. They don't assemble the pieces because it is easier to move them separately than to maneuver the size and weight of the finished stairs and shelves into the root cellar. The dowels that will hold the pieces together will be pounded in by hand. As they are doing their woodwork the girls are cooking, charging batteries, and clothes washing. After two hours the electricity goes off. Electricity for the town and surrounding farms is supplied by hydroelectric power. The plant is located in town at the confluence of the two streams that run up into the hills.

The town has long been where it is because of the falls where the two streams merge. Only the hospital and the mercantile have power twenty-four hours a day. The hospital uses the electricity for various medical needs and the mercantile primarily for refrigeration. Both also use electricity for food preparation. During the day, roughly from 5 A.M. to 5 P.M. the lumber yard, glass factory, tool and die/metal working shop, and the repair shop share the remaining electricity. Then at 5 P.M. the electricity is shuttled at two-hour intervals to four sections of the town, one of which includes the farms upstream of town, and two areas downstream, including Eli and Tohlee's farm.

This particular day Cassie's house happens to be first in line for electricity. Once the electricity goes off everyone enjoys dinner and then Tohlee and Eli have to return home for evening chores. They are late, but the long evenings of early June will give them enough time. Before leaving they verify that in a few days Cassie and Jed will ride their bikes to the farm for a longer visit. As they are riding back home Tohlee is still curious about Eli and Jed's conversation.

"Can you tell me how and why the lack of individuality in this country caused the problems it did?" asks Tohlee.

"How it caused problems is a spiral of lack of individuality and exploitation of that lack by hierarchical organizations," begins Eli.

"So people were led and their weaknesses encouraged but all along they could have focused on their Constitutional freedoms instead of conformity and obedience to the powers that held sway over much of their society," says Tohlee.

"That's right. The people's drive to conform, their drive to see individual value in things with no power to create individuality, was exploited and encouraged by hierarchical organizations over centuries. In this country organized religion was the biggest influence in its first couple centuries, but then government, the military, and big business followed suit. It really wasn't until mass media came along that the effect became as all encompassing as it did."

"And mass media was a tool that all those hierarchical organizations used for their own benefit," says Tohlee.

"That's right. The idea is that organized religion caused people to look to the leaders of churches and those churches established value systems for religious and ethical structure. My perspective is that individual development of religious belief and the establishment of individual value systems is necessary for people to reach their potential. I believe that human potential is reached through individual growth, not mass conformity."

"And how did mass religion increase the problems the country had?" asks Tohlee.

"All the large organizations, the government, military, big business, public education, as well as organized religion, all of them contributed to the focus of truth being outside the individual. Truth was farther up the hierarchy, not in the development of an independent perspective. There was one administration leading the country, one business a person's income was dependent on, and one person in a classroom who taught. Relying on an established leader of a church, leader of a country, leader of a business, general in the military, or teacher in public education all contributed to a focus away from the individual and towards an organization with a leader."

"Those examples always have someone else above the person you're dealing with," says Tohlee.

"That's true for all hierarchical structures. If you buck the system hard enough you'll end up dealing with an authority higher up the organization. If you disagree with someone in front of you, they will stop presenting themselves as the truth and point you up the hierarchical structure. When a sergeant defers to a colonel who defers to a general, or a priest defers to a bishop who defers to a pope, or a teacher defers to a principal the concept is the same. The individual has been caused to look out from themselves toward an authority that holds truth and validity. That truth and validity was a product of the hierarchical system. The higher up the system a person was, the more valid their perspective was presented and perceived to be, even though popes and presidents can be wrong. Over centuries, popes supported the Inquisition, looked the other way when there was genocide in neighboring countries, or child molestation in their ranks. Presidents lied to their people to promote war. They started war for false reasons and a hundred thousand unarmed women and children died. Bucking these hierarchical structures identified a person as a troublemaker, a loner, a criminal in some cases, a nonconformist, a heretic, guilty of insubordination and even treason. You were either for them or against the power of their structure."

"Okay, so how did the mass categorization and conformity of individuals in this country amplify the problems the country had?" asks Tohlee.

"When external pressures weighed on the people who were dependent on structures outside themselves they naturally looked out from themselves for help. But existing structures failed them in many ways. As war was being waged on multiple battlefields around the world, oil producing countries refused to or couldn't, because of their own concerns, support this country's dependency on foreign oil. The financial cost to people in this country was very large. Everything from driving to work to the food that was eaten took more of a family's resources. Medical care and rebuilding after weather-related calamities became more expensive. Heat, light, and raw materials all increased in price. The entire economy ran on oil in one form or another and when that supply was cut in half everyone suffered. For example, people didn't have discretionary income for childcare or for gas to drive to work. It became cheaper to stay home than to go to work. Because of this, people who were employed at lower paying jobs like housecleaning and childcare lost their jobs. The numbers of poor people increased due to the loss of jobs and through the loss of discretionary income to the point where only bare necessities could be afforded. This change was always blamed on another country, or terrorist organizations, or God's actions through nature, but never on the political choice to be energy dependent."

"Why did oil producing countries refuse or were not able to supply this country with oil?" asks Tohlee.

This country had been interfering with those countries' politics for many years because of the choice to be dependent on their oil. At the same time those countries were being told by Christians and Christian leaders in this country that their religion was inferior and not the truth. The U.S. militarily invaded and attacked a half-dozen Middle Eastern countries. The people of those countries resented the interference in their politics, the belittling of their religion, the invasions and occupations of their countries, and the killing of unarmed civilians. Countries that weren't directly invaded saw the result of being an energy supplier to the U.S. At the same time other countries were developing in a way that enabled them to be able to afford the oil that had been going to the U.S. When the governments of the countries that had been supplying the U.S. with oil faced internal turmoil, they were either overthrown or chose to sell their oil to other countries. Some countries kept selling this country oil and paid a huge price when they squashed the dissent from their own people. In a relatively short time, conditions in this country worsened to the point that oil-producing countries were blatantly invaded and occupied for their oil. This was originally tried in the Middle East, but it was too far away and there was a religion-based uprising, so this country had to discontinue that tactic. Those people identified themselves with their religion more than their country, so an attack on an oil-producing country in the Middle East became an attack on Islam. That caused World War IV which drained this country's resources."

"Just like World War III as the author called it. The U.S. was considered the victor, but at a terrible cost to itself. The major battles of the Cold War or World War III, however it's named, Korea and Vietnam, took a huge toll on this country. Not only were this country's resources used for war, but scientific advancement focused on developing the weapons of war which gave a taint to scientific learning. A huge toll was exacted through dividing the populace as well. The divisions caused by the war in Vietnam lasted for generations. People focused too much on the result of winning, not on what could have been if resources had been used for purposes other than war," says Tohlee.

"That's exactly what I'm talking about. First we paid the Middle East for their oil. Then when the cost to them in political, economic, social, and religious freedom grew too much, they used our money against us. They used the money we gave them for their oil to buy the weapons they used against us in World War IV. Even more incredible is the U.S. also built the weapons that the Middle East bought with our money from the sale of their oil to wage war on us. That part of World War IV grew until the U.S. military invaded and occupied some of the oil-producing countries so the U.S. could wrest their oil from them. Through this entire period the cost of this country's military increased and the cost to soldiers' families increased. Taxes went up to pay for the increased use of the military just when people's discretionary income went down. A draft was instated to provide the soldiers needed. Many people went along with these changes for the sake of the country just as they had been conditioned to do. Even after blatant invasions and occupations of oil-producing countries for their oil, many people thought the country was just doing what it needed to survive. But not everyone agreed with these actions of the country so schisms developed which deeply divided the country. Also, in this country and most others weather patterns were changing on an overpopulated world. Drought and famine caused the mass upheavals of millions of people, greatly stressing not only the countries they were from but also the ones they migrated to. In this country less food was produced and greater demands were placed on raw material sources from within the country. Even landfills were mined for what had been discarded in times of perceived excess. As they were conditioned to, people looked to religion to help them. But their god didn't put gas in their cars, or bring their children home from war, or stop tornados and hurricanes, or floods and drought. Their government didn't help either. No matter how many people this country killed in foreign lands it didn't decrease the cost of gas or food or medical care. Those costs increased at the same time the government was asking for more taxes, more soldiers, and more sacrifice.

All these various costs on the populace of this country caused hardships. Problems that had always been present, but under control, exploded. Problems between the haves and have-nots, between races, between religions, and between those who had said for years we must change our actions and those who said to be American is to support our current administration all exploded. A thousand local civil wars erupted in this country. People who had looked outside themselves for their truths lost their familiar structures and support. Those structures and support didn't fill their needs anymore and without them their behavior degraded to a level equivalent to their own individual development, a level of development that had been inhibited for many generations by the very same hierarchical organizations that failed them. That failure of individual development was so total that people couldn't follow the simplest of individual teachings. They failed at the most simplistic and common value known to humanity: Do unto others as you would have them do unto you."

"Oh, Eli, we've lost so very much as a society and a species. Wars have taken such an enormous toll compared to what could have been. Who won and who lost is such a shallow perspective on something as total as war. The cost of war was never measured in what may have been, what could have been done with the wages of war if we had spent our future more wisely. Religions have divided people and fueled intolerance compared to freedom of religion.

Nationalism pitted countries and societies against each other and rejected a view of humans as one species dependent on one planet. It's been two centuries since humans went to the moon and now the moon is almost as far away as it was for people a hundred years before we ever landed there. People die of diseases now that used to be curable. It's good for us to have learned that humanity doesn't just grow in a steady upward climb. The price we've paid to learn that we, not a God, or a government, or a cabal that supposedly knows what is best for us, are in charge of our own destiny, has been enormous."

"I agree with you that these problems could have been avoided if this country had chosen to export its clean air, clean water, energy, medical, and computer technologies freely for humanity instead of exporting a dependency on foreign energy and exporting a military to support that dependence," says Eli.

"We have ourselves and Anoo. We tend the garden of our lives and give what we can to others. I am so thankful for our life together, Eli, for blue skies and rain, summer heat and winter's snow, dogs and flowers, Anoo's smile and growing strength, individuality and contentment, learning and intent. Peace to you."

"Peace to you, Tohlee."

The rest of the trip Tohlee and Eli enjoy the quiet of the evening and the clip-clop of the horse's hooves. They care for their animals when they get home and then enjoy a cup of hot tea on their porch as the dark of night grows around them. First Jupiter shows, then, with the appearance of the first stars, they decide to spend the night outside.

Mateen and Anoo have spent the afternoon wandering near camp, meditatively quiet, and sitting on the cut bank looking over the lake and the slopes beyond. Some of the daytime animals are moving around in the mid-afternoon because the heat of summer hasn't arrived yet to cause the torpor of a midsummer's day.

"What's that deer doing over there, Mateen? Is she looking for something?"

"I don't think so. Her ears are pointed forward, but do you see the magpie over to the side in the oak brush?"

"Yes, and there's another deer there too. Hey! The magpie just landed on the back of the doe. Now it's hopping on her. What's going on?"

"Keep watching. Do you see the way the magpie is looking around the ears?"

"Hey! Now it's pecking at her ears. Why doesn't that hurt her? Aren't her ears sensitive?"

"Yes, but it's not pecking at her ears. It's looking for ticks and then pulling them off the doe and eating them."

"Oh yum, I wish I had some ticks to eat!"

"You would if you were a magpie. Ticks are small before they've fed on an animal's blood. But after they've fed and are full of blood they're as big as the end of your finger. They are a big, rich food source for the magpie. Plus the doe knows the magpie is ridding it of an irritant."

"Is that another symbiotic relationship, Mateen?"

"It certainly is, but of behavior, not habitat as with the lichen."

"That's quite a coincidence after what we were just talking about, isn't it?" asks Anoo.

"Yes it is. You'll find with experience that coincidences like these are what nature truly is for a woodsman."

"What do you mean?"

"The coincidences and timing, the choices you make to go here or there and the things you see when you do are going to be the moments in nature that mean the most to you. The times when you feel the most connected to nature are going to be gifts of timing and intent caused by your own experience."

"What are gifts of timing caused by my own experience?"

"You already have a good eye and experience with wildlife. That's why you saw by the way the doe was standing that she was doing something out of the ordinary. Once a person becomes familiar with the common in nature their eye will more easily pick out the unusual. Another person might have seen the deer and thought it was just another deer sighting. They wouldn't have kept watching to see what she was up to. By choosing not to watch, they would have missed the experience of learning about this interaction of deer and magpies. Other times you could watch a couple of deer for hours and they wouldn't do anything out of the ordInary. You realized because of the set of the doe's ears, through your experience from watching deer, that something out of the ordinary was going on. It was that experience that caused you to appreciate the opportunity in front of you and so learn about these animals. That is how one turns their own experience with nature into an art."

"What do you mean art? This isn't like painting or music."

"I mean it's the same process. Most great painters or musicians put a lot of work into their craft. Their work and effort causes the development of their abilities. It is a development that turns them into artists instead of people who paint or play music. Their abilities and experiences give them a perspective that causes an appreciation of others' abilities. An appreciation that allows them to see or hear the subtleties other artists are putting into their craft. Just as your increased experiences and abilities in a setting such as this, will show you methods of survival and adaptation in wildlife that another person might walk right by without noticing."

"Hey Mateen, so, when they're artists like painters, they can appreciate what they don't know about an artist who is a musician. They'd appreciate the effort the musician made to be able to sing or play an instrument, right?"

"You're exactly right. The expert painter's appreciation of an expert musician would be based on the painter's own efforts and ability in their own discipline, giving them a unique perspective on another's expertise in their own discipline. And isn't it interesting the coincidence that brought us to this point in our conversation, Anoo?"

"Do you mean the coincidence of nature?"

"Yes and also the coincidence of a teacher."

"Of a teacher?"

"Teachers can become artists through their ability to determine when a pupil is ready to learn a particular lesson, or by determining which example will demonstrate a concept to a particular person. In a case like that a singular occurrence can appear to be coincidence to the pupil because the pupil isn't aware of the groundwork prepared by the teacher before the actual occurrence."

"I think I see what you mean," said Anoo.

"You can think about it more when it's right for you. Did you see how after the magpie checked over the older doe she landed on the yearling doe?"

"Yes, but the yearling didn't like the magpie hopping on her. She got nervous after a bit and twitched her skin so that the magpie flew off her."

"That's right, but she saw what the older doe let the magpie do and she'll be more tolerant next time. Then she'll notice that her ears feel better after the magpie works them over and she'll associate the magpie's behavior and this spot with something beneficial for her."

"So, she'll learn from the older doe's actions and then the older doe's actions will be passed on to younger generations?"

"That's exactly right, Anoo."

As the sun starts to drop towards the hills across the valley Mateen prepares a stew of dried vegetables and meat over the fire. Anoo comes back from a walk and they both eat and relax around the fire. Mateen throws some green branches onto the fire so that the smoke from them will keep the mosquitoes away. They haven't been bothersome during the day, but now, with evening coming on, they are starting to become more active. After cleaning up the dinner dishes the campers spend the rest of the evening in meditative silence, stretching and watching the sunlight leave the sky and the stars come out between the clouds. Mateen goes to sleep while Anoo stays up until the clouds cover so many stars that he loses interest in watching the night sky.

DAY FIVE

Just before daybreak a shower passes over. It isn't enough moisture to supersaturate the soil, but it is enough to soak in a couple inches. Mateen wakes early and gets the fire going to take away the damp chill in the early morning air. Before he adds wood to last night's fire he moves some still warm coals to the top from under an inch of ash. Then he puts some dry grass on the coals and blows the grass into flame. After Anoo wakes Mateen starts cooking breakfast as they stay near the fire.

"I'd like to talk a little bit about how the mind works, Anoo."

"You mean having individual thoughts?"

"Yes, but from a little different perspective. You see, some people, more so in the past but there are still some now, consider the mind to be a sponge. A sponge that soaks up information from the world around it and then when there's enough information soaked up they think a thought will drip out."

"That's not a very appealing image. It makes thoughts sound like earwax."

"Good one, Anoo! What I mean is that to me, the mind is a fire waiting to be lit. A fire caused by the sparks of thought. Think about it like this fire in front of us. First it was wood piled up. That's the mind waiting to be lit. Information is fuel for the mind, waiting for a spark. There is a great deal of potential in the wood. Just as there is a great deal of potential in the mind for acquiring information, learning facts, and gaining experience. But the real beauty and usefulness of the wood as heat and light doesn't come out until the fire is lit. Its potential doesn't manifest until the heat and light locked up in the wood comes out through fire. Just as the mind's potential doesn't manifest until information and experience come together."

"How do information and experience come together? How will I know if that ever happens to me?"

"It already has happened to you. Every time you say "Aha, I've got it!" Every time you have the feeling that a light bulb has switched on in your mind. Those are the sparks of a mind waking up, of a fire being lit. When that happens to you, remember it and realize that something good has happened. Reinforce the event so that you will increase the likelihood that it will happen again. Those sparks of ideas will come together and create their own momentum. Those ideas will come together into concepts and pathways, into perspective."

"How come some ideas cause the light to go on and some are just gaining information?"

"That is a good question and I really don't think I can explain it fully. But the way I look at that is through neurons and synapses. I'd say that when the light bulb goes on, a new synapse is created or used for the first time. A new electrical pathway in the brain has been created. Using synapses over and over again doesn't require the charge that creating one to begin with does. On the other hand, new ideas need to be reinforced. New pathways have to be used to realize their potential. A thought that is a new idea is different from thoughts that are just brain activity, just repeated use of an established pathway. That distinction is similar to having your own independent perspective compared to merely being able to repeat what others around you already know."

"You just came around in a circle again, didn't you Mateen?"

"Yes, I did. There is a great deal of depth and potential in thinking for yourself. That is why there is more than one way to explain the concept."

"When you talked in that circular way my whole head felt like it was turning."

"That was you, changing your perspective. That was you, turning on the wheel of life."

"The wheel of life?"

"You are the center of your perception, the center of your ability to take in information. You have a perspective, a way of looking at and valuing the world around you. When your perspective changes the center of your perception is still you. So, when your perspective changes around your perception, it feels as though you are turning."

Mateen stands up and looks around. The sky is partly blue and partly cloudy. A cool but light breeze is moving the air. Anoo sits quietly and comfortably. Mateen chooses to just let some time pass.

"What have you been thinking about, Anoo?"

"I'm not sure I was thinking. I was just trying to understand."

"There is a lot to understand about who and what we are."

"Where does potential come from?" asks Anoo.

"The potential of this wood to become fire comes from the energy of the sun. This fire is the sun coming back out of the wood. The potential of a person comes from the unused capability of the mind and the unused capability of the being that is a person. That unused capability of a being is the ability to perceive and act from a more comprehensive perspective and to give good feelings and support to others, to give respect and freedom so that another can learn of their own potential."

"We're great big circles aren't we?" asks Anoo.

"That we are. And the more we turn, the more perspective we have. The more we have individual thoughts, the more momentum we gain and so the more energy we have. The more energy we have, the more potential we have to support a change in perspective and round and round we go."

Mateen stretches his arms up above his head and then his legs, one by one, up on a stump. Anoo wanders off into the woods for a break after taking a big drink of water. After a half hour or so they meet back up.

"Here's an example of merely a piece of information and information that contains a string of concepts with it, Anoo. During the Civil War of the early United States there was a soldier in the Union Army named General Thomas Jackson. He became famous during one particular battle because of the way he deployed his troops. He put his troops behind a stone wall at the edge of a field. The Confederate soldiers of the opposing army chose to attack General Jackson's troops by crossing the open field between them. This was a disastrous mistake because General Jackson's men were protected by the stone wall and so presented a very small target to the Confederates. The Confederates, being out in the open, were much more exposed to the rifle fire of the Union soldiers. Because of the deployment of his troops General Jackson won a decisive victory and earned the nickname "Stonewall Jackson". That nickname later turned into the phrase "stonewalling" which means to present an unyielding front to one's opponents."

"So his actions became a whole idea called stonewalling?"

"That's right. But I'm not through yet. During one of the first battles of the Revolutionary war a smaller number of colonists battled with a larger unit of British soldiers. The British soldiers were used to confronting their opponents out in the open in a very ritualized way. The colonists knew that if they confronted the British soldiers in the way the soldiers were familiar with, the colonists would lose. So the colonists waited until the British soldiers were marching down a road with trees on either side to start the battle. The colonists shot at the soldiers from under the cover of trees while the soldiers were in the open on the road. Because the colonists deployed themselves in cover and the British soldiers didn't, the colonists won a great victory. What does that have to do with General Jackson?"

"The Confederate soldiers made the same mistake the British soldiers did."

"That's right. If the Confederate general, leading his troops that day, had learned about the mistake of the British troops, he never would have sent his men across that open field. The idea of a mistake that repeats the error of an earlier time is captured by the phrase 'those who don't learn from history are destined to repeat it'."

"So knowing about General Stonewall Jackson means knowing about the idea of stonewalling and that I should learn history?"

"That's right. If you don't learn from history, you'll repeat the errors of earlier people just as countries, societies, or armies will repeat the errors of earlier countries, societies and armies."

"Wow! That's interesting, but what is the "merely a piece of information" in all that?"

"Well, I'm not done yet. The concept that people who don't learn from history are destined to repeat it is based on the idea that there is nothing new under the sun. The only way a person who didn't learn from history could repeat history is if the situation they were in had already happened at an earlier time."

"So, knowing General Jackson's nickname means knowing about the idea of stonewalling, which can take me to the idea that I should learn history so I don't repeat mistakes and that someone sometime has been in a similar position as me?"

"Yes, but not just that someone sometime has been in a similar position as you. I also mean that different countries, societies, and people each follow their own common themes that reoccur throughout time. Your parents and I want you to develop yourself as an individual so that you can have a perspective beyond those common themes. A perspective that is individual because of the depth of your understanding. Not because of a simple shuffling of common tastes or perspectives. Learning about the common threads of different countries, societies, and people allows you to learn to recognize the unusual when it is in front of you. Just as earlier today you recognized the behavior of that doe as something out of the ordinary and so paid attention and learned about an unusual behavior of that individual animal and how it was passing on that behavior to its young."

"You circled me again, Mateen! Now my head is really spinning. But you still haven't told me what the "merely a piece of information" is."

"The "merely a piece of information" is that General Stonewall Jackson's first name is Thomas. With that information you go nowhere. With an understanding of his nickname you're off on an adventure of learning."

Mateen and Anoo decide to drop down next to the lake to watch a family of mallards feed. They stay a little way back from the cut bank and quietly circle around until they are at the water's edge but behind a willow while the ducks are a short distance out into the lake.

"What are the ducks feeding on?" asks Anoo.

"The adults are filtering water through their bills and the little ones are eating insects."

"Are the adults eating insects too?"

"Well, not necessarily. They're filtering out plant and animal material from the water. They're more likely to end up with plant material, but they don't exclude the animals."

"Why are they more likely to end up with plant material if they don't try and exclude the animals?"

"Why do you think?"

"I don't know. If they're not trying to get one more than another, then they should get the same amounts of each."

"Always check your conclusion against your suppositions."

"What does that mean?"

"That means to verify that your conclusion makes sense. Then, check if there is something wrong with your suppositions or if you're leaving important suppositions out."

"So, my conclusion is that they'll get the same amount of

plant material as animal material and the supposition is that the conclusion is so because they're not trying any harder to get one or the other."

"That's right. Your supposition is that they're not trying any harder to get plant material than animal material."

"So that supposition is wrong because I'm not agreeing with you?"

"Ha ha, I like that, Anoo, but no, you're not wrong because you're not in agreement with me. Remember that no one is right because of who they are or what position they hold. Your supposition is not the only relevant information on the subject. Your conclusion is based on only one supposition while there are other factors to consider. You also need to take into account that right from the start there is more plant material in the water than animal."

"Oh yea, I guess I knew that plant material always outweighs animal in a system. So then, even though the mallards aren't trying any harder to get plant material than animal, they end up with more plant than animal because that's what's in the water they're filtering?"

"That's right, Anoo."

"What are the little ones eating?"

"They're eating insects."

"Oh yea, you said that. Why are they eating insects and not filtering water like the adults?"

"Well, they are doing some filter feeding but the insects are more important for them. The adults are maintaining their lives while the little ones need to double their size many times over this summer. If they don't, they won't be able to fly south for the winter."

"Why does eating insects make it easier for the little ones to double their size many times over?"

"It's the higher protein content of the insects compared to the protein content of the food filtered from the water."

"So the little ones need protein material for their bodies to double in size and the adults don't need protein material to maintain their lives?"

"The adults need some protein material to maintain their lives. They just get enough of what they need from filtering water without directly going after the insects."

"Some ducks eat fish, don't they?"

"Yes, but the ones that primarily eat fish, like mergansers, aren't filter feeders like mallards. That doesn't mean a mallard will pass up a fish if it happens to get one. I saw a female mallard catch a minnow once. It was full winter when they need more energy to maintain themselves compared to the summer. She brought the minnow out of the water with half of it sticking out of her mouth and clucked her delight at her catch so the other mallards around her noticed what she had. When the others saw what she had, they immediately started towards her to take it from her. She gobbled it down before they got to her."

"So she was showing off?"

"She was not only showing off, she acted in a way that could have created envy."

"Did the other mallards feel envy?"

"I don't know. They might have just wanted the food for themselves and were motivated only by hunger which doesn't need to include the feeling of envy. Or perhaps what would have been a feeling of envy was immediately used as the action of going toward the female's catch. To decide that the mallards felt envy is called anthropomorphizing. That means assigning human characteristics to animals."

"Isn't that what we do with dogs? For instance, when you said my father's dog has feelings?"

"With the mallard I only saw that behavior once. With your father's dog I've seen it many times. Plus, I've seen it with my own dogs and other people's dogs besides. So, I'm more comfortable with conclusions about dogs and their feelings than I am with basing a supposition and a resultant conclusion on only one behavioral occurrence like with the mallard."

"But didn't you see the mallard show off her catch only one time?"

"That's a good point, Anoo. In that case, my conclusion that she was showing off came from a direct observation of her actions, not an interpretation. The mallard brought her head out of the water with the fish showing in her mouth and clucked which attracted attention to her and brought an immediate response from the other mallards nearby. I guess I'm jumping to the conclusion that she knew what the other ducks' response was going to be when they saw the minnow. I assumed that she had seen similar behavior before in her life and had also reacted in the same way as the other mallards. My conclusion was that she was showing off. That's what I based my interpretation of the other ducks' drive to act on. I explain that drive as hunger and possibly the feeling of envy. That's why I said she acted in a way that could have created envy, but stated she was showing off."

"But now you're not sure if she was showing off when she clucked?"

"That's right. I still think it is more accurate to base conclusions of animal behavior on direct observation than on deciding their actions are based on feelings that humans would understand. But now I realize that even the conclusion that the female mallard was showing off was an interpretation that could be questioned. Perhaps her cluck was meant to tell the others nearby about a potential food source as a hen mallard would do with her brood."

"What do you know about mallards now?" asks Anoo.

"I guess I'm going to stick with my original supposition that she was showing off, but I've increased my need to see similar behavior again for validation and I've decreased my confidence in telling the story as an accurate interpretation of mallard behavior. I only raised the possibility of envy, so I don't think I need to change my perspective on that. But the actual occurrence of mallard behavior has not changed and remains an enjoyable wildlife observation. For me, it is an observation that raises the possibility of understanding mallard behavior without being definitive."

"There's a porcupine over there," says Anoo.

"Yes, and it looks like he is eating forbs."

"What are forbs?"

"Forbs are any herb that is not a grass."

"What's an herb?"

"Herbs are any plants that aren't woody."

"Oh, I thought porcupines ate pine bark?"

"They do in the winter. They eat pine bark and other kinds of bark also like Gambels Oak. Bark is their survival food. But, in the summer, when forbs are available, they'd rather eat them than pine bark."

"Oh, I guess I would too. I thought herbs were medicinal plants?"

"Some are. That's another definition of the same word."

"Words can have more than one definition?"

"Yes, they can. And the meanings of words, which aren't the same thing as their definitions, can change over time or in different parts of the country."

"Oh."

"Have you ever heard a porcupine sing?"

"Porcupines can sing?"

"They sing in the spring when they're looking for a mate."

"Is it a real song?"

"It's more like holding one long note."

"Who sings? Is it the male or the female?"

"I don't know because I never looked."

"I guess that would be kind of risky."

"Kind of, I'd say so! Let's catch some of these fish for lunch."

"Okay. Is it midday already?"

"It's only midmorning. There's still a lot of day ahead of us."

Anoo goes back to camp and gets their hooks and line. They walk around the lake and up toward the inlet where the ground rises up gently from the upstream edge of the lake. Willows are growing in the boggy ground near the water. They cut new willow stems to use for fishing poles and rig them up with their line and hooks. It's midmorning but cloudy and still cool with a little breeze blowing downstream. The cooler air from higher up in the hills is moving down the drainage, making the breeze. Usually that cold airflow down the drainage is over by midmorning in the late spring. But today it is hanging on longer than usual because of the clouds. It looks like it will rain some more later in the day because the clouds are building as the sun warms their tops.

"What are we going to use for bait today?" asks Anoo.

"Let's go upstream a little and look underneath rocks that are in shallow water for the larva of insects."

"Just any old rocks?"

"Flatter is better and under a couple inches of flowing water is better too. You don't want to try the rocks embedded in the muck of the stream bed. Try the ones that are resting on other rocks so they get some water flow running underneath."

"Okay. It looks like lots of these will do."

"I think you'll find some bait pretty quick," says Mateen.

"Do we want to use these little wrigglers, aren't they a little small?"

"Yes, those are too small to put on a hook easily. Keep looking, you'll find some good ones."

"Oh, these are bigger. I bet these will do!"

"That's what we're after. Trout love those. Just carry the rock back down to the lake and if we don't need all of the larva we'll put the rock back in a similar place. That way what we don't use for bait will have a chance to grow up. We'll fish where the stream comes into the lake, where the current of the stream slows as it meets the deeper water of the lake."

"I think the water is even colder here in the stream than it is at the end of the lake where we swam," says Anoo.

"It is a little bit. The running water of the stream doesn't have as much time to warm up as the more still water of the lake. It's better if we walk out into the lake in the stream water because the running water of the stream will help cover up the disturbance of our walking. Toss your line out in front of you a little bit, right about where the ripples of the stream end and the still waters of the lake start."

"Hey, I've got one already!"

"Bring him in and I'll hold him. I cut this thin willow twig to use to hang our fish on. Four should be enough, I think they'll all be bigger than the brookies from the pond the other day."

Tohlee and Eli wake as the sky is lightening to the east. To the west the clouds are heavier and look like rain. The clouds move over the hills steadily as a constant wind pushes them. Down near the ground errant breezes move branches seemingly without pattern. The disturbance in the upper air is reaching down and out from the growing clouds.

"Good morning."

"Good morning to you, Eli. Did you sleep well?"

"Very well, I had a fun jumping dream."

"A jumping dream, not a flying dream?"

"This was running a few steps before jumping up into the air and gliding along until my feet came close enough to the ground so I could run and jump again."

"That sounds like fun, unless you were running from something?"

"I think I was just running and jumping for the fun of it."

"Nice, are you ready to get up?"

"In a few minutes."

"OK, what will you do after morning chores and breakfast? Put the new stairs in the root cellar?"

"Later on this morning I will. I think the rain will hold off for a few hours so I'll get some gardening work done first and then go in the root cellar when it rains. What will you do?"

"I will garden too and then I'll make sure everything is out of your way in the root cellar. When it rains I'll be upstairs. I have some cloth to measure and cut before electricity tonight."

"It's easier for you to use the electric sewing machine than the peddle model, isn't it?"

"It's definitely faster. I want to finish several blouses before Cassie comes, so she can take them to the Mercantile to sell for me. That's what they said they needed when I talked to them yesterday. Cassie will let me know when they sell and if I should make more or if they need men's shirts or pants or whatever. Then I want to finish the embroidery on the blouse I'm making for her. I think she'll love it."

"I'm sure she will. You've been working on it for awhile now and it looks beautiful. You showed me the bouquet on the back when you finished it. I also saw the start of two flowers on the front."

"Those flowers are what I want to finish today. They're pretty close to done. Give me a long hug before we get going."

"Mmm, Tohlee, being less than a quarter inch from you is one of my delights in life."

After catching enough fish for lunch, Mateen and Anoo clean them and go back up to camp. Anoo stirs up the coals and lays some small twigs on them. After he blows on the coals the twigs flare up into flame. Quickly he adds some larger sticks and in short order has a nice fire going. Mateen has wandered off into the woods but is back by the time the wood has burned down to some nice coals.

"What do you have, Mateen?"

"Onions and morels, I thought we'd cook them up with the fish."

"Where'd you get them?"

"The onions were on the other side of the trees where there's a small meadow. Onions like these like to grow in the open. I dug up some of the bulbs just like a skunk had done last night. Although I used a short stick and he used his claws. I dug up the ones that were about to flower. The cutup leaves are almost as good as the bulbs. But my favorite part is the soon-to-open flower buds. The morels were coming up in the aspen grove. We'll fry each up right in with the trout, but I also think that the onions are just as good raw."

"Did you leave some for the skunk?"

"There were a lot there. Some with flowers that had already opened and some just starting to form flower buds."

"What are we going to do after we eat?"

"It looks like rain, so let's just hang around camp and see if it clears up a little in the afternoon. Even if it doesn't, we'll go sneak around after it rains while the ground is soft and quiet to walk on."

As Mateen and Anoo eat their lunch of wild trout and onions a light rain begins to fall. Mateen cleans up the dishes as Anoo takes the bones and skin from the trout down to the stream. He puts them in two different spots that he hopes will attract crayfish so he can catch some for dinner. After that he goes out and cuts a few more dead branches for the fire. They both have their rain gear on and because the rain is light and the day has warmed into the upper 60's, they decide to sit in the rain and feed the fire.

"What do you think the term 'preconceived perspective' means, Anoo?"

"It's when a person thinks they understand something before they've learned about it."

"That's pretty much right. I want to try and explain how a person's preconceived perspectives of the world affect the way they perceive themselves. First, I want to say that preconceived perspectives are formed through improper thinking. They are formed by affirming the accuracy of a concept before the information supporting the concept is analyzed. Or, put another way, a conclusion is reached before the suppositions supporting that conclusion have been evaluated. Or, put still another way, the drive to reach the comfort of a conclusion exceeds the drive to validate one's suppositions."

"So, those people are starting from a conclusion instead of seeing what conclusion can be derived from their information?"

"Well said, and that's exactly right. I want you to understand that some people take less care in checking the validity of their conclusions than others. Those people are more likely, than people who check the validity of their conclusions, to function from preconceived perspectives. But, understand that all people at times draw conclusions based on unsubstantiated suppositions. The difference in people comes from their willingness, or lack thereof, to learn and then change their perspective. Once a person decides an unsubstantiated conclusion is correct, they often hold back from themselves any information that would show their conclusion is actually incorrect. That's why it's easier to check your suppositions the first time around than it is to change your perspective on actions already taken, or beliefs already expounded on. And that's why freedom of speech and the press is so important."

"So, it's better to take into consideration all the information first and then arrive at the conclusion. Because it's easier to learn, think, and decide than it is to back up and start again."

"That's right, and restricting information causes a mind to become narrowly focused and inflexible. For years people thought that the world was flat and the sun revolved around the earth."

"If the world were flat wouldn't the water run off?"

"I think so. I think those people decided that after the water ran off, it ran back on. They couldn't explain how that worked but they decided it must work that way because the world is flat and there is water on it. So they were adjusting their suppositions to fit their conclusion."

"They were thinking backwards and that is improper thought. Plus, if they had really thought about the idea they would have known water doesn't run uphill."

"That's right. There were sailors who said if the world is flat why does the hull of a sailing ship go out of sight before the sails do? If the world is flat the whole ship would look smaller and smaller until it couldn't be seen anymore."

"But how did the sailors see their own ship's hull go away before their sails did? I don't get that."

"It was sailors still on shore and other people ashore watching a ship sail away who noticed that a ship's hull goes out of sight before the sails do. Thousands of years ago a man named Aristotle concluded that the world was round because the shadow of the earth that crossed the moon during a lunar eclipse was curved."

"Didn't people see the eclipse and agree with him?"

"Many did in his place and time. Then, governments, religions, and societies changed and much of Aristotle's thought was replaced with superstition and unsubstantiated conclusions. Many years later the upper hierarchy of the Christian Church promoted the idea that belief gave a truer version of reality than observation and deductive reasoning did. The Church was convinced that humans were the center of the universe, the whole reason the heavens and Earth existed, and the hierarchy of the Church determined the truth for its followers. They promoted the concept that the sun revolved around the Earth because humans were the center of the universe and they promoted the concept that their Church was the only way to an everlasting life.

"So the Church and the believers in the Church thought that since people are the center of the universe and the universe was all about people that the sun must revolve around the Earth. And, if that weren't true, then other things the Church taught might not be true also. Like that their Church was the only way to everlasting life."

"That's the conclusion that the supposition that humans were the center of the heavens and Earth led them to. Because the unsubstantiated conclusion that the sun revolves around the Earth was reinforced by the hierarchy of a church, it took a long time and there was a lot of resistance to change the idea. The Church thought that if its conclusions were questioned then its validity would be questioned. The believers in the religion needed the structure of a religion as much as the Church needed the believers. Followers and leaders are links in the same chain and so subject to each other's weaknesses. The Church and its believers weren't willing to learn anything that caused them to question their choice of and the truth of their religion. All learning was filtered through the view of the Church. The Church's definition of valid learning supported the Church and from their perspective it was heresy to question the teachings of the Church and so the Church itself."

"So the church and its believers all ended up with narrow inflexible minds because they adapted and restricted their suppositions to support a conclusion?"

"It was amazing how far they were willing to go to avoid admitting their teachings might not be accurate."

"How far did they go?"

"The Catholic Church went as far as torture, executions, and burning people at the stake. Any hierarchical church though stands on the same error in its base. The Catholic Church in particular actually believed their truth was so great that it justified torturing and burning people at the stake. They believed their version of God was so accurate and absolute they could do things that would, by any reasonable person, be considered truly evil. Things like burning at the stake and execution for the guilt of improper perspective from the Church's point of view. They thought their own actions would ultimately become good if it caused the heretic to renounce his beliefs. They actually thought a truly evil act would be seen by their God as good if the act supported their Church's hierarchy and beliefs."

"That sure is a long way to go. The hierarchy of the Catholic Church actually thought they were their own judges and truths."

"And that, Anoo, was in the name of Jesus of Nazareth who said that any place two believers come together is a church."

"How did they ever allow themselves to go that far?"

"Followers and leaders are links in the same chain and so each is dependent on the strengths and weaknesses of the other. Just as a chain is only as strong as its weakest link followers and leaders will drag each other down by their own weaknesses. They can reach high points to be sure. But they will ultimately break away from their base and drift into irrationality and a loss of perspective. That is why individual thought is so important. The choice of people to conform into a flock of sheep and adjust their thinking to another person's standard or to the standards of a church or group has dragged humanity down for thousands of years."

"Why has that gone on for so long?"

"Because the individuals and organizations involved did not seek out the results of their errors. They recognized their errors to some degree but then chose to stop only certain behaviors instead of rooting out all that had been built on that error. Individuals who create their own perspective can stand on their ability to create their own perspective while they adjust their base when errors are learned and acknowledged. Followers and leaders gloss over their errors and plunge on into the future of their shared dependency."

"What base did they break away from?"

"That base can be in many forms. But for individuals or flocks of people their base is the value systems that are chosen to be held. Changing a value system requires the rooting out of the original value system and looking at one's actions taken from that value system through the perspective of the new value system."

"So when errors based on value systems are glossed over you mean the value system appears to be changed. But if past actions aren't looked at from a new perspective people are really keeping their old value system, just acting a little differently."

"That's right, they're keeping the original base they were functioning from. Glossing over an error like that does not create or strengthen the ability to hold one's own value system. And it does not cause the humility necessary to want to change one's perspective and so grow into a more encompassing new perspective."

"So they changed their behavior but not the value system that caused the behavior which means they didn't change their base."

"Well said, Anoo. In this case the base is a person's individual connection to God. The new value system should have been that God has given each of us individually all that we need to live a life here on earth, in the physical realm, and to cause us to grow spiritually. The break from the base I'm talking about was caused by people choosing to put a hierarchy between themselves and their individual connection to God. By letting someone or something determine one's own value system. By letting someone or something determine one's own perspective. To worship a false idol, so to speak, from the perspective that God is a living spirit in all individuals, a living spirit that reaches to the individual directly and not to books or buildings or church hierarchies."

"So the base of a hierarchical church's perspective includes the idea that they can legitimately be between individuals and their connection to God."

"And that is why the hierarchical churches attract people who lack faith in themselves."

"But if they changed that perspective then people wouldn't be dependent on hierarchical churches. The people would grow away from them."

"That's right, and that is an example of the problems encountered and the stumbling blocks people put in their own way when belief systems are built on unsubstantiated conclusions. In this case, it was the hierarchical church's belief that God will come to people more purely through their hierarchy and their established belief structure than through the individuals themselves."

"You circled back around again, Mateen. So individual thought is the way out of that?"

"I believe that when God made man in his image, the image humans were made into was that of self-determinate beings. Not a being that walked on two legs or that can communicate in writing or that has opposable thumbs. Because once a being is self-determinate, as God must be by definition, no other image is as total and encompassing in creating identity. No greater gift could possibly have been given to humanity. Don't throw away God's gift of self-determination for what seems to be the security of a flock of sheep. If you do, you'll end up as schizophrenic as the people who think that their beliefs alone will lead to a true version of humanity's condition on this earth. You'll be as divided as people who see heart and mind, body and soul, reason and feeling, as being at right angles to each other. You will crucify yourself."

"Why is that schizophrenic or crucifying one's self? Shouldn't the heart be followed?"

"The heart should take precedence for some goals and the

mind for other goals. But don't split the two apart. Use one to support the other. If you follow only your heart, you'll end up giving the areas of life where the mind is truer, more direct, or has broader perspective, to others. If you follow only your mind, you'll end up losing the base of feelings that connects you to other people as equals sharing in life. If you put yourself on either of those paths, you'll extend part of yourself at right angles to the rest of yourself. You will end up crucifying yourself. Once you extend yourself at right angles to yourself by splitting your heart from your mind you can't move forward without drag from the part of yourself you caused to be out of alignment with the rest of yourself.

If you follow only your heart, you'll end up believing that the heart is good and the mind is secondary - that God made the mind but only the Devil uses it. That is what people in the past believed as they left their homes to drive to church in a car that they couldn't build and that ran on fuel they couldn't make. People with an immune system shored up by vaccines that their limited view of biology couldn't create.

If you follow only the mind, you'll lose the compassion and companionship that makes the heart whole enough to encompass your own humanity. People have allowed their beliefs to split heart and mind, body and soul, into separate things. They caused themselves to become socially accepted schizophrenics. They were socially accepted because they were the norm of society. Their beliefs caused an error in themselves that has taken away the ability for them to heal themselves. This has gone on for thousands of years and even permeates this country that promotes individual freedom as its foundational principle."

After Mateen and Anoo finish their talk, they have a snack of dried fruit. The rain has let up but it is still cloudy and looks like it is going to rain more that afternoon or evening. Heavy clouds hang low in the sky. Water drips off the trees and splats on the ground unevenly as branches are stirred by little breezes.

"If we go for a hike now won't we just get rained on again, Mateen?"

"It's going to rain some more I'm sure, but it might hold off for a little while. I'm hoping for an evening thunderstorm. I think the sun is going to warm the air this afternoon and then lift the clouds into thunderheads. I think we're going to see a nice light and sound show this evening. After a rain you're more likely to get wet walking through wet grass that soaks your pants and shoes than you are from a passing shower. Did you waterproof your boots well before we left?"

"Yes, I used Father's beeswax concoction. He says to heat your boots up a little over room temperature and the wax too. That way it'll soak in well and cover the whole boot evenly."

"Well let's go see how they do. The ground is going to be nice and quiet for walking. The breeze has been coming out of the southwest pretty consistently with this storm. So we'll walk into the breeze and see what we can sneak up on."

"In the afternoon there usually isn't as much moving around compared to the early morning or evening though," says Anoo.

"You're right about that, but after a rain, especially when it's overcast, animals will move around more than they would on a sunny dry afternoon."

"Why is it different to them?" asks Anoo.

"I think it is a few things. I think that plants taste better and are easier for the herbivores to eat when they're covered with water. For most animals and some little guys especially, like mice or rabbits, it's dangerous to go to water. So they'll take advantage of the water that has come to them from the sky by eating the wet plants. When the little stuff is moving around feeding, the foxes and coyotes will be moving too. They have new mouths to feed this time of year and so are more likely to be hunting in the daytime rain or shine. The rain is added incentive for them to go out and hunt. That goes for animals that have good night vision too. The bright afternoon sun isn't comfortable to be out in for them, but an overcast day is okay. If we stayed under trees after the rain stopped, we'd get dripped on just like a deer would."

"I guess there are plenty of reasons why critters would be moving around now." says Anoo.

"That there are, so, let's head into the wind and see what we see. We'll move along pretty fast at first, but then we're going to slow down. When I'm really sneaking I go about a quarter mile per hour. That way I can move and not make any sound and I'm more likely to spot an animal before it sees me."

"Why is it more likely you'll see them before they see you?"

"It's easier to see movement when you're not moving and it's easier to see movement when you look in one place and notice movement around where you're looking. Try looking at an ant hill for ants sometime. If you look around the ant hill you'll see some ants. But the movement of your eyes and the ant's movements have to be in different directions to each other for you to see the ants. There has to be contrast. If you look at one spot on the ant hill and notice movement with your peripheral vision you'll see a lot more ants."

"And you won't learn as interesting things about wildlife behavior if you're watching an animal that knows you're there, right?"

"That's right. Let's go take a look around."

Mateen and Anoo set off at a regular walking pace for about a mile and then they start to slow down. As they slow they pay more attention to what they are going to step on and how they are going to get through, or around, the vegetation in front of them without making any noise. Not making noise becomes harder as they move off a main game trail and let their direction be determined by the breeze instead of ease of walking. Mateen moves around some clumps of vegetation and through others. If he sees twigs on the ground that could snap he goes around them or even bends down and moves them out of the way, clearing just enough space for a foot to fit in. If he can hold branches out of the way and find a soft spot for his feet he will move through clumps of vegetation, knowing that when he comes out the other side there may be an animal that hasn't smelled him because he is downwind and can't have seen him through the thick clump of vegetation. After moving through the wet undergrowth off the main trail for awhile, Mateen and Anoo slow to a crawl. Both are observing rather than thinking. Their quiet minds and energy are focused out away from themselves toward the world around them. Mateen is doing this with many years of practice and Anoo by allowing the attitude of Mateen and the details of his movements to guide his own movement. When a new line of sight offers an opportunity to see an area that hasn't been visually examined yet, Mateen stands still and slowly looks over the new ground. Then he moves forward a step or two and looks again. At one point, he slowly lowers himself to one knee and points with his chin over to his right and a little ahead. Anoo eases himself behind Mateen and looks in that direction. At first he doesn't see anything, but then a willow bush moves abruptly. A branch dips down and then pops back up. The ears of a deer appear just under the branch. A young buck moves out from the willow bush and then ten feet in their direction. He is about fifty feet away and is looking around and chewing. Pretty quickly he drops his head down and circles up some clover with his lips and jaw, pulling the mouthful free as his head comes back up. He looks around as he chews. After taking another few steps he pulls a few new leaves off a wild rose. As he moves forward, he constantly looks ahead and also turns to look behind once in awhile.

It takes ten minutes for the deer to cross in front of Mateen and Anoo and another five to move off far enough that Mateen thinks he can start walking again without spooking the deer. They move up about twenty-five feet and see where the young buck crossed in front of them. His feet did not leave a lasting impression in the ground spongy from the recent rain. But grasses and forbs are bent over and moved aside from his passing. Then they keep going about a hundred yards. As they slowly move on, Anoo looks back and sees the young buck reaching down for another mouthful of plants. The buck is doing the same thing he had been doing as he walked by them with the same level of attention. Anoo knows that the deer hasn't realized they are there and isn't going to.

Mateen stops and motions Anoo to go first. Anoo slowly picks the places to put his feet and chooses the ten and twenty-foot-long pathways through the underbrush ahead that offer the quietest movement. As he slowly moves ahead he makes sure to stop and look around for animals in front of him. He doesn't want Mateen to spot an animal in front of them that Anoo hasn't seen first from his forward vantage point. Anoo moves forward another hundred yards and the concern of Mateen seeing something before he does is replaced by the world opening up in front of him. At one point he starts to go faster when a clear path opens up in front of him. Mateen makes a small mouse squeak sound that turns Anoo around. Mateen motions to slow down and looks in Anoo's eyes. Anoo has the thought that just because a path can be walked quietly and quickly doesn't mean it is the right time or place for that quicker movement.

Anoo moves ahead slowly and sees a shrubby hillside to his right come into view. As he moves forward he can see down to the base of the hill where there is a small lush meadow with willows and a small water hole. He squats down to look closely at the meadow, watching. After a minute a coyote comes out from behind a willow and moves a few steps forward. Its ears are pointed forward and it looks very intent. It hunches its back legs under itself and quivers a little as it waits. Then it launches itself farther up in the air than its movement forward. As the coyote comes down, its mouth is pointed down towards its front feet. It moves its feet around and sniffs, then looks ahead. It slowly stalks ahead a few feet and then waits. After watching the predator stalk its prey for a few minutes Anoo can feel the tension from the animal and tell when the coyote is relaxed and has decided not to spring or has decided its prey is close enough for a leap. After a few attempts the coyote leaps and puts his head down between its paws, flipping a fat mouse up into the air. The coyote leaps forward and hits the mouse with its paws as the mouse hits the ground. After another toss it eats the mouse and then hunts its way out of the little meadow.

Mateen and Anoo enter the meadow after they are sure the coyote isn't coming back. They find the place where the coyote caught and ate the mouse. They see the crushed grass where the coyote first stunned the mouse and then again where the mouse was mortally wounded. Anoo moves to the side of the meadow and up the hill a few feet. He looks in the direction the coyote went but can't see it. He looks down at his feet to walk quietly back to Mateen and lets out a gasp. Mateen hears and walks up to him.

"What is it Anoo?"

"Is that what I think it is?"

"It sure is, that's a stone arrowhead. Pick it up and clean it off."

"It has the tip broken off."

"They were projectiles. If the arrow missed its target, it would hit the ground and the arrowhead might break or it could break when it hit a bone. A broken arrowhead would have meant some work ahead around a fire crafting a new one, but that wouldn't be so bad if the break happened from successfully supplying food for a family for a week."

"If the break happened because of a missed shot the hunter would be hungry and he would also have to make a new arrowhead," says Anoo.

"That's right. But no doubt a hunter would have carried a half dozen arrows when going out for a hunt."

"Do you think this one was a good break or a bad break?" asks Anoo.

"I don't know, but you found it after watching a coyote's successful hunt. The coyote was finding food for its family just like a Native American was doing hundreds of years ago."

"I hope his hunt was successful also, Mateen."

"I do too. We're out here in the hills finding some of our food in the same place the coyote is finding his and where a human hunter found his hundreds of years ago."

"It's another circle, isn't it? One that started thousands of years ago and we're still a part of."

"That it is. Hold the arrowhead in your hand and relax like you're trying to see with your ears," says Mateen.

"It's like I can feel something alive in my hand but I can't see anything in my mind."

"That's okay. When you find similar tools in the future, relax and feel and concentrate on the lives of the people who made and used those tools. Be quiet and take all day if you want. You may end up seeing an image of their lives and hear the murmur of their voices. What should we do to honor the hunter that was here hundreds of years ago and also the hunter who was just here? We should honor the memory of that long ago hunter and honor the hunter we just watched."

"I don't know how to do that."

"I think you should put the arrowhead into a medicine bag as a symbol of the history of the hunter and the hunted that began an eternity ago and we are a part of today and future humans will, hopefully, be a part of an eternity from now."

"I don't have a bag like that."

"I have one for you. I made it out of a part of hide from a deer I shot and tanned last year. I knew we would be going on this walk and so I made it for you."

"Thank you, Mateen. I don't know what to say."

"You can put your emotions into the bag along with the arrowhead and with your respect for and your understanding of the hunters and the hunted."

"Thank you again, Mateen. Do you have a medicine bag?"

"I do. I made mine many years ago. I don't always carry it with me, but I certainly would on a trip like this."

"Do you have it with you now?"

"Yes, sometimes I wear it around my neck but usually it's in my pack. When I'm at home I keep it in my room with my collections and memorabilia from my walks."

"What's in yours?"

"Usually medicine bags are personal and not talked about. But I think it's fine between you and me. You have an arrowhead that represents hunters and hunted. I have an elk's tooth which represents all the lives I've ever taken to sustain my life. I also have a water worn pebble for the cycle of water on earth. Water from the oceans rises into the air and comes down to water the plants of the earth. Through plants breathing the water goes back into the air and falls as rain again. Then the water runs down a river and back to the ocean again. I also have a fossil that represents all the life on earth from before human's time, during human's time, and after humans are gone. I have a dried flower as a symbol for the beauty of the natural world. I carry these things with me to help me keep my perspective on my life and the earth I live on. Now you have the start of your own medicine bag. I wonder what else you'll find that will go into it?

"Let's sit for awhile and observe this place. Let's sit and feel the earth grow up into us as we become quiet inside. Let this place fill you with the perspective of time, of hunter and hunted. Let that perspective imprint in you like the first scent of an elk entering your sinuses. Make this a familiar place you can come back to when you need comfort or direction. Then, in your future need, hold your medicine bag next to your heart and you'll find the strength of all that is here, now, and long ago."

The sun is coming out and going back behind the clouds as Mateen and Anoo look out over the little meadow from just up the hillside. Violet-green swallows come out and are catching insects that had started flying as the afternoon began to warm. The swallows abruptly change direction a foot or two as they fly over the meadow, seeing and catching insects too small for Mateen and Anoo to see from where they are. Butterflies fly from one flower, swaying in the light breeze to the next. Squirrels chatter at unseen intrusions into their territory. A chipmunk runs past them and comes back a few feet, stopping, pushing up on front feet and peering. The chipmunk knows the humans are not from here but also that they are a part of all that is here.

After watching for awhile Anoo gets up and walks to the other side of the meadow. Mateen follows as Anoo bends down and picks up two orange feathers from a flicker. He holds them up for Mateen to see.

"They're feathers from a flicker. It looks like something caught it as it flew over this meadow. This broken, leaning tree was used as a plucking post to prepare the flicker for the hunter's meal. The whole process is a larger version of the swallows around us catching insects."

"What do you think ate him?"

"My guess is a goshawk."

"They're beautiful feathers, Mateen. They're here because of hunter and hunted, but to me they're for the beauty of flight and the beauty of individual birds."

"Put them in your medicine bag and then lead us back to camp, Anoo."

As Anoo slowly leads the way back to camp, the movement of branches out of his way, the choice of where to put a foot down, is done with almost no loss of concentration on what is going on around him. They stop often to watch. A bluebird catches a large bug in front of them and flies off toward some bushes to feed its young in the nest. Under a thick shrub a rabbit settles itself down over a grassy spot. It looks like it is just sitting, but actually it is suckling its young who are living in a shallow depression in the grass lined with rabbit fur. A hawk had seen them as they crossed a clearing and screamed out a warning at their presence. Anoo and Mateen move so slowly and quietly as they pass through some trees that a squirrel runs by and goes about its business without taking notice. Mateen tells Anoo that you know you're sneaking through the woods well when squirrels don't bother to chatter at you for entering their territory or when hunters like foxes catch up to you and pass you. When they are within sight of camp they sit down and take a break.

"Have you ever found an arrowhead, Mateen?"

"I've found quite a few at one time or another. I found one spear point that was used with an atlatl and is over ten thousand years old. It was made by a Native American who lived on the giant mammals at the end of the Pleistocene Age. It was near the end of the last Ice Age and there were mammoths, giant sloths, beaver the size of bears, and bison much larger than present day bison. I was awed by the beauty and the quality of that spear point."

"What's an atlatl?"

"It's a tool for throwing a short spear. It gives added leverage to the hunter, resulting in a longer, more accurate throw. Which means the hunter can strike his prey from a safer distance."

"You know a lot about those long-ago people."

"Not compared to all that could be learned on the subject, Anoo."

"Oh ho, you got me there, Mateen."

"It is easier for me to identify with more recent peoples who hunted the animals I'm familiar with, using bows and arrows, weapons I've hunted with, than for me to identify with the people who made that spear point to hunt animals that I've only seen as bone turned to rock. The environment of those long-ago people and many of the animals around them would have been new to me. But the quality of that spear point showed true artistry in its making. So I can identify with the artistry that was put into that tool. A tool that they needed for their survival and therefore I can make a connection with those long-ago people through that artistry and their need to hunt."

"I think I want to make an atlatl and a spear with a stone point and use it to take an animal for meat for the winter."

"That would be quite a challenge. You could also learn how those long-ago people tanned hides for clothing that allowed them to live at the end of an Ice Age."

"There's so much to learn, so much that has been, so much breadth to humanity."

"And to yourself as an individual, my friend."

"What else have you found that connected you with past people, Mateen?"

"I found a bison skull once. It was practically whole so I took it home to clean it up and put in my collection room. As I cleaned it up a piece of bone broke off from one of the sinuses. When I pulled it out I realized it wasn't bone, it was an arrowhead with a broken tip. I stared at it in my hand and felt the hopes and pride of the hunter who had shot the arrow and killed the bison. He was a hunter who left his family to find food so that they would survive and thrive. He succeeded in his hunt and was proud to bring home the means for his family's survival. The arrowhead was hundreds of years old. It was from a time when hunters had horses and bows. I could feel his excitement as he galloped across a plain chasing the bison. He ran his horse up to the bison and shot it in the ribs, then pulled his horse away so he wouldn't be charged by the bison. He did this several times and then moved his horse even farther away. The bison ran for several miles until it couldn't run anymore. As the bison stood facing the hunter, the hunter moved in close and tried to shoot it in the eye to kill it. Instead, he hit it in the nose, breaking the tip off the arrowhead and probably killing the bison, but not as quickly."

"You could tell all that from holding the arrowhead in your hand?"

"It was almost like watching a dream play out in my mind, but as much with feelings as with visual scenes. I wondered later if the arrowhead was intentionally put in the bison's sinus after it was dead as some sort of ritual. That version is certainly possible but I like the version that came to my mind while I was first holding the arrowhead."

"What other things have you found?"

"I found a mano stone once."

"What's a mano stone?"

"A mano and metate are stones for grinding seeds and nuts."

"Did they have grains like wheat and rye too?"

"Not specifically, but the grain of wheat and rye is the seeds of those particular types of grass. Just as corn kernels are the seeds of the type of grass we named corn."

"Corn is a type of grass?"

"Yes it is, and Native Americans first started the domestication process of the grass they named maize which then became the grass we named corn. The mano stone is held in the hand and grain is crushed in between the mano and the metate. The metate is a larger stone that sits on the ground. When I held the mano stone in my hand I could feel the life of a camp going on around me. There were numerous people going about their business involved in the life of a camp and an extended family. It was the kind of camp the bison hunter would have left when he went on his hunt. The kind of camp that would really appreciate the benefit of all the meat a bison can provide. People have been living in these hills for a long time and their history can be found in the tracks they've left."

"Arrowheads and mano stones are the tracks you mean?"

"Yes, I'm using tracks to mean indications of life that were here before we were. That might mean hours ago for deer tracks, hundreds of years ago for one kind of arrowhead, 10,000 years ago for a kind of spear point, and many millions of years ago for some fossils."

"Are there fossils that are millions of years old around here?"

"Over on the southwest side of these hills there are. We'll go over there in a couple days and try and find some."

"Wow, I'd love to do that! Can you understand those fossils the way you can understand the tools of the people in the camp or the hunter who used the arrowhead you found?"

"Not in exactly the same way. But you can have connections all the same."

"Just how can you hold an arrowhead or mano stone in your hand and tell what was going on when the person from hundreds of years ago was using it?"

"I don't know, Anoo. It's something that happens that I don't understand. It's something to experience and try to understand later."

"What did you think after you had time to try and understand it?"

"I decided that even though I taught myself to appreciate and remember the experience I didn't learn enough to know how it actually happened."

"How did you teach yourself to appreciate and remember the experience?"

"I told myself that it was a good experience and that I wanted to prolong and develop the experience. Then, when I found other tools I held them in my hand and tried to be quiet in my mind while letting imagery unfold in my mind."

"But you didn't decide for sure how the whole experience was possible?"

"No, I didn't. I just could come up with a few hypotheses."

"What are they?"

"Once quite a few years ago I was sound asleep and I had a very vivid dream. I was working on a road that runs from a hydroelectric dam down to Denver. It was early spring and during the day I would drive a van along the road looking for damage to the power line running from the dam. In my dream a large piece of ice blew off a tall power pole and fluttered down through the air in my direction. It looked like it was going slowly but as it got closer it seemed to go much faster and then it smashed into the windshield of the van with a very loud noise."

"So wait, you know how to drive and you heard sound in your dream?"

"Yes, I had to learn to drive for that job. And yes, hearing sound in a dream has happened to me at times, but not commonly. The loud sound abruptly woke me up from the dream. I remembered everything that happened in the dream and then I went back to sleep. When I first woke up in the morning I immediately remembered the dream and replayed it in my mind. I got up and made breakfast and went outside and loaded up the van for the day. As I was driving down the road I recognized the layout of the power poles in front of me from my dream. I didn't know what to do. I needed the work so I wasn't going to turn back. The dream hadn't been comfortable for me. It was very abrupt and shocking. But I kept going anyhow. As I got closer to those poles I slowed the van. When I was under the poles a large piece of ice blew off the top of one and fluttered down towards me just like in my dream. I slowed the van even more but that ended up causing the ice to smash into the windshield. The windshield shattered, looking like a spider's web from one side to the other."

"You didn't drive off the road?"

"No, I didn't. It was a steep section of road and going off would have been disastrous. I don't know if I'd have survived if the dream hadn't caused me to slow down."

"It's incredible you had a dream at night that became your waking experience the next day. But what does that have to do with understanding how you can know what people were doing in the past just by holding one of their tools in your hand?"

"The scenario of my dream and what happened the next morning were exactly the same, not similar, but exactly the same. It was as though time repeated itself or as though time was not linear."

"What do you mean that time wasn't linear?"

"It was as if the past, present, and future weren't in a line at that time. It was as if those experiences of my life were circular, I was at the center, and I could reach out and play different sections of that experience. Having the dream was as real as the future occurrence. Remembering the dream after the event was as real as the actual event. Maybe unbeknownst to myself I played a part of my life before it happened and so caused myself to deal with a potentially deadly situation in as safe a manner as possible."

"But how could you have done that?"

"I don't know how I did it or why it happened to me. It's something that happened in my life that I haven't been able to understand fully yet. But maybe with the mano stone or the arrowhead I was at the center of the actual experience of the people involved and that experience played back to me as a waking dream."

"Your dream experience seems even harder to understand than being able to see the lives of people who died hundreds of years before by holding the same tool in your hand that they held in theirs."

"It does to me too. One is realizing what was and the other is realizing what will be. This is another way I've tried to understand why I've seen images of people in the past by holding on to one of their tools. The tools they were holding were in their hands for a relatively long period of time. The mano stone may have been used for a hundred years, or at least dozens, and used by many different people over those years. The process of using the stone took a lot of concentration and the product from the stone was very valuable to the people. The arrowhead was probably made by someone with a lot of expertise and experience. A craftsman who used a lot of intent and concentration for the hours it took to make the arrowhead. Then the arrowhead was attached to an arrow that had also been made by hand. The wood of the arrow was straightened and feathers attached. The entire process was a work of art created by a master craftsman over many days."

"How did that make it more likely that you could see those people's lives in your mind?"

"I don't know exactly, but it would have to do with the energy focused on the tools by the people who made and used the tools. Remember at the beginning of our walk when I said that I think independent thoughts and emotions create soul?"

"Yes, and I still don't know what that means."

"I don't mean that any casual thought or feeling can create soul. I mean that intent and clarity can cause thoughts and emotions to reach an energy level where soul is created. When I say created I mean that energy is focused by the physical individual and that energy then adds to or becomes a part of the existing soul. The energy connects with the existing soul. I think those people whose tools we've found lived their lives in a way that the energy of their lives lasted beyond their individual time spans on earth. In their own souls as they continued on after their life on earth and in the tools they made and used that remained on earth."

Mateen and Anoo walk the short distance back to camp as the late afternoon sky darkens with the thunderheads of a coming storm that is moving towards them from the west. Mateen puts some dried carrots and peas In water and goes foraging for some fresh food for a little variety from the dried meat, vegetables, and nuts they'd brought with them. Anoo cuts some more wood before it rains again and then goes down to the stream below the lake and catches some more crayfish. When Mateen meets up with Anoo an hour or so later the storm is almost upon them. He's picked some more wild onions for the crayfish, a nice batch of strawberries for dessert, and a handful of last year's rosehips for evening tea. Anoo has a couple dozen crayfish for dinner and has rigged up a tarp next to the fire pit so they can have a better view of the coming storm. Mateen drops off his food and then goes down to the stream above the lake and fills up a couple pots with water. When he gets back to camp Anoo has the fire burning hot. Mateen cuts the rose hips into pieces and sets them to soak in some water. After dinner he will pour in some boiling water to finish the tea. Then he cleans up the onions and strawberries. He puts the onions in a pan and fries them up, adding the reconstituted carrots and peas when the onions are close to done. Anoo drops the crayfish a half dozen at a time into the pot of spiced boiling water. It makes for a nice meal they eat quickly as rain starts to fall around them and the intervals between the lightning flashes and the booms of thunder shorten.

"That lightning branched to the tops of those two hills, Mateen."

"I saw that too. I've seen lightning come down into a valley and turn at a ninety-degree angle and strike a rock outcropping before."

"Do you think lightning really only strikes a spot once?"

"When the lightning strikes, the discharge of electricity evens out the positive and negative charges. If the storm leaves quickly enough there won't be enough time for the positive and negative charges to build again. But there are rocky mountain tops, isolated hills, and other physical structures that are struck by lightning over and over again throughout a summer season or over the years."

"What causes the thunder?"

"It's supposed to be because the lightning expands the atmosphere and then the boom of thunder is caused by the atmosphere rushing back in to fill the vacuum caused by the lightning."

"Is that what you think happens?"

"Pretty much, but there probably isn't a full vacuum. It's probably just that the air is superheated. Air expands when it's heated. That's what makes a hot air balloon rise. Then the lightning, which is the source of the heat, is abruptly gone and the atmosphere quickly cools and therefore rushes back together causing the thunder."

"I guess that's pretty much the same thing isn't it?"

"Just a difference in how much of the atmosphere is left after the lightning passes through. One storm I was watching had lightning bolts that lasted longer than any others I've ever seen. I could spot the lightning bolt and lift up binoculars from my lap and see the bolt through the binoculars."

"What did the bolts look like?"

"Not much different, just closer and brighter. I'm sure if I saw a close bolt in that way it would have hurt my eyes. But this storm was miles away. Another time, in the fall, I never saw the bolt of lightning but I heard the rumble of thunder. It got louder and louder and then slowly faded away. By the time it stopped rumbling it must have lasted several minutes. I don't know if it makes any difference but it was a foggy day and the clouds were very low to the ground."

"My father and I were watching a late fall storm blow in. There was no snow on the ground but flakes were flying through the air. Then there was a big boom of thunder and after awhile some more booms too."

"I like thunder snow too. When there is enough of a difference in temperature between an incoming storm and the air around you, the storm can have enough energy for lightning - even when the storm is cold enough to snow."

"You sure know a lot about a wide variety of things, Mateen."

"Thank you. I've never stopped enjoying the learning of new things. I've never stopped changing my perspective on the world around me when I learn something new. One thing about me is I like to learn about what I am interested in at that particular time. I'm a lot quicker to accept a change in my perspective when I've learned something I chose to learn. I don't enjoy learning on someone else's schedule."

"You mean like at a school?"

"That's what I mean. I've never understood how the most advantageous time to learn Math is from 9 to 10 A.M. and then History from 10 to 11, for example. I think individual interest determines the most advantageous time to learn and natural curiosity will cause a breadth of learning in most people. Your parents teach you about a wide variety of subjects. But they push or back off on those subjects depending on how you are accepting the learning and also depending on how nice a day it is."

"I'd like to go to a university some time, I think."

"You'll have to go to a city for that. By the time you're at university level of learning you can choose your own subjects of study to a much greater degree than traditional schooling for younger children."

"So I'll have more freedom to learn about what I want to learn and should enjoy learning from being in a school in a few years than I would now?"

"That's the idea. Schooling that is applied to many people at once is more rigid than individual learning. That's why learning for oneself is as enjoyable and efficient as it is."

"That's why I should choose my own books to read when I'm out of school and ask questions of my mother and father and you too."

That's exactly right. Another thing I've found is that no matter what I learn about a subject, I can still enjoy and be awed by the beauty of the earth around me."

"What do you mean by that?"

"Some people think understanding the processes behind an image or event takes away from experiencing the beauty of that image. For me, I can appreciate the beauty of a colorful flower swaying in the breeze at least as well after learning about the chemical process of photosynthesis as before I knew about it. Photosynthesis gives the plant the energy to grow the flower whose color I enjoy. It doesn't change the color. Understanding the dynamics of air flow between low and high pressure systems doesn't change the movement of a flower as a breeze moves through a meadow. Just as an artist can appreciate the beauty of a painting by another artist even though he understands how the artist used brush strokes and textures to create the effect of the painting. In the same way a musician can appreciate another's song for its beauty at least as well as a person who hasn't developed the expertise of playing a musical instrument."

"It seems to me that an understanding of how those things work would increase appreciation for the things themselves, not decrease it."

"That's what I think. What else do you think about this subject, Anoo?"

"Well I guess, oh I see, I guess if I realize what I don't know about a subject it's wise to keep my mouth shut and if I choose to learn about the subject, I can appreciate it even more. I'll still find just as much beauty if not more in the world around me as I did before the learning. You circled me around again, didn't you?"

"You're an enjoyable person to talk with, my friend. You'll also find the more you learn about some subjects the more precision you'll see in them. Details coming together in precise ways have a beauty all their own that a vague understanding can never appreciate. I'm going to turn in."

"Good night to you, Mateen."

"Good night to you, Anoo."

After eating dinner Tohlee and Eli go out on the porch and enjoy some of Eli's hard cider. It's raining and there is some thunder and lightning, but the storm isn't particularly violent on the farm away from the hills.

"I love to watch these nice soaking rains from our porch, Eli. I think it's a great idea to have the porch go all the way around the house. Each side has its own identity; east side for sunrises, west for sunsets, south for winter sun, and north for cool in the summer. Plus, there is always a side alee."

"I bet it's a windy stormy evening in the hills," says Eli.

"You think they're all right, don't you?"

"I'm sure they are. They have a very good tent and their raingear and footgear is just as good. Anything that does get wet they can dry out tomorrow. And Mateen can get a fire going and keep it going in a downpour."

"How do you think Anoo is doing?" asks Tohlee.

"I imagine he's very interested in what is around him and full of thought from what Mateen has to say. I suspect that we think about him more than he's thinking about us."

"Our child is growing up. This walk is supposed to push the process along some, but he is still a boy."

"Boy and young man overlap at his age for different categories of development. He's ready for a walk to develop individuality but not ready yet to give his heart to a woman," responds Eli.

"That will come after he knows more about his own heart and mind. I wonder who she'll be. A girl from somewhere around here or do you think he'll go to a university and meet someone from a thousand miles away?"

"I don't know. There is a lot to gain from a university if you're interested in the right subject. Personally, I have nothing good to say about the city-states they're located in."

"I feel the same way, but there is no telling where his life will lead," says Tohlee.

"I remember when you were pregnant and we decided if it was

a boy we'd name him Anoo because our life was going to start anew when he was born."

"And it certainly has. I remember when you told me you wanted to raise our child with the two and twenty-two rule. As you put it, there are things parents have to tell their two-year olds and ways you have to treat them because of their age. But if the parents are still treating their children along those lines at twenty-two, it is a statement about the parents' character, not the need of the child."

"And I think there's a gradual change over the intervening years in that parental attitude towards the child, not lines drawn in the sand. I think you've been an exceptional mother, Tohlee, and you are a warm, delightful woman to be married to."

"Thank you for that, Eli, and for all the many things you do that fill me with the energy of life, with love, desire, contentment, calm, and peace. Thank you."

Day Six

"Wake up, Anoo, there's something I want you to see."

"Okay, I'll be right out. What are we going to do?"

"We're just going to the beaver ponds a little upstream of the lake. We won't be long."

"Stop here, Anoo. We have a good view of the closer pond from up here on the hillside."

"What's that beaver doing?"

"He's pushing mud into a little pile with his chest, and then he's holding it with his front arms and using his back legs to push himself up the side of the dam where he works the mud between and on top of the branches that he's already put on his dam."

"Wow! That's incredible. Look! That one has a rock and it's putting it on the dam just like the other one did with mud."

"Beavers are amazing animals. They build dams so that ponds will form behind them. Then, in one of the ponds, they build a lodge to live in with entryways below water level for their protection and with a ventilation hole in the top. They also cut down trees and stick branches from the trees into the mud in a big pile on the bottom of their ponds so they can eat throughout the winter."

"If a person didn't know what the beavers were doing and why they were doing it, that person could look at all this and just see some critters moving around in a pond they wanted to fish in or watch the reflection of clouds on the water."

"I think so too."

"What are we going to do today? Will we move to another place?" asks Anoo.

"I think we'll stay here one more day. I'm thinking this morning fog will lift and we'll have a nice morning. I do think we'll get some more rain in the afternoon or evening. Let's go back to camp and eat something, then take a walk."

After Mateen and Anoo eat some dried fruit and nuts they clean up camp. They hang everything that got wet from last night's rain on some branches to dry and ready their packs for a day away from camp. They walk uphill on a south-facing slope covered with large shrubs. There are a lot of Gambels oak with plenty of serviceberry and chokecherry too. The oak often grow in clumps ringed by snowberry several feet tall, making it difficult to walk into the clumps. In the openings between the clumps are smaller shrubs like bigtooth and silver sage with some scattered hawthorn. After walking up the hill between the clumps of shrubs for awhile they slow and then stop and stand. As their disturbance abates the smaller birds and chipmunks resume their activity. Soon there are bird chirps and leaves rustling all around them. Mateen is in front and starts to walk forward a few steps every minute or so. Soon he stops and points as a small bird hops into a clump of oak. Mateen and Anoo can hear leaves rustling as the bird looks under them for insects. A bird with a dark reddish spot on its side comes around the clump of oak from the other side. The first bird comes out of the clump, hops and flies ten feet to the next clump of oak. The red-sided bird flies to the far side of that clump and perches on a dead branch at the edge of the clump.

"What are those birds doing?" asks Anoo.

"The greenish bird that hopped into the oak clump is a green-tailed towhee. The bird staying on the outside is a rufous-sided towhee. As the green-tail hunts for insects inside the clump of oak, the rufous-sided is waiting to see if any insects get away and run or fly out of the clump."

"Does the green-tail know what the rufous-sided is doing?"

"I'm sure it does."

"Do you think it cares that the rufous-sided is taking advantage of his work?"

"I don't think so and it's possible he likes it."

"Why would he like it?"

"Maybe the rufous will move insects into the clump as it moves around the outside or maybe the green will move an insect out of the clump and the rufous will move it right back in to where the green has another chance."

"So they're helping each other hunt?"

"They're helping each other, but they're not really working together. It's not like they'd share their kill like a mated pair of foxes will when they hunt together. One fox will wait before going into a thick area for the other fox to get into position at the far end of a draw or brushy area. Then one will move toward the other, increasing the chances that one of the pair will make a kill. What these birds are doing is opportunistic but not cooperative hunting. One's actions may benefit the other, but the green-tail would probably be hunting the same way if the rufous was outside the clump or not."

"I see, so that's opportunistic, but if they change their hunting behavior to reach a common goal that's cooperative?"

"That's right. For these birds there is no more cooperation than when blackbirds look for insects that wild horses kick up when the horses are on the move. In that case it's more obvious the horses aren't getting any value from the disturbed insects. It's entirely the blackbirds taking advantage of the opportunity the horses' actions may create and the horses would be on the move whether or not the blackbirds were there."

"Will we see wild horses?"

"We'll probably see some over on the southwest side of these hills where we'll go look for fossils."

"When will we do that?"

"I'm thinking we'll go up toward the tops of the higher hills tomorrow. We've seen a lot of the riparian zone down low and the shrub zone around it. After we spend a few days up in the high country of aspen and spruce-fir, we'll drop down the other side to lower and drier country."

"Okay, it's kind of hard for me to think about songbirds as hunters. I think of hunters more like coyotes and foxes."

"They're hunters that go after smaller prey. Think about the robins in your front yard. You may not think of them as hunters because they're only catching earthworms. But if you were the earthworm moving through the soil an inch underground and a robin's beak pierced through your roof and ripped you in half as the hairs on your body gripped the walls of your home, you'd think you were being hunted and taken as prey."

"I guess so, when you put it that way. What's that large bird over there?"

"That's a marsh hawk. They have pretty narrow wings for a hawk and a white patch at the base of their tail. They hunt flying lower than most of the other hawks about their size."

"He's going right around those little clumps of serviceberry."

"Instead of being up higher in the air and looking over a relatively wide area for movement like red-tails or swainsons hawks will do, the marsh hawks fly low and look around to the far side of a shrub or a small clump of shrubs for prey. The far side of a shrub for a marsh hawk is usually the uphill side."

"Why's that?"

"He'll fly towards the shrub from the more open downhill side where the prey would be more exposed and therefore not as likely to be. Then he'll pop around the shrub to see what has come out from the center of the shrub to the outer edge on the protected side. The area of ground that is covered over and shaded by the shrub but doesn't have the stems of the shrub itself."

"Hey! He just dropped down to the ground. He turned really

quick and closed his wings and dropped down to the ground. There he is again and he's got something in his talons."

"He's got his breakfast or breakfast for his young. Whatever mouse or ground squirrel-type animal that he's got was under the edge of the shrub where a high flying red-tail couldn't see it. But the marsh hawk that flies around the shrubs and looks on the far side cannot only see it, but is so close to its prey that when he does see it he can drop on it quickly. As soon as the mouse or ground squirrel spots the marsh hawk, it's going to jump into the shrub to put some branches and leaves between it and the hawk. That will cause the hawk to lose sight of its prey and so increase the chance of escape for the prey. In this case the prey didn't get back into the shrub soon enough."

"Why would the mouse or whatever it was leave the center of the shrub and go to the edge area?"

"Take a look at this full-grown serviceberry right here. It's made up of hundreds of individual stems an inch or two around. You see how underneath in the center there isn't much vegetation growing? There is too much shade from the shrub itself and it's too crowded from the many stems. So inside is mostly leaf litter like you heard the green-tailed towhee rustling around in, looking for insects. The stems on the outside of the shrub lean away from the center. That causes an overhang where there is more sun than the center but not as much as right out in the open. That means the half-shaded edge of the shrub is moister than the sun-baked ground surrounding it. So there's more room for plants to grow than in the center of the shrub and more moisture and protection from sun and wind than farther away from the shrub. That makes for a better habitat for growing plants than the center-shaded portion of the shrub and also better than the open, dryer meadow area away from the shrub. Better habitat for a variety of different plants like these grasses and valerian here. That means more food for the mouse or ground squirrel to eat, but also increased risk from the animals that prey on them when they move out of the center of the shrub to feed."

"And this area with bare ground is a deer bed, right?"

"That's right. They like the shade and cover of the shrub but are too big to go right into the shrub just like us. Just like the wide wings of a flying hawk and the body of foxes and coyotes. That's why the much smaller mice live in the center of the shrub but have to come out to the edge to feed."

"Do you think the hawk is a male?"

"I've been saying it is, but it's really hard to say. Female hawks are larger than the males, but it's real tough to tell which is which unless they're next to each other. It's like when you have to look close to tell if you're looking at a crow or a raven when they're some distance away. You have to look close with binoculars to see if the beak is really big compared to the head, which then is a raven. But when crows and ravens are together, like when they're feeding on a carcass, then the difference in body and beak size is obvious. Let's keep going up the hill and see what else is going on."

Mateen and Anoo continue to slowly walk up the hill. They watch where they put their feet when they step so they don't make noise or slip on the muddy ground. After making sure their feet are secure they look in all directions for anything of interest. Anoo makes sure he steps and stops when Mateen does so an animal looking in their direction is no more likely to see movement than if there were only one person moving up the hill. One person's movement with two sets of eyes and ears increases their chances of seeing something before it sees them. He stays slightly behind and to the side of Mateen so they each have an unobstructed view. The clouds have lifted but not enough for direct sun to fall on them.

"Ooh, Mateen, who would do this?"

"It's not a question of who if you are thinking there is a person up here sticking grasshoppers onto hawthorn thorns. A shrike caught the grasshopper and then stuck it on the thorns. It's common shrike behavior and may be for food storage or so the grasshopper softens up a little before the shrike comes back to eat it. It also may have been stuck here to show other shrikes this area is currently being used by a shrike. So to a male shrike it's a warning and to a female shrike it's an invitation."

"Unless this one is female, then the warning would be to other females."

"That's good thinking," says Mateen.

"Why does it need to have the grasshoppers soften up?"

"A shrike isn't a big bird. Maybe it can't swallow large grasshoppers like this one whole. You would think it could tear them up even if they were freshly killed. They are big enough birds for that and they do have a sharp beak. So maybe they like the grasshoppers better from a taste standpoint after they've aged a few days."

"So the shrike could have torn up the grasshopper into pieces it could swallow, but chose not to. Maybe it wasn't all that hungry and was saving the grasshopper for another day."

"Otherwise it would have taken the trouble of tearing up the grasshopper? That's good thinking and maybe so, Anoo. It may also have chosen to use the grasshopper as a sign of its territory, like I said. But, as you're saying, if it were hungry, it would have just eaten it. Saving the grasshopper for another day is known as caching food."

"If the grasshoppers age a few days wouldn't they be dried out and tougher like elk jerky is compared to fresh elk meat?"

"Maybe, but I think they would get soft first and so be ready to fall apart into smaller pieces before they get really dry. They're not made of material as tough and stringy as muscle is."

"Should we wait and see if it comes back? I've never seen a shrike."

"We could, but it's probably off somewhere else. They do have a fair size home range. Or it could be feeding its young and there are plenty of other food sources around for it to find that are smaller and so better to feed its young. If it were saving the grasshoppers for another day because it wasn't hungry, maybe it wouldn't come back at all."

"Then it would have killed unnecessarily."

"When it killed it wouldn't have known it wasn't going to be hungry in a few days. The drive to eat will always come, food may not. It killed when the opportunity was there and then stored its kill. Only hindsight would show if the killing was unnecessary. Especially in the fall, grasshoppers dried on a thorn may last well into the winter. Maybe the shrike was planning ahead farther than we're thinking and maybe it wasn't planning at all. Maybe it was acting instinctively. It might have been acting in a way that has helped other shrikes generations ago and it doesn't even know why it was doing what it was doing."

"So it just felt like stabbing a grasshopper onto a thorn? Or it just did it without any awareness, just instinct? And maybe it would be in the same area later on and just happen to find a grasshopper on a thorn ready to eat? When a bird acts on instinct is it having a feeling?"

"I think that in this case the bird is having a feeling that causes instinctual behavior. Let's sit and watch for awhile. Maybe it will come back and you can see what they look like. Your comments bring up two categories of behavior and thought I want to talk about. One is feelings and the other is evolution. In this case you brought up a specific area of evolution; the ability for behavior to be inherited. For feelings you brought up the area of basing one's actions on past patterns rather than awareness through the thought process."

"When did I say all that?"

"You brought it up with the combination of your last comments. I want to talk about a lot of aspects of evolution, not just the ability to inherit behavior. But first I'd rather talk about feelings."

"The feelings that cause instinctive behavior like the shrike might have been acting on when it sticks grasshoppers on a thorn?"

"Yes, but all aspects of feelings."

"How many aspects are there?"

"More than we'll cover here today. There are emotions of love and hatred, there is the feeling when someone is looking at you when your back is turned, the feeling that you'd like to watch a sunset or take a walk, the feeling that life is growing shorter, the feeling that you should contemplate the situation you're in before acting."

"The feeling that I didn't have a clue what I was getting myself into when I asked about a shrike?"

"Yes, that feeling too. Almost all feelings are reactions to things around you. I prefer to act with intent not to react. But that doesn't mean feelings are always secondary to intent. It means each has its place and its perspective."

"How do you decide if you should apply feelings or intent to a situation?"

"That's a good question. The answer depends on the type of situation you're in. If you're talking about any situation that is quantifiable or defined, you are better off applying intent through learning than relying on feelings. Any situation where there is time to reflect, you should think before you base your actions on your feelings."

"What's a quantifiable situation, Mateen?"

"Any situation where an answer can be learned is quantifiable. You are much better off measuring the space a board will go in before cutting it than you are accepting a feeling as an accurate perspective to base the length on. You are much better off first learning what elk feed on, when they are actively feeding, and when they rest, than you are walking into an area and feeling your way towards them. It is better to walk a mile in a person's shoes, to take the time to learn that person's perspective, than to pass judgment on them with a feelings-based negative conclusion."

"That seems pretty obvious."

"You'd be surprised how many people choose to act on their feelings rather than choose to learn about the subject that they're using feelings to base conclusions on. You'd be surprised how many people decide through a feeling that they know enough about another person that they can suggest what is best for that person, even though they haven't learned about that person's individual perspective or situation in life. That's one of the reasons I say correctness, accuracy, truth, whatever you want to call it, is based on the content of what is said, not on who's talking. That's why I say if I feel like going to watch a sunset I will, and if someone else feels like I should go watch a sunset, they can take their presumption elsewhere. That's why if a stranger starts a conversation with a criticism, I decide my time is better spent somewhere else. If people kept track of the accuracy of their feelings-based presumptions, they would find they are more often in error than not. If people accepted how often their feelings were wrong, they would learn humility and increase the need to learn before speaking of their presumptions. But instead many people fall for the common human error of keeping better track of when they're right than when they're wrong."

"What does that mean?"

"It means that people often find it more comfortable to accept and remember when they are right rather than when they are wrong."

"But a lot of times a person's feelings about another can be right, can't they?"

"The more feelings are applied instead of available learning, the less valuable perceptive feelings are. Basically, perceptive feelings are best applied after learning and communication and reflection, not as an emotional reaction. Beyond available learning not one's own learning. You can't feel your way to a better treatment for an illness, compared to the diagnosis a doctor's learning will provide just because you waited to trust your feelings until you had exhausted your own knowledge of the subject. The more feelings incorporate experience, the more valuable they are. But not a biased experience where one forgets when they're wrong and only remembers when they're right. The more feelings can be explained, the more valuable they are. Don't use feelings to avoid learning, learn instead. Don't use feelings to make presumptions about others, communicate with them instead. Don't say "I'm right because I feel like I'm right;" explain your feelings-based perspective.

A perspective that can't stand the light of a clear verbal statement isn't valid enough to expect another to value. If you think you're right because you feel like it and don't explain what your feelings are based on, then you reduce everyone around you to "don't think, obey." "Don't think, obey" is a corruption of individuality. People who make presumptions about others based on gestaltic feelings that are based on experience can often be right. They can be right often if they incorporate experience with an unbiased perspective. The problem is when people who interact with others through their feelings are most likely to be wrong when they are dealing with a person who has used their intent to create individuality. They are most likely to be wrong when they are dealing with a person who holds an individual value system as compared to a society-wide value system. That's because the individual is functioning outside the established norms found in society. Feelings-based presumptions are based on familiarity with the norm. I find more truth in intent and individuality than I do flocking like sheep in a society-wide system. I believe individuals have contributed more to society than masses of people ever have."

"What's a gestaltic feeling?"

"I'm using the term "gestaltic feeling" to refer to a feeling that is a conclusion and that is more than the sum of its parts. People who react to life through their feelings often are most comfortable with feelings coming to them "out of the blue." They choose not to be aware of the steps they are going through to reach their conclusions that show as a feeling. Those feelings are based on an accumulation of minutia, an accumulation of subtleties of body language, and comparisons to other people in similar situations. The problem with this methodology as I said is most often shown when dealing with people who do not fit the norm. People who hold their own individual value system and have developed their own independent perspective because of applying their intent are not able to be categorized by common ranges of values. This country's constitution gives the right to be free from governmental oppression to individuals, not to society as a whole. This makes an independent perspective and independent value systems legitimate from a constitutional and therefore a societal perspective. People who categorize individuals into generalities belittle individuality. They belittle the very same individuality that their lives are dependent on. This is because individuals are responsible for the discoveries, ideas, and applications of ideas that our society, as well as past and future societies, depend on. Masses of people did not harness fire or electricity. Masses of people did not domesticate dogs or livestock. Masses of people did not make wheels and axles. These things were the products of ideas of individuals who applied their intent to a problem or a vision of the future. Then these same people passed their learning on to others so that other individuals could build on earlier discoveries. Don't belittle individuality for the ease of a generalized conclusion. Don't flock like sheep for the ease of not developing your own independent perspective. Don't choose to feel instead of learn, feel after you've learned. Don't belittle the gift of life you've been given by choosing to be one of the masses in a free society. Don't belittle this country's constitution by being a pawn for the current government or choosing to conform to societal values."

"Okay, Mateen, I'll try not to."

"I'm not done yet. This country's constitution has been around for more than 350 years. Current administrations have come and gone dozens of times. These days the current administration is found in the city-states or more locally. None of the current administrations have rejected the original Constitution of the United States of America. It is more patriotic to support the Constitution than it is to support the current administration. Disagreement with the current administration is fine. Not applying the freedoms of the Constitution on an individual level is to not live up to the gift this country gives all its citizens."

"I think I understand, Mateen."

"People who react to life through their feelings and do a better job of remembering when they're right than when they're wrong often become very quick at reaching the feelings-based conclusions they consider perceptive wisdom. A pattern or methodology repeated over time will decrease the speed it takes to reach a conclusion, but will not increase the correctness or accuracy of the conclusion. Familiarity of use increases speed, it does not increase the breadth of one's perspective."

"You're saying to learn and change, and to continually incorporate experience into individual perspective."

"That's right. Create your own individuality and then rebuild yourself through learning and experience. You'll make your life an adventure. Push yourself beyond learning and experience and you'll find the magic of the earth, of timing, of your own potential, of the gifts life can bring, and the gifts individuals can give."

"And how am I supposed to do all that?"

"Focus your efforts on possibility and potential, not familiarity. It is a lot easier to use the wheel someone else created than it is to fill the need for a wheel with the object that is a wheel."

"Now what does that mean?"

"It means that gaining familiarity with established patterns is not the limit of your potential. Familiarity with established patterns is what all the sheep in the flock accomplish. People often confuse the ease of familiarity with the effort of creation or invention. Don't let the choice to surround oneself with the familiar breed contempt for creators and inventors. Don't limit yourself to the comfort of familiarity. Choose to learn and to apply intent to make yourself more than you are, to create who you are. If you do that, you'll find that the gift of your life is the greatest experiment imaginable."

"My life is an experiment?"

"If you want it to be it can be. Your life, my life, all the life around us is the greatest experiment in intent and creativity imaginable. Life is always changing, always testing limits, always growing into unused spaces. Do the same with your own individuality and the magic of the earth, the life around you, and your own potential, will never diminish."

"Wow, okay, it will take me awhile to put that into perspective. But right now I'm still wondering something else."

"And what is that?"

"Is it common for animals to cache food? Or is that rare like animals using tools?"

"A lot of animals cache food. Ants and beaver we've already talked about."

"Oh, that's right, the grasshopper and the ant that I brought up and then the beaver putting sticks at the bottom of their ponds for winter feeding."

"Then there are squirrels and caches of nuts, pikas and hay, bees and honey, jays and suet, dogs burying bones, there are many examples."

"So that means some insects, birds, and mammals cache food. That makes it a lot more common than tool use. Have you ever seen an animal using a tool?"

"Depending on the definition I have a few times. I saw a seagull repeatedly drop a clam on a rocky shoreline once. It dropped the clam from fifty or sixty feet up, then flew down and picked it up. Then it flew back up and dropped the clam again. After the third drop that I saw, the clam's shell was broken open enough that the seagull could eat the insides."

"So the tool was the rock the seagull was dropping the clam on, kind of like an anvil. I can see how that is tool use. The height above the rock generates the force of the hammer, used against the rock which is the anvil. I guess that is really two tools and more abstract than a hammer and anvil actually," says Anoo. "What other examples have you seen?"

"I've seen both hairy and downy woodpeckers in my yard take a sunflower seed and wedge it in a furrow in the bark of a locust tree. It then cracked the seed and ate the kernel inside."

"So that's like what chickadees do with their feet. They hold the seeds in their feet to crack the seed open," says Anoo.

"That's right, and I think the woodpecker isn't built in a way that allows it to strike a seed held in its feet like a chickadee can."

"So the woodpecker is compensating for its build by using the furrow of bark as a vise."

"And the woodpecker was repeatedly going back to the same furrow each time it cracked a seed," says Mateen.

"So it figured out a process that worked and kept using it," says Anoo. "Have you seen any other examples?"

"A couple different times I've seen skulls jammed into a badger den."

"Who would do that and how does it help them? Was something trying to bury the skull?"

"I don't think so. Both times it was very early spring. I think in the early winter the badger took the skull to its burrow. Then went into the burrow and pulled the skull partly into the burrow, wedging it against the sides of the opening of the burrow."

"You mean like a door to its burrow for the winter?"

"That's what I think."

"Couldn't it just have been food for when it woke up in the spring?"

"There really wasn't much food content on either skull. There was hair and skin on it, but very dried up and rotted away."

"Then the badger would have had to go out looking for a skull when it knew it was ready to hibernate," says Anoo. "That's planning ahead to use the skull as the type of tool that is a door. I guess a door is a tool anyway. Animals are really interesting when you look close enough at them."

Mateen and Anoo walk down the hill towards their camp. They are both walking quietly with their feet and being quiet in their minds. They'd reached a conclusion to their talk and no longer want to discuss; they want to be. As they near a stringer of willow they see a small bird flying up into the air fifty feet or more and plunging down to the willows before arcing back up into the sky. They stop and watch and listen to the trilling of the bird's wings. As they slowly move closer, to where the bird is arcing back up from the bottom of its dive, the bird lands on a willow branch ten feet in front of them. As they watch, the bird is quartered towards them. Periodically it slightly lifts its beak and turns its head farther from them. As it does this the sun reflects off the rose-colored patch under its chin. They watch the glint of color against the blue sky as they stand in shin-deep green grass next to the eight-foot-high wall of brown-stemmed, green-leaved willow in front of them. After a few minutes they circle around the bird, making sure they don't come closer than the ten feet the bird originally allowed. As they start to move directly away from the bird Mateen stops and slowly moves his arm up and points. Anoo moves closer and looks into the willow where Mateen is pointing and his eyes slowly focus on a female hummingbird sitting still on a branch. They politely give her space and slowly move down the line of willows. They reach a place where two stringers of willow come together and the six-inch-wide streamlet they've been following becomes a foot-wide gurgling stream. On the upstream side of where the two streamlets come together the willow stringers reach out to each other into a patch. As Mateen and Anoo circle the willow patch an elk calf comes tottering out of the willows and stumbles into the rocky little stream. It steadies itself and then lowers its head and drinks. After drinking and lifting its head a few times it stumbles out of the stream and back into the willows. Mateen and Anoo slowly move on until they are back at camp.

"That was a broad-tailed hummingbird displaying for its mate, wasn't it?" asks Anoo.

"Yes, they're the hummingbird that trills its wings as it flies. The male trills its wings that is, and the female was the one sitting hidden inside the willow."

"So only the male trills and you knew what it was doing and so were looking for the female as we walked."

"That's right."

"Do you think the male knew he was showing us his chin patch?"

"I do."

"Why do you think he was showing us?"

"At the time I was just appreciating the gesture. I don't know why he was doing it. He was sharing a very important part of his life with us. I think he was willing to do that because we were a part of the earth around him and not a disturbance."

"Not a disturbance because of the way we were walking and by being quiet in our minds?"

"Yes, we weren't intruding ourselves out into the world around us. Our footfalls didn't send vibrations through the earth. We didn't break twigs that cracked vibrations out into the air."

"So a way to see the gifts of nature is to not intrude into that world but to be a part of it?"

"I think that's absolutely true."

"And the way to become an individual is to apply intent out into the world around us? That doesn't make much sense."

"The two things are different but I would say it is more accurate that becoming an individual is applying intent out into parts of yourself you haven't developed or become aware of yet. Merging with the background of nature and projecting your awareness out is a way to observe without affecting what you are observing. You can use the world of people to measure your individuality and also develop your individuality through the challenges of interaction with people. Just try to make those interactions and challenges positive not combative. Don't butt heads with others to define who you are. Don't use a negative view of others to support your independent perspective."

"Or I'll link myself to others like a chain which is only as strong as its weakest link."

"Well said."

"Are we going to talk much about how to use the world of people to measure one's individuality?"

"Not really, it isn't an area I've applied myself to and I know enough not to try and talk about things I don't know about or haven't experienced myself."

"That elk calf was very young, wasn't it?"

"I don't think it was more than a couple days old."

"Was it born late?"

"A little, but it should be fine."

"Where was the mother?"

"Farther in the willows I would think."

"Do you think she knew we were there?"

"I do and I don't think she was very comfortable with the whole scenario."

"Why do you think she didn't try and chase us away?"

"Partly because of the way we were moving and partly a fear of people I would guess. I walked into an aspen grove once and walked right up on an elk calf that was lying in the grass. As I stopped and looked a cow elk started barking at me."

"Barking?"

"That's the best description I can give. It's not exactly the same sound as a dog barking but it's abrupt and focused. I started to move away slowly and another cow elk popped its head over a small hill and started barking at me too. I moved farther away and a third cow came to see what the disturbance was, saw me, and started barking also."

"So you were pretty much surrounded by barking cow elk?"

"Yes I was. It sounds funny to say, but that's what happened. As I moved farther away I bumped into another calf in the grass. Once I had left the aspen grove I thought about what had happened and decided there was a group of elk in the grove, maybe a dozen cows or maybe more, and the grove was where they went to have their calves. They may have been going to the same grove for generations. Or maybe they change locations a little every year so predators don't focus on one particular grove. In the grove they were relatively close to each other where they could keep an eye on each other and protect each other."

"Were you thinking they would chase you?"

"I wasn't concerned for my safety but I didn't want to disturb them any more than I had so I left."

"We only saw the one calf today."

"I think that patch of willows wasn't big enough for more cow calf pairs. And since this particular cow had her calf a little late the cow may have missed her chance to be with the herd for the first week or two of the calf's life."

"But then she'll catch up to the herd as the calf gets bigger?"

"I would expect so."

"And just because you saw the one group of cows and calves doesn't mean that all cows with calves always group that way?"

"That's right. Keep in mind that we're talking about cows with, I'd say, less than one or two-week-old calves that were using that calving area. After that the calves can move around well enough that the cows will start to move around with their calves."

"So they don't smell up an area so much it attracts predators?"

"That's right."

"I saw a deer chase one of our barn cats once."

"Tell me what happened."

"The deer was looking forward and its ears were pointed forward too. It started walking toward where it was looking. As it walked, it picked its feet up in a really exaggerated way and put them down solidly. Then fifteen feet in front of the deer one of our cats came running out from under a bush and ran all the way back to the barn. The deer didn't see that and kept moving around in the bushes for a few minutes. Then I saw there was another deer watching the first deer from about twenty feet away."

"What time of year was it?"

"Springtime, like around now, I guess."

"I'd say the first deer you saw was the yearling doe of the doe that was watching and the watching doe had a new fawn in the bushes that it was keeping an eye on as the yearling doe chased the cat away."

"Like when you said that a yearling doe will stay with its mother helping out and learning about how to be a mother deer."

"That's right."

"I was surprised the deer even cared about something as small as our barn cat."

"That's why I think there was a newborn fawn nearby. I don't think a grown deer would be concerned with a barn cat otherwise."

"I see. And I guess that's an example of how I watched the deer but didn't understand why they were doing what they did because of a lack of experience."

"I think so. But you were interested enough to watch and remember, to note the occurrence as something special. Then you put the pieces together later."

"But with your help."

"With my help, yes. But you didn't gloss over the whole episode at the time. You knew you were watching something interesting and you paid attention. Then, that experience or observation was built upon later. The process works with or without me to help you."

"I guess so, but I like these times now where you help me build on my experiences."

"Thank you for saying so and I am enjoying our time together also. But do keep in mind the process will work for you with or without the help of others."

"Okay, I pay attention when I notice something out of the ordinary and I can learn about it later. My familiarity with what is happening around me allows me to identify what is out of the ordinary which means there is something interesting to learn about."

"It may take years before you learn the who or why of something you've seen. I once found the scent sacks of a skunk out in the woods still connected by the tubes that the skunk uses when it sprays."

"And that's all, no other parts of the skunk?"

"That's all that was there. I learned years later that great horned owls will kill skunks and eat all of them but the scent sacks."

"Even the fur?"

"Well I didn't see any fur around so I guess so. Coincidentally enough the first time I saw a grasshopper stuck on a Hawthorn thorn I had no idea what a shrike was or that they stick grasshoppers on thorns. Years later I learned the rest of that story."

"And now you've told me, so I don't have to wait for years to learn."

Mateen and Anoo eat a quiet lunch together and then Anoo wanders off to find a comfortable place to sit. When he is settled he thinks for awhile about what Mateen said and what they had seen together. Then he decides to just listen with his eyes closed as Mateen has shown him. He enjoys the warmth of the afternoon, the sounds of insects and birds, and the smell of moist earth. After listening for a time he stands and takes a look around before settling back down and taking a nap. When he wakes he sits up and watches the world around him. The quiet of a good sleep stays in his mind. After watching time and the life around him pass by, he gets up and slowly walks back to camp.

As he walks it seems his footsteps are as unobtrusive to the life around him as his mind is quiet. When he gets back to camp Mateen is not there so Anoo readies the food and fire for the evening meal.

When Anoo wandered away from camp Mateen decided to take a nap and when he woke he stretched for awhile. After stretching he sits and meditates. His eyes are open and his mind is alert yet quiet. Then he rises and goes to a small stand of aspen just up the slope from camp. He slowly moves through the stand, noting some interesting phenomena to show Anoo. After awhile he sees that Anoo is back in camp so he goes down and joins him. They eat as the sun is starting to lower in the sky. After eating and cleaning up there is still plenty of light. Mateen leads Anoo up the hill to the aspen stand. They move into the stand and wait a short distance from a tree about eight inches in diameter with a small hole in it. After a few minutes a flicker flies up to the hole, lands on the edge and then goes inside. Mateen and Anoo can hear the excited chirps of other birds inside. The chirps quiet after the flicker looks outside and then flies off. Mateen and Anoo wait for a little while until the flicker returns. This time they can clearly see the body and legs of an insect in the flicker's bill. After the flicker goes inside, feeds its young, and then flies off again, Mateen moves over about twenty feet and points to an aspen that is about four inches in diameter with a very small hole in it. Around the bottom two thirds of the hole there are about eight large ants. Their back feet are right on the edge of the hole and they are facing out. They all have very noticeable mandibles. As Mateen and Anoo watch, several ants, about half the size of those next to the hole, move up the trunk of the tree in single file. They pass by the larger ants and enter the hole. Mateen moves his finger against the bark of the tree an inch from one of the big ants. It immediately moves towards his finger and then stops as Mateen moves his finger away. Then Mateen walks about fifty feet from that aspen to a thick patch of grass. Some of the grass is fresh and green and some is dried and brown from last year. He kneels down and points to a dozen small holes, each about six to ten inches apart. Then, before getting up, he points to several spiders near the holes. They walk back to camp as the sky starts to show the orange and light reds of early sunset.

"I know what the flicker was doing; it was feeding its young. I could hear them chirp when the adult brought food."

"That's right. Did you know that some kinds of ants live in cavities in aspen trees?"

"No, I didn't, and why were the ones around the hole so much bigger than the three that came up the trunk and then went into the hole?"

"They're the same species of ant. The ones arrayed around the hole are soldier ants whose job it is to protect the colony. The ants that came up the trunk of the tree had been out foraging. That's their job to do for the colony."

"So they're different sizes with different jaws but the same kind of ant?"

"Yes, and then there's also a queen ant in the cavity that lays eggs for the colony."

"Do the ants that go out foraging get lost?"

"I'm sure they do sometimes, but they find their way by following a scent trail laid down by ants that went down the trunk of the tree earlier."

"Then where do they go after they're down the tree?"

"They're looking for food or going to a known food source."

"How do they know a food source has been found?"

"The ants that found the food source leave a scent trail with a different odor than the odor of a main travel way. That's an advantage they have over bees. Once an ant finds a food source it can leave a different scent trail back to the aspen tree. Then ants coming down to the base of the tree will find a scent trail telling them to follow it to food. Bees fly to their food sources and so can't leave a scent trail."

"So how do bees tell others in their hive where to find food?"

"They do a dance."

"Oh c'mon, they do not!"

"Yes, they do. They'll land in front of the hive and do a dance by turning around in a particular way and buzzing their wings. Other bees watch the dance and fly off to the tree or shrub or patch of flowers that is actively producing nectar that day."

"So the bees watch the dance and change that into a direction and distance and go flying off?"

"Beekeepers have seen it happen many times."

"That's pretty incredible."

"Yes, it is. I've also had flocks of finches coming to my bird feeder. Then the food runs out and I don't get around to filling the feeder for several days. After I fill the feeder I've watched several different times as one finch shows up and just looks at the full feeder and then flies away. Less then fifteen minutes later I'll have a bird feeder surrounded by a flock of finches."

"That's pretty incredible too, but I think it's more amazing that insects can communicate like that. What kind of spider lives in those holes in the grass?"

"Wolf spiders, they're the ones you often see carrying an egg case around with them."

"Those were bigger than the ones I usually see."

"Wolf spiders can get big. It depends on how much food is available for them. I once caught a very large one that I first saw on the window of my cabin. I decided it got as big as it did because it had a good food source as a young spider. That caused it to grow fast until it became large enough to eat grasshoppers. After it started eating grasshoppers it got really big."

"How big is really big?"

"When I caught it, its body was as large as my thumb and its legs spread out as large as my palm."

"Did you let it sit in your hand?"

"No, I didn't. When I caught it I put a canning jar up next to it and shooed it into the jar with a stick. At first it didn't move and then when it did, it jumped into the jar before I could move. I had no idea what I was dealing with. If it had not gone into the jar it could have jumped up my arm and bit me before I could have moved, it was so quick. I was just lucky it jumped into the jar."

"You wouldn't have wanted to be bit by a spider that big, I bet!"

"Definitely not, it had mandibles three eighths of an inch long and as big around at the base as pencil lead. They were shiny black, curved, and extremely tapered to a very fine point. When I first caught it I cut a couple slits in the thin metal top of the canning jar with a heavy knife. The spider would jump up to the top of the jar, hook a mandible over the slit in the metal top and twang it so loud I could hear it across the room."

"Wow, I'm going to think twice about laying down next to that patch of grass we saw. How do you know it ate grasshoppers?"

"I'm not positive what it ate in the wild, but after I had it in the jar a couple days I moved it to a terrarium. I put grasshoppers in with it and at first it wouldn't eat. Then it most have gotten really hungry or got used to its new home and it started to feed. When I'd put a fresh grasshopper in Wolfie would jump across the terrarium in two bounds, grab it in its jaws and hold it up in the air until it stopped kicking. I don't even think the poison of Wolfie had time to work before the jaws by themselves killed the grasshopper."

"Wolfie, you named your pet spider?"

"Yes, I did. I didn't keep it for very long. After a couple weeks I let it go. But I let it go a lot farther away from the cabin than where I first caught it."

"I would have too!"

"Let's watch the rest of the sunset. Tomorrow I think we'll move up higher into the hills to the spruce-fir zone."

"Okay, how far will we go?"

"I think we'll probably go about five or six miles in distance and two or three thousand feet in altitude."

Tohlee and Eli start the day with the morning chores and then have breakfast together and talk about their day. Eli is going to set some stepping stones in his garden. He removes them every fall so slugs and other critters won't winter under them and so they'll be out of the way when it's time to turn the soil in the spring. The stones aren't needed for planting because he moves around on wide boards to distribute his weight and so keep the soil from compacting. But after planting, the stones come in handy as a travel way and as a place to lay tools.

One section of the garden is for perennials like rhubarb, asparagus, and strawberries, but most of it is tilled every year and crops rotated. The corn and wheat patches are tilled every year and switched every three years. Eli is also going to put up some trellises for the tomatoes, spaghetti squash, beans, and the other plants that need them. They need to go in before the plants get too big and fall over.

Tohlee has decided to sew early in the morning and then go out in her gardens after it warms up a little. Her gardens are set up more permanently with gravel pathways and stones. She has a higher proportion of perennials to annuals than Eli does and only turns over the sections for the annuals each year. She does redo a small percentage of perennials each year when they become overmature. The gardens surround all four sides of the house, lining the porch which goes around the entire house. This provides four different habitats for the wide variety of plants she grows.

Around midday they get together for a light lunch and decide to go down to their swimming hole in a few hours. After working awhile after lunch, Eli puts away his tools and packs a blanket, some water, and towels in his daypack for the walk to the swimming hole. Tohlee meets up with him and they walk down to the river with the dogs. They talk a little as they walk and then fall into a comfortable silence. When they get to the gravel bar next to the swimming hole Eli spreads out the blanket and they take off their clothes and go into the water. After a refreshing swim they get out and dry each other off and warm in the sun. Tohlee is standing in front of Eli as they look at the water. Tohlee turns and kneels in front of him. When he is ready Eli sits down on the blanket and Tohlee turns her back to him and kneels in front of him. She rises up and then slowly lowers herself down onto him. With a few movements and a final wiggle she stretches out her legs with Eli deep inside her. As Eli feels her warmth soaking into him he reaches around her and puts his left hand under her left breast so he can feel her heartbeat. He puts his right arm around her and holds her right breast in his hand. Tohlee wraps her arms around Eli's and squeezes. The distinction between their bodies blurs as their attention goes inward. Their awareness joins like their bodies and goes down to where their bodies are together. The feeling warms them both and their attention rises up to the center of their bodies. Tohlee can feel Eli's heartbeat against her back and Eli can feel Tohlee's heart under his hand. Together their awareness rises up from their hearts and separates as their energy ascends into their heads.

Their eyes open at the same time and they look out around them. It is the same river, greenery, and blue sky as before their eyes closed, but somehow it is different now that they are together. They see the ripples of the fast water as it enters the pool. They look downstream a little and across to where the shade of a willow darkens the water. An unseen trout rises from below, dimpling the surface and taking an insect from just below the surface that has drifted up from the gravel bottom of the pool. They both watch the spot and after a minute or so the fish rises and dimples the water again. After watching the fish feed a couple more times their eyes move downstream to where the pool narrows, the water speeds up, and then turns and goes out of sight. They look at the turn of the water until the whistling wings of a mallard brings their eyes up.

They follow the bird as it flies past them and then look up at the cottonwood trees across the stream. They watch small branches and leaves move in the errant breezes of the afternoon. Their eyes shift to the right and follow a puffy white cloud as it goes behind the canopy of a tree. As they watch, blue patches of sky peeking through the green canopy change to white. The white of the cloud shifts with the green canopy as gaps in the canopy shift with the breeze. They continue to watch until the cloud comes out from behind the tree. They look at a willow as the song of a wren reaches out to them across the stream. Their eyes focus on the bird as it comes out on a branch from deeper in the tall shrub. They close their eyes and listen to the song. They feel the energy of each other's awareness. They are together yet next to each other. With a calm awareness time passes. They open their eyes and look to where the sun has noticeably lowered in the sky.

Tohlee leans forward as Eli pushes her up with his hands on her hips. They stand with his arms around her and shift their weight from one foot to another. They feel the stiffness leave as they slowly move their arms and legs. They walk forward, feeling the gravel under the calloused soles of their bare feet. They feel the cool water rise up their legs and they rinse off. After they dry off with the towels Eli packs up their clothes, the towels, and the blanket into his pack. They put on their sandals and walk back home hand-in-hand. The sun warms the left side of their bodies and the breeze cools the right as they walk. Eli feels the fur of one of Tohlee's dogs as it brushes past him. They see their home come into view and Tohlee squeezes Eli's hand. When they enter the coolness of their unheated house they dress. Then they go into the kitchen and start making a light dinner. Slowly the process of forming words in their minds comes back to them and Tohlee turns to Eli.

"You give so much depth to my life. You're the time I take to watch a butterfly flutter in the breeze on a warm afternoon."

"You're the first step I take outside in the morning, when I smell the hay in the barn, the soil in the corral the horses have disturbed."

"You're how I feel when I watch a bee moving from one flower to another."

"You're the feeling of morning mist reaching into my nostrils."

"You're the leaves of a tree stretching up to the sun."

"You're the sound of biting into a crisp apple, the explosion of taste in my mouth, the feeling of the juice running down my dry throat."

"I love you, Eli."

"And I love you, Tohlee."

Day Seven

As the sun lightens the sky Mateen and Anoo eat breakfast and break camp. Mateen leads the way as they walk across a slope, gradually climbing. They leave behind the cottonwoods and willow scattered with blue spruce as they climb out of the drainage. Patches of tall shrubs and small aspen on the slope gradually change to groves of larger aspen. Individual ponderosa pine transition to groves of pine trees with open ground between well-spaced trunks. They walk through an aspen grove that already has a two-foot-tall undergrowth of grasses and forbs beneath straight un-branched white trunks, reaching sixty feet into the air to a canopy that allows scattered beams of sunlight to reach all the way to the ground.

Other groves of aspen they pass through have only ferns making up the undergrowth. One grove has an understory of fifteen-foot-tall chokecherry so thick that they are glad it has a nice game trail going through it. Some stands of ponderosa pine give the appearance of a tended park. Meadows become more infrequent as they climb. They start to see stands of lodgepole pine as subalpine fir shows up as understory trees in aspen stands. A north-facing slope is thick with Engelmann spruce and subalpine fir, mixed together with down trees scattered about.

They haven't taken a break as their pace has been steady, not fast, the climb continual, not steep. They are ready to rest after climbing over the down trunks of two-foot-diameter spruce and fir. As they remove their packs they see the ground in front of them level out into undulating folds and realize that the hardest part of their climb is behind them. They stretch and cool down before sitting on a fallen log to rest and enjoy a snack.

"Will we go much farther today?" asks Anoo.

"Maybe another mile or two, we've come out onto a plateau that is in between the two streams that join at town. This whole area is relatively flat for miles around. There are lots of little hills and small drainages, but the whole area stays between nine and ten thousand feet. This is a very well watered and green area in the summer so we'll see lots of wildlife."

"Does this plateau get a lot of snow in the winter?"

"It often has five or six feet on the ground by late winter so many of the animals drop down to lower elevations in the winter."

"That's when we see the largest herds of deer, elk, and sometimes moose at home."

"In the spring they move up to this higher country and stay through the summer and fall. Then as the snow starts to build up in early winter they drop down off the plateau and go to south and west-facing slopes with less snow and good sun exposure. The elk may go all the way out onto the plains. The deer like to drop down to the lower shrubby hills but usually don't go all the way out onto the plains. The moose are so long-legged they don't mind a few feet of snow and they like to be near willows, so they stay up the highest in the winter."

"So they don't move as far as the elk in the winter. But we saw that one moose down below and some recent sign of elk, too."

"Not all the animals move at the same speed. The elk might take six weeks to wander up here from the plains. The moose haven't gone as far but still take a couple weeks to come up. The deer take a little longer than the moose because they start from farther down and need more snow to melt up above than the moose do. Most of the animals don't race up here as soon as they can. The lower elevations green up earlier and the animals like to recover from the winter on fresh greenery. Cows stop to have their calves along the way. Some of the older animals go slower and feed longer down below. It's the big bulls that come up first. They go to the south-facing meadows up here that lose snow first and don't care that they have to walk through a couple feet of snow to get to those open meadows."

"So it's more of average behavior than an absolute rule," states Anoo.

"That's right. If all the elk or moose did exactly the same thing, the entire herd could fall victim to severe weather or disease. It would be easier for predators to target them and the overall herd could suffer. If some individuals didn't wander farther than others, new areas wouldn't be populated."

"So an entire herd is at greater risk without individual variability built into it."

"Not only an entire herd can be at risk, but an entire species can be at risk also. If a bird like a snail kite in Florida is completely dependent on snails for food and something happens to the snails, all the kites are threatened. The snail kite is a very specialized feeder. They can be considered to be overspecialized if the populations of snails drop and the kites aren't able to find a secondary food source. Some individual kites may be better at finding a secondary food source than others because of a better ability to adapt to changes in their individual lives. Or, some kites may have lived on the fringes of snail habitat for generations and have had to utilize a secondary food source often. Those can be the individuals that survive a crash in snail populations."

"And so those individuals can cause the whole species to survive."

"That's exactly right. Salmon are another example where individual variability is a plus for a species. Most salmon return to the one stream they were hatched from, but a small percentage won't. Without that small percentage salmon wouldn't be able to spread to new rivers. If they don't spread to new rivers and something happens to their home river like a landslide cutting it off from the ocean, the entire species can die out."

"So that means individual variability can be an advantage to a species when it's physical like the ability to adapt to various places or food sources and it can be an advantage for a species like humans when an inventor creates something new that positively affects everyone."

"That's right, for people especially, it's not only inventors but artists who show new perspectives, or writers and teachers who give the inspiration to others to learn and try new things or to think new thoughts."

"Like new perspectives that cause the wheel of life to turn inside us."

"You're an intelligent boy and a delight to talk to."

"Thank you, Mateen."

"Now let's move on. I want to find a place to camp with a nice stand of spruce and fir to block the west wind."

"That's because it will be colder up here at night than down below. So we'll need lots of firewood too, don't you think?"

"Yes, we will and we'll want a small stream nearby for water also."

Tohlee and Eli wake early as usual and tend to chores around the house before breakfast. Eli turns the horses out in the pasture for a morning meal as Tohlee pumps water from the well for themselves and the dogs and cats. When she is done Eli brings over the wheelbarrow with a large tub in it. He fills the tub and tips it over into the horse trough. After two trips it is filled for the day. Tohlee gathers eggs from the chickens and gives the chickens and turkeys some stale bread. They go inside and have a breakfast of green chile sauce over potatoes with omelet sandwiches. As Tohlee cleans up, Eli goes out and opens up the chicken and turkey coops. The dogs know their job and so they go out fifty to a hundred feet from the flock and act as outriders, alert to danger and ready to protect the birds. Two cats tag along as Eli moves the flock along the barn. As he comes to strategically-placed boards and rocks he turns them over so the birds can look underneath for slugs, grubs, or worms. After moving past the barn Eli moves the flock between gardens and out into one of the orchards. Small early spring grasshoppers are on the menu now as well as any other insects the birds can find. The dogs stay out wide, looking for fox or coyotes or any other critter big enough to hurt the birds.

It wasn't hard for Eli to use the dogs' territoriality and respect for him to teach them what he wanted them to do. After a few years the pattern has become well established and the newest dog to the farm quickly learns what is expected of him by following the lead of the older, experienced dogs. Tohlee often goes along but this morning she is getting the house ready for Cassie and Jed's visit tomorrow.

As Eli brings the flock back to the barn Tohlee meets up with him. It has been a good morning's hunt and the birds are ready for a break and water so they willingly return to their coops. As Tohlee and Eli finish shooing the birds in, the dogs tear off down the lane, barking an alert. The dogs quiet quickly as they recognize Caleb and Laurel, the neighbors from the next farm upstream. One of their horses is pulling a cart with two calves and three piglets inside. After a friendly chat and learning everything is going well, Eli stakes the calves out in the tall grass of the front yard as Tohlee takes the piglets to the sty. Eli and Caleb plan to meet up that afternoon so Eli can help Caleb with some carpentry work and fencing and then also after Cassie and Jed's visit. Tohlee will meet up with them all for some drinks and more in-depth catching up after this afternoon's work.

"What do you think of this spot?" asks Mateen.

"It has a view to the east and the thick spruce/fir stand you wanted to the west. There's plenty of dead wood on the trunks that's drier than what is on the ground. The line of willows at the bottom of the hill must mean there is water down there. I think it looks like a good spot."

"I agree; if the tree stand were smaller we would make a little leanto out of spruce and fir branches to shelter the tent and fire ring. But there's no need for that here as this stand is large. As you look up the stream you can see it starts just a couple hundred yards away at the base of that small hill. We'll check for any recent beaver activity at the stream and if we don't find any we should be able to drink the water without boiling it. The farthest up the stream where there is still good flow will be the best spot and maybe the stream starts at a spring right at the base off the hill."

"That would be best of all because there wouldn't be an opportunity for critters to poop and pee in it before we drink it, right?"

"That's right, and nothing will ruin a trip like amoebic dysentery. I don't want to have to go through that on this trip."

"Me neither, Father said he had giardia once and that was enough for both of us."

"I second that notion. Once I was down on the southwest side of these hills, that's where we'll go look for fossils and wild horses, and I was very thirsty. It was a hot day and I went up a small branch stream."

"There are streams away from the hills but it's dry too?" wonders Anoo.

"Streams flow out of these hills into the much drier flatlands. I knew I didn't want to drink that water, but I thought if I moved up a small branch stream I might be able to find some water I could drink without boiling it. I got to a place where the stream was only six inches wide and was gurgling down a small hill. The water looked really inviting, but I decided I just wasn't willing to take the chance. I walked up to the top of the small hill and there was a small beaver pond right at the headwaters of the little stream."

"And beavers are one of the main carriers of giardia."

"That's right, but not only that, there also was a recently dead and bloated bison floating in the pond."

"Oh yuck, it's a good thing you didn't drink that water! What did you do?"

"I went back down to the main stream and set up camp, started a fire and didn't get to drink until I boiled some water."

"You must have been really thirsty by then."

"I was very thirsty. I made sure I drank enough water to pee clear urine and I made sure I had plenty of water for the next day too."

"Why did the bison die?"

"I guess he went into the pond to cool off and got stuck in the mud."

"That would have been a slow way to die."

"Very slow, it would be better to be taken by wolves I think."

"I understand. There are worse ways for a prey animal to die than to be taken by a predator."

"Okay, Anoo let's set up camp and get organized. I'll set up the tent and fire ring while you get wood and dig a couple poop holes. Then we'll take a break before going for a little walk around so we know our surroundings."

Mateen quickly clears an area for the tent and sets it up. Then he clears the ground around the tent of branches as well as any branches attached to trees that could poke a person when they move around camp at night. Then he sweeps bare the area around the fire pit which he builds from nearby rocks. A short distance from the fire pit on the opposite side from the tent he makes another pile of rocks and clears a small area there also. In the meantime Anoo has dug a couple poop holes and is carrying a third armload of branches into camp when he sees what Mateen is doing.

"What are those stones for?" asks Anoo.

"At the lake we swam at least once a day to keep clean. Here we're going to build a little sweat lodge with a frame made of willows from along the stream and then our tarp thrown over the frame to hold in heat."

"Oh, a quick one like the permanent one at the farm. So we'll put these rocks in the fire and heat them up before bringing them into the lodge."

"That's right, then we'll pour some water over some of the hot rocks and sprinkle some sage or fir needles on the dry rocks for the fragrance. Some of the rocks we'll use to hold the edges of the tarp down, too."

"That will be great, I'll dig a little pit in the lodge for the hot rocks so they don't roll."

"And then if you would, cut a couple of short-forked sticks to move the rocks into the lodge. I'll cut the willow for the frame and then we'll make it together."

"Sure, will we take one today?"

"Let's have a little rest and a walk around first, then we'll get a fire going for a sweat before dinner."

"Okay, how will we make the frame of the sweat lodge?"

"I'll cut some long willow stems and then we'll push the big ends into the ground about five or six feet apart. Then we'll bend the tops toward each other and tie them together with a couple feet of overlap."

"I see, and then it will be strong enough to hold up the tarp."

After completing their camp preparations Mateen and Anoo stretch and slow down from their hike and work. They take a nap and wake refreshed as midafternoon passes. They have the rest of their water from yesterday and go for a walk so that they'll be familiar with the area near camp.

"This is pretty much a spring, isn't it?" asks Anoo.

"Pretty much, maybe it's more of a seep as the water first comes from underground as this wet soil and doesn't become this small stream until after it goes over the edge of this little basin holding the wet soil."

"I don't see any beaver or other animal sign."

"I don't either. There's water everywhere up here this time of year. Maybe this little stream gets more animal use in August when snow melt is long gone and other streams farther away from their source dry up. Let's fill our water bottles at the basin edge for our walk and leave the pots here to fill on our way back. We'll grab some of this sage then and there's obviously plenty of fir at camp. In the morning we'll pick strawberries from the patch we passed."

They walk up the little hill above the seep and stop just below the crest. They stand side by side and take another step up. First they see the near side of the top of the hill they are walking up. They take another step and can just see the top of the ridge on the other side of a larger valley than the little one they set up camp in. They take another step and more of the far side hill comes into view. They see a buck moving down the hillside. They wait a minute as the buck drops out of sight and then they take another step. The buck hasn't come back into sight but more of the valley below has, so they wait and look carefully at all the new ground exposed to them. They quickly scan over some openings in the aspen. Then they slowly look around the edges of the openings. Nothing else is moving so they take another step and then another. The buck comes back into sight as a hawk screeches a warning to the valley of the intruders. The buck takes a quick look around and keeps going towards the stream at the bottom of the hill. Another step and the valley bottom comes into sight. The stream is fair-sized with willows and beaver ponds as far as they can see up and down the valley. The hawk screeches again and then can be seen as it leaves its perch and flies down the valley. The buck looks around once more and then walks down almost to the water. He nibbles on some plants as he looks around, his head dropping to the greenery and then quickly up to look around. After a few mouthfuls and checks he goes to the water and drinks. Then he moves upstream, going in and out of the willows until he doesn't come out of one patch.

"I think he's bedded down," says Anoo.

"Me too, let's not go down into the valley and disturb him. We know we'll be able to get plenty of brookies from a stream like that. Let's drop back down from the crest of this hill and then around the seep to the spruce/fir stand. We'll go around it and so circle camp."

"Did you see the redtail hawk in the tree?"

"Not until it moved. They're very hard to see not moving in a living tree unless they're silhouetted against the sky. But it saw us as soon as we moved above the skyline though."

"Why didn't the buck care more when it screeched?"

"The buck didn't know why the redtail screeched. A problem for the hawk may not be a problem for the buck. He did take a look around each time. But for all he knew the redtail had seen another hawk intruding on its territory. That wouldn't be a concern for the buck."

Mateen and Anoo slowly move around the top of the bowl that holds the seep. As they walk they keep to little game trails and check for tracks. As they move around the spruce/fir stand they find themselves on a rocky narrow ridgeline looking down into another valley.

"Let's sit on these rocks and watch the valley below us for awhile."

"Those rocks were tipped over by a bear, weren't they?"

"They were, we'll probably keep seeing them along the ridge top. What do you think it was looking for?"

"Some kind of creepy crawlies, I guess."

"Me too, they're not very particular. What else did you see?"

"Should we be concerned that a bear moved along this ridge recently when we're camped just on the other side of the trees?"

"Probably not, this entire area is bear habitat just like the last two places we camped. If we moved camp we'd just end up at another place bears use. We can hang our food up in a tree away from camp a bit. Other than that we'll just make sure camp is kept clean and as odor free as possible. What else did you see as we walked?"

"The main trail through the saddle at the end of this ridge was used by elk and deer recently. The tracks on the trail up this ridge that look like little moccasins were from a porcupine. Father has shown me those before in dusty soil. He says their claws often don't show. There were some small mice-sized animals moving around in the meadow too."

"So nothing to be concerned with but the bear that may be a mile away or more now?"

"I didn't see any other sign to be concerned with. And you're saying the bear may have been just moving around his territory. It's not like this is his home stand of trees?"

"We'd have seen sign around the camp area if he frequented that particular stand of trees. I think he just uses this ridgeline as he moves from one place to another. What else shows we've chosen a good place to camp?"

"Well we talked about the water nearby and the trees breaking the west wind. The view to the east is really nice and there's lots of firewood. What else are you thinking?"

"This rocky ridge is the highest point around and our camp is far enough below the ridgeline that the trees around camp are lower than the trees up towards the ridgeline."

"So that means lightning probably won't strike the trees at camp. It will either strike the rocky ridge or a tall tree up at the top of the stand."

"That's what I was thinking. It's also nice to be camping off the main drainage so that we won't be as likely to disturb the animals that are comfortable using the main drainage."

"And it was just a short walk for us to see into this drainage and the first one with the hawk and buck."

"That's right, let's keep going along this ridge and then drop down at the end of the stand and then back to camp. Keep your eyes open for anything else we should be aware of as we camp here. More strawberries and onions would come in handy."

"Hey, I remember seeing mint at the seep!"

"Then we'll have some fresh mint tea for our stay."

After Mateen and Anoo get back to camp Anoo goes to the seep and picks some mint for tea and sage for the sweat lodge before filling the pots they'd left there with water. When he gets back to camp Mateen has a fire going.

"Let's sit around the fire as we get some nice coals burning and heat up rocks for our sweat," says Mateen.

"Okay, what should we talk about?"

"Let's talk about people you'll run into in life."

"You mean like future friends?"

"I mean more like how to tell if a person will help you grow in life or is more concerned with their own agenda for themselves."

"So more like what kind of person I should be wary of, someone I should be hesitant to value as a friend."

"That's what I mean. We've talked about how your parents and I want you to think for yourself to develop an independent perspective. So I'm going to tell you about ways people show they're not interested in your individual thought or perspective."

"You mean like the way some people act or the things they say."

"That's what I mean and also the value systems some people hold. One example is when people ask leading questions."

"What's a leading question? Was that one? Or that one? Or?"

"Good one, Anoo, and no, those aren't leading questions. You don't want to annoy me with meaningless questions, do you?"

"No, I sure don't, I was just having fun."

"And I just asked you a leading question."

"You mean when you asked if I wanted to annoy you?"

"What I said was "You don't want to annoy me with meaningless questions, do you?". If I had asked "Why are you asking me those questions?" that would not have been a leading question. When I asked "You don't want to annoy me with meaningless questions, do you?" I was pointing you to the answer I thought was the right one."

"You were pointing me to saying "No, I don't want to annoy you". But I didn't want to annoy you, I was having fun."

"It's the form of the question that matters. It's that I was leading you to the answer that I wanted to hear. A lot of times people who use leading questions to elicit a desired response will start asking leading questions that most anyone would be in agreement with. That develops a pattern of agreement with the questioner who then asks the question they intended to ask all along and also in the form of a leading question."

"Then the person answering responds in agreement almost without thinking of what they really think the answer should be. So that would be too much leading and not enough interest in my perspective."

"That's right, it is too much like don't think for yourself, just agree with me. It is too much like don't think, obey. Don't you agree?"

"Yes, I do, even if you didn't just ask me another leading question."

"Another way people promote the concept of "don't think, obey" is when they think they are right because of the position they hold, not because of the content of what they are saying."

"What do you mean by position?"

"I mean a position like that of a teacher, or parent, or someone higher up than yourself in an organization, or someone older than you. No matter who they are they must be able to prove their point or validate their perspective to be right. Otherwise they are functioning from a "might makes right perspective." In this case might is the position they hold. Might doesn't make right, might means a person gets their way. Presidents have started wars based on false information. Popes have looked the other way when genocide was committed on people of other religions. Those actions were not justified by the individual's position. Those people were not right because of who they were."

"You mean prove their point or validate their perspective in writing or by saying it?"

"Any correct or accurate perspective or piece of information can stand the light of day through clearly stating or writing it. Be wary of people who think they're right because they feel like it when you and everyone else on earth have their own feelings. Be wary of people who think they're right because they've managed to form an opinion or repeat someone else's opinion. Everyone on earth is full of opinions."

"And my feelings and opinions are as valid as anyone else's."

"That's right, correctness, accuracy, or truth, whatever you want to call it is determined by the content of what is said, not by who's talking."

"So instead of expecting people to be obedient a person should make their perspective clear and let other people decide for themselves if they agree."

"That's right, and along the same line be wary of people who think they're right because of their age. People who think they're right because of their age never intend to change their mind if someone older than they comes along."

"They just want me to change my mind so that I am in agreement with them."

"That's right. And watch out for people who think that they're right based on a simplistic line of reasoning or an undefined line of reasoning. Those people are termed fanatics."

"And a person is a fanatic when they...?"

"My definition of a fanatic is a person who thinks their beliefs negate the concern of hypocrisy. They are people who think their actions are legitimized by their beliefs and yet if others acted towards them the way they act, they would find fault with the others."

"What's an example of that?"

"Fanatics think they're right because they find truth in their own obedience or lack of thought. So a fanatic will say something like "it's the truth because I read it in the Bible," or the Koran, or the Bhagavad-Gita, or the Talmud. Fanatics find truth in the person talking, such as a political or religious figure, or where they read something."

"Not in the content of what was said or what was written."

"That's right. From my perspective a fanatic is someone who walks the straight and narrow by narrowing down their sources of information and then proclaiming their righteousness. I think a person should walk the straight and narrow by focusing their intent on a mature value system that they have created and then not straying from that value system."

"And you think a mature value system is based on the concept of do unto others. Specifically, don't do violence and don't tear down other people's capabilities for the sake of your own ego. Acknowledge and appreciate other people's gifts. Don't tear them down to avoid your own feelings of inadequacy or failure or that you haven't tried as hard as you could have."

"Well said, Anoo. Let me emphasize the creation within creating your own value system. Don't use the feelings that are reactions to life when creating your own value system. That is how a person adopts the established value systems of society or another person, thereby limiting their own individuality. The value system I'm talking about is the way you value or interpret those feelings. The process of determining how you value or interpret your feelings is the action of applied intent. That action takes you deeper than the reactions of your feelings. It establishes the base that you use to evaluate your feelings. In so doing you become your own truth and validate your own individuality."

"Are you saying the process of creating your own value system is an action and using an action to establish your value system inherently changes that value system?"

"That's right. That is in comparison to the people who use reactions to interpret their feelings because they've chosen to adopt an existing value system."

"I think there's a whole lot there I need to put into perspective or action on a level beyond conversation."

"Well said again. So let's go on with our conversation. There are people who think something is right because it is just the way it is. Nothing is just the way it is in a free country except for the laws of physics. People who think something is just the way it is either don't understand their perspective well enough to say what it is or they know the simplicity of their perspective will be exposed if they explain themselves."

"Their perspective can't stand the light of day through clearly stating it or writing it down."

"You're onto this now. A very ugly form of the same idea is when a person says "oh, you wouldn't understand it anyway." Poor or simplistic communication causing a lack of understanding is the fault of the communicator. Being vague is often just a method people use to hide their own lack of understanding. You should also avoid people who think they're right because they're angry or who think their anger is additional proof of how right they are."

"That would make for an unpleasant conversation."

"I agree completely. You should be wary of people who change the topic of conversation in the middle of a conversation without saying they are. This is a technique most often used by people in an effort to make it appear as though they weren't wrong. It's a technique often used by people who think their feelings are the truth and so can't be proven wrong. If they're proven wrong they won't be wrong just on that particular subject. Their methodology of determining the truth, their own feelings, would be shown to be wrong. Oddly enough, those people are avoiding exactly what they need to make their feelings more truthful, humility."

"I'm not sure I follow that one."

"A person may make the statement that the death penalty is a legitimate form of corporal punishment. A rebuttal would be that people innocent of the crime they were being punished for have been wrongly put to death. If that person had been sentenced to life in prison, their innocence may have been discovered through evidence learned after their conviction. The first person would then say they feel that all murderers deserve to be put to death, don't you agree?"

"That's a leading question."

"It's a leading question designed to cover up the change in the conversation from the legitimacy of the death penalty to how the first person feels about the crime of murder."

"And feelings aren't categorically right or wrong, they are

individual truths so the first person can't be wrong now that he's changed the topic of conversation to how they feel."

"Now you've got it, that was very well done. An aside to that example is that when a government applies the death penalty it is basically throwing up its figurative hands in frustration and saying "what you've done is so wrong that we're going to do it too.""

"That's an irrational reaction."

"That it most certainly is. To go back to people who think their feelings are the truth you should be aware of people who don't listen to the specific words you say but rather choose to get an impression of what you're saying. Their impression of what you are saying is often vaguer than your individually thought out communication. The listener will feel like they understand you but they have simplified what you said to their level of understanding."

"Then they wouldn't really be following what I was saying."

"That's right, and communication with them on that topic will diverge at that point. They'll be talking about how they feel about the topic while you'll be talking about the information that supports your position on the topic. This often leads to disagreements. Nothing has caused more disagreements in relationships between people or countries or religions than poor communication which includes poor listening. Lack of understanding or lack of respect for a different perspective or position often starts with poor communication."

"And communication is both expressing your position and listening to the other person's position."

"Well said, Anoo. People who think listening is choosing to have an impression of what someone is saying often jump to their preferred conclusion with their impression."

"And if they're jumping to their preferred conclusion, they are thinking improperly because they are letting their conclusion weigh more than the concepts leading to that conclusion."

"That's very good, Anoo. People who think their feelings are the truth often say "they speak from their heart." It can be surprising how often people who speak from the heart have to spin their words once they realize what they actually said."

"Spin their words like saying "that isn't what I meant" and then changing what they said?"

"Yes, and then they have to think about what their heart actually meant to say."

"It sounds like it's better to think before you speak,"

"It often is. People who think their feelings are the truth and then realize they were wrong often say that they thought they were right."

"So when they're wrong they were thinking, but when they're right they're feeling?"

"Yes, and that's a common way for people to make the mistake of doing a better job of remembering when they're right than when they're wrong. They deny the error of their feelings by blaming their own thinking."

"And if they accepted that their feelings were wrong, that would be humility."

"That hopefully would cause humility in them which hopefully would cause them to not rush to a conclusion based on their feelings."

"And that's because feelings are individual truths."

"That's right; feelings are much more likely to be based on a person's experiences and value systems than on divine inspiration."

"What does that mean?"

"Some people think their feelings are a truth as valid as divine inspiration but I think everyone's perceptive feelings are filtered through their own value systems and expectations. Perceptive feelings are much more likely to reach a conclusion from an expected list of possibilities than a novel conclusion. The expected list of possibilities of a person who has not intended to develop their individuality will not have the depth necessary to encompass a person who has intended to develop their individuality."

"I think I'll have to think on that for a while, Mateen."

"Well, I'm ready for a sweat, my young friend."

"Me too and I think these rocks are ready."

"So do I, but let me finish with one other example of people to be wary of."

"Okay I'm ready, but my head is pretty full right now."

"Just one more and that is to be wary of people who find truth in generalities."

"What is a generality?"

"A generality is men are like this or women are like that. Fat people are lazy. Asians are good at math. Young male blacks are violent. Blondes are empty-headed. It's categorizing people by type, not looking at them as individuals. The more a person develops their individuality the more they abhor generalizations."

"Isn't that a generalization?"

"Hmm, basically yes, the idea is to not extrapolate. Extrapolate means to take a small amount of data and apply it to a large set or grouping. Just because one fat person is lazy doesn't mean another doesn't have a glandular condition or it doesn't mean thin people can't be lazy."

"If I'm an individual I'll want to be respected as an individual."

"That's right, you won't want to be grouped and then have the effort of your individuality glossed over. You'll respect others' individuality by looking for it in them, not trying to categorize them"

"If I say something specific I won't want it to be grouped into a vague feeling. If I've made the effort to hold an independent perspective I want that effort recognized, not trivialized by lumping me with others based on some aspect of my appearance."

"I am very impressed with you, Anoo, and am delighted to have your company on this journey, both this trip and this life. Let's have a sweat and relax and let our conversation sink into a mind cleared of everything but our awareness."

Mateen and Anoo, using forked sticks, carry the hot rocks over to the frame of the sweat lodge they lashed together out of willow branches. They drop the hot rocks through the frame of the lodge into the shallow depression which Anoo had dug. Anoo places their tarp over the framework and weights it down with unheated rocks. Mateen tears the sage Anoo gathered into different-sized pieces and they both strip down and go into the lodge. Mateen gives a couple larger pieces of sage to Anoo and then sprinkles some smaller pieces on the rocks at the edge of the pile. They quickly began to smoke. Then he sprinkles some water onto the center of the pile of rocks which fills the lodge with steam. The heat of the rocks and the humidity from the water combine with the aroma of the sage inside the lodge. As they break into a sweat they gently slap the larger sage branches against their chest and arms, putting an even stronger smell of sage in the air as the gentle slaps help open their pores. After a few rounds of sage and water they go out of the lodge and feel the cooler air outside on their skin. They pour the cold water from the pots over themselves relishing in the shiver of abrupt temperature change. They go back into the lodge and repeat the whole process. After the second rinse they stand outside and let the breeze cool and dry them. Mateen puts a meal on the remaining coals of their fire and lets it heat up. Neither feels like putting clothes on their freshened skin until after they eat and an evening chill comes to the air. They haven't said a word since their conversation before the sweat. Mateen stretches and Anoo gazes into the fire and then walks to the edge of camp, looking at the colors of the sky. The first stars begin to appear to the east as the colors of the sunset fades. They spread out their bedrolls and gaze at the stars. Sleep comes easily and is deep with intervals of dreams. As a dream rouses one of them the night sky is watched and the area around camp checked with probing senses. All is well and sleep comes again.

Tohlee makes some crisp flat bread in the afternoon and then gets together some of their best wine, a few bags of herbs, some flowers, and a five-pound bag of wheat flour. Eli's dog is with him at Caleb's, so Tohlee's two dogs accompany her on the walk to the neighbors. Tohlee and Eli produce a variety of plant goods. Tohlee grows a variety of medicinal and culinary herbs, flowers, and house plants with a variety of uses. Eli grows many kinds of vegetables, berries, grapes, fruit and nut trees, as well as corn and wheat. Caleb and Laurel have a garden and berry patch as well as some fruit trees in the front yard. That is enough to help feed a family of five, but they don't grow crops at the scale that Tohlee and Eli do. They especially don't grow wheat, corn, and nuts. What they specialize in is dairy cows and pigs. This makes for complimentary production between the neighbors. Dairy products, calves, and piglets go to Tohlee and Eli as corn, wheat, nuts, and herbs go to Caleb and Laurel. Whenever an extra pair of hands is needed each household knows they can count on the other. The walk is about a half-mile and so, very shortly, Laurel's dogs are running down their lane to tumble into a ball with and then go running off with Tohlee's dogs. Laurel greets Tohlee at the door with a big hug and a kiss.

"Hi, Sweetheart, come in."

"Hi, Laurel, I brought some wine and snacks."

"You two should stay for dinner. What a lovely bouquet!"

"Thank you and we'd love to. Let's get these in some water. How's the work going?"

"I took some water out a couple hours ago. They'd finished putting the shelving Caleb had prepared into the shed and did some repairs on the barn roof. They were about to start on repairs to the corral. That's them pounding spikes for the corral. Next time they'll work on the pasture fence. We really appreciate the help. It makes the job more enjoyable and is lots faster."

"We really appreciate the calves and piglets. Where are Timothy and Deirdre?"

"He's helping and she's up the road visiting. She'll be home for supper."

"Have you heard from Matthew?"

"The summer mail has made one turn. We sent letters in early May and just got some back a few days ago. This month's mail just went out."

"How is he doing? This is his third year, isn't it?"

"He's just finished his third year. Then he'll work full-time all summer again. After he graduates he's planning on coming here for a little while."

"That will be nice after four years of not seeing him. Will he be able to stay and work?"

"There's some call for an electrical engineer here, as you know, but I think he likes the city. He's planning on staying here after graduation long enough to see if the power plant and the whole electrical system can be made more efficient. But then he intends to go back and work in the city."

"That will be hard for you."

"It will be, but there's only so much here if you're not devoted to the land."

"Maybe later in his life he'll want to be back in our quiet little town working part-time on the system."

"I'd be delighted if, after gaining experience working for the big plants, he brought a wife here and took over our little plant. I wish the city was a healthier place for him to live."

"What's it like for him? Does he go into much detail in his letters?"

"From a health standpoint my biggest concern is the smoky air."

"I've heard about their inversions and the amount of wood and coal smoke in the air," agrees Tohlee. "What about his day-to-day life?"

"He has three meals a day but they're not even close to extravagant. We eat much better here. For him it's mostly starches with a minimum of meat and vegetables and spices."

"Oh, I forgot about that. Please send some spices to him from me next mailing. I'll bring you some more in a few days."

"Thank you so much for that. He says that's the way about three quarters of the people in the city eat. The other quarter does allright but not any better than we do. His dorm room is heated, but small, and shared by three other boys. They have electricity until 10 P.M. every night and then its lights out for the whole campus. There's electricity during the day for most classrooms but not the dorms, and there's heat during the day for classrooms but not after 8 P.M.

There's usually hot water by the afternoon from solar heat, but it's minimal."

"What about drinking water?"

"There's some in the dorm and the cafeteria. You can't drink the running water. He seldom gets out of the city or even off campus. But on weekends when the weather is good, groups of students will arrange for bikes and pedal out of town."

"It sounds so barely comfortable. And that's the way it is for most people there, not just the food situation?"

"Yes, right in the city. As soon as you're out of the city it's wood heat and wells with minimal electricity."

"So outside the city it's similar conditions to here, but they're in mostly grasslands."

"Besides that, the biggest difference is that the wood is brought in from the mountains and so is costly. The people just outside the city have more land to grow food but they don't eat any better. After obtaining necessities by trading food or other commodities they produce to people in the city, they trade what's left for wood. No one has enough gas for anything but work vehicles. The medical and dental care is better than here and more available for everyone because of the student programs. There is a big library on campus and they do have some computer capability on campus also."

"I think we're much better off here."

"I do too and especially you guys. Eli, and you too, just have such a knack for plant production. I know Eli goes around teaching other people when he can. But there is an intangible something that gives quality and quantity to his produce others have a tough time matching."

"Well, you guys have the same ability with your animals. They're always easy for us to work with and I hear the same thing from others who work with your stock."

"Thank you for that. It's too bad some people even in our little town have a tougher time than we do. We do try to help others with raising stock as you guys do with plant production."

"The biggest bonus to our lives here are the intangibles like freedom and beauty. That's above and beyond our kids, dogs and cats, and a glass of wine."

"I agree. How's Anoo doing, have you heard?"

"We haven't heard. I'm sure everything is fine. Both Eli and I are using this idyllic time of year to avoid dwelling on his absence."

"It is an opportunity for you two to have couple time. And what an amazing adventure it is for him. I think Timothy is envious."

"We're really thankful that Mateen is taking him. It's such an important time for a young person."

"Yes, before the whirlwind of hormones takes control but after individuality has really started to develop. It's interesting how some children can seem so mature and broad in their perspective and then hormones come along and they have to start over."

"I've been thinking that is just as it should be."

"What do you mean?"

"I think the maturity and breadth of perspective in some children isn't truly theirs. I think it is emulation of the parent. Then hormones force the child out of the established perspectives of the parents and into a brave new world of individual development."

"So the disruption caused by hormones is a necessary breakdown of the norm so an individual perspective can be built in its place?"

"I think so, necessary physically and opportunistic individually."

"It is an advantageous time for individual development and yes, necessary because of the depth of emulation children naturally have towards their parents."

"I think also necessary because of the depth of potential in individuality."

"I think it's good you're giving Anoo a line in the sand so to speak. He's on his own from a child-parent perspective and in different surroundings while being exposed to a different perspective, that of Mateen's. I do realize he's been away before."

"Yes, but you're right, not for this long or with the potential for this much change in the focus of who he is or of where his identity comes from. Matthew is having the same opportunity through being away at school."

"I agree, the same potential for growth is there, it is just a little more drawn out from a timeline standpoint. Four years to have a profession and to start one's own life as compared to an event over a few weeks in Anoo's life."

"It is two different methods or opportunities for two different Individuals, each process and individual with their own potential. I guess for Anoo this is more of a ritualistic beginning to his adulthood, a line in the sand as you said. I think it's better than a number like eighteen."

"Caleb and I will have to think of something similar for Timothy and Deirdre."

"The female version could be an interesting twist. But let's have some wine while the men are working."

"That's an excellent idea, Tohlee, you should visit more often."

After a while Caleb, Eli, and Timothy stop work for the day. After cleaning up at the water trough they join Laurel and Tohlee on the porch. Everyone has drinks with Tohlee's crackers and Laurel's cheese for an appetizer. After a bit, Deirdre walks up the lane to the great enjoyment of all the dogs. To everyone's amusement she indulges them by rolling around on the ground with them in a big puppy pile. After greeting everyone she tells them what's going on with the neighbors a few farms up the road where her friend Kirsten lives. Then everyone heads inside for the evening meal.

"Would you be so kind as to give a blessing for us, Eli?"

"I'd be honored, Laurel."

Everyone holds hands around the table with heads slightly bowed in respect and eyes open in awareness of the food before them.

"From the history in the seed, to the blossoms of yesterday, from the fruits before us today, to the energy of life tomorrow, we offer our respect and appreciation."

With a chorus of "To Life!" and a clinking of glasses everyone enjoys a good meal and conversation. After a last drink on the porch and promises to meet again for work, food, and friendship, after Cassie and Jed's visit, Tohlee and Eli return home.

Day Eight

Anoo wakes up, stands, and stretches. He sees Mateen on the ridge where they looked down and saw the buck yesterday. He is standing with his shirt off and his arms outstretched as the first rays of the sun wash over him. Anoo watches the sunlight come down the branches near him until the sun reaches him too. When he looks back Mateen is halfway to camp.

After a light meal that includes fresh strawberries, they ready their packs and set out for a walk. They head about a mile to the south at a good pace and then slow down as they reach a small streamlet. Slowly they follow the streamlet up into a stand of spruce and fir where the streamlet is barely running through shaded moss-covered rocks. As they follow the streamlet farther into the tree stand Mateen starts to point out areas where the moss is flipped over. After they go a little farther they notice hand-sized areas where the moss is turned over every few feet. When they reach a spot where a large subalpine fir tree has fallen across the streamlet they move up the side of the little draw they are in and rest on the trunk of the fallen fir tree near its base.

"What turned over the moss?" asks Anoo.

"It was a black bear."

"How do you know it was a black bear and not a grizzly?"

"There's a possibility it was a grizzly, but I've followed that kind of sign before and found black hairs in the bark of a tree that had fallen like this fir."

"You mean from the bear's belly rubbing against the tree as the bear went over the tree?"

"Yes, and also where one had gone under a tree and rubbed his back up against the tree. There was quite a bit of hair on the tree that time as though the bear had stayed under the tree and rubbed back and forth for a bit. I also caught up to a bear one time while following this kind of sign and it was a cinnamon-colored black bear."

"And black bears can be a bunch of different colors."

"Yes, they can. I've seen them very black, which is their normal color, but I've also seen cinnamon, blond, and some with patches of brown on the legs and then black over the rest of the body. I've also found tracks near the turned over moss and they've always been black bear tracks."

"And how do you know the tracks are from a black bear and not a grizzly?"

"The imprints of the claws where I could see them were close to the imprint of the toe. Grizzlies have longer claws that, when they show, are farther out from the toe."

"And this one is turning over moss looking for creepy crawlies in the wet just like yesterday one had been looking for them under rocks on the dry ridge line."

"That's exactly what I think. Critters like worms and grubs of various kinds."

"Do grizzlies eat that kind of stuff too?"

"They sure do. That's normal bear food at some times of the year. Once I came out into a meadow and found some rocks turned over and soil dug up. I knew it was from a bear. Then I saw where the bear had turned over an entire area about eight feet by sixteen feet. It was roughly a rectangle and the bear had turned the soil over a paw full at a time. The ground was almost worked as well as the garden soil your father prepares for planting."

"How do you know that was a grizzly?"

"I had been looking around the edges of the meadow as soon as I saw the bear sign. On one side of the meadow a little ridge rose up steeply with a bunch of ten-foot-tall alder growing on it. One of the times I checked the area around me I saw a brown spot in the alder I hadn't noticed before. I thought right away it was the head of a bear showing through the top of the alder. I'm sure it had been lying down and then stood up when it realized I was there. I didn't look directly at it because I didn't want to challenge or threaten it. It was less than two hundred yards away and would have been on me in seconds if it charged. I looked at it from the corner of my eye for a few seconds and then looked away. When I looked back a few seconds later it was gone. I couldn't see the alders moving so I knew it wasn't coming towards me very fast at least. I slowly and steadily moved away from it and never saw it again."

"You're sure it was a grizzly?"

"I got a good look at its face when I was looking at it from the corner of my eye and the face was definitely different than a black bear's face. There was much more forehead above the line of the nose than what a black bear shows."

"Do you think we'll see a grizzly?"

"We might, they're up here. There aren't as many as black bears, but we might."

"If it turned over soil like my father does for a garden then does that mean plants would grow well there?"

"Yes it does. Some types of plants like areas where the soil is disturbed. The disturbance allows seeds to get right down into the soil instead of sitting up above the soil on leaf litter."

"So the bear is altering its habitat kind of like a beaver does."

"In a similar way, yes, the bear probably doesn't know what kind of plant will grow there, but its actions will help a variety of different plants. It's kind of like how the process of freezing and thawing of the soil in the springtime helps plants in general."

"How does the ground freezing and thawing help plants? I would think plants don't like frozen soil."

"They don't like ground frozen solid. But in the spring when the soil is thawing there is a period where the soil thaws during the day and then freezes again at night. I don't mean the deep freeze of the winter but up near the surface in the top couple inches of the soil. What do you know about water as it freezes into ice?"

"When water freezes it gets lighter and so floats on water."

"And why is ice lighter than water when ice is water?"

"Umm, I guess because water expands when it freezes into ice."

"That's right, and because ice is expanded water, it is lighter than liquid water."

"Okay, so how does that help plants grow?"

"When the water in soil freezes at night and expands, it pushes the soil apart. Then during the day when the ice melts the soil is left pushed apart. At that time of year, where there is good amounts of organic matter in the soil, you can find places where you can see little furrows in the soil. Those furrows can be a half-an-inch across and an inch deep, sometimes more and sometimes less. I've found places where I could push my finger two inches into the ground and where I left tracks a half-inch deep in soil softened up by the action of water freezing and thawing."

"Why does organic matter help? I know that's little pieces of dead plants and stuff."

"The organic matter holds water up at the top of the soil. If the soil is sandy, the water would run down into the soil."

"You mean beneath where the freeze/thaw is going on?"

"That's what I mean. And why does it help plants to have those little furrows in the soil?"

"Well, like you said, when a seed falls in that furrow it means the seeds are actually in the soil instead of above it."

"That's right, and that means the seed is in more constant contact with water than it would be above the soil. The sun and wind can't dry out the seed or the seedling as fast when it's in the soil compared to just an inch or two away on top of the soil."

"So that's a microclimate like you were talking about with the fawn lily."

"You are a smart guy," says Mateen.

"And the freeze/thaw pattern helps any plant like the grizzly helps any plant when it exposes bare soil. The grizzly isn't planting the plants for future use, it just happens to help plants as it's looking for grubs."

"Well said. Have we had enough of a break?"

"Yes, I'm rested and ready."

"Good, why don't you take us through this stand of trees and then wherever you think we'll find something interesting? But remember which way you're going so you can lead us back to camp."

"Okay, who knows what we might see?"

"Who knows indeed, my friend?"

Anoo leads the way through the spruce/fir stand and down a short steep sagebrush hillside into a stand of aspen. Toward the end of the stand the aspen mix with some large lodgepole pine. Anoo looks up and sees a large nest made of twigs. The twigs are obviously too large for a smaller bird to have flown up into the tree. Some of them are an inch thick and two feet long. He looks down at the ground and sees splotches of bird poop and also downy feathers several inches long. He looks at Mateen who points up the hill. They go about fifty yards from the tree up the hill to where they are just below the height of the nest and find comfortable places to sit.

"What kind of bird do you think made the nest?" asks Anoo.

"A large raptor, but other than that we'll have to wait and see."

"The poop and feathers must mean there are chicks in the nest right now."

"That's right, I'm sure the parents are out hunting. If we wait a little bit I'm sure one will come back and we can see what kind they are."

After waiting a short time they see a head or two show above the edge of the nest. Then a chick some eight inches high jumps up on the edge of the nest. It's half down and half feathered as an adult.

A second bird can be counted now that the first can be fully seen. The first spreads its stubby wings and flaps as the second squawks. After some more activity the chicks go back out of sight in the nest. A short time later an adult lands in a nearby tree and calls. Immediately the chicks jump up on the edge of the nest, squawking repeatedly. The adult flies to the nest and the chicks peck at what looks like a small mouse in the adult's mouth. With some thrusting of its head the adult gets the meal down one of the chicks. The chick that didn't get to eat actively jumps around the adult. After looking around for a few minutes the adult flies away.

"What kind of birds are they?" asks Anoo.

"They're Cooper's hawks."

"It looked like the adult brought a mouse to the chicks."

"I think it was a mouse, too. Coopers will hunt mice and birds and maybe even large insects like grasshoppers in season and animals up to the size of rabbits."

"That makes for a lot of possibilities for a meal."

"It does, they'll focus on what is easiest to catch or most abundant at the time. I think they're very smart birds."

"Do you think they're smarter than other birds?"

"I'm not sure if they're any smarter than other raptors. I say they're smart birds because I had one hanging around my cabin one winter. I put out sunflower heads your father gives me for songbirds in the winter. So there are usually small birds around the cabin. One particular year I saw a Cooper's chase the birds around my yard several different times."

"Did you see it catch any?"

"I saw it catch a couple and miss a couple, too."

"What kind of birds was it after?"

"Any kind of small songbirds like finches, sparrows, chickadees, or goldfinches. One particular day I was out on my porch and there were plenty of songbirds feeding on sunflower seeds. The Cooper's hawk came around the corner of my cabin at full speed right in front of me. It passed ten feet in front of me with a wingtip pointed at the ground and the other at the sky, that's called banking. It was going so fast it had to bank at ninety degrees to make the turn around the cabin. It shot right into the songbirds that had started to scatter as soon as the hawk rounded the cabin. Some of the songbirds flew into a spruce tree right next to where I set up the feeding area. The Coopers went right into the branches of the tree after those birds. The songbirds went flying out the other side of the spruce and got away as the Cooper's was jumping through the branches trying to get to the other side of the tree so it could fly again."

"So the little birds got through the spruce tree faster than the big bird?"

"That's right."

"That sounds like the little birds were smarter than the big bird."

"They're smart too for choosing to eat where they had an escape route available to them, which is one reason I put the sunflower heads where I do."

"Why else do you put them there?"

"So they're nice and close to me which gives me a good view of the birds when they feed."

"And why does all that mean that Cooper's are smart birds?"

"It's because of the speed and direction of the Cooper's attack. I think that because the Cooper's attack was so fast and accurate it must have set up its attack ahead of time. First its attention would have been attracted to the small bird activity around my back porch. It may have made a couple of poorly executed attacks on the birds as a learning experience other days. Then I think it learned the area of my backyard enough to know it could come unseen around my cabin at speed and be in the middle of the birds in an instant. It would have waited and watched from a nearby tree until there was a lot of activity at the sunflower heads. Then, leaving its perch in a way that wouldn't disturb the songbirds, it built up speed and shot around my cabin directly into the flock of birds. It didn't get a bird that time but the next day it might have."

"So you think it thought ahead, planning its attack to its best advantage, and waited for the best time to make its attack?"

"That's what I think."

"Okay, I can see how that's smart. That's what people do too when they hunt."

"That's right; the best hunters don't just wander around, hoping to bump into prey. The best hunters use past experience and knowledge of their prey to put themselves in the most advantageous position to make a kill."

"It is smart to learn about one's prey and plan ahead," agrees Anoo.

"And the actions of those smart predators change the behavior of their prey. The songbirds knew they wanted an escape route available as they fed. Prey animals know that feeding and going to water are more hazardous activities than resting in a thicket. Have you seen flocks of small birds jump up and fly away to shelter a half-a-dozen times for no apparent reason as they feed?"

"Yes, pretty commonly."

"Don't look at them as overly nervous or silly. Another bird that wants to kill and eat them can be on them in an instant as they are out in the open feeding."

"And that bird can be one that is smart enough to think ahead about the best way to kill and eat them."

"That's right, why don't you quietly take us up the hill away from the nest and loop us around back to camp? I always prefer to circle around rather than just go back the way I already walked."

This time circling back to camp doesn't show the hikers anything out of the ordinary. But the odds of an interesting sighting go up whenever a new route is taken compared to retracing one's steps. After arriving back at camp Mateen and Anoo eat the food they had taken with them and then Mateen settles in for a nap as Anoo quietly relaxes around camp.

Tohlee and Eli are up at their normal daybreak. Besides her usual morning chores, Tohlee finishes readying the house and preparing food for Cassie and Jed's visit. Eli now has the addition of two calves and three piglets to care for this morning. The calves are easy to feed as they are just moved to different spots around the house and in the orchard as they mow down the grass. A water bucket is moved around with them. Their manure is shoveled up and added to the manure pile. This is a daily chore of Eli's along with the horses, chickens, and turkeys' contributions.

Every year he starts a new pile. As he needs fertilizer for the various gardens, fields, and orchards he digs into the oldest pile. He makes sure he uses manure that is at least three years old. That way the undigested seeds in the manure will have had time to sprout in the warmth of the manure pile and so not sprout in his worked soil. Also, the high nitrogen content in the bird manure is evened out with the other animals' manure. The daily compost from the house, vegetables going soft in the root cellar, as well as trimmings from the gardens mostly go to the piglets. The leafiest trimmings go to the chickens and turkeys. As the growing season progresses, there will be more and more trimmings available for the fast growing pigs.

A little before noon Cassie and Jed ride up on their sturdy three-speed bikes. They are greeted with much enthusiasm by the dogs after they make sure the visitors are known to them. First there is a little settling in and then some lunch. After lunch Jed helps Eli with some light work as Cassie does the same with Tohlee. After a few hours everyone gets back together to walk down to the swimming hole. After a swim and warming in the sun Tohlee and Eli's pattern of making love in the afternoon sun gets the better of them. They excuse themselves and go down to the end of the gravel bar. Their often quiet meditative joining is replaced by physical pleasuring due to their unavoidable audience. After a short time pretending not to notice the coupling just down the bar Cassie and Jed decide it is indeed a wonderful way to enjoy the beautiful afternoon. Afterwards a nap and then a quick swim are in order for all. Back at the house they all decide it is time for wine and appetizers.

After his nap Mateen sees that Anoo has been busy. He has gathered more firewood and water as well as more mint and sage. He also wandered around until he found some onions and then cut some willows that will be rigged for fishing.

"Let's go cut some more willows."

"Sure, Mateen, what will we use them for?"

"We're going to dig two small trenches with our trowel that we brought for digging poop holes. Each trench will be about a foot long, a couple-inches wide, and about four-inches deep. We'll put the fat ends of the willows we cut into the trench at a little bit of a backwards angle and tamp dirt in around them. Then we'll each need two branches about two-inches around and about two-feet long. Those will be lashed together with another branch almost two-feet long and not quite as thick as the two other pieces. Lashed together they'll look pretty much like a U. The open end of the U we'll bury a couple inches in the ground a couple feet back from the willows. The closed end of the U we'll lash to the willows."

"We're making chairs."

"Or backrests, but yes, that's right."

"What should we actually sit on - just the ground?"

"Do you want to sit right on the ground?"

"I guess I'd rather sit on something softer and warmer."

"And what might that be?"

"A shirt would work, but it would get dirty and damp. Small needle-covered fir branches would work. But I guess they'd have sap on them. What about some dried grass?"

"I think that's a good solution to the problem."

After cutting the willows and thicker branches the holes are dug and everything is lashed together and secured in the ground. The ground of the seat is cleared, smoothed, and loosened up with the trowel before being covered with several inches of dry grass. Only about an hour has passed when Mateen and Anoo sit down on their grass cushions and lean back against their willow rests.

"Let's talk about dreams and sleeping," says Mateen.

"Okay, I'm thinking you have something particular in mind? Not just about having a dream?"

"You're right, I'm thinking of a few different areas of dreaming. Most dreams are entirely visual and when there is talking there doesn't seem to be sounds coming into the physical ears."

"That's because dreams are happening inside the head."

"And when awake the ears hear another person talking, but it's the brain that interprets the sounds that are heard as language with meaning."

"So when a person is dreaming they are not hearing words with their ears, they are hearing from where the sounds from talking become words with meanings."

"That's very good," says Mateen. "The same thing happens with the visual side of dreams."

"Because a person sees things in dreams but they have their eyes closed."

"That's right, and when awake the same process is followed for sensations from the skin, smells, and taste. There are stimuli from outside the body onto the body and the mind interprets those stimuli. It is the mind's interpretations of those stimuli that create our version of everything around us. So if the process is the same, why don't people feel sensations on their skin, smell, and taste in dreams?"

"I guess I don't know, but it seems like they should be able to."

"Well I've felt sensations on my skin, smelled, and heard sounds other than words in my dreams."

"Were they just parts of regular dreams?"

"No, they were parts of dreams that were more intense or memorable than regular dreams. When I've heard sounds other than words and smelled in my dreams, I've always woken up wide awake when it happened. When I've felt sensations on my skin it didn't cause me to wake up, but it did cause me to be aware that I was in a dream and so the dream was very real to me."

"What do you mean by being aware that you were in a dream?"

"It's like when I've flown during a dream."

"Flown like a bird?"

"I guess it would be similar from a sensation standpoint, but without wings. Sometimes when I realize I'm flying, I realize I'm dreaming, but I don't wake up."

"Like if you're flying you must be dreaming, but if you're talking to someone how would you know if you're awake or asleep?"

"That's a good thought. I've realized I was dreaming as I was flying, I've felt myself leave the ground and fly, and I've decided I wanted to fly and made myself take off."

"How did you do that?"

"I kind of jump and then try and feel myself moving. I sort of remember what I felt when I realized I was flying in other dreams. For practice and familiarity I've gone back to the ground and lifted off repeatedly. I've even jumped and gotten off the ground and then kind of dropped back down to the ground chest first and pushed off the ground with my hands and moved back up into the air a few times before I really got going."

"What did it feel like?"

"It felt like there was a world around me that I was above and it was ending up behind me because I was moving forward. Sometimes I've gone slow and watched things go by and other times I seem to have a destination and I don't pay attention to what's going by me, but about where I want to be. If I get going too fast and everything around me blurs, I often end up losing my awareness that I'm in a dream. Then the dream becomes just any old dream that I don't remember."

"And you don't get to find out where you were going so fast?"

"That's right, and I think it would be very interesting if I could do a better job of keeping my awareness of being in a dream while flying fast and so realizing where I wanted to get to. I've also skimmed over the ground with both my feet held steady like I had run and was sliding on ice. Then I stopped and started again so I could get comfortable with the feeling. I chose to slide over water so I could feel the texture of what I was on change and how I had to adjust my weight pushing down so I skimmed on the water instead of sinking in it."

"So being aware you're in a dream can be learned or developed?"

"I think so. One of the ways I've tried is to reinforce the dream after I wake up. I try and remember details of the dream or bring the dream fully into my conscious mind by being able to put the dream into words. I also try to remember the feeling of enjoyment I have when I'm flying."

"What else do you try to do?"

"When I realize I'm in a dream, I try to act by my own choice or with intent."

"You mean if you're flying or not?"

"Yes, any dream. Lots of times when I do, the same thing happens to me as when I fly too fast."

"You lose the dream you're in and kind of go back to sleep?"

"Yes, but other times the dream gets more vivid and it seems like it's as real as my waking life. Then I try and lengthen the dream. Not just see a scene, but walk a few feet in different directions and so watch the scene from different perspectives."

"Your dreams can be every bit as real as when you're wide awake?"

"Yes, every bit as real. Sometimes I have trouble determining if something happened when I was awake or asleep. When I can be in a dream and lengthen it, or choose to act in it, make it clearer, I wake refreshed and whole. A few times I've felt like I was in a dream and the people in it were having the same dream I was. One time I thought I was in someone else's dream and I turned to him and said "Hello, Bill." Bill turned to me with a very surprised look on his face."

"What happened then?"

"I think that I so surprised him that he woke up because all of a sudden the dream turned off. I woke up myself, remembered what had happened in the dream, then went back to sleep."

"That would mean the dream really happened then. I mean, if you both had the same dream and both woke up from the same dream."

"It would have been a shared experience, but I've never run into Bill since then to see if he did have the same experience. I've also had 'out-of-the-body experiences'."

"What does that mean?"

"Sometimes it's when you perceive the known physical world but in a place where your body isn't. It can refer to being in a dream where you see someone you know and then you verify with them that they were doing what you saw them doing when you were sleeping. Or you can go someplace in your dream that you've never been to and then go there physically and compare the two perspectives. An out-of-the-body experience doesn't have to take place on a physical part of the earth, it can be one of those strange dream places, but you become so aware that you're there that your surroundings become as real to you as a place on Earth."

"Does it matter what the person was doing when you verify their actions with them?"

"Not if you can tell them what it was and they can remember it. I've realized that I was in a dream and I was in my own bedroom. I floated up to the ceiling and moved through it and sat on my roof. Everything I saw around me was what I see when I'm awake, except I was seeing it from my roof."

"So that really happened? I mean, you were dreaming but aware of what was happening outside your cabin the same as if you had been awake?"

"It seemed like it. But there is a difference there than if I had verified what was happening with someone else. There is the possibility I was just remembering in the dream. I know what my front yard looks like, even from the roof. I've been up there doing repair work and looked around. Also nothing happened that I could wake up, go outside, and verify. All I saw was the plants that are in my yard."

"Have you ever thought what was in your dream was happening to waking people, and then told them and had them verify your dream?"

"I never have. But a fellow named Robert A. Monroe wrote some books about his out-of-body experiences and he did verify some of his experiences with other people. He wrote his books even though he was ridiculed by some people because they thought he wasn't telling the truth or was just dreaming the way most people consider dreaming."

"Do you mean how dreaming seems to have no connection to the world we know when we're awake?"

"Yes, as though we're separated between our waking and sleeping selves, or the dream is so symbolized that it may have meaning based on our waking life, but the actual circumstances of the dream are nothing that can be directly seen in our waking life."

"It's too bad Mr. Monroe was ridiculed just for telling people about what was happening to him."

"Yes it is. He wrote his books so that if other people had the same experiences, they wouldn't be afraid to develop them or try to verify them. They would know others have had the same experiences and be comforted. They would know that those experiences are known to be within the realm of a human's potential. And that's why I am telling you about my experiences."

"Thank you, Mateen."

"I've also had the same dream multiple times."

"Do you mean on the same night?"

"I mean on different nights. Although I have woken up, remembered the dream I was having, fallen back asleep and returned to the same dream."

"When you have the same dream on another night, is it because the dream is really important for you?"

"Those dreams haven't seemed to be any more important than other dreams. They do create an opportunity to become aware you're in a dream while you're dreaming though. There is something about remembering as you're dreaming that causes awareness of what you're doing."

"There sure can be a lot more to dreaming than just having a dream."

"Yes there can. Sometimes the dreams I remember with the most detail are the ones that are the brightest."

"The brightest like sunlight?"

"There is brightness to the dream, but the source of that brightness is not above like the sun. It seems to come from all around. When I have dreams that are brighter than others, more detailed, out-of-body experiences, or when I remember dreams well, I always feel more rested when I wake up than when I'm not aware of my dreams."

"You mentioned that before and I didn't follow up on it. But that's kind of odd. That you're more rested from dreams where you're the most aware, the most awake."

"It is odd and wonderful. When I awake from those dreams I bring the clarity of my awareness during those dreams into my waking life. Let your dreams, imagination, and self be free, Anoo. Live your life with integrity, honesty, and awareness of the consequences of your actions. If you do, you'll create a base to your life you can explore from, create from, change your perspective from, and change your capabilities from."

"Can you give some examples of living with integrity and honesty?" asks Anoo.

"An example of living with integrity would be to only take credit for what you deserve, not for what you don't. Even if you think you were somehow slighted in the past and so are overdue for credit. For honesty one can speak honestly, for example, to straighten out a past deception. In which case the honesty will hurt or have negative repercussions. It is not honest to say that the sky is blue because of the absence of negative repercussions. The sky is blue is a true statement. It is telling the truth. Being honest is an effort or action, not a statement. Living your life with honesty is to live it in a way that will not cause you to be open to the reproach or hurt, of having to be honest after the fact."

"Be honest now or it will hurt later," says Anoo.

"Honesty is a burden only when it is used in hindsight. When it is lived in the moment, it is a clear, shining light," says Mateen.

"What is living in the moment?"

"It can be the quiet awareness of stalking through the woods. It can also be the living of your own perspective and value systems. It is not reinterpreting the past or predicting the future. It is determining the present through the value systems you have chosen and taken responsibility for."

After everyone returns from the swimming hole Eli gets out a cask of wine as Jed sets some Adirondack chairs and a couple small tables out by the fire pit. Tohlee and Cassie get some snacks together and after a few minutes they all gather at the fire pit.

"I think your wine gets better every year, Eli."

"Thanks, Cassie, I keep refining my technique but I'm sure I'm missing details."

"You mean details like how long to leave it in the cask?"

"From that all the way back to if the vines need extra water and when and how long to keep the grapes on the vine. The sort of decisions I make every year. But I think I need more experience to adjust my decisions to the weather of that particular year to bring out the best in my grapes."

"That would make for a fun, but long term, experiment," says Cassie.

"It sounds like you need to develop the intuition of a master vintner," says Jed.

"It does, it would have been a real advantage to a novice like me if more vintners had written about the details of their expertise."

"The kind of experience that is usually passed from master to novice directly in the field," says Tohlee.

"That experience is too often kept private or as intuition as Jed said. Being able to communicate one's perspective by the written word can benefit more people. Not everyone is in a position to live an apprenticeship."

"I'll keep my eyes open at the library for a book that might help you."

"It would be a great help to me if you could find something, Cassie."

"I can make some inquiries. Have you read the book Jed gave you?"

"I've read parts of it. I especially like the perspective on the organization named Christianity."

"Which ideas in particular, Eli?" asks Jed.

"There were quite a few. I thought an important one was the way the Bible has gone through many different translations and versions over centuries. The faithful consider all those human-caused variations to have been accomplished through the divinity of an all powerful being."

"So they can validate their belief that Christianity is the one true religion and the Bible is the written word of that religion," says Jed.

"That's seems an odd belief to put faith in when even the disciples didn't agree on how to interpret the teachings of Jesus of Nazareth," said Tohlee.

"And as far as we know Jesus never told them that understanding him required that they agree among themselves. It would seem individual application of his teachings was expected," says Eli.

"Many Christians have focused on the perspective of Paul as the one that appeals to them the most," says Cassie.

"I think that's where the idea of worshipping Jesus instead of living his teachings comes from," says Eli

"Jesus never said to worship him," adds Tohlee

"Christians who have chosen to follow the teachings of Paul towards Jesus of Nazareth should be called Paulians. Because they've chosen the perspective of Paul towards Jesus of Nazareth over applying the teachings of Jesus to their lives," says Jed.

"Most Christians don't even think about the teachings of Jesus of Nazareth, they focus on his birth and death instead," says Tohlee.

"Which brings up another point I liked," says Eli, "and that is that many Christians say you can't pick and choose the parts of Christianity or the Bible that appeal to you. If you don't accept the whole religion and the whole book it's based on, you aren't living the truth."

"And yet many Christians choose to accentuate specific parts of the Bible that appeal to their predetermined perspective. John 3:16 is a good example. Many Christians point to that one section as the one basic truth Christianity stands on," says Cassie.

"It's a small section in one of the Gospels. Did the other Gospel writers not consider it important or was Jesus telling secrets to one disciple?" wonders Jed.

"And why is that one section, which carries so much truth for some Christians, written by a narrator and not shown as an actual quote from Jesus the Christ?" wonders Cassie. "Who actually wrote it?"

"So the concept of Divine Intervention during the various translations and versions of the Bible doesn't end there. It must be extended to the various focuses on and avoidances of particular Biblical teachings adopted by some sects of Christianity. If their version of Christianity is to maintain the status of the one true religion for all of humanity," says Eli.

"No sect of Christianity is following all of the aspects of the different disciples' perspectives on Jesus of Nazareth because their Bible doesn't even include all the Gospels," says Cassie, "someone chose one disciple's version over another."

"That was done at the Council of Nicea held by the Emperor Constantine." says Eli. "The gospels chosen by people at the council to be in the Bible were the ones that most supported the belief of the divinity of Jesus of Nazareth which was supported by the hierarchical church. Some of the gospels excluded from the Bible, like Mary Magdalene's and Thomas's, supported the perspective that one should seek God within their individual self. That learning and knowledge could bring one closer to a godlike state of being."

"If God is found within your individual self, then the hierarchy of a church is not necessary for an individual to bring himself to God," says Jed.

"The hierarchical church in an effort to protect its own hierarchy convinced the Emperor Constantine that the Gnostic perspective of seeking individual truth was in error," says Eli.

"And of course that appealed to an emperor who was at the height of his own hierarchy," says Jed. "Constantine was an emperor who wanted conformity in religion so there would be conformity in the society he ruled."

"The Gnostic perspective of finding God through individual truth then became what the hierarchical church was against," says Eli.

"The hierarchy of the church became its own truth over time," says Jed.

"The Catholic Church in particular tortured in God's name, turned a blind eye to genocide, and covered up for child-molesting priests," says Eli.

"The hierarchy believes its own power can overcome any barrier, including its own ignorance. To put it another way, the hierarchy believed its own power could overcome its unchristian behavior," says Cassie.

"When the hierarchy is the truth, protecting the image of the hierarchy becomes more important even than the welfare of children," says Jed.

"As bad as all hierarchies are, the worst ones decide the top of the hierarchy is more godlike than the lower rungs as compared to hierarchies that just see the top as more correct," says Tohlee.

"The people higher up in hierarchies always fall victim to the concept of absolute power corrupts absolutely by deciding that the structure of the hierarchy has more significance than the actions of the people who comprise the hierarchy," says Cassie.

"A hierarchical church's version of Christianity can be shown to be skewed from the teachings of Jesus of Nazareth by looking at how little of Christianity is connected to his teachings and how much of Christianity has been determined by people well after his death," says Eli.

"That's why I say I have a problem with Christianity but not with Jesus of Nazareth," says Jed.

"The hierarchical church's version of Christianity is more focused on being a sheep in a flock than on individual application of the teachings of Jesus," says Tohlee.

"A flock that pays dues to belong to a congregation," says Cassie.

"A flock that has a person as a leader and a building that is holier than where one lives their everyday life," says Jed.

"Even though Jesus himself didn't go to church and said that any place two believers come together is a church," says Tohlee.

"The kingdom of God is inside you and all around you, not in buildings of wood and stone. Split a piece of wood and you will find me, turn over the stone and I'll be there, said Jesus in the Gospel according to Thomas," says Cassie.

"The tolerance and benevolence directed at fellow humans necessitated by embracing the concept of freedom of religion on an individual level is more Christian than arguing, debating, or being in a quandary about the correctness of one dogma or doctrine over another," says Jed.

"I think that anyone who puts a person, be they named pastor, preacher, priest, guru, imam, pope; or anyone who puts a book, be it titled Bible, Koran, Talmud, Bhagavad-Gita; or anyone who puts a building labeled church, temple, mosque, between themselves and God, worships a false idol," says Eli.

"That's a strong statement," says Jed.

"It is, and there is a matter of degree involved," says Eli.

"One person's false idol is another's lack of faith in themselves or lack of desire to break from the flock," says Tohlee.

"And when an individual acquires a new truth, the source of that truth, be it experience, person, or book, is only the source of one piece of the greater truth the individual is building," finishes Eli.

"The source of the information that is used to build individual truth is just that, a source, not the truth itself," says Cassie.

"The truth is not an item to be acquired, but a relationship to be built," says Tohlee.

"That's what I'm saying," says Eli. "Truth is a process to be built and that is why I consider the tolerances built into this country's constitution to be a greater source of truth than any particular written document, or person, or building."

"Because it opens up the freedom to learn individually and find individual truth," says Tohlee. "And one's connection to God should be individual because the connection is inside oneself, not outside. That's why even hierarchical religions pray inwardly."

"Hierarchical religions need to bring the source of their believers' truth out from the individual so that people can be caused to flock around something," says Jed. "People can't flock around their individual connection to God."

"If people weren't caused to flock around symbols like books, beads, altars, crosses, buildings, or titles of people in a hierarchy, what then would organized religion stand on?" says Tohlee.

"The power of forgiving a person of their sins," says Jed.

"Giving forgiveness to an organization causes forgiveness to be a reward from the hierarchy. If life is lived with an awareness of the God within, forgiveness is not a power that can be held over an individual. That is the difference between being atoned by an authority figure and living at one with God, living in at-one-ment," says Eli. "I'd rather be judged in heaven than rewarded with forgiveness by a symbol of authority on Earth."

"If people didn't flock, organized religions couldn't collect enough dues to support their clubs," says Cassie.

"Organized religions need a clubhouse for their members to flock to once a week or the flock won't pay dues to their club," says Tohlee.

"The bigger the flock, the greater the conformity in the religion and the more diluted the truth, from my perspective," says Eli.

"The greater the conformity the greater the need to force people into a group through the threat of punishment and the promise of forgiveness," says Tohlee.

"What a vicious circle," says Cassie.

"Where would Christianity be without its devil and its organization?" says Eli.

"It would be made up of the teachings of Jesus of Nazareth, not the constructs of people who came after him," says Jed.

"Constructs like worshipping Jesus of Nazareth and belief in the Virgin birth," says Cassie.

"Both are cases of people creating tenets of Christianity instead of focusing on the teachings of Jesus," says Eli in support.

"Rally around the Cross, boys, and worship your Savior," says Tohlee sarcastically.

"Humanity was supposed to need saving from the condition of original sin," says Cassie.

"God is the source of all there is including original sin. Original sin is the awareness of good and evil," says Eli. "An awareness that was ultimately created by God and then that burden was lifted from humanity by Jesus of Nazareth."

"Do we then worship our Deliverer or live our lives beyond good and evil where the gift of Jesus of Nazareth has brought humanity?" asks Jed.

"The hierarchical church says worship your Deliverer but the Deliverer did not say to worship him," says Cassie.

"The hierarchical church has tortured in God's name, started wars in God's name, turned a blind eye to genocide in God's name, and turned a blind eye to child molesters for the sake of its own hierarchy," says Eli. "I would rather use the religious freedom granted to the individual citizens of this country by this country's constitution to create my own religion than follow a religion established by other people in the name of Jesus of Nazareth. A religion established by people who then believe that the religion they have created in the name of Jesus of Nazareth will exonerate them from the atrocities they commit themselves or choose not to notice as others commit them."

"In the book that I read the hierarchical church also chose to have the book of Revelation included in the Bible," says Jed. "The followers of the hierarchical church then, in our recent past, helped create the problems that beset humanity by actually thinking that Armageddon was something good and wanting it to happen."

"They actually thought that plagues and war that killed a billion people so that supposedly 50,000 could live with Jesus was an appropriate application of the concepts Jesus promoted to love your fellow man and to live in peace with your fellow man," says Eli.

"I think the Book of Revelation is a book of evil," says Jed "because what happens to humanity in the book is so opposite of the teachings of Jesus of Nazareth. Yet, according to the hierarchical Christian church what happens in the book is considered to be necessary for Jesus to live with humanity. Well, I think the idea of an exclusive Jesus of Nazareth, one who excludes the majority of humanity through famine, plague, and war, is a corruption of his inclusive 'love your fellow man'."

"A corruption that deserves the term evil," says Cassie.

"The idea of 50,000 people living with Jesus after Armageddon was made up by some guy in the 1850's and he named it 'The Rapture'. Then an entire branch of Christianity adopted the idea as their own and made it a basic tenet of their religion," says Jed.

"People have a real ability to use time to pretend a human concept is God's truth," says Cassie.

"I'd rather create and be responsible for my own destiny than live the destiny for humanity the hierarchical church has included in its version of the Bible," says Eli.

"When we live our own individual religion and strive to be the creators of our own perspective and destiny, we are entirely counter to the hierarchical church," says Tohlee, "because we are completely out of their realm."

"That is how they set up their own rules," says Eli. "Truth, good, being right is following an organized church's hierarchy while being false, evil, and wrong is precipitated by self-determination and finding God for and within oneself."

"If violence and destruction are not caused by the devil, but are actions of individual responsibility, the concept of being contrary to the hierarchical church becomes a difference in value systems, not the difference between good and evil," says Jed.

"So how did you set up your own religion, Eli?" asks Cassie.

"Let's get into that after dinner," says Tohlee. "Cassie and I will get the food ready while you guys start a fire for a moonlight sweat."

After their talk Mateen and Anoo decide to catch fish for tomorrow's breakfast rather than for dinner. They eat more of the food they brought with them and then clean up camp. The sun is just starting to set as Mateen says he will stay around camp for the evening. Anoo decides to find a place to sit looking over the nearby valley and stream. He chooses a place that gives him a good view but also hides the small movements he makes while getting comfortable from the eyes of the wildlife he wants to watch.

He sits with his eyes closed at times. Other times he looks into the valley. At all times he is meditatively quiet in his mind. He is surprised when he sees a doe and fawn out in the middle of an opening without having noticed them as soon as they had come into the open. He thinks about it and decides that he didn't miss them but that they must have just stood up. He notices a fox out of the corner of his eye as soon as it comes into sight from behind a large patch of willows and watches as the fox hunts its way downstream. He watches bees on flowers right in front of him and songbirds flitting from one shrub to another along the stream. He notices the movement of a small pine and watches until a porcupine shows itself. The movement caught his eye because it couldn't have been caused by the light breeze that is starting to move down valley. Whenever his legs or back get a little stiff he dips his head down below the low shrubs in front of him and lies on the ground. Then he moves his legs and arms around to get the blood flowing. As he does this he makes sure his movements don't show above the low shrubs. Toward dusk he watches two bull elk come over the hill and drop down to water and then graze in the thick riparian grasses. The sun sets behind him as the first stars and Venus show in the darkening sky. He listens to a pair of coyotes howling the start of the males evening hunt with the accompanying excited yaps of their pups. Anoo turns and sees that Mateen has the fire going. He gets up and goes toward the fire for a sweat and then some stargazing. He and Mateen will end up falling asleep out under the stars without having said a word.

The sun is lowering in the sky after the couples finish their meal and clean up. Rocks are heating in the fire for a moonlight sweat. Everyone settles in around the fire with glasses of wine as Eli starts up their conversation where they had left off.

"I decided that a religion contained three parts, Cassie; a code of ethics, values and or beliefs, and a perspective on a supreme being. The code of ethics was quick and simple to start. Do unto others as you would have them do to you. Most importantly, that eliminates physical violence."

"It covers all the "thou shalt not" in the Bible in one statement," says Tohlee.

"It's a very simple and powerful code that even now way too many people aren't physically comfortable enough or developed enough as individuals to live," says Eli.

"It's too bad people have to wait until after death to have their actions judged," says Cassie. "Instant karma would be so much more effective in creating good behavior. Can you imagine how quickly people's behavior would change if for every hurt they caused they were the ones who felt the pain?"

"Like Arthur C. Clarke's example in "Childhood's End," says Eli. "If everyone who went to a bull fight for entertainment felt the sword in the heart like the bull does, who would go back for a second round of that form of entertainment?"

"Who would find benefit in a physical fight if they felt the hurt back on themselves that they were causing others?" asks Jed.

"What country would send out its military if the same death and destruction they caused happened equally in their own nation?" asks Tohlee.

"Or find righteousness and heroism in military conflict if what they caused happened equally in their own country?" adds Eli.

"Instant karma would take the intervention of a higher power," says Cassie.

"Humanity's history is too full of war and self-destruction for us to wait for or to expect a higher power to intervene in our affairs," says Eli.

"We have to be our own higher power as individuals and as societies," says Cassie.

"We humans have to teach ourselves how to be humane," says Jed. "We got off on an interesting tack there Eli, but please go on."

"There are exceptions to 'do unto others' like when someone has already not kept that rule with you, say, by breaking into and entering your home," says Eli.

"But it's a rule that when everyone really makes an effort to follow, people's day-to-day circumstances change enormously toward the better," says Tohlee.

"That's right, it's a broad generalized statement that avoids the need of writing a Talmud-like book about specific circumstances," says Eli. "My perspective on a supreme being is that when God created humans he created…"

"She!" says Tohlee.

"Okay, she, but the use of he was just a conversational convenience. When she created humans she created us in her image and then gave humans dominion over all life on Earth. I believe the image of God that God made humans into is that of a self-determinate being and dominion over life on Earth means responsibility for life on Earth."

"So the image is a potential, not a form like being two-legged," says Cassie.

"Self-determination, by definition, can't exist while acting out a part in another's plan," says Tohlee.

"Yes, and that takes away the complications that arise from looking at ourselves as beings on Earth that are subservient to an all powerful master," says Eli.

"You mean the complications that are explained away by

hierarchical religions with the flippant statement that God works in mysterious ways?" says Jed.

"Yes, all the complications like why does God allow wars or sickness? Why does God allow natural disasters like hurricanes or earthquakes? Why does God allow people to hurt others?"

"It's because we live God's gift of self-determination to us when we are responsible for ourselves and when we create our own destiny and circumstance," says Tohlee.

"That's right, we can't be self-determinate beings while God is protecting us from Earth's processes or from ourselves. And that leaves the values and/or beliefs portion of creating a religion. I found that the most challenging. Not because of the difficulty, but because of the sheer numbers of examples of values and beliefs that I have."

"What about faith?" asks Cassie.

"Faith and belief run through the whole structure of the religion. I believe that doing unto others will create a society that is positive and beneficial to all. I have faith that individuals applying the concept of doing unto others in their individual lives will cause that behavior to spread throughout humanity. I believe God created humans in her image and I have faith that humans can live that gift in a way that will honor the giver. I believe it is better to have a structure built on learning to base feelings on than it is to use feelings to try and overcome one's ignorance. I believe it is better to communicate with others and learn of their circumstance before using feelings to make determinations of their character. I have faith that God gave us all that we need to successfully accomplish all we have been put on Earth to accomplish, both as individuals and as a species."

"What you don't have faith in is the need for Jesus of Nazareth to save people from themselves or from God's gift of life to them," says Tohlee.

"I believe that seeking salvation from an entity or hierarchy, rather than living one's life in a way that doesn't require salvation, corrupts the gift Jesus of Nazareth gave humanity when he took away original sin from humanity while on the Cross," says Eli.

"I believe that God's truth is lived through individuality and that grouping in commonality limits an individual's potential," says Tohlee.

"I believe that all religions are cultural variations of humanity's truth and that there is no one true religion for all the different societies and individuals on Earth," says Jed.

"I believe that all humans will be given the gift of judgment in the afterlife," says Cassie.

"I believe that a God that would punish an infant in any way because the child's parents did not put the child in a ceremony is not a just God," says Eli.

"I believe that the concept of punishment from God on an individual for actions taken while learning how to develop an independent perspective and value system is a myth. A myth created by established religion's drive to increase its flock through fear, not fact-based on the actions of God towards an individual," says Jed.

"As long as the actions are within the bounds of the Golden Rule and non-violence," emphasizes Cassie.

"I believe that the concepts of angels in Christianity, the ancestors in Eastern philosophy, and the spirit guides of Native Americans, are different societies' perspectives on similar phenomena," says Tohlee.

"I value the creation and living of one's own religion over the adoption of a hierarchical religion," says Eli.

"So, saying one holds a particular value is the same as saying one believes in that value?" asks Cassie. "And saying one values one concept over another indicates faith in that concept?"

"That's the way I see things, Cassie. We're talking about individual values, not laws of physics," says Eli.

"In that case," states Cassie, "I believe that choosing to create and live one's own religion is a better choice to make than to choose to give the responsibility for one's own religion to an established construct."

"I believe it is better to put one's faith in one's self than to put faith in the values or decisions of other humans," says Eli.

"I believe it's better to make one's own mistakes than to avoid choice by choosing to belong to a club," says Cassie.

"I hold the value that individuals are responsible for their own decisions including the decision to let another decide something for them," says Jed.

"I hold the value that the questions whose answers are most able to create an independent perspective have been put into religion and glossed over by the hierarchies of those religions," says Tohlee.

"I hold the value that bringing rationality into religion creates a stronger base for belief than mindless obedience and blind faith," says Cassie.

"I hold the value that individuals have made discoveries of greater benefit to humanity than the accomplishments of people en masse," says Eli.

"I believe that the accomplishments of people en masse couldn't have occurred without individuals to organize them and individuals to direct the group's methodology to accomplish their task," says Jed.

"I believe that it's better to act in life than to react to life," says Cassie.

"I believe that it is better to take responsibility for one's feelings than to consider the world around oneself as the source of one's feelings," says Tohlee.

"I hold the value that one's feelings are more the result of individual experience and the values one holds than the result of an unbiased interpretation of what is happening around oneself," says Eli.

"I believe that when one passes judgment on another that one is saying more about their own values and character than about the one they are passing judgment on," says Cassie.

"I believe that a person's feelings when used to judge others are based on their own experiences and value systems, not divine inspiration," says Jed.

"I believe that using feelings as a base for negative criticisms is a coarse and ugly level of functioning," says Tohlee.

"I hold the value that one can legitimately tear down an existing philosophical construct if one can build a replacement of similar or greater breadth," says Jed.

"I believe that more personal development comes from looking at the source of evil as individual humans than comes from looking at the source of evil as coming from a deity," says Eli.

"I believe that the split between body and soul, heart and mind, and reason and feeling, is socially accepted schizophrenia," says Tohlee, "and that those splits need to be joined in order for an individual to achieve their human potential."

"I believe that one should never trust a wise man who can't dance."

"I believe that we should get the instruments out and have a moon dance and then a sweat before another moon dance and then another sweat."

All agree and they quickly reconvene with Eli's drums, Tohlee's guitar, and Jed's mandolin. They play a variety of songs, some for the benefit of Cassie's voice, others for the individual musicians, and others for the whole group. After quite a few songs they decide to have a sweat. Rocks from the fire are placed into the lodge and buckets of water are readied for cooling and rinsing. The air in the lodge quickly heats up as water is poured on the hot rocks. Sage is smudged and slapped against skin. When everyone has heated up and broken a sweat they all go out and whoop and holler as they pour buckets of cool water over each other. Then they go back into the lodge to start the process again.

The third time they come out of the lodge instead of cooling down Eli picks up a drum and Jed a didgeridoo. Tohlee and Cassie begin to dance around the fire in the moonlight. As the dancing continues places are traded so everyone can dance or play as they want. Soon the beat of the music and the often eerie vibrations of the didgeridoo lead to dancing with wilder and wilder abandon. The women love their men and delight in their desire for them. Eli and Jed are attracted to the provocative moves and lusty need in the women's dance. In between the fire and the men the women stand sideways and bend over, showing the men the silhouette of their hanging breasts against the firelight. They flip their long hair over their heads as they bend down and then back behind them as they straighten up. Dancing to the other side of the fire where the light shines on their sweat-covered bodies they raise their breasts up to their men, massaging them, while inviting the men with their lips and tongues. Then they dance back in front of the men where they turn to the fire and with hands on their knees they shake and sway their backsides. Both men are standing and erect, stomping their feet on the ground in time to the pounding drum and the wailing trilling didgeridoo. The women dance back to the far side of the fire where one holds her arms up above her shoulders while the other stands behind and raises her sweat-soaked breasts to the men. Then the women circle around the fire, bending over in front of the men and pushing back against them. After a short joining they dance around to the other side of the fire.

Sparks fly as wood is added to the fire. The dogs howl with the coyotes on the nearby hills. Moonlight casts a pale glow on the entire scene. They dance and play and stomp and join through the night as the moon crosses the sky.

Day Nine

Mateen wakes up and gets going before Anoo. After washing his face and readying his pack he wakes Anoo. As Anoo prepares for a walk Mateen stands to the side of camp and looks around. When Anoo is ready he goes over and stands by Mateen. They both look out for a few minutes and then head south as the sun is beginning to light the sky to the east. They walk at a slow but steady pace along game trails on a small ridge. As it becomes lighter they stop on a rock outcrop overlooking a shallow valley. They can tell the sun's rays are just overhead and will soon be down to them. Removing their packs, they wait. After a few minutes a spot appears just above the ridge to the east, quickly becoming too bright to look at.

Mateen stands with his arms outstretched, his hands just above his hips, his palms towards the sun. Anoo's arms are pointed down with his palms to the sun at thigh level. His chin is up and he is looking above where the sun will appear. They wait and feel the sun's rays coming down to them. They feel the rays push against their faces and go down to their palms. Anoo opens and closes his hands, feeling the sun come and go from his palms. They watch as the line of sunlight drops down past their feet and into the valley. Mateen turns, dons his pack, and walks over the top of the ridge, dropping down into the shade on the other side. Anoo follows, first feeling warm while walking over the ridge and then cool as he drops down below the sun and into a thick stand of spruce and fir. Mateen uses a long and thin opening to move them farther into the stand of trees.

Soon they are stepping over two-foot diameter trunks fallen to the ground, the sires of the heirs standing seventy and eighty feet above their heads. Mateen stands on a log, looking for a way ahead where they won't have to climb over trunks jackstrawed on top of other trunks. They wind around and up and over the logs. The air is still, cool, and damp. Mateen points to his right. He brings the back of his hand to his mouth and makes a high-pitched squeak. Anoo sees quick movement above a fallen log and then a moment later sees grass and flower stems move below the log. Not ten feet in front of him a sharp-nosed face comes out from under the log. Two feet of long body follow the face out from underneath. A pine marten moves forward and puts his front paws up on another down log. Mateen squeaks again and the face tips to one side - just like a questioning dog. Anoo squeaks and the face quickly turns to him. The marten jumps up on the log and moves towards Anoo. It stops five feet away and then Mateen squeaks. The marten turns and looks at Mateen, then hops off the log, wiggles under another, and isn't seen again. They keep going until they reach a small opening in the fallen trees not much larger than a room. Removing their packs, they sit on a down log. Around them other down trunks are stacked up two and sometimes three high. Looking up from the down trunks they see the living trees reaching up as high as eighty feet.

"He sure wasn't very afraid of us," says Anoo.

"Martens are rare and specialized, but not shy. They are rare because there aren't numbers of them in any one place like a herd of elk in a meadow. Even in their prime habitat like this tree stand they are spread out to a low population density. But when you do bump into one, they aren't shy, so you often get a good look at them. They'll readily come closer when you squeak like a mouse. They are intelligent, curious, fun-loving critters."

"Why do you say they're fun-loving?"

"I have them around my cabin sometimes. I've watched them go up on my roof after a fresh snow. They'll go to the top and push themselves down the side until they fall off and drop eight or ten feet into the snow on the ground below. Then they'll climb the tree next to my cabin and do it all over."

"They're just having fun?"

"Just having fun as far as I can tell."

"And why do you say they're specialized?"

"They've evolved into an animal that needs these big trees. They would be too slow and wouldn't have a place to hide out in the plains or a large meadow. They use their long bodies to wiggle through small openings to find prey and protected places to sleep."

"Small spaces like underneath these logs I can understand that. But if they're spread thinly how do they find each other to mate and how then do the young travel to new places so they can have their own stands of trees to live in?"

"Those are good questions. They make those trips on dark nights. It's a similar need to beaver when they have to leave an overpopulated stream in search of another with more available habitat. Or like tiger salamanders waiting to move until a warm dark rainy spring night comes along. The move is necessary for mating and dispersing of high local populations. But leaving their specialized habitat is very dangerous. They often don't live through the attempt."

"But when they do they can establish whole new local populations. Like the small percentage of salmon that don't go back to their native streams."

"That's very good, Anoo."

"But why did they evolve into such specialists to begin with?"

"They filled an available niche. They found in the trees a refuge from predators and an available food source. Over a long span of time their bodies adapted to their habitat in such a way that it makes it very difficult and dangerous for them to leave their habitat."

"Like a fish out of water or a bird that can't fly."

James Nelson Caulkins

"That's right."

"Okay, but how did they know to change their bodies like that?"

"They didn't know. It's more like how a tree's roots reach out to water. The tree doesn't know which direction to send its roots out. The roots go out in all directions. When a hard clay soil is reached, the roots can only grow slowly in that direction. When a nice rich loam is reached, full of worm holes, the roots rapidly grow through that type of soil and even down the worm holes. When a water source is found, the roots grow larger and a main root becomes established."

"So the tree didn't know which way to grow its roots, but when a direction worked for it more roots and thicker roots grew in."

"It's the same for the marten. Martens as a species didn't plan ahead to become long thin animals that can't run fast but can wiggle through little openings. They evolved that way during the process of fitting into the habitat they had found that could support them safely."

"So fitting into their habitat caused them to develop the way they did. So they're a product of their habitat."

"They are certainly at least in part a product of their habitat. It's kind of a chicken and egg thing."

"You mean which came first, the chicken or the egg?"

"Yes, and from an evolutionary standpoint what came first was an animal very similar to a chicken but a little different."

"It's not like the chicken or the egg materialized out of nothing."

"That's right. It's like the puzzle of if a tree falls in the forest and there is no one there to hear it fall, does it really make a sound?"

"And does it?"

"From a history of life-on-earth standpoint, trees have been around for two hundred million years. The earth has been around for twelve billion years. The idea that trees and earth need people to do what they do when one crashes into the other is a little too egocentric a perspective for me."

"Okay, it's too much like thinking the Sun revolves around the Earth. But how does that go back to martens?"

256

"Trees existed way before martens. An animal similar to a marten lived in the trees long ago and over time developed into what we today call a marten. So the habitat shaped the animal, but there was an animal living in the trees to begin with that became genetically shaped by its environment into what we call a marten."

"Okay, I see. The marten didn't materialize out of nothing. There was something similar to a marten first and there was a forest somewhat like the forests today."

"Yes, that's right, and what about the roots of the tree?"

"The roots of the tree looking for water?"

"The marten didn't adapt itself to the forest through its own intent. Like the roots of the tree reaching for water, the marten reached out evolutionarily in many directions. The variations of marten that evolutionarily reached out are caused by sexual reproduction and mutation combined with which animals lived long enough to successfully reproduce. So both its habitat and genetic diversity caused the marten to evolve the way it did."

"So what was going to become a marten reached out genetically and behaviorally in many directions in the forest and what survived the test of time is what we call a marten today."

"And that, Anoo, is what is known as evolution. Life forms that change over time into new species because the ancestral life form needed to change because its environment changed. Its environment changed because of climate change, a change in the tree species of the forest, or a new predator moved into the forest, or a familiar prey species became less common."

"I guess something is always changing, but some changes are bigger than others. Some changes make an animal evolve like a new predator and some changes allow an animal to change like a newly available food source."

"Well said. What matters is having the time for the changes to occur. If there is a fast and major change, like a lot of new volcanic activity, many types of life forms may go extinct. If the change is slow enough, life forms can adapt and can become a new species that ends up very different from its ancestors."

"Like animals similar to elephants can become whales, and fish with thick fins can come out of the water and walk around for so long that they become reptiles, then the reptiles become dinosaurs and they become birds flying."

"That's right, if there's enough time. I personally have seen catfish in water so shallow their backs were out of the water and when they moved, they moved with a much exaggerated S in their backs as they swung one and then another pectoral fin in front of themselves so that they could move forward."

"If the whole process takes so long, how do we know for sure it happened? Well I know fossils are one way."

"Fossils are one of many ways."

"Then I know there is radiocarbon dating too, like they do at the universities."

"That's right, but there are other ways. People have genetically changed many types of plants so that they will produce more food. Corn or maize started out a plant with a much smaller seed head than it has now. People reinforced traits in the plant that caused the plant to grow into the food we know as corn. Your father does something similar when he saves seeds from the food plants that do best in his garden and then replants those particular seeds. That type of genetic manipulation is applied evolution."

"The genetic variation found in wild plants is used by people to change plants into a type of plant that grows more food for people."

"That's right, but not just plants, animals too. When wild animals are domesticated, the animals people allow to breed are the ones that are the tamest and so the least threat to the rancher. They are the animals that give the most milk or grow the fastest."

"And so when people use the natural variation in a plant or animal to intentionally genetically or behaviorally change plants and animals through deciding who breeds with whom or what seeds get planted in a garden, people are applying evolution through their own genetic manipulations."

"Very well said, and how else is evolution shown in the world around us?"

"I guess I don't know."

"Well what allows evolution to work is time. So how is time shown in the world around us?"

"Well the radiocarbon dating, which is the time it takes for radioactive decay."

"How else on a global scale is it shown that the earth has been around long enough for non-human-caused evolution to occur?"

"Oh, it's shown by the movements of the continents."

"That's right, people have gone to northeastern South America and to westernmost Africa and looked some miles inland away from recent ocean-caused erosion and found the same geologic layers on each continent."

"How do you know that really happened, don't you have to have faith that's where they really went and that's what was found?"

"I do, but the faith is in their colleagues who would have yelled foul if the people didn't really go or if they didn't prove what they found there. No matter how much you learn from the sciences, you will end up with faith and belief when trying to prove the age of the Earth and evolution. But that is after learning about the fossil record, radioactive isotopes, and many other things. After that much learning the entirely belief-dependent notion that God made the world in six days is not very convincing."

"It seems like a choice to believe in a book as truth rather than make the effort to learn."

"That's how I see that choice. How else is evolution shown in the world around us?"

"I guess I don't know."

"It's shown by how much like people some animals are and by how much like animals some people are."

"So it's like how my parents' dogs learn what is expected of them and how the dogs have feelings and opinions towards each other and us? And how animals use tools like that seagull that used the rocky shore as a tool to break open clams?"

"That's what I mean right there. You have animals with feelings and opinions and that use tools and, as we know, they communicate with us and each other. Most people don't do any better. Most people react to the world around them through their feelings. Most people don't learn as much as possible and communicate that learning before acting. Most people choose faith over learning as shown by how few people apply rationality to religion."

"How are feelings a reaction to the world?"

"Those feelings are about the world out away from the person having the feeling. The feeling is how the person is assessing what is going on around them and then those feelings are what some people's actions are based on. Animals, just like most people, use their feelings and opinions to assess the world around them and to determine a course of action. What animals don't do as well as some people is think ahead, plan, take a variety of unseen factors into account, and then choose to act accordingly. Animals can hunt cooperatively but they can't debate the merits of moving to an unknown place. Through communication of abstract circumstance the ability of people to assess the merits of a future choice and develop a plan to accomplish that choice is spread to the group for consensus and so shared responsibility. That's how people function at a level above animals. That's why I say if a person wants to function above the level of animals they have to function above their feelings and opinions. They have to be able to explain the perspective behind their feelings and opinions."

"Because animals have feelings and opinions too, but people are capable of more. If a person doesn't explain the perspective behind their feelings and opinions they just drag everyone around them down to don't think, obey."

"That's how I see this. And how does tool use fit in? Most people can't make the tools that they need to live the way they do. If people couldn't give little green pieces of paper to the people who have learned through their intellect to make tools, most people's tool use wouldn't be much above animal tool use."

"So you're saying that people can learn to function above

animals, but they have to try. It's not an inherent difference. And when people think they are a step above animals, that perspective is often based on their chosen value system or based on the merits of a small percentage of innovative individuals, not on their own individual development or that of masses of people."

"That's right, I'm saying that evolution is shown to be true in ways other than fossil records and plate tectonics. Evolution is also shown to be true by the minor degree people function differently than animals. How it is through the work of only a small number of individuals that enormous benefit has come to a majority of humans, seemingly showing we are all more than animals. But at the same time people are peering out at animals from a societal window they don't know how to make or sustain."

"God gave people capabilities and responsibilities that are more advanced than animals, but not so much a given ability, rather a potential."

"That's how I see it - as a gift of potential to humanity and many people degrade that gift by considering it a statement of fact. The conclusion that people are inherently better than animals is made by the same people who are acting like grunting apes when they think they are right because of how much anger they feel. It is made by the people who are acting like grunting apes when they reproduce uncontrollably. It is made by the people who are acting like grunting apes when they soil their own nests with pollution. It is made by the people who are acting like grunting apes when they use the love of God as a rationale to wage war on people who hold different beliefs."

"And the way people can actually function above animals is by thinking and intending and benefiting others through their innovations."

"And also they can appreciate the independent perspective that the thought and intent that results in an innovation that benefits others springs from. Let's keep on walking."

After a few hours' sleep everyone at the house is stirring. Eli is taking care of his morning chores while Jed restarts the fire and heats rocks for a sweat in the cool morning air. Tohlee prepares a light breakfast for all as Cassie cleans up after the night's activities. The light breakfast is enjoyed with large amounts of water still cool from the well and flavored with dried cherries and raspberries from last year. Their bodies are replenished but they keep drinking water throughout their sweat. Buckets of that same cool well water thrown on each other wipe the last of their late night from them. While Eli and Jed stand warming in the morning sun Tohlee and Cassie wash each other's hair. After washing their hair the women dry off with towels heated by the fire. Then they brush each other's hair and rub lightly scented oil into their skin. Afterwards with a conspiratorial smile they laugh and run to their men. Using their oiled bodies they oil their men's skin too. After everyone's skin is glistening in the morning sun the women go inside and the men walk around the gardens and orchards.

"It looks like everything is growing well, Eli."

"It's been a good start to the growing season. There haven't been any late frosts and there's been a nice mix of rain and sun."

"I saw all your seedlings are out of the greenhouse."

"All the seeds I sprouted early have been moved outside as seedlings and almost all the beds that get planted directly from seed are sown and most have sprouted."

"Is that bed one that hasn't sprouted yet?"

"Some rows haven't sprouted and some aren't planted yet. That's where I sow my different beans like these that are up. Next to them are rows that haven't sprouted and then rows I haven't planted yet."

"How often do you plant your beans?"

"About every two weeks from mid-May to mid-July."

"Do they ever get frosted?"

"Some do every year because I push the season on either end. I make sure I have enough seeds for a double planting each year. Then if the whole year fails I have enough to replant the next year.

Since I seldom have a year that bad for any of my crops, I end up building up a stock of seeds. After about five years I either swap the seeds at the farmers' market in town, or if I still have too many older seeds, I give them to the animals. They love old bean, pea, and corn seeds. The smallest extra seeds I mix in with the pigs' regular food."

"So you grow food in your gardens and orchards, and scraps and leftovers go to the animals or compost. The compost ages for a year and then goes back into the growing beds. The manure ages for several years and goes back into the growing beds. And in the fall you kill the animals for their meat grown from your garden plants."

"That's basically right, especially for the pigs. The cows also eat grass from the yard and orchard, not just garden and orchard leftovers. The chickens and turkeys also forage around the grounds for insects. And we always keep some chickens and turkeys through the winter. But yes, the plant crop supports the animals as the animals support the plants."

"It's a good system, Eli."

"It's been around for thousands of years and yet people are still learning and refining and trying new things."

"It's been around since Adam and Eve."

"You like that idea also, Jed? That Adam and Eve weren't the first people - they were the first gardeners?"

"It was the Garden of Eden after all. And the whole idea that the second generation of humanity sired a third through incest doesn't appeal to me."

"I think God chose to give humanity a better start than that."

"The hunter gatherers were and are capable of incredible learning, understanding, and culture. But there are things that their methodology of survival inhibited."

"Like libraries. But they did have doctors and medicine, teachers, laws, food storage, protection from the elements, more than enough to consider them human. Most religions and societies frowned on the people who were different from them."

"That's true, the idea that humanity started with the God of

Abraham's influence on humanity is very egocentric, but not at all new. To establish their own identity societies and religions have long proposed the idea that their system of belief is the only true one or that their society gives their members some special attributes, lifting them above other humans."

"Identity should come from the individual not from the religion or society the individual belongs to."

"Well said, Eli. Where did the wood we worked on at Cassie's end up?"

"Right over here."

They walk over to the root cellar which is under the barn. At the bottom of the stairs Eli moves a large mirror into the sunlight coming down the stairway and aims the reflected light down to the end of the root cellar.

"The stairs are where most of the wood went but some also went to these shelves."

"You do nice work. What do you have down here?"

"This section is for vegetable and herb seeds. I store them in the cool while other seeds, usually from plants that haven't been domesticated as long, may need to be where they will be below freezing for a time."

"To prepare them for sprouting just as some seeds sprout best after going through the digestive tract of an animal?"

"That's right and that's one reason why the animal manure is aged for several years. To give ample time for seeds that lived through the digestive process to sprout and die in the warmth of the decomposing manure pile. Then they won't sprout in my growing beds. And that's why I don't put old seeds or plants that have gone to seed into my compost. The shorter time it takes to move my compost into a growing bed doesn't always give enough time or heat to sprout seeds."

"So you keep seeds out to begin with. And here are your fruits and vegetables."

"They're from last year and will end up going to the pigs before this year's crop is ready to be stored."

"And do the canned and dried goods go to the pigs too?"

"They'll go to the Farmers Market first and if no one has a need, then they'll go to the pigs."

"I think this attachment on your dry goods jars is great."

"It is too moist down here to leave dried goods out in the open. So I use these canning jars to seal out the moisture."

"So you attach a vacuum device to this nipple and suck out all the air from the jar after you fill the jar with dried fruits or herbs?"

"That's right, there is a filter on the inside of the attachment to keep the dry goods from being sucked up into the vacuum and I seal the lid with beeswax."

"There must be a valve to keep the air from going back in."

"Yes, it's inside between the filter and the nipple."

"Where did you get the lids with the attachment?"

"I went to the metal shop in town and told them what I wanted. They worked out the details of attaching the whole piece to the lid and putting the filter and valve inside the attachment. When people in town saw them they wanted some too so it's turned into a nice little business for the metalworkers."

"That's great, you should think up something like that for us leatherworkers in town too."

"I'll certainly try. Let's go get something for lunch."

"Sounds good, that light breakfast was great as a pre-sweat meal, but I'm ready for more."

Eli and Jed leave the root cellar and walk over to the house. As they do, they see Tohlee and Cassie working in one of Tohlee's herb gardens. They stop and watch Tohlee and Cassie bend over and move around the garden. After a little bit they realize they've been noticed and as the women turn laughing at them they become aware of their own nakedness.

"Are you two spies enjoying the view?" giggles Tohlee.

"Absolutely, we are delighting in the beauty and attractiveness of two exceptional women," says Eli.

"Do you think they want sex or food?" asks Cassie.

"With a comment like that it's sixes," says Tohlee.

"Actually we were heading to the kitchen for something to eat," explains Jed.

"Food not us," sighs Cassie.

"Yes for now, but a little food will increase our stamina," says Eli.

"I guess we're going to have to get them drunk again," says Tohlee.

"Or take them down to the swimming hole," says Cassie.

"Or get them drunk at the swimming hole," continues Tohlee.

"Or serve them food while they get drunk at the swimming hole," says Cassie.

"That's it! We'll feed, water, and wash them so all their needs will be taken care of," laughs Tohlee.

"Except the need to ravage us," says Cassie.

"That's right, we just need to get only one thing on their mind to avoid confusion," says Tohlee.

"Do you mind that they're talking about us like we're not even here, Eli?"

"No, not the way this conversation is going."

Mateen and Anoo slowly work their way through the rest of the spruce and fir stand. Sometimes they go over logs, sometimes they walk on a trunk for fifty feet, and a few times they even duck under logs that have fallen on other logs. Here and there they stop among small groups of eighty-foot-tall spruce where a half dozen trunks two feet in diameter are growing within twenty feet of each other in a roughly circular shape.

Underfoot there are so many chewed-up pieces of spruce cones their feet sink several inches down into them. They stand quietly and feel the presence of the life forms. Their eyes are drawn up to the tops of the trees where the sun has awoken the needles and the trees are bright to their eyes. Mateen walks to a trunk and puts his arms around it. Anoo does the same. After a time they continue walking while maintaining the meditative silence and awareness that holding the trees brought to them. At one point they stop and watch as two pine grosbeaks move through the trees crossing in front of them. As they near the edge of the stand they slow even further because the gaps in the trees are showing a wet meadow and some willows instead of more tree trunks. They move out of the trees and into the wet meadow. Their feet push down into moss and water squishes out from underneath. Anoo turns and watches the moss rise back up, erasing their passing. He looks ahead and sees Mateen pointing at the ground. As he moves up he sees large deep footprints punched into the moss with small pieces of moist soil scattered between the tracks on untrodden moss. An image of a cow moose comes to Anoo's mind. Mateen keeps going across the meadow and up into a stand of aspen. They sit in a small clearing, warming in the sun.

"Think about how much time each day we have been spending talking about particular topics, Anoo."

"It seems like a lot."

"Think about the actual time spent."

"Well I guess it is really only a few hours a day. But it seems like more."

"We're spending a few hours a day talking about some specific topics while we're out on a two-week trek which was intended to give us time to talk."

"Do you think we're not talking enough?"

"Actually what I want you to realize is that the relatively short amount of time each day we're spending talking specifics is enough. Even when an individual is creating their belief system and a code of ethics it doesn't take up all day, every day. Then, once a person is comfortable with their own individually developed base to live their life, that person spends even less time a day maintaining and restructuring that base."

"What do you do with the rest of the day?"

"Take walks, feel a breeze on my face, talk to a friend, work, reap, sow."

"So an individual who creates their own perspective or value system isn't in a constant effort of creation. Usually they're just living their life?"

"They are usually just living life from within their own structure instead of living life from within another's structure or an organization's structure."

"And you're saying that an individual's life holds all the same elements as any other person's, like a mate, children, work, hobbies, and passions."

"What we've talked about will in no way diminish your ability to live your life. What we've talked about is meant to help you create a structure to live a full life from, a structure that will lead to freedom of beliefs and a perspective that can only come from the individual application of a value system. Once created, that structure will take no more effort to maintain than the effort a follower needs to make to belong to their chosen hierarchy. And yet, you will perceive your individual life and the world around you from an independent perspective that a follower will never achieve."

"You mean while I'm working or holding my child or wife, just like anyone else?"

"That's right."

"And what will make my life so different are the values I choose to hold?"

"The values you hold as well as the perspective that holding your own values brings to you."

"And these values are ones you've been talking to me about?"

"The values I've been talking to you about and that I have been living, modifying, and building on for more than fifty years."

"You've changed values from where you started?"

"Values should be fluid to learning. You should be strong enough to get out of your own way and rearrange the base you have chosen to stand on when you have learned something new."

"If you are rearranging your base, who are you when you have stepped away from your values to rearrange them?"

"You are your ability to live your own value system and create your own base."

"So, after creating and holding my own values long enough, I'll become the ability to hold my own values, not just the values themselves?"

"That's what I'm saying, Anoo. Creating and holding your own individual value system will result in the creation of your own perspective. That creation process, along with time and familiarity, will end up allowing you to pull your perspective inside yourself to the point where your identity is not the perspective created by your own individually created value system. Your identity will become the ability to create your own perspective and value system. At that point you will be able to separate yourself from your base to the degree that you will be able to restructure your base, and after that restructuring, you will expand yourself back out to your own perspective."

"I'm not at all sure I followed that. Which values will end up with my identifying me with my ability to create my own value system and perspective instead of my own actual values and perspective?"

"I could ask you the same question, but I think a little summary is in order. The value system that truth, accuracy, being right comes from the content of what is said, not by who is talking is a good one to start with. Another is the idea that the closest connection to your God is found within you, not by going outside yourself to a book or building or to a religious authority and then to God. Then there's the belief that evolution and the geologic age of the Earth is a more accurate synopsis of the planet Earth and the life on it than is the Christian story of creation. Then, there are the indicators of people who do not live these values."

"You mean the people who think they're right because they feel like it or because of the position they hold."

"That's right, the people who can't explain why they're right and so they feel anger when their so-called truths are questioned.

They are a negative to the people around them because the people around them must give up the validity of their own feelings to fit in with the person who thinks they're right because they feel like it. Instead of communication being an interchange of concepts, talking to those people is an exercise in "don't think, obey". Those same people's anger is a defensive mechanism because they don't want to hear explanations of how lacking in substance their perspective is. Those people aren't strong enough to step back and examine their base. They can only accept and agree with the various structures they've chosen to adopt. Because of this, a conversation with them about specific values is a threat to their identity, not an opportunity for learning and growth."

"So their own choice to belong to established structures instead of creating their own structure is a choice that feeds on itself."

"That feeding on itself creates a dependency where originally there may only have been a little need for guidance. Once that dependency is created and maintained it is very difficult to overcome. Instead of exposing themselves to a concept that would cause them to see the results of their own choice to rely on established structures, those people often restrict their exposure to information so that they experience only that which they already agree."

"Which then takes away the changes from new learning that could come to them and results in the restricted perspective of a fanatic."

"Well said, Anoo. I used to think that with age all people would end up learning the same things. Some people would learn some things earlier than others, or quicker than others, or due to different circumstance, but that with age the learning would end up coming together to a similar perspective. Now I think that there are values an individual can hold and build on for years that a conformist or a user of established structures will never reach. Because they'll never ask themselves the right questions to create growth in themselves, they've chosen to pass up the opportunity for that resultant growth for the apparent security and noticeable lack of choice found in an established construct. They are the people who can stand in a vegetable garden or look at a lake or a small forest and never ask themselves the questions that will lead to a lifetime of learning."

"Wow! Mateen, that was a really big circle you took me on. What are these right questions that create growth?"

"You're welcome. The questions that contain the power to create individual growth have primarily been put into the realm of religion and downplayed through obedience and superstition by religious authority. Many people have decided that melding themselves into the various established thought constructs found in society will lead them to the greatest learning available. That choice requires a loss in individual perspective that I think often can't be overcome by age. When an individual learns and changes by building on their self-determined value systems, they develop a perspective that cannot be duplicated by a conformist following or adjusting themselves to the constructs of others. In other words, those followers become dependent on the weaknesses of their leaders who are themselves, dependent on their followers for their own validity."

"They are each links in one chain and therefore only as strong as the weakest link. You're doing too many circles for me, Mateen."

"You're fine. When people choose to meld themselves into established constructs they have an initial surge of learning and comfort. Compared to them at that time a person who learns for themselves will appear insecure and slow because that person is questioning the constructs around themselves, not adopting them. That individual is giving up immediate learning and the comfort of belonging for the greater learning that comes from self-determination. It is self-determination through the choice of which values an individual holds that creates the ability and identity with process required for a person to be able to step aside from themselves and rearrange or revalue their base. Without the ability to rearrange one's own values a person becomes dependent on the established structure they've adopted for growth and change. Those established structures are inherently slow to change and grow compared to the capabilities of an individual. My experience has shown me that there is much to learn beyond the averaged and conformed values that are necessitated by trying to be a truth to masses of people. That learning can never be found by conformists because the choice to conform restricts the development of individual ability that is necessary for learning beyond one's comfort zone. My experience has shown me that there is so much to learn that no construct begun in youth can be so accurate and comprehensive that the revaluing of one's base isn't required as one learns throughout their life."

"So the questions that create growth are the questions whose answers become the base I will perceive the world from?"

"That's right. Questions like, how much does God play a part in your daily life? Or, should you create your own religion or code of ethics as the freedoms of this country allow? Should you give up the responsibility for your afterlife to an organized religion? Is it better to be an actor in someone else's play or to write your own?"

"I think I need to walk now, Mateen."

"Then let's walk. I am not expecting from you the obedience of immediate agreement. You will incorporate what I've said into your life as it is right for you. You will incorporate into your life what I've said to you as well by taking a walk or sitting and meditating as you will by the two of us debating the merit of my words or my method of explanation."

The day has warmed nicely so even the light gardening work the two couples have been working on has become a little uncomfortable under the afternoon sun. It's quickly decided that a wine and cheese picnic at the swimming hole is in order. Food, drink, and towels are packed up for the walk. Shoes are put on but there is less need for clothes now than when everyone stripped down for a morning sweat. The walk to the swimming hole causes everyone to kick their shoes off and run into the cool water. After some swimming and splashing everyone relaxes on the gravel bar under the warm sun.

Wine and cheese are passed around as the sun takes the water's chill off their skin.

"You mentioned earlier, Jed, that you could use some ideas for leatherworking jobs."

"That's right, Eli. We keep reasonably busy with standard work but some new projects or products would be nice."

"What sort of items are the standards?"

"Shoes and boots are definitely the standard. But we do a lot of belts, mittens, and gloves too. Pants, vests, and coat requests come along often enough. The more out-of-the-ordinary projects are things like drive belts for various pieces of machinery or tool belts for specific jobs. There's one fellow at the shop who specializes in saddles. We all make traces, harnesses, and reins, as well as bicycle and buggy seats. We usually get a couple orders a year for tepees."

"Are you usually using cowhide?"

"For the heaviest work, but there are other types of skins we use. The tepees are made from bison and we make bison bedding with the hair left on. We use deer leather for gloves and other light flexible items. Then there is sheep hide as an insulated fleece and even rabbit with the fur on for liners. Rabbit is the thinnest leather we have commonly available to work with."

"How do people usually pay for the work the shop does?" asks Tohlee.

"Usually barter of one kind of commodity or product. But we do get some people paying in gold or silver coins or with copper ingots. A rancher might slaughter three cows in the fall. He wants a couple pairs of boots and new reins and so will take the hides to the tannery. The tannery will charge him one hide to tan all three. Then the tannery passes all three tanned hides on to us while keeping track that one hide is their's and the other two are the rancher's. We make boots and reins out of one hide and they go back to the rancher. Our boot work is worth more than the one hide not accounted for, so the rancher throws in some of the meat from the slaughtered cows. We either pay the tannery with the meat we earned from the sale of boots to the rancher or we give them a finished leather product for their tanned hide."

"So the rancher is putting in three raw hides to start this process. Then the tannery turns the raw hides to tanned leather. They get to keep one of the tanned hides as payment for their work, leaving the rancher with two tanned hides. The rancher comes to you guys and you turn one processed hide into two pairs of boots and some reins. The rancher gives you the last tanned hide and some meat for the leather work you've done. You pay the tannery for the one tanned hide they received as their payment from the rancher, with meat you received from the rancher. Then you'll have a cowhide available when someone without their own source of leather needs a pair of boots," says Tohlee.

"Or their payment is credit with us that we and the tannery keep track of."

"Okay, so the tannery ends up with the value of one tanned hide that they get back in one of several forms from the leatherworkers. The leatherworkers end up with the value of one tanned hide and some meat, and the rancher ends up with two new pairs of boots and some new reins," says Tohlee.

"That's about it except that the rancher has also gone to the butcher with the meat from the three cows. He needs some of the processed meat for the leatherworkers. He also has to pay for the meat processing with some of the meat. He pays for the leatherwork with a quarter of a cow and the meat processing with three quarters of a cow. That leaves him with two cows' worth of processed meat at the butcher's. The rancher takes a half-a-cow's worth of meat for himself, leaving one and a half with the butcher. The butcher stores and sells that meat for the rancher for a fee. A metal worker might come to the butcher for meat and pay with a copper ingot. The rancher has all the meat he needs so he either ends up with a credit with the butcher or he accepts a copper ingot for the meat the butcher sells for him minus the butcher's fee. When the rancher needs some metal work done he takes the copper ingot to the metalworkers and trades that for some horseshoes or whatever."

"And so right here in our little town we have commodities, products, credit, and money," says Tohlee.

"I can't believe people used to use little green pieces of paper as money," says Cassie.

"People not only used little green pieces of paper for money, they also thought that those pieces of paper separated them from responsibility for their actions. People actually thought that if they gave green pieces of paper to a butcher it would mean they weren't responsible for the death of the animal that their green pieces of paper were buying pieces from," says Eli.

"Like people who would buy a leather belt and think that it was really the people who ate the animal who were responsible for its death. As though there is an animal out there alive and well except missing a belt-size piece of skin," adds Tohlee.

"Isn't it just better to realize we're omnivores who take life to live life?" observes Jed.

"Everyone should be thanking and respecting any animal whose life is taken to satisfy their needs. Thanking and respecting on an individual level meaning this one person and this one animal. Thinking that the taking of the animal's life is the responsibility of someone else demeans the animal," says Eli.

"We have to thank plants too because carrots and radishes have to die for us to eat them. Even if a person could go a week without indirectly killing something for food or clothing that person would step on a bug when they went next door to brag about how they hadn't taken a life to survive that week," says Tohlee.

"I'd rather do my own killing whenever possible. The humility that grows in me when I take a life leads to greater respect for all life," says Eli.

"So much death goes into one life over the years. It's not just the chicken we eat for dinner. It's the fifty bugs a day the chicken ate for five years too. After all, that's what morphed into the chicken breast we eat," says Cassie.

"And eating eggs instead of the chicken doesn't change

anything. Even if the eggs are unfertilized, there wouldn't be eggs if the chicken wasn't eating bugs," says Tohlee.

"Eating an unfertilized egg is just putting a step in between the taking of life and eating. It's no different than putting little green pieces of paper between yourself and the taking of life," says Jed.

"If a person ate only bread there would still be the taking of life by the action of plowing the field the wheat for the bread was grown in," says Eli.

"Or the bugs the horses that pull the plow inadvertently eat when they graze and eat egg cases that are laid on grass stems," says Tohlee.

"Or the grasshoppers the horses step on before the morning sun has warmed them enough to be able to move out of the way," says Jed.

"Or the cabbage looper butterflies on my cabbage family plants that I kill with bacillus thuringiensis before the crop is even ready for harvest," says Eli.

"Or the bacteria that gets sucked into our bodies when we breathe which adheres to mucous membranes and are spit out or swallowed and digested," says Cassie.

"I think that's a graphic enough example. We take life when we breathe, move, and eat. That's what happens when we live in a world as full of life as we do. There's life in the soil, the air we breathe, and living on our skin. We can't help but take life as we live, but we can be aware of the consequences of our actions all the way down to the breaths we take," says Tohlee.

"Awareness leads to compassion, denial leads to self-delusion," says Cassie.

"And realizing we have to take other life to live our life and choosing to take that life with awareness, compassion, and respect goes a long way toward taking away the issue of right or wrong in how we sustain ourselves with food," says Eli.

Mateen and Anoo have slowly moved through stands of trees and across meadows. They stay in the shade when possible and move across openings only after standing at the edge and watching for a few minutes. On the edge of one meadow they see three young cow elk and they follow them into the trees. They stop when the elk stop and move only when the elks' heads are down. One of the three animals is usually looking around. But at times all three heads are down or all three animals are moving forward and not looking behind. Anoo moves around Mateen and moves swiftly but silently down a well-worn path towards the elk. He covers a hundred feet in several dashes and finds himself within thirty yards of the last elk in line. He crouches behind a small snowberry as the two elk in front move apart about thirty feet and look all around. The elk closest to him turns and looks out over the meadow. All three are looking intently and smelling. Anoo doesn't think they've seen him, but at only thirty yards away any errant breeze could give him away. The animals are alert, but he hasn't seen any abrupt movement that might mean he was scented. All three elk separate even further with the one closest to Anoo moving towards him. Anoo is kneeling behind the snowberry and looking up at the elk as it sniffs and looks out over the meadow. The other two elk continue to look in different directions and sniff the air. After several minutes all three move back together and lie down. Anoo keeps the snowberry bush between himself and the elk as he backs away. He sees Mateen at the edge of the meadow and slowly moves over to him. They slip quietly away so as not to disturb the elks' rest.

"I thought they had scented me at first," says Anoo.

"So did I when the one moved towards you. But they were only looking around extra carefully before they bedded down. When they split apart the farthest, they were getting different vantage points to check the area."

"They're lucky I'm not a cougar."

"Or a hungry bow hunter."

"I didn't know they looked around like that before bedding down."

"They know they're more vulnerable lying down and that their ability to see, smell, and hear will be compromised lying down compared to standing up."

"Do other animals do that too?"

"Most herd or flock animals rely on the numbers of eyes, ears, or noses around them to alert the whole group of danger. But some animals like crows and geese will set guards for the group. Those individuals stay where they have a good view of or perspective on the group and the area around the group. They'll stay there alert for danger, but unable to feed until another guard replaces them. It's similar to a wolf pack that leaves an aunt or uncle wolf to watch the cubs when the pack goes off to hunt. The pack will bring food back to the guard as well as the pups."

"That shows a lot more social structure than I realized they had."

"As I've said before, animals know each other as individuals even if we see them as a herd of elk or a flock of geese. It changes things for a hunter when he realizes the animals he's hunting have a social structure."

"How does it change things?"

"When a human hunter becomes aware of the social structure, or feelings, or intelligence of his prey, it tends to create a need to ritualize the hunt. A tribe or community will have ceremonies to indicate when it is okay to hunt. For example, a traditional fall hunt for elk takes place after the young of the year can survive on their own and before the hardships of winter causes a herd of animals to severely impact their range."

"So the young can take care of themselves within the herd if their mother is taken in a hunt and the numbers of the herd are lessened just before the hardest time of year to find food."

"That's right, and so a tribe will have a fall hunting ceremony to indicate that time of year has returned and to give the hunters permission to interrupt the social structure of the animals and to lessen the effect on the hunters of that disruption."

"And that effect on the hunter is because the hunters are aware of the intelligence, feelings, and social structure of their prey?"

"Yes, and that awareness I'm talking about comes after learning all sorts of things about how the animals live their life."

"So a hunter might learn first about where and when some animals go to water, but after learning enough facts about the animals he'll realize how in-depth their social structure, intelligence, or feelings are."

"That's right. Rituals of hunting are connected with a need in the hunter to justify the disruption to his prey base that his killing to survive will cause. A disruption that the hunter is causing in animals he feels a kinship to, has compassion for, and depends on."

"What are things a hunter learns about his prey that cause him to need a ritual to balance the disruption of his hunt?"

"Once I was hunting in the early fall and I heard two deer run away from me. I couldn't see them because they were on the other side of a clump of Gambels oak from me. I thought I had spooked them and so lost my chance to kill one of the deer. Then I heard them run across in front of me. Then they ran right at me before running away off to the side of me. They ran back and I could hear them coming to a gap in the oak just thirty feet in front of me. A doe and a fawn came through the oak thirty feet in front of me and broadside to me."

"It sounds like the perfect opportunity for a shot."

"It was, but I saw the deer's tongues were hanging out of their mouths. I realized that the doe and fawn were running back and forth as they played tag. The doe was helping the fawn develop the ability for quick starts, stops, and turns, by pitting herself against the fawn through a game of tag. I couldn't bring myself to shoot the doe while she was playing tag and so I let them go on about their business. In that case, the time of year was good, but the individual animals involved weren't the right ones. Another time, a friend of mine shot a young cow elk in a meadow. Out of respect for her life I put my hand on her just after she died. I saw imagery in my mind of the elk out in the meadow jumping around because she had become pregnant for the first time. A full grown cow with a calf watched her from the trees, wanting the young cow to be with them in the trees. But in the young cow's exuberance over her first pregnancy she stayed in the meadow too long and the hunter saw her and killed her."

"You saw that in the same way you've seen a hunter on horseback take a bison. And in this case, it would have been better if the hunter waited for an animal that was in a better social or life position to be taken."

"That's right, like the time I watched a small herd of antelope for most of a day, waiting for an opportunity to get close enough for a shot. After several hours they bedded down and I was able to get closer to them. I walked, crawled on my hands and knees, and then on my belly, until I was close enough for a shot. By then the animals were up and looking around because they knew something wasn't right. I shot one and the rest all ran away. By the time I waited a little bit and went to the downed animal, the rest of the group had come back and were standing, looking at me and the downed animal from thirty feet away."

"What did you do?"

"I knelt beside the animal and thanked it for being worthy prey and becoming my sustenance. Then I shooed the rest of the herd away before I cut up their friend."

"And that meant it was a good animal to take?"

"It did to me. Another time I was hunting for grouse or a rabbit. I didn't want anything as big as a deer. But a deer stepped out of some trees and stood broadside to me just twenty-five yards away. She was looking away from me but knew I was there. I raised my gun up for an easy shot but I didn't shoot. I wasn't prepared for such a big animal, I just wanted a dinner and breakfast the next day. She moved away and I kept hunting for a few minutes. I then thought maybe I wouldn't see a grouse or rabbit so maybe I should have taken the deer. I turned in the direction she went and took a step. She snorted from seventy-five yards away and I knew she was aware of my change of intention and that I would never see her again. In that case I should have taken the deer when she chose to put herself right in front of me. In less than two minutes my indecision made the right animal to take the wrong one."

"Did you see a rabbit or a grouse?"

"No, I ate camp food until the next day's hunt. Another time, I stood waiting for an animal to come by and found myself walking to a different position without having thought I should move. A minute later a deer moved in front of me that I wouldn't have seen from my earlier position. That one I took."

"So the tribal hunting rituals you mentioned came about because when people see animals as individuals they develop an affinity towards the animals. Because of that affinity hunters want to sustain themselves and their people in a way that minimizes the disruption to the animals they depend on."

"They also want to disrupt themselves as little as possible. Compared to sneaking through the woods with a clear head and full awareness, a bad kill is very disruptive. An injured but not recovered animal or taking the wrong animal will disrupt one's ability to have a clear mind. If you are mentally distracted when you hunt, your success rate will drop. That's why some tribes have other rituals that are designed to bring a hunter back into alignment with the clear-minded awareness a hunter needs to be consistently successful."

"Rituals that include a sweat lodge."

"Okay, Anoo, take us back to camp."

It doesn't take long to get back to camp at a steady walking pace. They've only walked about five miles from camp throughout the day. So after a little more than an hour Mateen is at camp readying the fire for dinner and a sweat. Anoo goes down into the nearby valley where he catches some fish for dinner. They relax around the fire as dinner is cooking.

"I'm going to repeat myself a little here," says Mateen. "When you create your own perspective by choosing your own value systems, you are setting out on the path of an individual. At the same time you should hold value systems like the Golden Rule that respect others. Individual development should not be at the expense of others. But also realize that others have no right to expect you to become less than what you could be just so they don't have to see themselves from a different perspective."

"What are some other value systems you've lived and changed over the years?"

"I used to have a definition of thought or mind that started with brain activity, then above that came thoughts where the light comes on, then above that are divinely inspired thoughts. Now I think brain activity just means you're not dead. A person can have a million thoughts about what to wear or what sports team has the best chances to win, and those thoughts will never equal one thought where the light comes on. Thoughts where the light comes on are meant to be daily occurrences. And thoughts I used to think were divinely inspired are just the way the mind feels when it's been energized by enough sparks from the quality of thought that we perceive as a light going on."

"So that's a shift in perspective?"

"That's a chosen change in values because of a change in perspective. How my mind feels when the light goes on didn't change. I changed how I valued that feeling because of a change in my perspective."

"And that change in perspective was?"

"That God made us in his image and that image is that of a self-determinate being. Living in God's plan for humanity is to be self-determinate. God can't create self-determination in humanity. By the very nature of self-determination we have to grow into it through our own actions. Self-determination comes to individuals first and through them to society. The freedoms in this country are granted to each individual not to society as a whole because of that truth. My perspective changed when I realized I could not live my life with self determination while God was giving me revelations. What I had identified as revelation I chose to value as an individual's thought process when 'the light goes on.' That change in perspective is that Thou art God. The perspective that sees this is human and that is God separates us from ourselves to the effect of cutting ourselves in half. That change in perspective is that we should act with God, not under Him, for we are God. Our image of God is our selves that we haven't learned to incorporate into our perspective of ourselves yet. There is the God who is with us all day everyday as the Creator of all life in the universe and as the Sustainer who connects our souls to our bodies when we're in the physical. And there is a religious image of God where organized religion has erected a barrier named God, separating us from our own individual potential."

In the early evening Mateen and Anoo enjoy a trout dinner. After cleaning up camp and making sure there's plenty of firewood they relax around the fire. The fire had been allowed to burn down for cooking over coals and then was built up again, and now has burned down again. Mateen puts the sweat lodge rocks into the coals as Anoo stretches. Then Mateen goes through his version of Tai Chi. He starts out very slowly but increases speed until his movements are closer to a martial arts kata. He doesn't follow an established pattern. If some muscles are tight, he'll work them longer than others. If he's loose and relaxed, he'll move faster or push harder. This evening he feels good and his movements take on the flow of a dance. Hand follows hand as foot mirrors foot. Each side of his body is treated equally. At times he has to pause as he realigns his feet with the weight of his body and the leveraging weight of his outstretched arms. He feels for the balance points where a foot pushes down on the ground just as an arm fully extends. His weight is mostly on the balls of his feet with just enough weight towards the heel for stability. After a quick turn he refocuses his eyes forward, turning the blur of a quick head movement into the next point ahead he is reaching out towards. He keeps going until he's worked up a light sweat and then slows down to just stretching. All the while his mind has been clear and focused. He is putting the quiet mind of meditation into motion. The light exercise has him ready for the deep cleansing heat of the sweat lodge. Anoo has already placed half the heated rocks into the sweat lodge. They go through the heat and cool rinse cycle three times, making use of all the heated rocks by the last cycle. After the sweat Mateen stands just outside the firelight, looking into the darkening night. In the direction he's looking a wolf howls. A minute later Mateen turns and walks to his bedroll. Anoo sits by the fire in a meditative silence. He works on the thoughts of the day in the back of his mind as he watches the colors of the flames come and go.

The couples enjoy their afternoon at the swimming hole. By the time they're ready to leave it's late afternoon. The evening chores at the farm are out of the way quickly with two extra sets of hands helping. Dinner is light and eaten standing up around a table outside. Everyone circles around the table as various fresh fruits and vegetables are spiced and dipped. The elk and antelope jerky go well with pickled green tomatoes and jalapeno peppers from last year. The fire is started before the cooling evening creates the need for clothes. Hard cider and wine replace the food on the table as the musical instruments are brought out. It won't be as late a night as last night, but the sweat lodge, music, and dancing will be just as enjoyable.

Day Ten

When Anoo wakes, Mateen is not in camp so he restarts the fire and readies himself for the day. The sun will soon be over the low ridge to the east. There's a chill to the early morning that won't last long as it looks like it will be a mostly sunny morning with the possibility of thunderstorms in the late afternoon and evening. As Anoo finishes readying his pack Mateen walks into camp with some fresh strawberries.

"Good morning to you, Mateen."

"And to you my friend."

"What will we do today?" asks Anoo.

"We're going to plan and talk and walk."

"What is our plan for today?"

"The plan will include tomorrow. Today we'll walk and talk much like yesterday. Tomorrow when you wake I will have started hiking over to the southwest side of these mountains. We'll meet up over there."

"How will I find you and where am I actually going?"

"As you know we're on a high rolling plateau between the two forks of the river that flows through your town and your parents' farm. Town and the farm are to our north. If we were to go to the east or west we'd drop down from the plateau and cross one fork of the river or another and then climb the hills on the other side of that fork. On the other side of those hills are smaller and smaller hills, leading out onto the plains. To the south of us is a line of ridges and mountains making the highest headwaters of the river that runs through town. On the other side of those mountains the ground drops quickly down to the plains. There is one ridge that runs roughly southwest from the southwest side of these mountains out onto the plains. That's where we'll meet up again tomorrow afternoon."

"How will I find that ridge and how far away is it?"

"Today we'll hike in that direction and I'll show you the pass you'll take over the mountains. Through that pass you'll head southwest and that will take you out onto the ridge I'm talking about."

"How will I find you on that ridge?"

"If we have to we can build smoky fires to show each other where we are. But the ridge is only about a mile wide as it comes off the mountain and about five miles farther it is only about a quarter-mile wide. As you walk down that ridge keep your eyes open for my tracks and I'm sure we'll find each other."

"So I'm going from here to the end of this plateau."

"That will be about five miles."

"And then I'm going through a pass."

"That will be a couple miles up and then a little farther down the other side to the ridge."

"Then I'm going about five miles down the ridge to where I meet up with you."

"That's it, and total it will be about fifteen miles with some uphill as you go up the pass."

"What will we do when we get there?"

"Tomorrow night we'll have dinner and a fire."

"Okay and then what will we do?"

"We'll talk and walk and look for fossils and wild horses and petrified wood."

"Is water easy to find?"

"We'll be fine this time of year, but it can be quite dry later in the summer. It will be warmer down there. We'll pretty quickly go from spring to summer by moving over there."

"How long will we stay?"

"A couple of days."

"Then what will we do?"

"We'll go back through the pass together and then I'll head back to my cabin as you head back to the farm."

"Separately?"

"Yes, I'll move along pretty quickly and you can take your time and enjoy the land and think about what we've talked about."

"Okay, that sounds interesting, what will we talk about today?"

"Similar to yesterday, there's still some perspective there I haven't reached with you yet."

"Okay, what are you thinking of?"

"I'd like to expound on the effort conformists make to find truth in the hierarchies they have chosen to surround themselves with."

"They find so much truth in their hierarchies that they give people above them the right to be right without proving their points."

"That's exactly right, and I am telling you the value system that says truth, accuracy, being right, whatever you want to call it, is determined by the content of what is said, not by who is talking, is a value system that individuals hold."

"I think I understand that. How far will conformists go to find truth in hierarchies?"

"If there are a group of conformists outside of an established hierarchical structure, they will build their own structure by choosing a leader, and a pecking order, beneath the leader. Instead of a group of individuals who will defer to whoever in the group has the most knowledge or experience with the concern at hand after showing that knowledge by proving their point, they will defer to their leader."

"So the conformists are so dependent on functioning within a hierarchical structure that they will build one to be within when they find that they are in a situation where they could create or build whatever they wanted."

"That's right and I am saying that if you find yourself in a situation where you are free to create or build what you want, then be strong enough to build an individual structure that won't fall apart just because the hierarchies around you have faltered."

"And, be strong enough to step away from your own individual structure so you can rearrange your structure as you learn," says Anoo.

"Well said. Hierarchical structures are too slow to change and adapt to new learning for an intelligent individual. Hierarchical structures restrict learning that would cause them to rearrange. There's more that I want you to understand. People are so dependent on hierarchies for the structure around them and are so afraid to rearrange themselves that they've chosen to function within a hierarchy of knowledge."

"What is a hierarchy of knowledge?"

"A hierarchy of knowledge is dependent on the idea that a person can learn by being open to the accumulated human consciousness around them."

"I don't know what that means."

"It means that conformists find truth in the generalized concepts they can tap into through a telepathic-like merging with the human consciousness around them. And, I say, when conformists merge with the consciousness around them, all they gain are generalities, the weakness of being a link in a chain, and the comfort of being one in a flock."

"And you would rather learn at your own pace, build what structure is right for you, and be responsible for yourself to the point of being responsible for your own immortal soul."

"You are an intelligent young man. When people choose the seeming wisdom of a hierarchy of knowledge, they see themselves within a caste system of knowledge. Where if one has conformed themselves to a level of the existing structure, they have learned the generalized concepts of that level. Not through the learning of specific concepts, but through merging with the human consciousness found at that level. If one hasn't learned the generalized concepts of that level through such a merge, that person is beneath the others who have learned the generalized concepts of that level of the hierarchy they are in."

"So the conformists are trading the light-bulb-going-on type of individual value of thought for the generalized knowledge of the average around them and the ego-driven view of themselves being above others in a societal hierarchy," says Anoo.

"I am thoroughly impressed by how much conceptual ground I can cover with you, my friend. I'm not saying the whole concept is false, I'm saying it has limits and it is not a concept designed around mental or individual fluidity. I am saying that when a conformist merges their awareness with the generalized consciousness surrounding them what they get is the generalized average knowledge of the people around them. They do not get the specific information someone who has chosen to learn about a subject will have. Their being conformists causes them to find truth in the most common perspective, not the specific knowledge of whoever has chosen to specialize in that subject."

"You're saying that I should give myself the chance to have my own specific knowledge and individual value systems and not to choose to conform myself to an existing structure for a quick generalized version of knowledge that will limit me in the long run."

"That's what I'm saying. By the very definition of average there are some above the average."

"And you're saying the best way to function above that average is through an independent perspective, not by succeeding in being at the top of the hierarchy," says Anoo.

"That's right again. I'm also saying that there is some truth to that version of knowledge, just as there is some truth to the feelings people use for their version of perceptive truth. Similarly to how people can increase the accuracy of their own perceptive truths by realizing how often their perceptive truths are wrong compared to when they're right, a person in a hierarchy of knowledge must take an objective look at the hierarchy they're in to evaluate the weaknesses their hierarchy is built on. They have to be able to step away from the hierarchy to see it objectively. They aren't living their lives in a way that has taught them how to step away from themselves and rearrange their values before growing out into a newly created perspective."

"That realization you're talking about would give them the opportunity to rearrange their value systems and therefore their perspective through the truth of humility. That truth is the humility of knowing that one's perceptions are not as accurate or as encompassing as once thought. Or that the hierarchy of knowledge, one was so impressed with that they chose to join it at the cost of their individual freedoms, contains serious flaws."

"Well done. An individual can increase their own knowledge or change their perspective by learning how much more there can be to their individuality as compared to what will come to them through merging with the generalities of human consciousness surrounding them. In other words, a person who has chosen to conform to the generalities around them will not learn how much their perspective of their own potential is created by the value systems they have chosen to conform to and therefore are looking out from."

"If a person hasn't learned how much they don't know, they won't value what they could know."

"Well said. The value systems from which we view the world are all that separate us from people one hundred thousand years ago. People one hundred thousand years ago were as mentally capable as we are. We couldn't function in their society any better than they could function in ours because of the different value systems involved. Just as a conformist's value system won't mesh with an individual's. The same stimuli or thought or perception will be interpreted differently through different value systems. Conformists want one value system for everyone in order to increase the apparent correctness of their perspective and to reduce the effort of encompassing new possibilities. But, we live in a country that has given many freedoms to the individuals who make up the country. In this free country we have the right to think whatever we want to think and hold whatever values we want to hold."

"Just start with the Golden Rule and build from there," says Anoo.

"And realize that true evil comes from dragging people down to your level for your own comfort, not in worshipping an entity with horns and a pitchfork."

"And don't do violence."

"That's right. In addition you shouldn't tear down anything that you can't rebuild better than it was, at least from your perspective."

"And the freedoms of this country are granted to the individual citizens of this country, not to the society as a whole," says Anoo.

"Live your life as an American by living the freedoms of this country on an individual level. Don't limit yourself to being a citizen of the United States by merely adopting the existing value systems and perspectives held by the majority of people around you," says Mateen.

"Individual freedom is a greater truth than conforming to the averages of a generalized society," says Anoo.

"Well said Anoo, and keep in mind that the Golden Rule doesn't cover all possibilities it's just a good start as you correctly said."

"What possibilities doesn't the Golden Rule cover?" asks Anoo.

"An example is that I don't think it is impressive for a person to manage to have a feeling or an opinion," says Mateen.

"But some people will expect you to be impressed with their feelings or opinions even if they can't prove their point," says Anoo. "Which can't ever square with your value system which is a reflection of your valuing thought over obedience."

"I think you're ready for a walk now."

Mateen and Anoo set out for the pass with a full day's supply of food and water. They decide to make a full day of the ten-mile-round trip so they won't have to hurry. Their route is basically southwest through the undulating top of the plateau. Sometimes the easiest way is along the top of a little ridge and sometimes along a water course. When they are on the high spots they can often see down into drainages where a variety of animals are moving around in the early morning light. When walking along the watercourses they are going slow enough to bump into animals, but too fast to see them before being seen.

From one high point they watch a young bull moose for a few minutes. He's down on his knees grazing, because the grass hasn't grown tall enough for him to reach it while standing up straight. From another high point they see a coyote that is moving so purposely in one direction they guess it is heading to its den. They decide to follow it and after about a half a mile, they hear the excited yips of pups and a howl from an adult. After a quick sneak to the top of a little rise they see the animals next to a couple mounds of dirt. They watch as the coyote that was out hunting throws up a meal in a couple different spots and the pups quickly race for it. The other adult heads downhill towards water and a quick mouse hunt. The hikers ease back the way they came and then continue on. After about a mile they are dropping down towards a watercourse when they see the tops of willows moving. As they stop to look they feel a breeze at their backs. After just a few seconds the willow movement abruptly stops, then moves quickly straight away from them. They watch as a large black bear emerges from the willows and runs straight up the steep hill across from them. In no more than a few seconds the bear crests the hill and is out of sight.

"Wow! Mateen, that was impressive. I'm glad he went away from us."

"Me too, Anoo, and that one was so big I think it must be a he."

"He was so big and powerful it seems really odd that a smaller female with cubs could drive it away from her cubs."

"It does, unless you consider how smart bears are."

"In what way do you mean?"

"It's not that the larger male couldn't kill the smaller sow. If a large boar and a mature sow actually fought it out, the larger male would certainly come out ahead. But the boar is smart enough to know that it may very well receive an unacceptable level of injury because of the encounter."

"What's an unacceptable level of injury?"

"Any predator taking prey that isn't much smaller than it is runs the risk of injury from the prey's hooves or teeth. Predators often get bumped and bruised taking larger prey. But bumps and bruises are an acceptable level of damage for the resultant food source. In the case of the boar and sow, the boar knows it can kill the sow but also knows the risk of unacceptable damage to itself is high."

"So you're saying unacceptable damage is something like broken bones that will weaken the animal even after the food source from the conflict is consumed."

"That damage could be a swat to the face that takes out an eye or breaks a jaw or a hit that breaks ribs. Just surviving the encounter isn't enough to justify the encounter. And what is it about the sow that makes her such a threat of unacceptable damage to the boar?"

"She's protecting her cubs."

"But how does that make her such a threat to the larger boar?"

"She's willing to put everything she has into protecting the cubs."

"That's right, she's willing or she is applying her intent. She intends to damage the larger boar. Remember when we talked about how animals have feeling and opinions as a way for me to explain to you the similarity between people and animals?"

"Yes, you think the similarities indicate a common ancestry, or proof of evolution, and that humans are different from animals only when you compare the creative few individuals that have really furthered humanity through discovery or reason to animals."

"Well said. I think that God's gift of self-determination to humanity is a potential, not a right. And so now I'm saying that besides having feeling and opinions, animals can also apply intent just as people do. And I may as well throw in the ability to dream, also."

"Like when dogs are asleep and it looks like they're running in their dreams by the way their legs twitch?"

"Exactly, and I may as well throw in the ability of all female mammals to lactate and that all mammals have hair."

"More similarities than differences until you get well into an academic level of learning or well into changing one's perspective through intent," says Anoo.

"Well said again. Also, animals are very perceptive. I remember when I was young, a friend of mine who was close friends with her cat. One time a few of us were leaving her house and she saw her cat ten feet up a tree with all four legs hanging down around the branch she was on. She said something to the cat about how silly it looked. The cat didn't understand the English words but realized by tone of voice its owner and friend was making fun of it."

"How do you know the cat realized that?"

"Because as soon as my friend's back was turned, the cat bounded down the tree, ran behind her, and scratched her with both front paws as it bit her behind the knee."

"Was she hurt badly?"

"No, the cat didn't intend to hurt her badly, just give her a message that it didn't like that behavior by its friend. The owner said the cat had never done anything like that before. Another time I was reading a book about British Columbia and cougars. The author said cougars often kill by stiff arming prey from the side. They hit the prey so fast and hard with their two front feet it knocks the body of the prey to the side so abruptly that the prey's neck beaks. Just as I was walking by my pet cat I was wondering if that was really a cougar's technique as it seemed so incredible. My cat jumped out of the chair it was on, bounded across the floor and stiff armed me in the foot with both of its front feet. I was amazed at how I could feel the paws hit my foot through the leather boots I was wearing."

"So you think the cat somehow knew what you were wondering?"

"It had never done that before and never did it again. Just the one second I was wondering about it."

"That seems like more than coincidental timing," says Anoo. "I think I need to walk on that one for awhile."

"I think the timing was more than coincidence, too. Let me back up a little bit. I'm sure you've seen one of your barn cats or a fox play with a mouse they've caught?"

"Sure, plenty of times."

"That play is based on the idea of prey being able to hurt the predator that has taken it. That quick grab and toss is designed to injure the prey before the prey can injure the predator. After enough injury to the prey, the predator will be able to dispatch the prey without injury to itself."

"I see what you mean," says Anoo. "But some of the play is just play for fun, just as animals are capable of feelings and opinions, one of the feelings they're capable of is having fun."

"Well said, my friend."

"I think I'm ready to walk for awhile."

Mateen and Anoo continue walking to the pass they will go through separately the next day. During the next mile of walking they see some raptors and songbirds as well as smaller critters like a few chipmunks and one golden-mantled ground squirrel. The bigger animals have sought cover now that it's toward late morning. As they top a rise Mateen points out the pass, now only a mile ahead. The southern end of the rolling plateau they're on transitions to peaks and ridges eleven to twelve-thousand feet in elevation. It's this high end to the south that causes the two branches of the river to flow north where they come together at Tohlee and Eli's town and then flows past their farm five miles farther downstream. It's also what keeps the southern end of this high country from sending water out onto the surrounding plains, except in intermittent streams.

Mateen knows it is the right time of year for the larger of the streams to still be holding water. Anoo sees that the pass is the lowest spot to the south at around ten-thousand five-hundred feet. They'll have to climb about a thousand feet to go over the pass tomorrow. That will mean about five miles of rolling terrain to cover first, then a thousand-foot climb, and then a five-mile drop down to the scrub lands which will feel like the middle of summer compared to where they've been. After going a short walk farther to get to the top of a higher hill, they stop and take a break.

"So, all I do tomorrow is go through the pass and drop down the other side?"

"You'll go through the pass and move to the west or to the right-hand side of the drainage that flows south from the pass. That western side is a long, steadily dropping ridge, running out onto the plains. We'll meet up down that ridge."

"Okay, and you'll leave first thing in the morning?"

"I will and I think it'll take you about six hours walking steady, but taking breaks to get there."

"It looks like it could rain this afternoon or evening."

"Maybe so, but I don't think it will make for a socked-in day tomorrow. Plus, when we're down the other side it probably won't have rained there at all."

"Then we'll be in scrub country with horses and antelope instead of trees and wet meadows with moose, elk, and bear?"

"That's right, that's what a drop in elevation will do. Tomorrow we will be a good thousand feet lower in elevation than where we started at your parents' farm."

"And that's why it's scrubland instead of the tall shrubs around my parents' farm?"

"That, and also the soils are heavy with clay at that edge of the high country."

"It'll be a first for me to see the wild horses and find fossils too, you said?"

"We'll find fossils and petrified wood as well as seeing the horses."

"That will make for an interesting experience. Mateen, I was thinking about your cat that hit you in the foot with his stiff-armed paws."

"What interested you about that story?"

"Well, it's like the cat must have had some sort of telepathic bond with you."

"That's the way I see it."

"So you think it did. People can have telepathic bonds with animals?"

"With animals and, of course, that includes other people."

"Do you think that happens often?"

"It does to me, although I don't know that it happens to everyone. I do think it's common. With animals I think it's more of a shared visualization. For many people it's an empathetic connection."

"What type of connection would that be?"

"An empathetic connection is where two people share a feeling and that allows the listener to understand the situation or condition the teller is in without words."

"And what's visualization?"

"Animals don't communicate verbally like people so their minds don't concentrate into a concise communication based on words like humans can. When an animal concentrates on something, in its mind it sees a picture. When people are empathetic, they get an impression of what another is feeling or experiencing. When people are telepathic, they hear words in English - just like we're talking now."

"In English and so you hear words in your head, not through your ears?"

"If you're telepathically communicating with someone who speaks a different language, then you'll still hear them in English."

"How does that work?"

"I'm really not sure."

"Can you telepathically communicate with anyone?"

"Not anyone. A person who is comfortable being part of a group often is sending out telepathic communications to the group even though they're unaware of it. Those thoughts can be picked up by others outside the group."

"What sort of thoughts are those?"

"They're usually pretty mundane and have to do with keeping contact with the group for the comfort of the participants. When a person who communicates telepathically is in contact with a person who is comfortable with empathy, a connection exists that is different for each participant. The empath will receive the communication as an impression or feeling while the telepath is hearing words. Empathy communicates the emotional condition of a person, telepathy can communicate the circumstances that caused that emotional state."

"So that would be the communication empaths' do out loud with English?"

"That's right. Two telepaths can have a conversation in English just like we're having now."

"Just like now?"

"Yes, they can rephrase something or change their minds or whatever you can do out loud."

"And that happens commonly?"

"If the people involved are telepaths or, more correctly said, are aware of their telepathy."

"Aware of their telepathy because it's there - even if people aren't aware of it?"

"Exactly, when you're comfortable with telepathy and can return to it by choice, you can be having a conversation with a person who isn't aware of their own telepathy and then you can choose to take the telepathic connection between the two of you away from your communication in English with that person."

"How do you do that?"

"It's hard to explain, but when you've developed your individuality far enough, you'll realize and be able to recognize the connections people subconsciously make all the time and you'll be able to choose if you want that kind of a connection with a particular individual."

"So you have that connection with a person who is empathetic but not aware of their own telepathic connections, and then what happens to that person when you turn off the telepathic part of the connection between the two of you during a conversation?"

"They will look at you like you're talking gibberish."

"Because of how important a role telepathy plays in regular verbal communication?"

"That's right."

"What if someone wants their thoughts to be private?"

"If you're thinking or talking about someone else, that is an invitation to them to listen. When a person thinks about someone else they create an identity or image of that person in their mind. The creation of that mental image of someone can be picked up by that person, allowing them to focus in on a conversation about them - even if the participants weren't intending to include them."

"Can the telepath focus on any conversation?"

"I imagine so, although I apply the Golden Rule to that idea and don't listen to anyone unless they're thinking about me. It seems too self-righteous to me to just listen to others. Also, it's often boring as most people's day-to-day thoughts are pretty mundane."

"You've tried doing it then and been successful?"

"Yes, and then I decided it was beneath me."

"What if someone is thinking about you?"

"I consider that an invitation to me to listen. If it wasn't an invitation, it would be the equivalent of two people telling you they're going to go talk about you, but you can't listen."

"Which would be a rude thing to do, and so you're helping those people be polite by listening?"

"I realize there's some self-justification there, but I do think it's my right to hear what other people are saying about me."

"Even if they don't know you're listening?"

"That's how I see it. A person can also hear conversations that will be important to them in the future. If you're going to have a conversation the next day with someone and they are preparing for that conversation today, it is also an invitation to listen."

"How do you learn to be telepathic?"

"Guidance from a telepath is one way. The telepath can tell you what they heard of your thoughts and then you have to be honest enough to admit that's what you thought."

"Why would I have to be honest?"

"For most people, it's not the common thoughts of the day that are communicated out from themselves. It's the more focused thoughts of problems or out-of-the-ordinary circumstances."

"And how would the telepath, proving to me they're able to receive my thoughts, help me become telepathic?"

"It would allow you to recognize the feeling of rapport that comes with a telepathic connection. If you have that rapport with someone and neither is thinking, neither will hear a communication, but the rapport can be felt. If you have that rapport with someone and want to communicate with them, think up! With practice you'll become as comfortable with that type of communication as you are with talking. Just like with talking, it may take some years to become proficient at it."

"But not everyone can do it?"

"Not everyone does, maybe everyone could if they wanted to."

"Why wouldn't a person want to?"

"People who are hiding parts of their personality or past behavior close themselves off from telepathy out of guilt or a desire to hide themselves."

"So past actions can interfere with current development?"

"They can, unless the person owns up to them. And when I say owns up to them I don't mean admitting them to themselves. I mean explaining the action to the person telepathy is desired with."

"So hiding something from someone interferes with telepathic communication just like it does verbal?"

"It interferes with telepathic communication just like it interferes with a friendship or a romance. Let's head back, Anoo, it's time for you to think some more in the back of your mind as we walk."

The two couples are up by first light. After some of the little bit of grape juice that didn't get fermented last fall they do the morning chores. The morning is a little cool with some fog along the river and a few scattered clouds in front of the low morning sun. It won't be long before the sun rises above the clouds and the day warms to early summer. Over an hour later they are sitting down to a nice breakfast of tossed salad with fresh herbs and scrambled eggs.

"How long will you guys stay today?" asks Eli.

"We're thinking late morning. Neither of us has any obligations until tomorrow, but there's things to do at home," says Cassie.

"Have you guys had any thoughts of living together?" asks Tohlee.

"We've talked about it, but we both like having our own places. We're only a five-minute walk apart," says Cassie.

"Cassie's place is bigger than mine so I usually go over there, but I still like to have my place where I can be undisturbed to study and meditate until I grok," says Jed.

"I like to meditate until I grok by the river. Sometimes I meditate on how hundreds of years after Heinlein's work there is still validity to his individually defined concept.

"Our place is so big we can find our own quiet places even when Anoo is here," says Tohlee.

"You guys are such a good couple Eli's need to grok probably coincides with your need to embroider, Tohlee," says Cassie.

"We all have our own methods of creating the opportunity to incorporate new knowledge or perspective and rearrange ourselves accordingly," says Tohlee.

"Cassie and I would be fine living together, there's just no real need at this point," says Jed.

"If it ain't broke, don't invite a man over to fix it, I always say," says Cassie.

"Good one, Cass," says Tohlee.

"She's as tough as nails, isn't she Jed," says Eli.

"Until she breaks one anyhow," says Jed.

"Good one, Jed," says Tohlee.

"Hey, whose side are you on?" says Cassie.

"As is always the case when dealing with a situation that does not include the possibility of violence, I'm on the side of my own values," says Tohlee.

"Now who's tough as nails?" says Jed.

"We all are by that insinuation. I think we all consider honesty stronger than allegiance in our day-to-day interactions," says Eli.

"I value my principles over the female's side in a relationship or a female's perspective in a conversation or Eli's opinion. I know we all live our lives in a way that won't support taking a position based on allegiance or values that aren't thought out. We're all strong enough in our positions that we don't need the supposed support of blind allegiance. On the other hand, if Eli ends up confronted by a person with an irrational ego and whose truth is their anger - we're a team together forever," says Tohlee.

"Our individuality will blossom again when a safer and less disruptive locale has returned to us," assures Eli.

"Do you think if we started living together we could keep our own individuality and be as close a couple as these two?" asks Cassie.

"I think we could work it out over time and I think your relationship is special, Tohlee and Eli. It's interesting how, when most people are in a relationship, it's the overall physical, emotional, spiritual, and personal joining that has the most meaning. But for a person who has intended their own individuality, whether in a relationship or not, what has the most meaning from a values standpoint is the actual holding of an independent perspective," said Jed.

"I think that speaks to how much a person has to bring to the relationship. A person without an independent perspective, whose values come from the society around them instead of developed individually, has less to bring to a relationship and therefore will find less depth in a relationship," says Cassie.

"Don't look for a mate to complete you, look for a mate who you'll be compatible with when sharing your individuality," says Tohlee.

"Individuals who've created their own independent value systems choose to share in a relationship, while some people require a relationship for their own identity, and that places too much of a burden on the relationship," says Eli.

"It makes it too hard for the relationship to be flexible through the normal ups and downs of a relationship, caused by the growth of the people involved, simply through living their lives, and so the individual growth caused by intent would be an even bigger strain," says Cassie.

"If a relationship can't grow with the growth of the individuals involved, the relationship is no more. If the individuals in a relationship choose not to grow so they won't grow apart, then they're no more," says Jed.

"The more individuality a person brings to a relationship, the more there is to share in a relationship. The deeper a person looks inside themselves for their own truths, the deeper a relationship can be. Eli likes to reach a grok level of understanding by himself; I do the same when I embroider. Women and men have different ways of doing similar things. Individuals have different ways of doing similar things. Separately, we've looked inside ourselves and chosen to live certain values. When those values are shared with someone, the need to have the particular expression of those values the same for each person in the relationship doesn't mean much compared to the sharing of the actual value," says Tohlee.

"Individuality comes from the values examined and chosen and lived. Not from the adoption of values held by the majority of people one comes in contact with. Even if, after examining one's values and determining there is no reason to change from the values that were adopted as a child from one's parents or nearby society, the process of examining those values gives individual validity to the values. That individual validity is then a stronger base to live one's life from and to share in a relationship," says Eli.

"Grow yourself first, and then bring what you've grown to the relationship. If the relationship is with another who's chosen to grow themselves, the individual quirks of personal expression are overlooked for the depths of the concepts shared," says Jed.

"Tohlee, you said women and men have different ways of doing similar things. Did you mean like how women tend to bond with women over a good conversation while men tend to bond with men through an activity?" asks Cassie.

"That's what I was thinking of," says Tohlee. "Like how women nest in the home and men in the tool shed."

"I think it's time for you and me to bond over your flower gardens while the guys bond over the next chore on their list," says Cassie.

The morning sun is warming when Eli and Jed go out for a chicken and turkey foraging trip. Afterward they walk along the river looking for the places feeding trout or pike lie in wait for food and the deeper more secure holes they rest in. Frogs jump off the bank into the water as they walk. They watch a blue heron standing in a slough off the main river and see its attention grabbed by something. A couple of slow deliberate movements later and the bill shoots out too fast for them to see and then it is back out of the water with what looks like a crayfish. After a couple of head shakes and some hard pinching bites the claws are pulled off and the heron throws its head back and down goes the crayfish. It takes off just after its meal and from ten feet up leaves a big splat of poop on the water in seeming disdain for the disturbance of observation.

Various fishing spots are noted and plans made for a visit that will include some fishing and, hopefully, a meal of fresh trout or pike. While the men walk along the river Tohlee and Cassie visit on the porch and in Tohlee's gardens. After awhile everyone meets back at the house where Cassie and Jed pack up their things and load their bikes for the ride back to town. Many hugs and kisses are shared before they are ready to go.

"Thank you for a very enjoyable visit, Eli."

"You're very welcome, Jed, it was a pleasure to have the company of both of you."

"If you would be so kind and afford me the time of a call tomorrow night, please Tohlee?"

"Of course, Cass!"

"And would you be so kind as to bring Anoo around for a visit when he gets back?"

"We'd be delighted, Aunt Cassie."

"I love you, Tohlee," says Cassie.

"And you, my dear sister."

"Will the dogs go with us, Eli?" asks Jed.

"For about a mile and then they'll come back."

"Bye, you guys!"

"Peace to you both."

It is mid-afternoon by the time Mateen and Anoo arrive back at camp. They covered ground quickly on the return trip as it is a time of day when most wildlife is resting out of sight. After freshening up with spring water they relax around camp. Anoo stands in the intermittent clouds and sun while Mateen stretches.

"What should we talk about?" asks Anoo.

"Whatever you'd like, my friend."

"I was wondering, if an independent perspective is so much better than a flock, or societal perspective, why don't more people have one?"

"There are a higher percentage of people with independent perspectives now than before the past troubles because of the problems that were caused by, and that people were led into, by their chosen hierarchies. Still, many people these days don't have an independent perspective.

A lot of comfort and much less effort is built into the choice to adopt or adapt to an established hierarchy and its existing perspective or value systems. From my perspective, the greater the comfort taken by conforming to an existing structure the greater the loss of individual growth. I don't think it matters if the structure is religious, military, political, or business related. The goal of theirs for you, which is your cost, to belong to their structure will most likely not be your individual development in the direction your potential would otherwise lead you. For some people that is an acceptable cost and return on their investment. The creation of an independent perspective has its own costs. With more awareness comes more responsibility, more clarity, more realization, more perspective, more change, more learning, and more desire.

There is a slippery slope aspect to the creation of an independent perspective. There is a "this feels good or right" aspect to creating one's own perspective, like when the light bulb goes on from a novel thought for you. With the openness and learning needed to begin to create your own independent perspective, the confusion of multiple possibilities arises. With the initial uses of intent, the awareness of responsibility and potential increases doubt. The cause and effect of applying intent creates information to assess current value systems or beliefs. Adapting to that learning requires change. A great deal of effort is required to incorporate that new knowledge into one's perspective. And a great deal of strength is required to individually hold the beliefs chosen and to let go of the beliefs that one grows beyond."

"Where does that strength come from?"

"That's the part about living the rest of life as decently as possible. Be aware of the consequences of your actions, don't do violence, don't deceive or manipulate, build a strong base in your everyday life for your individual applications of intent to stand on and to be assessed from. I think you'll find, like I have, that the slippery slope of creating one's own perspective is caused by the increased need for the feeling of strength and awareness that comes with successes along the learning path of individuality."

"If it feels good or right, isn't that because you're following an existing path? If a path is completely new to humanity wouldn't it be for you to determine for yourself whether it is a good path or not? If so, wouldn't someone or something have had to take the path first to cause it to feel good to an individual?"

"I think it does. I think that God creating us in his image as self-determinate beings and allowing us the freedom to create our own destiny on this marvelous planet is not compromised by the idea that God may have set up a system of reward through good feelings as one successfully grows along the path of individuality. The same is true if the pathway of good feelings was caused by someone coming along the same path earlier than you or I and determining that pathway to be good."

"How can that be if an independent perspective is truly independent or individual?"

"I think that's because of how broad the path of individual perspective is. It's like music. There are only so many notes, chords, and octaves. But when you throw in all the possible permutations of which notes come before or after, or with what chords, and include rhythm and syncopations and then the human voice and lyrics besides, the possible individual songs humanity can come up with are limitless, like the possible applications of individuality.

And people did come before you and walk the path of individuality. Royalty and shamans started out being who they were because of what they knew and understood that others hadn't yet. Started out that way, but then royalty became an institution and the breadth of shamanism was restricted and discredited until it was replaced by medicine. Medicine was only one part of shamanism. More importantly for you, we live in the country of freedom which was founded on individual freedoms, not the right of society to freely choose which value systems its constituents will hold."

"What happened to the people who did the very best at creating their own independent perspective?"

"I think they became our best teachers: Buddha, Confucius, Jesus, and Muhammad. Buddha was supposedly so comfortable crossing over into the realm found after death and coming back to help others that he did it many times."

"Are you convinced there is a life after death?"

"As I've said, I think thoughts and emotions of quality can create soul. I don't think quantity or repetition of thoughts and emotions can. Just as I don't think the individual choice of what to wear or how to cut one's hair can. The energy in thoughts and emotions that creates soul merges into the part of you that is not confined by the physical body. That part of you is called soul. It is the part of you that your awareness here merges into after death."

"Do you mean you're creating your soul out of nothing?"

"No, I mean I'm adding new energy to my existing soul. I'm creating more soul than I had before by living this physical life."

"And are you creating the energy involved?"

"No, I'm containing the energy through the way I live my life and then transferring it to the part of me beyond the physical."

"And you see that ability as either given to humans by God so humans can develop themselves, or it was discovered by successful individuals in the past and followed by others like us?"

"Yes, and followed by others like us along a broad path of potential and individual application. I think there is a part of me while in the physical that is in direct contact with the energy of my soul - because there is what I will call an aware energy in me that does not age and is always with me."

"I'm not sure what an aware energy is."

"Me neither, really. It's just a term to describe something I can find inside myself."

"Where is it in me?"

"I seem to have first become aware of the phenomenon when I was about your age. I'm going to say it was an existing pathway that I became aware of in my life and that I developed depth of that awareness through use."

"So as I learn to grow my own soul I'll become aware of the pathway used by energy to go from me to my soul beyond the physical?"

"That's my impression of the way things work."

"Wow, I had no idea I had the potential to be so incredible."

"You do and I do and the earth is and the whole universe is. There is an enormous amount of potential in your freedom. That's why I don't want you to limit yourself to the existing hierarchical structures around you. That's why I think life is the most incredible experiment ever."

After a sweat bath and a quiet evening Mateen says goodnight. Anoo stays up and watches stars come and go through the moving patchy clouds. He goes to sleep but doesn't sleep deeply. He wakes up more than usual in the middle of the night and finds himself seeking the presence of Mateen before he scans the night for dangers. He wakes up wide awake as soon as he hears Mateen get up. It seems like only a minute before Mateen has packed and heads out of camp. Anoo lies in the dark, wanting to be comfortable and go back to sleep. But he lies awake until he sees the first lightening of the eastern sky. He lies awake until he decides to get up and catch a fish for breakfast.

Day Eleven

It is still early morning when Anoo packs up and polices camp. He sets out for the pass at a slow but steady pace. He watches where he puts his feet and all around too. There are deer and hawks as well as the whistles of marmots from shrubby spots near meadows and picas from rocky slopes. Mice scurry across the path in front of him while spider webs stretch and break as his legs spring their traps. He doesn't follow the same path as yesterday but isn't far away either. Hills and stands of trees are remembered from the day before and tracks are crossed at times from yesterday's walk. There is no sign of Mateen's passing, not until Anoo gets to the pass itself does he see where Mateen has switchbacked up the steepest sections. It comforts him to see the tracks like a hoodoo can give comfort in the wilderness.

At the top of the pass he stops and has a snack. Looking east and west he sees the rocky, sparsely-treed slopes of the mountains the pass connects. Looking north he looks down on the high rolling plateau where they've spent the last couple days. The plateau seems to float between two ridges because of the valleys of the stream branches that come together in town. To the south he can see the long low ridge Mateen has told him about and he sees distance. He sees as far as his eyes can see. He sees the curve of the earth and distant mountaintops that barely break above the horizon.

As he meditates on the awesome expanse in front of him he

loses track of time. He is roused when movement far below catches his attention. His first thought is of Mateen, but then he quickly sees it is three bison miles farther than where he thinks Mateen is going to be. Motivated now by time and distance, he heads downhill into new territory.

"Hi, Mateen."

"Hello there my young friend, it's nice to see you again."

"And you too. It really wasn't hard to find you. I crossed your tracks climbing up the pass. After going through the pass and coming down to this ridge I just followed your tracks along the top of the ridge. I saw you from about a quarter-mile back. Have you just been sitting for a while?"

"Sitting and thinking. Take a break and sit with me. I knew I'd be able to see you from here as you came down the ridge."

"What have you been thinking about?"

"I was thinking how beavers alter their habitat in a way that benefits them and lots of other wildlife like we talked about."

"I remember, and what were you thinking then?"

"I was thinking how I'd seen squirrels prune maple and box elder trees in the spring."

"What do you mean by prune? I bet they don't have loppers like my dad."

"I would be extremely surprised to see that kind of tool use from squirrels. Their method of pruning is to walk along a good-size branch and knock little twigs off of that main branch. They'll do it early spring after the buds have swelled and they'll end up with a relatively thick scattering of broken twigs on the ground under the tree."

"Why do they do that? Do they eat the swollen buds from the ground?"

"Well that's what I was thinking about. How does that behavior benefit the squirrel and does it benefit anything else?"

"What did you decide?"

"So far I haven't come up with a good explanation. Most of my suppositions I've discredited."

"You don't think it's to eat the buds from the ground?"

"I haven't seen them go down and eat the buds or take them back up the tree to eat them. The twigs with buds just end up adding to leaf litter on the ground. Also squirrels like to eat up in trees. They run around on the ground to find food. But they like to take the food up into trees and eat there for safety's sake. Like when they knock cones from the tops of trees and go down to the ground and get them and bring them up a tree to eat them. But this seems to be just knocking the twigs down."

"So then, what did you think?"

"If I was leaving a bigger branch and pruning away smaller, I would expect the bigger branch to get even thicker and stronger. So maybe it's a way to make their travel routes stronger."

"What do you mean by travel routes?"

"I was sitting on my back porch reading and watching my friendly back yard squirrel as he came by every now and then. There was one spot in particular where he had to make quite a big jump to go from one branch to another in order to avoid going down to the ground. I was really impressed by his strength and agility. I'm still impressed, but after watching awhile I realized he often travels that way to get around the back yard looking for food. So as impressive of a jump and grab as he was making, I saw that to him that was the same old route and no more challenging with practice as my walking around in the yard is for me."

"I see, his ability and familiarity made a difficult jump a familiar pattern. So do you think that's why they prune?"

"They seem to prune the entire tree, not just travel routes, so I discredited that supposition. I also wondered if it was just to thin the tree out within the canopy to make it easier and faster for them to move around while in the tree. A tree they spend time in, not just travel through. But they don't seem to have any trouble moving around in thick trees, and thick trees give more cover from predators. On the other hand, if they don't knock the twigs off early, they would grow too big for the squirrel to knock off. I haven't been able to think of who else might benefit. So at this point it's an observed behavior, but I have to work more on why they do it."

"It sounds like you're leaning towards movement, not food or shelter though."

"That's right, but not conclusively."

"Maybe they don't know why they do it either?"

"That's a very good thought. It might be a behavior that all of that type of squirrel has, but it's only positive for the squirrel when it's in a particular type of tree."

"Maybe that type of tree isn't even around anymore, maybe it's extinct."

"That's another good thought. That behavior could have caused a positive effect in the past and is now in the genetic history of that species of squirrel, but it isn't a benefit any longer."

"Why would they still have that genetic trait if it was no longer positive?"

"As long as a trait isn't negative it can linger on past its usefulness. An example would be people's appendices and tonsils. We're all born with them, but we don't require them."

"I see what you mean," says Anoo.

"And what have you been thinking about, my friend?"

"Not that much, I guess."

"Well, you mentioned you crossed my tracks at times on the hike over here."

"I did in several places."

"Was there any particular place?"

"I crisscrossed your tracks quite a few times coming up the steep pass, then through the top I was right on your tracks. Coming down this ridge, I knew your tracks were just to one side of me or the other if I couldn't actually see them."

"So where the walking was more difficult or choices were limited we tended to the same route."

"That's right."

"When people come into an area that is new to them they tend to go where people have gone before. They travel along routes that the people who came before them followed for the same reason they're following them."

"You mean reasons like it's flatter or the shortest route is through the pass or there's less vegetation to force your way through."

"Yes, and the same holds for where people camp."

"You mean like water and shelter from the wind and deadwood for fuel."

"That's what I mean, so how would you use that information to your advantage?"

"I guess if I was looking for a place to camp and I saw a spot that had been used for camping before, I'd take a close look to see if that place worked for me too. If I was looking for a travel route through an area, I'd look for where people or animals also had gone through before me - just like we did as we hiked and looked for game trails to move along."

"And if more people used the area where we just were we'd have followed some of their trails too. And how could the opposite learning help you?"

"I'm not sure what the opposite learning would be."

"We've been talking about how people tend to move through an area using the same paths others used previously or camp in an area that was a good camping spot for others previously. Well, if you're hunting for food or something like petrified wood, how would you apply the idea we've been talking about?"

"I guess if I was hunting for food I wouldn't want to go where people go because the animals that people hunt avoid the places people commonly use. If I was looking for a piece of petrified wood to decorate my home or make jewelry out of, I'd have to go where no one went before me and had already found the piece."

"So you would want to go off the beaten path to find what people hadn't come across before or find places that are refuges for animals people hunt. You would go places that are not the most obvious or comfortable for people."

"You circled me again, Mateen, we're right back to where

the most interesting thoughts are found from an independent perspective or value system."

"That's exactly the concept I was explaining. And we're right back to you are an intelligent young man and it is very enjoyable to have these conversations with you. Do you see how you were onto a very interesting topic, but you hadn't yet thought it through all the way?"

"And you could help me with it because it is something you have thought about before, so had become familiar with."

"It's always nice after time off the beaten path to return to more familiar ground and to put into perspective what you've experienced. That is also the process of being able to teach others. A new thought or perspective or experience must become familiar to be able to put it into words so it can be explained to others."

"And without that familiarity to put the thought or experience into words, all that is left for the learner is follow me, do it this way, don't think about it, don't ask why, I can't explain it, just do it like I am."

"Well said, I think it's time to find a place to settle in for the night."

While Mateen and Anoo are looking for a place to camp Tohlee and Eli are just sitting down on the porch for a relaxing evening. They had a relaxing afternoon and evening the day before after Cassie and Jed left. Today was much the same. There is plenty of work to do around the farm, but nothing so pressing they can't enjoy their afternoon swim. Now, after a light dinner it is time to enjoy some wine and the sunset.

"I think Anoo is even farther away from us tonight," says Tohlee.

"Me too, and that's probably a good thing. I would say that Mateen thinks everything is fine and there's no reason to come back yet, so they went to a new place. Mateen likes the south side of the mountains down in the scrublands. I would guess they went there and it seems farther to us because it is and because there's a whole line of mountains between us and them that weren't there before."

"I think everything is fine too. I'm just feeling my own need to hug Anoo home, but he'll be back with us soon."

"You did a good job of focusing your attention here while Cassie and Jed were visiting."

"Thank you, Eli. I was surprised you and Jed didn't talk more about how this Country's troubles started, or maybe I was hoping you would."

"I was a little surprised too. I'd kept studying up on the subject just in case."

"What have you learned? It really is fascinating."

"Some hierarchies have been around forever like organized religions and monarchies. But the industrial-military complex in this country that so drove events before and into the troubles didn't come into its own until after World War II. There was a President Eisenhower who warned of the consequences of the industrial-military complex running this country. Then there was a President Kennedy who was assassinated by the complex because he wasn't in favor of using war to solve problems. After he was killed, the complex created the reasons for the wars they engaged in and allowed only individuals into the presidency who would support those wars. It appeared as though voting was democratic, but it was really economic. There wasn't a one-sided economic or societal advantage to a particular candidate because the same complex was ultimately behind each candidate. Democracy, after elections, was almost non-existent after an enemy labeled 'terrorism' was established. Then people were directed to think that being American equaled supporting the current administration whose motto was 'you're either for us or against us'."

"So, you're saying they used war to put the current administration in between the citizenry and the individual freedoms of the constitution. In much the same way as organized religions put their own structure and their own symbols in between people and their individual connection to God."

It's very similar. In both cases a small select group created an organization and created a need for the organization whether that be protecting the electorate or saving one's soul. It didn't matter as long as there was a dependency created. Then that dependency was exploited in the name of the country or God."

"That sounds like the same methodology, just different particulars."

"It is, and the oil companies did the same thing. They chose to have cheap available gasoline until the economy and people's lives were dependent on that commodity. Then they chose to have it cost more either in the form of wars, or loss of personal freedom and privacy, and threatened the populace with the loss of the commodity they had created the need for."

"They created the supply which produced the need. Then they produced the vehicle for the need, specifically the automobile. Then they created the wars that protected the supply. The wars created the need for the production of war material which they then blew up along with infrastructure so they could produce more."

"None of this happened overnight. The industrial-military complex part and the political machine to support it grew over a hundred years. People wouldn't have accepted the situation if it had been shoved on them all at once. The Catholic Church waited centuries and incorporated all sorts of values from other religions and belief systems into theirs before they were in a position to torture non-believers in the name of their god and get away with it. And before they were in a position to deny they were a haven for child molesters and get away with it."

"The values and belief systems you're talking about are like the Easter Bunny, Santa Clause, and Christmas trees?"

"Yes, but the biggest one was incorporating the Roman value system that their leader was God on earth. This was whole-heartedly embraced by the organization which created a seeming legitimacy to the organization most people weren't willing to fight. It also lifted the highest levels of the hierarchy to a position that made it very hard for constituents to disagree with."

"So we're back to don't buck the hierarchy because it's God's truth. Don't buck the administration because it's America. Don't conserve because excess is what drives the economy. Whichever the hierarchy, the methodology is manipulate the constituents for the hierarchies' good because the hierarchy is more than the individual, and defend the hierarchy from the individual for the sake of the people."

"That was the way things were until the troubles proved that the absolute power of hierarchies absolutely degenerate into self-serving manipulation and repression when the leaders of the hierarchies are created by the hierarchy, not by their own individual development."

Mateen and Anoo find a nice place to camp pretty quickly. They choose the base of a short, east-facing hill for a windbreak and to catch the morning sun. They go just around the hill a bit to where water running off the hill earlier in the spring went into a small ravine before going over a four-foot-high ledge. There is no water flowing at this time, but Mateen digs into the gravel at the base of the ledge and hits water after about two feet. He widens the hole and then lets the water sit and settle. Anoo has kept going after Mateen explained what he was going to do. He finds a thicket of plum trees on a north-facing slope farther down the drainage Mateen is in where the ravine levels out and widens. He gathers enough wood for a cook fire and evening comfort fire and meets back up with Mateen at camp. Anoo starts the fire and they finish up the spring water they brought with them. Mateen puts a pot on the fire for their evening meal of beans and jerky. After eating while sitting by the fire they boil water until their water bottles are full and there is enough left over for breakfast and cleaning up.

"Mateen, would you tell me more about what you think about life after death?"

"That's a subject with many perspectives. We've talked about living life in a way that grows soul. I think that living life with intent is the most enjoyable and productive way to live here in the physical. I also think it's the most beneficial way to live life from the perspective of how an individual's entire self, physical now for us and what we've termed soul, can gain from this physical experience we're in."

"And you've talked about perspectives that don't gain much for a person in the physical or for the soul like reacting to life through perceptive feelings."

"I wasn't saying there is no place for perceptive feelings. I was saying to use those feelings as a complement to acting in life through your intent."

"Okay, I think I understand that."

"And I was saying that the value systems one holds in life change when one acts in life instead of reacting to it."

"Which changes the way one interprets their perceptive feelings," says Anoo.

"That's right. When a person is out of balance by reacting too much to life and not acting enough, they think they are made to feel by other people."

"How are they made to feel?"

"There are many individual possibilities. Categorically it's shown by people saying something like "that makes me feel bad" or good, or glad, or whatever. What I'm saying is that you are responsible for the value systems that interpret your feelings; so ultimately, you are responsible for your own feelings. People who react to life through their feelings and are made to feel by their own reactions are victims of their own reactions to what is going on around them."

"That seems kind of twisted."

"I think being a victim to one's own reactions is a counterproductive way to live one's life."

"That makes sense when you say it, but I don't think I ever would have thought it on my own."

"You may very well have learned that on your own without me to help. Don't belittle yourself theoretically. At this time, put it into the category of it seems right but you're going to live your life and see how that perspective fits into it."

"Okay, so we started with life after death."

"We got off on a tangent there but a productive one I think. Let's go back to life after death. From my perspective when you are here in the physical not all of you is here. The part of you that is not in the physical is what you will go to when your physical life is over. The part of us that is not here in the physical is not bound by the type of time that the physical exists in."

"So that part of you is what warned you of the piece of ice that crashed into your windshield?"

"Yes, that was a real learning experience for me. As I've said, time in the physical is not as linear or as inflexible as one might think. Because the part of you that is not in the physical is not bound by time, that part of you already encompasses your past, present, and future. But you are here in the physical now. All that you are beyond the physical is focused on you here because the ability to intend is here with you now. You are a subset of who you totally are, but you are also the effort that all of you is focused on now. Once you are back with the part of you that didn't become physical you are not in a hell of torment or a static heavenly or ecstatic existence. You are still learning and growing and changing. There is no ultimate statement of you where you will stop developing and just be. Once you are reunited with the part of you that didn't become physical the ability to intend will return to the totality of you. That intent will then be used to see if you accomplished what the totality of you needed from this experience in the physical.

The judgment of your life here is accomplished by the totality of you, not by the Creator of the universe, or his representative. It is accomplished from the perspective of the encompassing you. You're like a scout reporting back to his commander. Telling what you saw and did while away and then viewing that from the perspective of all that you are. That perspective is one that can view your life here in the same way that you can step back from yourself now to assess and change your value systems. That perspective is what organized religion defines as a deity and so effectively cuts yourself in half. What we've been talking about these past days is my perspective on how to live and understand your life in a way that will cause the encompassing you to welcome you back with open arms."

Day Twelve

The next morning while Mateen and Anoo eat breakfast they discuss what they will do while at their new location. The day is going to be hot with clouds in the afternoon. Most likely any rain that falls will be up higher where they had been. Down at the edge of the plains where they are they will probably see only virga, the possibility of rain, but only the reality of higher humidity and breezes.

"You said we were going to look for fossils, and petrified wood, and wild horses down here, right?" asks Anoo.

"I did, I've found wood and fossils around here and the horses are usually around."

"I saw three bison yesterday out on the plains."

"We may very well see more today."

"Where do you find the wood and fossils?"

"There are a couple different things to look for. One is a particular shade of brown soil. Another one is where there is active erosion going on."

"What do those places look like?"

"That's like this cut bank here where it is falling down faster than plants can get a root hold in the soil. Another place is similar to where you gathered wood yesterday. Where a ravine opens up and flattens. Rocks will be washed down the ravine and then stop where the ground is flatter and the water loses force. Out on the plains it can be a flat pan where rain water or snowmelt washes the soil away from the rocks, leaving them exposed. There isn't enough elevation change for the water to move the rocks, only the soil around them."

"Or where freeze thaw pushes the rocks up to the surface in the spring like you talked about with soil and seeds."

"That's right. If I see something interesting I'll show it to you before I pick it up so you can see what it looks like on or half in the ground. That will help your eye pick out the unusual that we're interested in from the usual."

"That's the same method you talked about with wildlife behavior."

"You're right again and that's also right when looking for rare plants or mushrooms. Let's get our packs together and head out."

After a walk of a mile or so just for the exercise Mateen heads to a steep hill with scattered sagebrush and grasses. Just short of the hill they stop and watch various bugs, flies, and bees as they work in the bright pink and yellow flowers of a patch of prickly pear cactus. Then Mateen stands and looks at the hillside for a few minutes. He heads up the hill and to the left and stops in front of a couple rocks exposed on the hillside.

"Those are a nice color, Mateen."

"Pick them up and wipe them off."

"They're white on the bottom side and almost a root beer color on the top."

"Take a good look at the white part."

"It looks like bark. Hey! I can see curved lines on the ends. This is petrified wood!"

"Yes, it is, and a very attractive piece."

"But how did you just walk up here right to these two pieces?"

"Partly my familiarity with finding petrified wood, but mostly that's the magic found in rock hounding."

"The magic?"

"Or the artistry, if you want to call it that. It's a phenomenon beyond rational explanation. At least it's beyond my ability to explain. And yet I can repeat it like a scientific experiment."

"Did you see something from the bottom of the hill?"

"Not that I'm aware of. Other times I've been walking, looking for wood and veered off at a ninety-degree angle and dropped down into a little draw and found pieces of wood I couldn't possibly have seen from where I was."

"But how do you do that?"

"It has to do with intent and focus and clarity of mind. Remember when I talked about an aware energy that is in me and that I think is a connection with the totality of me?"

"You said soul at the time but yes, that's the part of you that doesn't age."

"That's right. When my mind is focused on that aware energy, magic happens."

"Is that the totality of you, talking to you like the warning of your ice and windshield accident?"

"I'm not sure. But I think it's more what happens when a person with a clear mind focuses their intent."

"How can a clear mind focus intent?"

"I would say the process begins with more daily uses of intent. With familiarity intent can develop into a mental structure instead of an effort."

"I'm not sure I follow that."

"I don't think I can explain it well. I can say, by my experience, a clear mind holding a structure of intent will take you to magic and that the phenomenon is repeatable. And I can say that no matter how much you learn or how rational you are, you'll never explain all that goes on around you or what you are capable of. There will always be magic at your perimeter."

"What else have you done with that clarity of mind and intent?"

"Lots of things connected with timing and fortuitous circumstance. The most incredible to me was when I stood on a hill on a night with no moon or clouds, only stars. I saw in the sky what looked like a small cloud lit by moonlight. I focused my clear mind around the intent that the cloud was the northern lights. A part of me challenged the cloud. My intent said if that is the northern lights, come and prove it to me. Within seconds the cloud had grown and moved over me and was an incredible display of northern lights. Then part of the lights came down to me and through me into the ground. I stood there with my arms out to my sides slightly raised and my palms up. I stood there and felt energy running through me into the earth. I stood there until I felt I was going to discorporate. I chose to stay in the physical where I was.

I came down off the hill and held my clarity of mind the rest of the night."

"I don't know what to say."

"Then let's walk."

After walking several miles Mateen stops at a small pan where rocks are scattered over a bare piece of ground. Some rocks are concentrated in particular areas and others are haphazardly scattered. He goes to one concentration of rocks and kneels down. Anoo sees the rocks are like a jigsaw puzzle. They are a little bit apart from each other, but look like they would fit together if moved closer to each other.

"What are these, Mateen? They look like they used to be together as one rock."

"They used to be together as a turtle shell some fifty million years ago."

"This is a turtle shell? I can see if they were together they would have been an oval shape."

"Look on the edges, the pattern is different than the top or bottom."

"I see, the edges are like little sand grains or something and the top and bottom are smooth. This one has a mark on it like a Y. Or, if I turn it upside down, it's like a, hey! It's a peace sign! I think this is going in my medicine bag and will symbolize the peace I want on earth for the next fifty million years."

Anoo is in awe of the find and stands and stares for some time. Then Mateen steps to the side and motions him to go ahead. Anoo leads the way for a quarter mile or so and stops next to a mound of soil with no vegetation on it and flat, hard clay surrounding it. He walks up to the mound and notices a small smooth linear rock poking up from the soil. He reaches out and pushes on it. It is firmly held in place, so he takes out his knife and works the soil loose from around it. He holds it up, noting that it is a little over an inch long and a quarter inch or so wide. Then he turns it over.

"Mateen, these are teeth."

"Yes they are. That's a fossilized jaw bone also around fifty million years old."

"A jaw bone of an early horse like you found?"

"Let me take a closer look. This isn't a horse, this is from an animal named hyopsodus or a tube sheep. They were kind of like a pine marten in shape, but they are thought to be burrowers and more omnivorous than a marten. You just walked right up to this mound and spotted it."

"You're right, I did. I wasn't even thinking after I found the peace sign turtle shell. Hey, that's what you mean, clarity of mind and intent. I know what you mean now. I did it too. Thank you, Mateen. Thank you."

Anoo moves off again with Mateen following. After covering a mile or so Anoo stops next to a few colorful, rounded and polished stones. As he looks nearby he sees there are close to twenty of the stones. They're all relatively close to each other and all have that polished look, but with different colors. In size they are all similar also, able to fit in a hand. Anoo knows the stones are different than any other stones he's seen so far today.

"What do you think these are?" asks Anoo.

"I think those are gizzard stones from an animal fifty million years ago."

"Gizzard stones, like the stones some birds put in their crops to help them digest grain?"

"That's what I mean."

"What kind of animal can swallow and hold several pounds of stones in its stomach?"

"My guess is a brontothere."

"What was a brontothere?"

"They were a mammal that looked a lot like a rhinoceros and which could be as large as an elephant. Some related kinds were twenty or thirty feet high at the shoulder and had skulls five or six feet long."

"That's gigantic. Not that one the size of an elephant isn't, but thirty feet high at the shoulder, wow!"

Anoo keeps hunting for interesting finds. He continues leading the way. In one place he finds broken pieces of clam shell that if whole must have come from a clam eight or ten inches long and six wide. Another find is a piece of petrified wood in a complete circle like a branch and with a knothole in it. In the knothole is a crystallized pocket of quartz.

Anoo walks up the hill in front of him and stops at the top. There, less than one hundred yards in front of him, are six wild horses. The stallion sees him as he comes over the horizon. With a stomp of a hoof and his head and neck down but nose up he urges his harem to move. They all break into a gallop and a couple minutes later are out of sight and a mile away. Anoo looks where they've gone until their dust has settled. Then he starts in a broad turn until he is pointed back towards camp. Mateen follows at a distance, knowing Anoo is walking with a clear mind and has lost awareness of him. Almost back at camp Anoo sees movement in front of him. A little head and ears are up above a clump of sagebrush. He takes another two steps and the movement becomes a jackrabbit standing on its hind legs. Then another one hops on its hind legs up behind the first, both standing almost three feet off the ground. Then they drop and run and are quickly lost to sight in more sagebrush. Arriving back at camp Anoo lies down on the ground with his arms outstretched, closes his eyes and melts into the ground.

Mateen watches over Anoo for awhile and then goes and gathers more firewood. When he comes back Anoo is sitting up and staring into the fireless fire pit. Mateen starts the fire and then sits down with him. Deciding it is time for Anoo to be actively thinking again Mateen engages him in conversation for the first time in hours and miles.

"That was a beautiful piece of wood you found. Not only is it a full round of a branch but it had that crystal pocket in it."

Anoo looks over at him until something changes in his mind and the ability to verbalize his thoughts comes back to him. He looks around as though orienting himself and turns to Mateen.

"I understand where the wood came from or when it was alive. That was around fifty million years ago like the turtle and the tube sheep. But how did it turn to rock and where did the crystals come from?"

"It's part of the same process. The theory is that the piece of wood fell into a mud hole or a swampy area. Some place where oxygen couldn't get to the wood. If no oxygen can get to the wood the decay process will be greatly slowed. The wood, as it's in the mud at the bottom of a swamp, becomes waterlogged. Minerals, dissolved in the water, soak into the wood along with the water. The most common mineral is silica, both on earth and to soak into the wood. Silica is what quartz is made of. Microscopic bits of silica then start to build up in the wood. Over time and through wet and dry seasons the wood becomes impregnated with silica or silicified. The water will move back out of the wood during the dry season but the silica won't."

"Why does the water go out without the silica it had with it to begin with?"

"I think the silica chemically bonds with the wood and that is a stronger connection than just being dissolved in water. Another possibility is that the wood is like a physical filter straining the dissolved silica out of the water. After enough time, depending on how mineralized the water is, the cellulose of the wood is replaced with silica. That turns the wood into rock. If the microscopic bits of silica are minute enough even the small details of the wood are preserved."

"Details like the shape of the bark and the rings of the tree?"

"That's right. Then other minor amounts of minerals in the water or in the tree, when it was alive, give color to the silica in the same way quartz can have many colors depending on its trace minerals."

"And why did the crystals form instead of solid silicified wood?"

"They grew in the knothole which was a space in the wood, not solid wood. As the silica concentration builds up in the wood and in the water in the knothole, the space of the knothole allows the crystals to form."

"Why did they form as crystals and not a blob of quartz?"

"If the silica filled the knothole it would be a solid piece of chalcedony which is water-deposited quartz. If the silica doesn't completely fill the space it can be quartz crystals, or perhaps chalcedony crystals is more correct, I'm not sure."

"What determines whether there will be quartz or chalcedony crystals?"

"I don't know. The two crystal shapes are completely different. I know quartz crystals have interesting electric properties. That's why they can be used in radios. So maybe there's an electric component to the formation. But I really don't know."

"So the wood has to fall into a muddy area or be swept to a muddy area and then mineralize before it rots. Then it lies underground for fifty million years until I come along and recognize it. That's a pretty amazing process."

"Yes, it is. And the hyopsodus jaw went through a similar process.

The mineralized wood can end up underground for millions of years and then the earth above it erodes away, bringing it nearer the surface. As it nears the surface it can come back in contact with ground water, mineralizing it a second time. This can give it another color or finish the process of mineralization if the wood was only half replaced with silica the first time around."

"That's a very long slow process."

"Yes it is, like the process of soil formation."

"Soil takes millions of years to form?"

"Well it can be thousands, but it doesn't have to. A volcano can spout out ash that is rich enough in nutrients that plants will grow in it almost as soon as it cools. A glacier can scrape soil off bedrock and then melt back away from the bedrock. The exposed bedrock then starts to weather from wind and sun and rain and the freeze thaw process. As it weathers lichens will start to grow on it. The lichens produce an acid that eats away at the rock. All of those factors break the rock down into little pieces. The lichens grow and die and break down also. Then a big rain comes along and sweeps the little pieces of rock and dead lichens into a crack in the rock where it builds up. As it builds up it becomes thick enough to support other types of larger plant life."

"So then, when those plants die and rot, that produces more material for other plants and animals to live in. So the lichens create habitat for other plants and animals - just like beavers do."

"That's good thinking, Anoo, very good thinking."

Mateen boils water and makes dinner as clouds build into thunderheads. At times rumbles of thunder can be heard from up on the mountains to their north. To their south, isolated thunderheads move from west to east. After nightfall, from the more elevated ridge they dropped off of to camp, Mateen knows they could see flashes of lightning from thunderheads a hundred miles away. A nighttime walk may be in order. As they eat Anoo begins to wonder.

"When I first showed you the hyopsodus jaw you looked at it to see if it was a horse jaw like you had found."

"I couldn't be sure until I looked closer at the teeth."

"You weren't just being polite because I thought a horse jaw could be that small?"

"No, the one I found really wasn't much bigger. The ancestors of horses fifty million years ago were way too small for you or me to ride."

"So they got bigger over time. Is that the way evolution works?"

"Not necessarily. Animals that adapt to the Polar Regions tend to be larger than their relatives in warmer climes. That's because larger animals have less surface area and so can retain heat more efficiently. On the other hand, animals have been isolated on islands and, over time, they've gotten smaller so they are less likely to eat themselves out of house and home. The smaller animals can also have a larger population on the limited space of the island than their larger ancestors. A larger population of a species has more potential for genetic variability, which is a positive aspect for species survival."

"So there are lots of possibilities for how species of life will evolve," says Anoo.

"I would say about as many as there are species. There are bitter tasting butterflies with a distinctive coloration and good tasting butterflies that have evolved a similar coloration so they can benefit from the other butterflies' bad taste to predators. There are the cowbirds of North America that lay eggs in other birds' nests. When the young hatch, not only do the parent birds of the nest feed the cowbird chicks, the cowbird chicks have the instinctual behavior to back into their nest mates, pushing them out of the nest to their deaths. That leaves the parents to care for just the interloper of another species."

"So there are all sorts of variations on the theme of generational survival like you said."

"Yes, the ancestor of the modern horse started out quite small and in North America. Then they expanded into Asia before dying out in North America. They reached their modern size in Asia or Eurasia, I don't remember which. Then people brought them back to the Americas as part of European society, colonizing North America. The horses we saw today are feral horses from stock originally brought with the Europeans. That stock then inhabited their original or genetic homeland."

"That sounds like the European starlings my father told me about that were brought into Central Park in New York City which grew into the billions of starlings found in North America today."

"It's very much the same."

"Why did people like starlings so much they took the trouble to bring them here?"

"I'm not sure, but I have heard a flock of starlings up in a tree squawking like crazy before settling in for the night. As I listened, I heard them mimic a rooster's crow and a pheasant's call and finally a horse's neigh."

"That would be different, hearing a horse's neigh from up in a tree. I wonder what advantage it is to the starlings to be able to mimic other animals' sounds?"

"I don't know. It doesn't seem like a meaningful communication for the starling like it would be for the rooster, pheasant, or horse."

"Because, to the other animals, it is a sound with meaning, but for the starling, it is only mimicking the sound."

"That's right, for the other animals, their calls are sounds with meaning like our words. For example, I've listened closely to a robin's call in spring and decided I heard it saying 'here I am, right here, look at me'."

"Do all robins make that same call?"

"No, this would be a male robin trying to attract a mate. That was only part of the call, the part I thought I could interpret. Sometimes I've heard each part repeated twice. Sometimes there's only two of the three parts or they're in a different order."

"Because all robins are individuals even if they look alike to us."

"That's right, and it may be there were different circumstances involved like the proximity or level of interest of a female."

"Animal behavior and evolution are incredible things," says Anoo.

"Yes, they are. Look at people's evolution. There wasn't one line of primate that gradually turned into what we would recognize as a human. There were many different branches of pre-humans and humans, most of which died out. Some of those branches our ancestors interbred with after quite a distinctive separation like Neanderthals and Cro-Magnon man, I think it was. Humans have been around a long time. Ever since our prehuman ancestors more than a million years ago had fire and fire-hardened spears we've been a distinctive animal. An animal that could defend itself from predators many times its size. A group of a half-a-dozen extremely well-conditioned prehumans with sharp sticks are a threat to most any predator."

"Because of the intelligence of the predator who doesn't want to incur an unacceptable level of damage," says Anoo.

"That's right. The distinction between prehumans and other animals and then humans and other animals has increased with more efficient tool making. Then, through our desire to change our appearance by making clothes, tattooing, cutting our hair. Along with that came art and music and complex verbal communication which then led to written language. We humans have an exceptional lineage."

"Life on Earth, the Earth itself, climate, and all the interactions between them mixed with human history and humanities and individual potential. What a wondrous mix and what an amazing gift to be here alive and perceiving this awesome world we live in and the amazing Earth we live on!"

"I couldn't have said it better, Anoo. I couldn't have said it better."

Mateen becomes lost in thought, so Anoo walks up to the ridge just above camp where he can watch the flickering lights of the distant thunderstorms. When he comes back down, Mateen is asleep.

DAY THIRTEEN

"Good morning to you, Anoo."

"And to you, Mateen, what do you have planned for us today?"

"I was thinking about yesterday and your final comment last night. And I was thinking I would head back to my cabin today."

"Today, you mean this morning?"

"Yes, after we have another talk I'll start back and get there sometime tomorrow afternoon."

"Just you?"

"You can come with me if you'd like. But I would like to suggest that you stay here or back up in the mountains for a day or two and think about things and be by yourself for awhile before you go back home."

"Okay, I guess that would be good."

"I'm certainly not concerned for your safety. You have proven yourself to be a very capable young man. I think a little time for reflection with no one else's input would be a good thing at this point."

"Okay, I guess so."

"A little apprehension is completely understandable."

"I'll miss you, Mateen."

"And I you, Anoo. I'll see you when I come down and help you and your folks with the fall harvest - just like every year."

"That will be good."

After eating breakfast and drinking some water Mateen gets his gear organized. When he is packed up they sit around the fire and boil more water until they have drunk their fill and have a full supply in their water bottles.

"What else do you want to talk to me about, Mateen?"

"I wanted to point out how throughout history it is the winners of wars or the perspectives of the largest religions that end up as popular truths. Those are the perspectives that are most easily found in written word or in common beliefs. The winners of wars are the mightiest, but they are not necessarily the most compassionate or with the broadest perspective on what benefits the human condition. The largest religions have the most popular appeal, but not the clearest truth of who, what, and why we are."

"As you said before, Mateen, correctness, accuracy, truth, whatever you want to call it, is determined by the content of what is said, not by who is talking."

"That is well learned and you can spend a lifetime living it and still gain from it. Many people assess the world and the people around themselves by putting information into the back of their head. I've suggested you contemplate things I've said in a similar way. I'm not saying the process doesn't work, I'm saying it can be overly relied on. People often take information and subtle cues and assess them out without their direct awareness. Then they wait for an answer that is usually in the form of a feeling. For you I expect the answer to be verbally communicated. When the conclusion is a feeling the process is the same that religion uses. Faith instead of reason, the truth is somewhere beyond you and when it comes to you - it is a feeling, not an explanation or a line of reasoning or a formula. The ultimate ending of that process is to perceive a thought where the light bulb goes on as a revelation from God."

"That's two different perspectives on the same phenomena," assesses Anoo.

"Clarity and awareness trump vagueness and disassociation," replies Mateen. "Learn and communicate, then feel from as informed a perspective as possible. Choose to build your own structure, don't adopt an existing structure. Use your subconscious when you have to, not as a substitute for awareness of the thought process. The more aware you choose to be of the processes that go on in the back of your head through intent, honesty, openness, and awareness, the more you can create the structure you assess others and the world around you with. The more you choose to grow that structure instead of having that structure be a reaction to the world around you. The quicker you will learn to change your perspective. The choice to change your perspective is a more efficient creator of wisdom than reacting to changes forced on you by a hierarchy you've chosen to adopt or by the happenstance of one's life. The awareness you create when building your own values structure opens up the area of the self that is most often occupied by religion. Don't worry, in the same way scientific learning can't cause beauty or the real magic of timing or gifts from nature to go away, the truest aspects of religion will remain."

After a short meditative silence Mateen stirs.

"I have delighted in our time together, Anoo. You are an intelligent and aware young man. I am sure your observations and thought will grow you into a compassionate man with a broad encompassing perspective. Now a big hug for me and I'll be off."

"Thank you, Mateen. Thank you for your time and effort to communicate your perspective with me. I know your perspective will grow in me as I learn and grow. Thank you."

"A few last things to think about later, Anoo. The walkabout we've been on is a short version of an adventure. An adventure is more of the same, just longer. There are days when travel or situations are difficult and other days much easier. There are days of ease and relaxation between days of effort, just like with our walkabout."

"You mean an adventure like when you sailed to Hawaii?"

"That's what I mean, an adventure of many months or more.

Another thing, don't be just a citizen of the United States, a person who leaves the granting of freedom to their government. Be an American, a person who lives and grants freedom on an individual level."

"Okay, Mateen, I understand that and will think about how to live it."

"Belief in the God of Abraham does not equal gnosis."

"I'll have to think about that."

"The more you intend, the better efficiency and being succinct feels, the more right it feels. There is more learning possible in life than efficiency can ever achieve. That is why life is the greatest experiment ever. Don't be afraid to learn and grow – you'll only become more of you. Don't be afraid to choose the path less traveled. That is where potential is greatest. Peace to you, Anoo."

"And to you, Mateen."

Anoo watches Mateen walk up the ridge until he is out of sight. Then he can't help but sit down and shed a few tears. After some quiet reflection he makes sure camp is organized and goes for a walk.

Mateen takes his time walking up the ridge. He takes a break before starting up the steep climb to the top of the pass. By the time he has finished the climb it is mid-afternoon. He takes another break at the top and then stands and faces his nephew's farm. He thinks of his nephew and builds an image of him in his mind.

Tohlee and Eli are back into the routine of their farm after Cassie and Jed's visit. It is mid-afternoon and time for a swim. Tohlee was going to get ready to go, but goes to find Eli instead. She finds him standing still and looking south.

"What is it, Eli?"

"Mateen let me know he is back up the pass and going to his cabin. He'll be there tomorrow afternoon. Anoo is fine and will be back in a couple days. All is well."

"Thank you for letting us know, Mateen. Why do you think he didn't contact you sooner?"

"It wouldn't have been fair to, or trusting of us in Anoo, if we mentally hovered over him on this walk. We entrusted him to Mateen and that was a good thing for all involved."

"Peace to you, Mateen, and thank you."

"Peace to you, Mateen."

After walking around for awhile Anoo heads back to camp. He has found a rock ledge with snail fossils. Snails so big they could have made a meal of escargot. He places a loose one in his medicine bag for the sheer beauty of it, for its symmetry and for the red flecks against the black coils ending at a solid white tip.

In the morning he will go back over the pass into the high country.

Day Fourteen

Anoo is up and moving at first light. He walks up the ridge to the base of the pass in little more than an hour. After about the same amount of time he is at the top, winded and ready for a break. He thinks of Mateen. He decides Mateen probably went back to their high camp by the spruce fir stand for the night. Then he will have roused early as Anoo had and is now several miles closer to his cabin. Anoo decides to go toward the western side of the high rolling plateau. He wants to see new country. He goes down the pass and then slows his pace, watching more than walking, but still moving a couple miles in a couple of hours.

He decides to go up a ridge. He knows he is going to the top but doesn't care when he gets there. He walks even slower, slowly enough to make no sound. When a game trail is going the direction he wants to go he speeds up a little. When he goes through brush he slows down. Birds fly by him. Chipmunks and squirrels go about their business around him. Sometimes they stop to look at him and sometimes he is no more to them than the plants and earth that are around them all.

As the morning sun becomes the hot sun of afternoon he moves toward a thick stand of aspen. He slowly moves inside the grove and feels the coolness of the shade and then stops to listen to the breeze rustling the leaves. He goes in farther and comes to the edge of a small clearing. There is a small patch of light in the center where the sun is above the tops of the trees. He stands in the sun for a few minutes before removing his pack and sitting down.

As he takes some dried fruit and nuts out of his pack and sets his canteen beside him, a western tanager flies into the clearing and lands on a branch at the edge. It sees him and chirps its displeasure. Anoo watches as the bird continues to display its agitation. When he moves his hand up to his mouth the bird became louder. As he sits and chews the bird quiets down. After a few minutes the bird flies a few feet into the trees and disappears from sight. It is back again soon and begins chirping its displeasure again. After a few minutes it leaves the clearing and Anoo eats some more and takes a drink. Now that he isn't moving, he enjoys the warmth of the sun and the sound of the breeze in the leaves. Again, the tanager returns to the same branch at the edge of the clearing and chirps at him. It flies back into the trees and is soon back on the branch, chirping at him again. After watching the pattern a few more times Anoo closes up his pack and stands. When the tanager leaves the clearing Anoo puts on his pack and moves into the trees in the direction the tanager has been going. He looks up the trunks of a few trees until he sees the small opening he knew would be there. After stepping back about ten feet for a better angle up, he moves over a foot to the side where the branches of another aspen cover his upper body and the trunk covers his right side. Within a few minutes the tanager flies up to the hole and goes inside. Anoo can faintly hear the demanding squawks of the young. The tanager's head soon appears again at the hole and then it flies out. Anoo moves off through the trees and continues up the ridge.

By late afternoon he is finally at the top. A pocket of spruce-fir trees are to his right and he angles over to them. There is a nice spot in the trees where a large spruce has fallen near a boulder almost as high as his head. Anoo clears the forest litter from near the boulder and gathers some wood from the fallen tree for a fire. He walks to where he can watch the sun go down and then goes back to his cleared area by the rock. The valley in front of him and the hills beyond are all in shadow, but the sky is still light.

Anoo sits while full dark appears and then returns into the trees to start a fire. He gazes into the fire, sitting on his sleeping bag until he feels like stretching out, and soon he is asleep. He wakes in a couple of hours and listens to the woods around him. The eastern sky is lightening. Soon the little past full moon rises over the horizon. He says hello and watches the moon shrink in size as it climbs higher and higher over the hills. He stirs his fire up once more before falling back to sleep again.

Day Fifteen

noo wakes before dawn and walks to a rocky knob above the trees where he slept. He leaves his sleeping bag in the trees. After standing on the rocky knob and seeing the light increase in the eastern sky he steps off the knob and removes his pack and clothes. He returns to the knob barefoot with the breeze cool on his skin. He becomes cold in the predawn chill and feels his skin thicken and his blood withdraw from the surface of his skin.

As the light increases around him the sky above brightens until he can see the rays of the sun. He can feel the energy going over his head. Minutes later as the rays come down farther he feels them touch the tops of the trees above him and to his side. He feels the trees respond to the energy. The rays drop down closer to his head as he stands facing the sun with his arms out slightly from his sides and his palms toward the sun. The rays are just over his head and then on his forehead. He shuts his eyes and sees the bright yellow and then pink of his eyelids. The rays warm his body and he realizes from a slight breeze that he is fully erect. His sight goes from the brightness of his eyelids inward. His attention goes inward. In his mind he sees green grass and blue sky, dark hair spins out in front of him as someone just to his side suddenly turns toward him. Bright eyes and a laughing smile appear in front of him. For a second he sees her face clearly and then she is gone. His sight returns to his eyelids. He realizes that his arms have raised and are crossed in front of him with the palms toward his chest, hugging the image in his mind. His entire body relaxes and he turns away from the sun and looks along the ridge. He knows that someday he will know her, but that will be another time and this is now.

Anoo walks along the ridge, leaving his clothes and pack behind. He drops down into a little gully, crosses to the other side and is at the bottom of a steep rock pile. He reaches out in front of himself and places his hands on the nearest rocks. He starts moving up the slope on all fours. He realizes how low to the ground he is and moves over to the side where a slight depression causes the rocks to be over his head. He moves up the depression from rock to rock while, now and then, looking above the rocks, scanning the hillside around him. He sees a deer near the edge of the rock pile a hundred yards away and his mouth waters. After watching the deer feed along the slope he knows which direction it is going and how often and for how long it lowers its head. The breeze is down slope and he knows he can slink within feet of the deer. But instead, he goes farther up the rock pile. As he nears the top there is a patch of moss in front of him and he goes to it. At the base of a large rock water drips from one patch of moss and falls onto another a few inches below. He moves closer and holds his cupped palm under the slowly dripping water. He watches as drop-by-drop his palm slowly fills. At last he drinks. An hour later he has had his fill and moves up to the top of the rock pile and sits.

He thinks of the deer he watched and considers the paradox of the predator. The predator must reach out with its awareness to learn where its prey is. Then it must draw close through observation of the prey's behavior without alerting the prey to its intent - without creating awareness of itself in the prey.

Then he considers other topics from the past days. There will be a point where feelings are the next step, but that point is after learning and communication. The feeling is a step in a process not the goal or a final conclusion. Okay, clear enough. The potential quality of thoughts and feelings reaches to the creation of immortal soul. I guess that's where I'll rest on the feeling that the potential is there for now. Except I have no doubt there is quality to thoughts and feelings that quantity will never reach. Okay, that's where the feeling the concept has merit comes from. Different people do the same things in different ways. Freedom of religion is the concept that embraces different people seeking truth in different ways. If freedom is restricted truth is restricted and fanaticism grows. Where's a God fit into that? The creator of the universe has encompassed the time span of billions of solar systems from birth to black hole. That creator has encompassed untold trillions of lives of intelligent beings. That creator gave humanity the gift of self-determination. The gift of responsibility through compassion for the Earth itself and all life on it and then wishes us well. Then how does the God that takes sides in a religious war fit in? Or the God that works in mysterious ways as a child dies because its parents won't seek medical help for it? Or the God that watches a tsunami kill hundreds of thousands of people fit in? That God lives in human consciousness. That is a God created in human consciousness by humans. A God created in human consciousness by people who don't want to accept the responsibility of the gift of self-determination. And that is the same circumstance as the devil – a being created in human consciousness by humans so they can avoid responsibility for their own actions against each other. I think I'll stand on that perspective and see if my experiences in life support it.

Each individual and all people are their own evil and their own God. I will not wait for the Great God to come from the sky and make everybody feel high. I will act as though humanity is its own best hope as I am the creator of my own future.

And just so, through many steps, and through time, I will become a determiner. I will become a person who creates and holds his own value systems and is aware of and responsible for his actions and circumstance.

After quite awhile Anoo stands and walks up the rock pile to the top and enters a large stand of spruce-fir trees that run along both sides of the ridge top. As he walks into the stand he feels the spongy softness of the needle duff under his bare feet and the coolness of the shade on his skin. He stands still and smells the aroma of the forest. Then he slowly walks through the trees.

A chickadee comes to a branch near his head and calls. He follows it to where it goes into a cavity in a dead tree and watches as it flies away. He walks in the direction the bird has flown and stops where he has lost sight of it. After a few minutes the bird flies back the way it came and Anoo waits. A few more minutes and the chickadee flies past and Anoo follows. Once again he loses sight of the bird and waits. The chickadee goes past a few more times until Anoo walks up to a tree that has broken in half. The top half is lying on the ground. He stops where he saw the bird land, peck around and turn back. Bugs are crawling out of the broken wood of the tree top. Some fly away and others crawl along the trunk. As Anoo watches, the chickadee returns and grabs three of the bugs in his beak, then flies off. When it is gone other bugs crawl out and fly or crawl away.

Anoo watches the bugs fly until he can't see them anymore. He knows this same activity is going on in other parts of these hills. The bugs that are grabbed by the chickadee become food for its young. Some of the bugs that fly away will become food for a flycatcher on the edge of a clearing. Some of the bugs will mate and lay their eggs in the cracks of exposed wood. Some of these eggs will be laid in wood soft enough that a woodpecker will chisel its way in and eat the larva before they are ready to fly. Other eggs will be laid in a tree that is too exposed to the winter wind for the eggs to survive until spring. But here and there, next year, the survivors will crawl out of their wood nests, avoid predators and fly away into an unknown world to find a partner and reproduce.

Anoo moves the short distance to the west side of the ridge and looks out. The sun will be setting in four hours or so. He sits to wait for the colors of the coming sunset. He knows from the scattered clouds to the west that it will be an exceptional sunset on one of the longest days of the year.

After full dark Anoo arises and stretches. He walks down to

where he left his clothes and pack and eats a light, late dinner. He walks up to the top of the rock pile and sets a pan under the dripping moss. Then he sits and watches the stars until the moon rises in the night sky.

Day Sixteen

Anoo wakes as the sun's rays fall on him. He drinks from his pan and waits until he has enough water to fill his canteen. Then he goes to where he left his sleeping bag and packs it up. He drops down in elevation to a stream and catches some crayfish. He pinches them in half and puts the tails on a rock next to his fire. As they cook he catches a couple brook trout with a fly Mateen tied and finds some wild onions.

It is late morning by the time he has finished eating. After a short nap and an invigorating swim Anoo angles up the ridge in a northerly direction. By late afternoon he is miles to the north and near the end of the ridge. He walks up to a very large aspen tree and sets down his pack. He reaches his arms around the tree and holds it. After awhile he can feel the sap in the tree reaching to the sun-charged leaves and down into the cool moist soil. As the sun sets he sleeps with the tree until morning.

Day Seventeen

Anoo and the tree slowly rouse in the early morning light as a deer walks by. By the time he reacts and turns his head away from the tree trunk to look at the deer, it has moved a hundred yards down the hill. Then the sun's rays reach the leaves of the tree and both Anoo and the tree speed up. After a light breakfast Anoo says goodbye to the tree and slowly continues north, dropping in elevation with the ridge. He stops at a spring, drinks and fills his canteen. He eats the last of his dried food.

After walking another mile he finds a spot with shade and nearby water. For a few hours, he waits there, to be present for the coming sunset. After watching the sunset and the stars come out of the darkening sky, he sleeps.

Day Eighteen

Anoo wakes and watches the moon set as the eastern sky lightens with the dawn. He drinks and slowly walks north until he can see where the two main stream branches converge at town. The air above town is disturbed with the thoughts and activities of the townspeople. He decides to stay on his side of the western branch and keep moving north. At midday he rests while waiting for some people to cross the ridge a mile in front of him. After they have crossed the ridge he walks down to the narrow road the people were traveling on. After standing and watching by the side of the road for awhile he crosses it and walks the last couple miles north. Coming to the top of a small hill where he can look out a half-mile east to his parents' farm, he looks out from the hilltop and sends out a hello from his mind to the homestead.

Seconds later the breeze brings him the neigh of the horses and the excited barking of the dogs. He sees his mother walk between the house and barn from her gardens and his father emerge from the barn and stand next to her. He feels their attention reach out to him and he is warmed. He knows that, as he drops down the hill, the dogs will meet him half-way down and that his parents will walk hand-in-hand down their lane to meet him at the road. He also knows the horses will be upset if he doesn't go to them and say hello as he arrives in the yard. He knows all this as he looks down. Just as he also knows that in time he will leave.

The adventure of his life is just beginning.

Appendix A

More concepts that the author has found can
help create an individual perspective.

I think that males need to incorporate a more female perspective into their perspective to reach their individual potential.

I think that females need to incorporate a more male perspective into their perspective to reach their individual potential.

I think that males need to be more compassionate and considerate of others.

I think that males should aid the sick and feed the poor before going to war.

I think that females need to apply more intent and to act more in life to balance the reactions to life that their feelings often are.

I think that applying intent in life changes the value systems that are used to interpret perceptive feelings.

I concur with Jesus that people should take the "log out of their own eye before taking the mote out of their brother's eye." If they did this, they would spend more time growing plants and watching sunsets than in conquering man or nature.

I believe that the Second Coming of Jesus was to Paul on the road to Damascus and he failed Jesus when he passed out.

I believe Paul's failure to maintain conscious awareness in the face of the Second Coming of Jesus set hierarchical Christianity on a path of subservience and worship for millennia.

I believe that evolution is a more accurate representation of the history of life on Earth than creationism is.

I believe that the future is not set - that our fate is what we make.

I think that people who believe that their anger is a statement of how right they are prove the theory of evolution because they are functioning at the level of grunting apes.

I believe it is better to live one's own destiny than to be an actor in someone else's play, no matter how supreme a being the writer is.

I believe that perceiving others through generalities is coarse and degrading to people who function as individuals.

I believe that people who find truth in generalities lack their own individuality.

I believe that when someone says "it's just the way it is" that it really isn't.

I believe that when someone says "in all honesty" or "to be perfectly honest with you," there isn't honesty involved.

I believe that God has seen a million intelligent societies and untold trillions of intelligent individuals come and go.

I believe there is more value in talking about concepts and ideas than in talking about people.

I believe that vanity, vanity, all is vanity, can be translated to ego, ego, all is ego.

I believe there is nothing new under the sun but individual application.

I believe that as Santayana said "those who cannot remember the past are condemned to repeat it."

I believe that the difference between us and people one hundred thousand years ago and between us and people a hundred thousand years from now is the value systems held within each society, not the intellect, or feelings, or capabilities of the people themselves.

I believe that societies have come and gone on Earth without leaving a written record whose perspective equals or exceeds anything known through recorded history.

I believe that the proof of human evolution can be found in the lack of individual development of humans who don't "do unto others," showing that we haven't raised ourselves very far above animals yet. And that proof can also be found in the feelings and intelligence of animals, once again showing we haven't risen far above animals.

I believe that a level of intent can be reached by a being in the physical that will increase the energy in the spiritual.

I believe that emotions can be reached by beings in the physical that increase energy in the spiritual.

I believe that the self one gives up when reaching nirvana does not include a loss of the awareness of who we are now, but does cause a change in perspective on who we are now.

I believe that structure created by intent, focus, or concentration is not lost through the realization of the state of awareness named nirvana.

I believe that what holds our awareness together through the realization of nirvana is caused by intent.

I believe my limits are not created by another's failings.

I believe that true evil is found in individuals who see someone more capable than they and then try and tear that person down to their level for the sake of their own comfort.

I believe that true evil is found in the actions of people who can't live the Golden Rule or who commit acts of violence, not in the whisperings of a nearly God-like being or the selling of one's soul to such an entity.

I believe the greatest trick the Devil played on humanity was to convince them he was responsible for evil in the world not individuals themselves.

I believe the philosophical concept that there must be evil in the world to recognize good is grossly blown out of proportion. A person living the Golden Rule needs no more than the knowledge of the concept of murder, rape, and violence, to know how wrong those acts are. They don't need the enormous numbers of occurrences throughout human history of those acts to see the value of good.

I believe that if the Biblical version of creation were accurate, then God must bear responsibility for the fall from grace of humanity. Because the fall happened within two days of His creation of the life-form that from the Christian perspective is at the center of creation, a creation that spans 15 billion years and billions of galaxies with trillions of stars each and many trillions of planets.

I believe the Biblical version of creation must include the creation of humanity as self-determinate beings or God would be responsible for humanity's fall from grace.

I believe that God intentionally tempted Adam and Eve with the apple through his grandiose statement "Whatever you do, don't eat that apple." That temptation was intentional because people had to go against God's will in order to begin the effort that would eventually lead to self-determination for all of humanity.

I believe that Jesus of Nazareth took the responsibility for original sin on himself and so absolved humanity's debt for original sin, not so we could go back to the way things were before original sin, but rather to allow the continued growth of humanity's development towards God's goal for humanity of individual self-determination.

I believe that the choice to be dependent on other countries' natural resources does not legitimize going to war to protect that chosen dependency.

I believe that the ultimate truth of war is the slaughter of unarmed women and children, not heroism on a field of glory.

I believe that truth, accuracy, being right, is determined by the content of what is said, not by who is talking.

I believe that might doesn't make right, instead it means that might allows a person in authority or government to get their own way.

I believe that learning is meant to be mental delight.

I believe that a gardener can put energy into a crop that can be passed on to others.

I believe that air, water, and soil pollution is no different than an animal soiling its own nest.

I believe the choice not to use birth control reduces people to mindless breeding animals.

ABOUT THE AUTHOR

James lives and works in Colorado with his wife Lorna and dogs Seven and Breeze. He enjoys gardening, camping, hiking, fishing, rock hounding, and videoing wildlife. With fifty plus years into appreciating the natural world his love and enjoyment for the daily and seasonal changes of an untended landscape as well as the day to day growth in a vegetable garden still fill him with awe and questions . He can be reached for comment at walkingforbreezes. com.